THE MYSTICAL BONES SERIES

VELOSAURA

VICTORIA
RIVERA

First published in the United States by Prosey Books, an imprint of Pocketful of Prosey LLC.

Cover art by TrifBookDesign
Maps and interior art by Daniel Brown
Layout, typography, and formatting by Victoria Rivera

www.toririv.com

First published September 28, 2024
Second Edition

*For Rocco and Bellamy,
my very own little dinos.*

Note From Author

This story is inspired by real-world places and the things, people, and languages in them. However, it is neither historical fiction nor an alternate history of Earth. It takes place in a unique setting that also includes dinosaurs and other prehistoric creatures from various geological time periods (as well as special breeds, hybrids, and a few fictional species). I have obviously taken creative license with the overall concept and many details, and simplified a few items for better readability, but I hope readers will feel as excited about this fantasy world as I do. I wanted to write a story that incorporates my passion for dinosaurs and my love of Latin America; this is my ode to both.

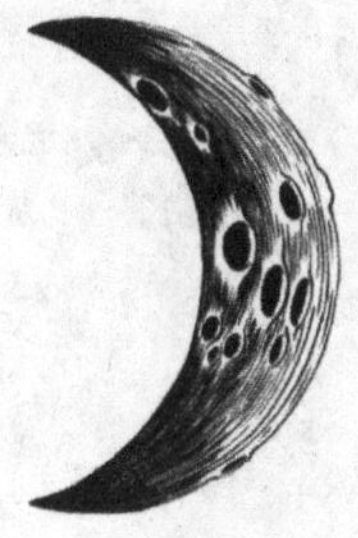

Some parts of this novel may deal briefly
with sensitive subject matter.

....

For a detailed list of content warnings, please visit:
www.toririv.com/cw

RUNAQA
GULF OF WAYAQA
Lake Weqe
Masi
TISQU
Silver City
Port Sach'ara
Port Anqas
ALETA
RUHPARIY
QHUSI
Willkabamba Mountains
Volcanic Region
SUMAQ
QOLQE
Urubamba Mountains
Ñansa
Lake Waylla
KANTUTA BAY
Lake Umiña
YUPA
UNU
Huandoy
ALLPA
Lake Sillu
AMACHAKUNA
GULF OF ALLPA
Tukukuq
Pirqa Mountains
ANQAS OCEAN
Mt. Wiru
Murkroot
THE TAIL

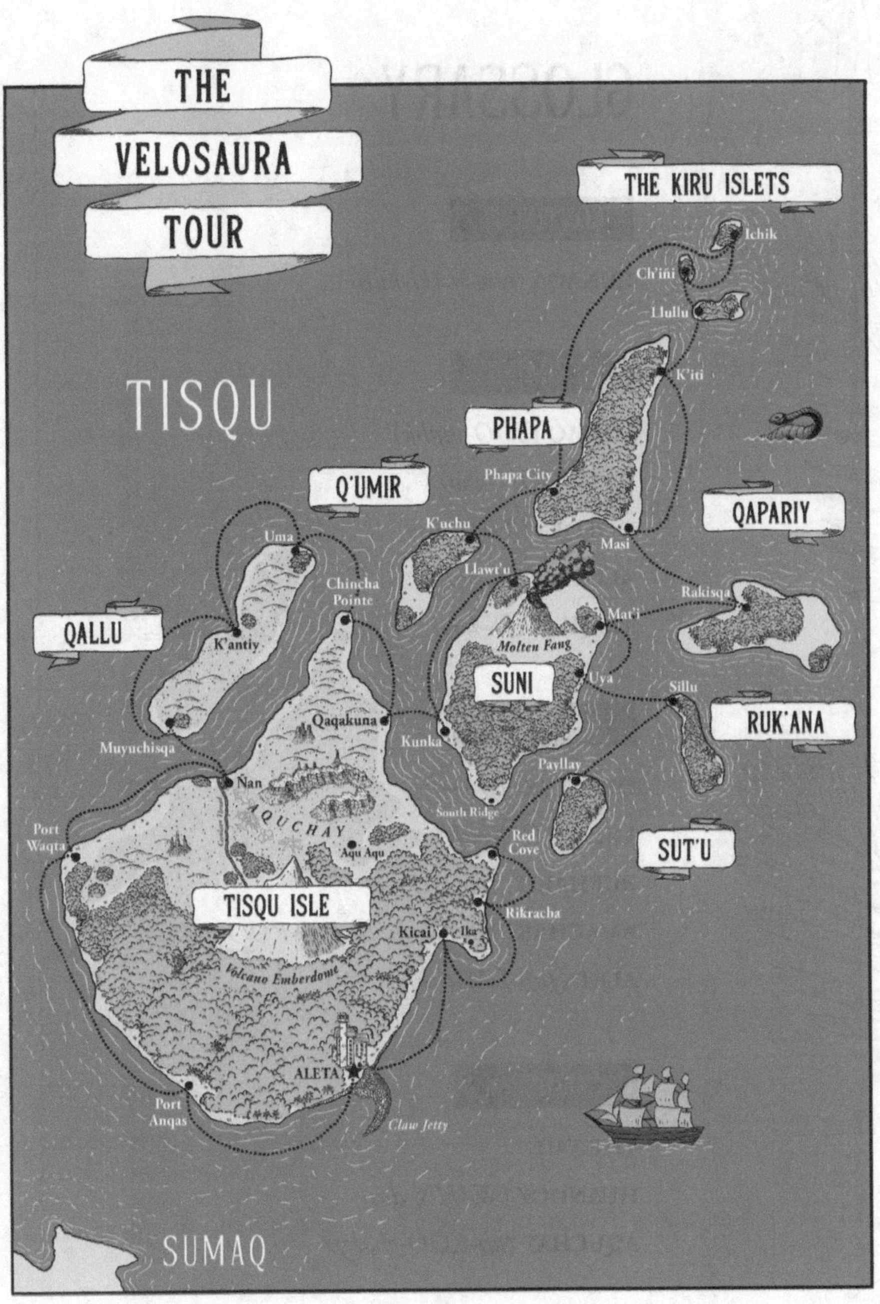

THE VELOSAURA TOUR
TISQU
THE KIRU ISLETS
Ichik
Ch'iñi
Llullu
K'iti
PHAPA
Phapa City
Masi
QAPARIY
Q'UMIR
Uma
K'uchu
Llawt'u
Rakisqa
QALLU
Chincha Pointe
K'antiy
Mat'i
Molten Fang
Muyuchisqa
Qaqakuna
SUNI
Uya
Sillu
Kunka
RUK'ANA
Nan
AQUCHAY
Payllay
Port Waqta
Aqu Aqu
South Ridge
Red Cove
SUT'U
TISQU ISLE
Rikracha
Volcano Emberdome
Kicai
Ika
ALETA
Port Anqas
Claw Jetty
SUMAQ

············· TOUR ROUTE

GLOSSARY

CONTINENT

RUNAQA *(roo-NAH-kuh)*

TERRAINS

SUMAQ *(SOO-mahk)*

UNU *(OOH-noo)*

QOLQE *(KOHL-kay)*

ALLPA *(AHL-puh)*

TISQU *(TISS-koo)*

CAPITALS

QHUSI *(KOO-see)*

YUPA *(YOO-puh)*

RUPHARIY *(roo-PAR-ee)*

AMACHAKUNA *(ah-mah-chuh-KOO-nuh)*

ALETA *(ah-LAY-tuh)*

OTHER

THE TAIL

HUANDOY *(WAHN-doy)*

AQUCHAY *(ah-KOO-chahy)*

QORA *(KOR-uh)*

NINAN *(NIH-non)* / **APO-KIMSA** *(AH-poh KIM-suh)*

SAKAY *(SAH-kahy)*

PAQARI *(pah-KAR-ee)*

QHAPAQ APO *(KAH-pahk AH-poh)*

QHAPAQ IZHI *(KAH-pahk EE-see)*

QUYA URPI *(KOO-yuh OORP-ee)*

KUY *(KOO-ee)*

REQ *(rek)*

WAYRA *(WAHY-ruh)*

GORGO *(GOR-goh)*

TUKO *(TOO-koh)*

CAPTAIN YANACHA *(yah-NAH-chuh)*

APO-HUK *(AH-poh HOOHK)*

APO-ISKAY *(AH-poh ISS-kahy)*

JAYLLI *(HAHY-lee)*

MICHIQ *(MIH-cheek)*

OLLAN *(OH-lun)*

PIDRU *(PIH-droo)*

TAMYA *(TAHM-yuh)*

HAKAN *(HAH-kahn)*

RIMAQ *(RIH-mahk)*

THALU MACHAQWAY *(TAH-loo muh-CHAHK-wahy)*

KUNAQ *(KOO-nahk)*

YAKU *(YAH-koo)*

TIKA *(TEE-kuh)*

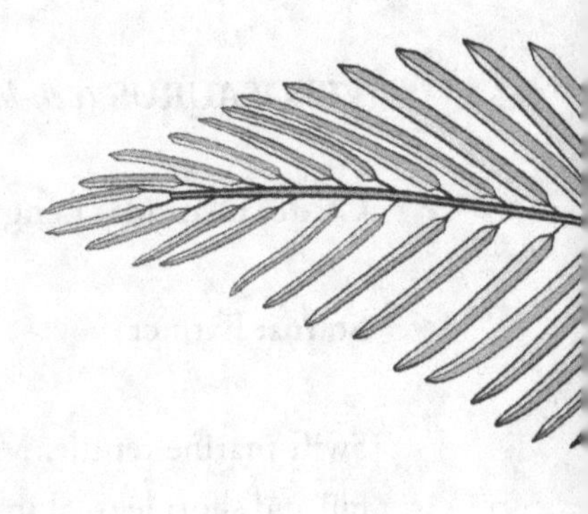

VELOSAURUS *(veh-loh-SOH-russ)*

Clade: Diapsida **Length:** 3-4 ft **Weight:** 30-40 lbs

Status: Extinct

Swift marine reptile. Medium thalattosaurian with long, paddle tail and short legs. Skin contained specialized cells with pigments that could expand or contract to create a range of colors in order to camouflage in response to predatory threats. Under extreme stress could also generate small electric shocks to defend itself.

The Runaqan Compendium of Reptiles

ONE

THE **RAPTORIVA CONSTELLATION TWINKLED** above Ninan as he rode slowly up and down Moriche Pier on raptorback, taking in the briny scent of the sea that churned over the coast of Tisqu's main island.

He scanned the night sky—which seemed so much bigger over the ocean than it did above the mountains—and visually mapped the outline of the flyer with its wings spread wide, the closest he'd been able to get to Qora (the mere, symbolic idea of her) in nearly three moon cycles. His father had made sure they never saw each other, sending Qora out to different cities for celebrity events whenever Ninan was at Kallpa House, and sending Ninan on pre-tour appearances with Paqari throughout the mainland whenever Qora made appearances for locals or tourists in Sumaq.

Sakay had delivered the cordshield message to let Qora know that Ninan had a plan, but now that the island tour aboard the *Velosaura* would begin the day after tomorrow, Ninan worried he'd given her hope for a future he wouldn't be able to realize.

As it was, Qhapaq Izhi was late tonight. The Unuvian qhapaq had sent Ninan explicit instructions to meet him here at this hour, but the man was nowhere to be seen.

Ninan had been gathering intel since Izhi had approached

him privately before the Venture homecoming ceremony. They were close to finding the location of Qhapaq Apo's growing dinosaur army—Ninan could feel it. Or maybe he just wanted to *believe* he could feel it, knowing that there was no way out of his arranged marriage if he couldn't.

Finding a location wasn't everything, though. Even locating his father's skyrock refinery hadn't gotten them far, since it was secured beyond what he or Izhi's spies could infiltrate.

"While skyrock tends to repulse reptiles, this formula somehow appeals to them."

Currently they were only able to track outgoing skyrock shipments to Tisqu, and always lost them upon arrival at obscure ports—different ports every time—random detours, and decoy shipments at transportation switch-points throwing them off the scent.

Finally, Izhi rode up on his own raptor, wearing a heavy cloak with a hood that obscured most of his face.

Ninan and Izhi dismounted at the same time and greeted one another in relative darkness.

"Apo-Kimsa," said Izhi.

Ninan gestured at the small cage attached behind Izhi's saddle, which rocked gently as the flyers inside jostled one another. "Are those the messengers?"

Izhi removed the cage and handed it over. It contained several common black microraptors, and then one gray pteromorph that could fit in his palm. Ninan was unsure of the purpose of the pteromorph; he only knew the microraptors would be trained to home back to Unu's capital so that Ninan could relay messages to Izhi from the ship; he was supposed to store them in the flyer hold aboard the *Velosaura*, where they would find a place among the other messenger flyers.

"They're subtly marked," Izhi explained, "on the bottom of the left foot, so you can be sure you've got one of the right ones. They're also trained to resist anyone who doesn't share your scent"—This explained the sash Izhi had requested from Ninan a week earlier—"and I expect any of the crew looking to use one of them to message Tisqu's capital will then simply opt for a flyer that is less hostile instead."

"And the pteromorph?" Ninan had never heard of anyone using something like that as a messenger. He supposed, with its hyper-flexible body—allowing it to bend and flatten itself to hide in crevices—it might be less likely to get picked off by a predator in transit.

"That's Tuko. He's a tracker. Very shrewd. Don't leave that one in the flyer hold; keep him with you until it's time to use him."

"A tracker?"

"Yes. Pteromorphs have eidetic memory. And if you look closely, you'll see he has scale-feathers—sceathers—which provide insulation and aerodynamic advantages, but also provide added durability for the type of work he'll need to do."

Tuko's sceathers shifted on his back, allowing him to vaguely reshape his head and push halfway through the cage bars, revealing silvery eyes. He nipped at Ninan's finger with his beak.

"What do I do with it?" Ninan asked.

"The first stop on your tour is Kicai," Izhi said. "I've just received intel that an obscure shipment should be arriving at Ika—some eight miles from Kicai's port—shortly after nightfall on the day you dock. In the evening, you must sneak away, procure transportation, and place the pteromorph with the shipment. He'll follow it to its destination, meanwhile stopping to gather bits of flora along the way. It's part of his nature to tuck scraps under his sceathers—typically to use later in nest-making—but we've exploited this behavior as a means of gathering a material trail. Once the cargo has remained in the same location beyond two sun cycles, he will home back to me just like the microraptors, bringing the materials with him. Since every region of the islands is known for its particular botanicals, it should be a relatively easy task to determine the path to the breeding and training base we seek."

"But the botanicals would only give us the general area, not an exact location."

"Yes, but most of the isles aren't many miles across. I'm confident that with a regional clue, we'll have no trouble finding what we're looking for."

"And how will he understand when he's supposed to begin tracking?"

"He's learned a command." Izhi leaned in and whispered it to Ninan. "Say that when you're ready for him to begin."

"That's it?"

"That's it. Although he's also trained to bite an enemy, if you need him to." Izhi lowered his voice and spoke behind his hand. "Just command him to 'sting.'"

Ninan glared at Izhi skeptically. "How will I get close enough to place him on the shipment?"

Izhi removed an additional package from the raptor's saddlebag and unwrapped it, revealing an article of clothing—a dockworker's uniform. "I won't try to tell you it's not risky, but … well, there's a lot on the line here, isn't there?"

Ninan thought of the countless human soldiers who would die if this war were to break out as planned. The countless potential civilian casualties. The grand destruction of buildings and lands. Meanwhile, his own friends in Thak were living with the looming presence of Qhapaq Apo's guards, all two hundred and four citizens under threat of death, simply to ensure Ninan's cooperation with the wedding.

Knowing these things had been enough to make him visit the sanctum weekly, back at Kallpa House. Even with so little faith in gods and spirits, he had knelt repeatedly at the altar embossed with the Three Crescents, and the High Shaman had read from the dinoleatherbound anthology that contained every canonical chant. The High Shaman would perform three chants each time: one for clarity of the mind, one for purity of the heart, and one for serenity of the soul.

After all those visits, Ninan could not say that his mind was clear, nor that his heart was pure. And his soul was anything but serene. Instead, he was clouded and full of rage and drowning in turmoil. But whenever the High Shaman had said, "Be thou now cleansed in body and mind," Ninan had always simply recited back, "Yes, Wise One."

It wasn't that Ninan had thought the smoldering bowl of holy wood or the monotonous chanting or the bundle of chakapa leaves could erase his pain or change upcoming events. It was that, in these desperate moments, the rites he'd been raised on were all he'd had. With so little he could do to stop the storm that threatened to destroy everything he held dear—and perhaps all of Runaqa as he knew it—there was nothing left but to plead with whatever supernatural forces might have some sway.

Then again, if gods could be swayed, Qhapaq Apo would surely win their favor, as he went to the sanctum every morning without fail. For someone who believed himself to be divinely sanctioned to lead not only Sumaq but all Five Terrains, it would follow that he must consistently go before the gods to plead his case and call upon their powers.

And so Ninan had continued to align himself with other potential powers, those which were more practical, and right in front of him. He hadn't forgotten, however, that Qhapaq Izhi had been the one to revive Takan—a man who had nearly killed Ninan on multiple occasions and would have succeeded, had Qora not been there to stop it—at the end of the Venture. Thus, these meetings and these assignments always carried a weight Ninan struggled to bear. But Izhi was right: It was a risk he'd have to take. In many cases, Ninan was the only person close enough to the source of the threat to get necessary information—at least without too much suspicion. Being on the tour would allow him the best access to this upcoming shipment.

"I'm told, they're referring to the refined skyrock product as 'dominite,'" Izhi added.

Dominite. Ninan turned the word over in his mind. Something that implied dominion. Control. He remembered that night in the menagerie—the night his father had threatened him into the arrangement—and how affectionate those dinosaurs had been, because that's what his father had wanted. But when his father wanted them to be vicious, they would no doubt be vicious.

His mother's words came to him like a sharp blade: *The qhapaq gets what he wants.*

"We still have yet to obtain a sample of it," Izhi informed him. "If you're able to do that while you're placing the tracker, it would be immensely advantageous."

"I'll see what I can do."

Ninan stared up at the stars again, looking over the silhouettes between them. Astrodon glowed with its bright saberteeth, and The Serpent sat coiled with its head raised and its eyes twinkling. A white band of thickly clustered stars flowed through the darkness—the great Sky River—from which the nearby astronomical creatures came to "drink." All the shapes were only approximations of their real-life counterparts, and some more vague than others. He locked onto the vague shape of the raptoriva once again—feeling all too vague in whatever shape he himself had begun to take these past moons—and remembered the look on Qora's face when she'd learned the truth about him. While he couldn't change where he'd come from, he could use the privilege that came with it to help make way for a better world.

"You know," Izhi said, "It's fitting that you're going to be on that particular ship."

"And why's that?" Ninan asked.

"Surely you're familiar with the creature for which it was named?"

Clinging to his raptor's reigns, Ninan nodded. "The velosaur was a swift thalattosaurian that could change color to blend into its surroundings to hide from predators."

"Right," said Izhi. "Likewise—although you are no match for your father's power—if you can disguise yourself in loyalty, and act like you belong in this highborn world despite rejecting it … you just might make it out alive."

TWO

"REST YOUR HAND ON THE SNOUT," the artist told Qora.

Qora eased closer to the enormous spinosaur head, severed from its body only eleven weeks ago—by her. A thick layer of resin coated the scales now and gave off a woody scent, one that had come to stoke the unpleasant coals of Qora's memory.

At least once a week, she was forced to stand here on the grounds of Kallpa House beside the spinosaur head and pose, to stare determinedly off into the distance or point her weapon while a sculptor or painter immortalized her. She would have been lying if she'd said she hadn't thought of aiming her new, showy, metal crossbow at whichever man or woman gave her direction on any given day, demanding that she lower her brows or puff out her chest or raise her chin.

It was barely tolerable even when she didn't have to touch the monster she'd murdered, but putting her hand on it brought everything back to her in flashes. Its jaws open wide, enormous and all-encompassing, the stink of its hot breath that carried the deaths of so many others before her, its teeth threatening to dig into her shoulders. Then the blade, the one Sakay had lent her—her only hope, her last effort, the way it had broken through the spinosaur's soft palate under her desperate plunge, its roar radiating through the bones of her arm as she had forced the blade deeper and twisted and wrenched it out to do it again.

"Chin up," the artist demanded, bringing her back to the moment. He pointed his brush upward.

Thankfully, this would be her last publicity task for a while. The qhapaq had promised her a few weeks' rest from riding in parades at city festivals, or laying the winner's medal on whomever took first place in the biweekly megaraptor races, or training to ride giant pteranodons so that she could majestically fly in and land on the city square platform before public speeches, or posing for these gratuitous portraits.

She adjusted the sleeves of the green bayeta jacket she wore, recreated by the qhapaq's tailor to match the one she'd worn during the Venture. Except this one was stiff and itchy, and jade in color, rather than the mossy green of the jacket she'd dyed herself, which was tattered and folded up at the bottom of a trunk at home. It wasn't something she liked to look at if she didn't have to, a reminder of how many times she'd nearly lost her life, a reminder of the boy she *had* lost. An ache took hold of her when she thought about Ninan, who would be out on the *Velosaura* soon, sailing the ocean between islands, so far from her that he might as well have been a dream. Did she ever cross his mind now?

I HAVE A PLAN. WAIT FOR ME? For weeks, she'd repeated those words in her mind, over and over until the individual sounds of them had lost meaning. It had only been recently that she'd stopped, wondering whether it was worth it to hold on to them. He was, after all, engaged to another girl. Paqari, princess of Tisqu, and beautiful enough that Qora wouldn't even blame him for going through with it. It didn't help that it was Ninan's own father who had Qora up on a pedestal for the public, working her weary to bring in more tourism as hordes of people came from all surrounding lands to see the spinosaur head—and its slayer—for themselves, or sending her out to Allpa and Qolqe for additional appearances, forcing her to wear the likeness of her own clothes as a costume. At least her family was well cared for, thanks to her winnings from the competition. That made all of this work important, she reminded herself.

When the artist finally dismissed her, she quickly picked up her satchel and ran off to the menagerie.

By now, the staff hardly paid her any attention as she moved across the courtyard and through the corridors. She'd been in and out of Kallpa House on an almost weekly basis and was permitted to spend as much time as she liked. Not that she *liked* to be here; she'd learned early on that the chances of running into Ninan were low, and she cared little for the art or the architecture—having seen it all often enough—but there was one place that did bring her a certain sense of comfort.

Qora entered the menagerie, following the stone path that snaked between the cages and holding her breath against the scent of ruck that rose up from the straw. Several keepers were shoveling right now, although it was impossible for them to keep up with so many reptiles, some of which were quite large. The faux habitats, however, looked stunning as always, with realistic red-rock walls or verdant jungle flora or tall grasses or watery pools. Living within them were miniature pink triceratops, multicolored iridosaurs, a microceratus with scales so shiny they looked like polished silver, some troodon-archaeopteryx hybrid that appeared to have more feathers than it knew how to handle, and a very grumpy dilophosaur with striped frills around its neck—to name a few.

The qhapaq's staff had bred at least half of the creatures here, while the other half were collector's items the qhapaq had discovered or seized from illegal trades. The Venture's spinosaur had surely come from some egg that the qhapaq's scouts had seized from beyond the Pirqas—the only place where the larger theropods still remained in nature—and raised it in captivity. It may have even been the source of the genetic material used to create the very sailbeast that had killed Qora's oldest brother, Ollan. She clenched her fists at the idea, an idea she'd had to wall off in her mind every time she came to Kallpa House for another assignment, every time she stood beside the qhapaq at a public event, every time the qhapaq called her "my champion."

Qora made her way to the west end, where a small green flyer perched within an ornate, gilded cage. The raptoriva squawked when it saw her, and flapped its iridescent wings.

Removing a small package from her satchel, Qora stepped close.

"Good morning, Miña." The flyer's full name was Umiña Mintasqa the Resplendent, and she certainly lived up to the glory of it with her raised chin and regal posture. Unlike Qora, Miña liked to strike a pose.

Qora set her satchel on the floor, then unwrapped the papyr crinkled around the package, and revealed several slices of dried mango.

Miña cocked her scaly head, paused dramatically, then darted forward as far as she could fit and snatched a piece. Laughing, Qora watched the raptoriva work her mouth around the fruit. She slipped two fingers into the cage and stroked Miña's head. "That's a good girl."

As she did every time she visited the raptoriva, Qora said a silent prayer to Sky Mother, begging her forgiveness. The poor flyer would be free if it hadn't been for Qora's attempt to trade her. Although, she had to admit, she didn't know what she would have done instead. Rimaq had been on the brink of death from theropox, and there simply hadn't been enough money for the sparkshade he'd needed to survive. As much as Qora regretted her choices, the events that had followed seemed to be woven into her destiny in a way she couldn't explain. As difficult as it was to constantly face the qhapaq, and the public, and the consequences of her participation in the Venture—not all of which had been negative, especially not her happy, living, littlest brother—she felt almost … *content* … to bear the burden. It was a high price. A sacrifice. What other way could there have been?

Still, the sight of the raptoriva behind these bars induced a pang in her chest.

"I'm sorry," she told Miña.

The raptoriva chewed through the leathery, dried mango, shredding it bit by bit in silence.

"Sorry for what?" said the qhapaq.

Qora flinched, then released a slow breath before she turned around and bowed. "Your Majesty." Her pulse raced as the qhapaq stared at her, some ten paces away, with his dark, muscular arms bared in a sleeveless red robe. Even though he only ever moved solemnly, he was built like a warrior, honed and postured as though he knew how to wield a blade.

He inclined his head and stepped forward, holding his scepter. "Such a fascinating creature, isn't she?" He glanced at the flyer. "Docile, meek—so long as no one threatens her. Then she will reveal her true and vicious nature."

Qora watched as the raptoriva tucked her wings and shifted within the cage. She imagined that the flyer would not *like* to fight, but that, with her place in the reptile hierarchy, she would do whatever she had to. Regardless, the raptoriva had now been reduced to a decoration.

"I am grateful to you for bringing her to me," he added.

Qora swallowed hard. "What?"

He smiled, although the expression didn't reach his eyes. "The raptoriva. She came to me by your hand. Did she not? That's why you have lingered here at Kallpa House today, why you visit my menagerie whenever you've finished with a portrait or a flying session, why you … *apologize* … to the little reptile when you think no one's listening."

Her heart hammered in her chest. Her face flooded with heat. *How long has he known?*

The qhapaq clicked his tongue. "Don't be fearful, champion. I'm not angry. In fact, I'm rather impressed that you, at such a tender age, were able to procure such a rare thing on your own. Then again, after all you managed to accomplish during the Venture, I suppose it should come as no surprise."

Qora didn't know what to say. She was too focused on keeping her breathing steady, on locking her knees in place. Gods, she was practically shaking. It wasn't as though Qhapaq Apo were some enormous dinosaur that could cut her in half with his teeth.

But of course there were *other* ways he could cut her in half.

"I believe," he added, "that she acted as a divine symbol—a harbinger for your championhood. Surely it was no mistake that she found her way into my hands just prior to your entry into the Venture. Surely it was no mistake that it was you who sent her to me, albeit unwittingly. In all ways, she stands for you, and you for her."

Qora nodded numbly. "I suppose she does."

He smiled again—that same, eerie twist of his lips. "If you're finished here, you are dismissed for your extended leave. I expect to see you again in two weeks for your appearance at the Heritage

Festival, and then for your fitting the week after in preparation for the Revelry."

"Of course." She nodded again, then cast a longing glance at Miña. It would be at least two weeks before she would see her again, too.

"Don't worry," said the qhapaq. "Miss Umiña Mintasqa will take a brief leave of her own." He snapped his fingers to the side, prompting one of the nearby keepers to look up from his shovel. "Take the raptoriva to the fields for some exercise, won't you?"

The raptoriva squawked, and Qora gave her a few final strokes down her back.

At least she'll get some fresh air, Qora thought as she bowed to the qhapaq in farewell and hurried out of his presence. But before she was completely out of earshot, she heard him add, "And don't forget her tether."

🌙🌙🌙

Halfway down the connecting corridor, Qora reached for the strap on her satchel, only for her hand to come up empty against her chest. She sighed and rolled her eyes, remembering she'd left it on the floor by the raptoriva's cage.

She returned to the menagerie, and as she approached, she heard the qhapaq's voice again.

"I appreciate your swift response to the threat," he said. "These matters must not be taken lightly."

Rather than step into his view, Qora halted, straining her ears.

"Certainly not, Your Majesty," another voice replied.

It was the Commander of Watch.

Qora knew his voice by now, too. He often came to deliver

reports, especially those pertaining to attempted security breaches in the skyrock processing facilities. Lately, he'd been showing up with wide, shifty eyes and perpetually furrowed brows, taking more frequent meetings with the qhapaq. Many a time, Qora had been summoned to Kallpa House for one champion's task or another—to practice a motivational speech or receive feedback on her progress with her pteroflight training—and had ended up having to wait for the qhapaq when the meetings had run long.

"Rest assured, I've implemented a number of new strategies to minimize any attempts at interception," the qhapaq told him.

"Of course," said the commander. "My concern, however, is that the increased shipments will lead to an increase in attacks, and that, eventually, we won't be able to stop them all. Our enemies are aware of the dominite now; that much is clear. They suspect what it can do, and I believe they're ready to lay down their lives for it."

Dominite? Qora thought. *Enemies?*

The qhapaq paused before he spoke again. "Very well. I will summon additional security officers from Ñansa to assist you. They have plenty of teeth to defend themselves, even if we borrow from their numbers."

"Thank you," the commander said.

Qora continued to listen until she heard their footsteps on the stone path, then turned to leave, abandoning her satchel altogether.

))) (((

One of the qhapaq's enormous pterobeasts delivered Qora to her home in its dangling gondola. Qora hated the attention it drew, with everyone outside the city gazing up at her as she flew over. She often put up the hood of her jacket so she didn't have to show her face, although the jacket itself was iconic now, and did little to keep her identity a secret. But at least no one gathered outside the house anymore, thanks to the novelty of her fame slowly fading, and the fact that she had purchased a new, more remote place to live.

With her winnings, she'd had a new house built on the several acres of land her family had once owned before her papáy's death. Long before the Venture, her mamáy hadn't been able to afford it without his income, and so they'd moved to a snug little place near the woods. This was an incredible feeling for Qora, recovering what they'd lost after so many years, and then improving upon it.

Once she landed and approached the front of the house, Qora kicked off her boots, practically before she was even all the way through the door. The stiff dinoleather, treated to look pretty rather than to be functional, had made her legs sore, nothing like the soft and supple dinoleather of her original boots, which were lined up in the entryway. Hakan stoked the flames in the oven while their mamáy patted corn dough into cakes and Rimaq swept the floor. It was a comforting scene, the three of them. The qhapaq had insisted Qora move them all to Kichka, to an even bigger house with tile floors and glass windows, but she continued to politely refuse. Now with plenty of money to keep them all fed and clothed and far away from indentured labor, they didn't belong anywhere but here. They definitely didn't belong in Kichka, Qora thought, with those showy stone walls and qompi robes.

The new house did, however, have two levels, so that each member of the family had his or her own room complete with carved-wood doors and troodon-feather bedmats. The meadow stretched out all around it, with plenty of space for alpacas so that Qora's mamáy could spin even more alpaca-fiber yarn—not that she needed to, but she didn't seem to know how to quit working. They'd even constructed a dinoshelter and purchased a couple of rhabdodons for transportation (although Kallpa House was only accessible by flight, and thus she'd had to rely on the pterobeasts whenever she was summoned). While the view from the property might have been practically nothing compared to what the qhapaq saw from the mountain castle looming over Qhusi, Qora thought the view from here was spectacular anyway, overlooking the stream and several small farms below.

"You're home in time to eat with us," Rimaq chimed, gripping the broom as he paused to look at her. His skin was rosy and taut, and clear of any pox. The residual sores had taken several weeks to fully heal, with lingering scabs, but now he showed no signs of his former illness.

Throwing him a wan smile, Qora sighed and peeled off the green jacket, tempted to leave it in a heap on the floor, but she imagined the qhapaq with his scrutinizing stare finding a single speck of dust on it and she hung it nicely on the set of hooks instead. Behind her, two compies scampered in from the yard and she nudged them out with her foot before closing the door.

Her mamáy nodded toward the jacket. "You should let me make you a new one."

"This *is* a new one," Qora reminded her, flicking the sleeve as it dangled.

Her mamáy clicked her tongue and plopped a disc of dough onto the ceramic baking tray in front of her. "You know what I mean."

Qora knew she meant well, that she was trying to help her find a way to reconcile her old life with her new one, but both held complications Qora wanted nothing to do with anymore. When she pursed her lips, her mamáy just said, "Think about it."

"There's nothing to think about," Qora muttered. With two quick tugs, she pulled the ties from the ends of her braids and combed her fingers through to unravel them. Anything to distance herself from the Raptoriva persona. Anything to help her forget all that and move on.

Her crossbow, on the other hand, was more difficult to ignore. It had its own hook by the doorframe, and although she never took it hunting anymore, it made her feel like Ollan was still with her. She spared it a melancholy glance before wreathing her littlest brother a tight squeeze. Thanks to her work with the qhapaq, she'd been given resources and assistance to distribute sparkshade to many *other* children to combat theropox too, yet another reason she had to remember to be grateful for her position.

When evening fell, Qora and the boys helped their mamáy take down the yarns that had been drying, and then each of them settled into some leisurely activity or another. Hakan, still thirteen but having grown another inch or so and built some muscle, sat in their papáy's old chair, whittling a small figurine, and from this particular angle Qora thought he was beginning to look a lot like Ollan. Rimaq, who had recently had his ninth birthday, looked much too grown up in a new tunic as he stroked the scales of one of the compies he'd tamed and taken to bringing inside. Their mamáy knitted a new shawl for herself and hummed absentmindedly while she did it. Qora polished her old boots even though she didn't wear them anymore, just for something to do.

The boots still bore the scars of the journey on which they had carried her, down through the foothills and across vast stretches of jungle. In many places the dinoleather was scratched beyond repair, and Qora couldn't help feeling like she was the same way, all cracked and worn so deeply that nothing could ever truly polish her up again.

"I think I need to take a walk," she finally said.

It was late and her mamáy didn't think it was a good idea, but Qora reminded her she'd seen much worse than the thieves who might accost her in the dark—and besides, she'd gladly give them a few coppers anyway, since she had them to spare and most everyone was struggling a bit these days.

Her walk was just an excuse, though, to go see the one person who really knew the full extent of what was going on in her mind right now. And she knew exactly where he'd be.

THREE

SAKAY FOLDED A STACK of colorful, geometric-patterned alpaca-fiber blankets in a way that showed them off for buyers. He stopped and ran his hand over his close-cropped hair, grazing the patterns shaved into the sides.

The Underground was fairly empty, with lanterns casting dim, flickering light across the dinosaur heads mounted on the walls. A few men sat at the tables playing a game with wooden tokens while they sipped pisco. Aside from the clatter of tokens and cups, the atmosphere was quiet.

Then a familiar face appeared at the entrance, and Sakay smiled.

Qora kept her head covered, likely out of habit. Sakay figured she wasn't especially worried about being recognized at this time of night. A good number of the traders who came in were from distant cities, unlikely to know her face as well as the locals. As always, she carried her crossbow.

He took in her appearance, hair down and loose, dark pants and hooded poncho.

She moved silently toward the back and caught sight of him, smiling in return. She eyed the traders warily as she passed them, pulling her hood more tightly around her face, but when she reached him he told her, "Don't worry. They're much more focused on their game than on anyone around them."

Qora released a pent-up breath. "Good to know."

"There was only one pachyrhinosaur horn left, so they're playing to see who wins it."

With the kind of addictive energy boost brought on by ingesting ground-up pachyrhinosaur horns (referred to as "pachyrhine") it was a tense game.

Qora raised an eyebrow. "Only one? Don't you usually keep a few extra in the—"

Sakay put a finger to his lips and grinned behind it. His skill in driving up the value of goods was why he was practically running this place on his own at the age of twenty. His uncle had entrusted him with the whole of the Underground on a regular basis while off establishing other trading posts along the coast.

Qora let her hood down and rolled her eyes, then moved to take a seat at the bar.

Shortly after, Sakay came around and slid a ceramic mug in front of her.

"No thanks," she told him.

He cocked his head knowingly. "Really? Sure looks like you could use it."

She leaned toward the rim and wrinkled her nose. "That's ... sharp."

"Takes some getting used to," he admitted.

The look in her eyes told him she was wallowing in misery, barely kept afloat by the peace of mind her winnings had brought her. She hadn't come in for a trade since before the Venture—because now, she didn't have to. Thankfully, she'd never have to enter those woods again, looking for a kill. She'd never have to be reminded of her lost brother—at least not by those surroundings. Still, he wished to all the gods he had another message from Ninan to give her, anything to assuage the other ache that certainly plagued her now. But he hadn't seen Ninan since the night after the homecoming ceremony, and he doubted he would again; a disinherited prince, reinstated, had few freedoms.

"Your hair looks nice like that," he said.

She pinched a section of the loose waves and glanced at it, then let it fall. "Thanks. I can't handle the braids anymore—and I really only needed them to keep my hair out of my face while I was hunting. Besides, people seem to have a harder time recognizing me without them, so … that's an advantage."

"I'm sorry fame and fortune is such a drag."

"I accept your apology."

As Qora took a sip of the drink in front of her, Sakay spotted yet another familiar figure entering the Underground.

He cast an apologetic glance at Qora and said, "Excuse me a moment, would you?"

Approaching the young man, having forgotten how tall he was, Sakay lowered his voice and looked up at him. "Kuy …"

The man straightened his lean form and flicked a bit of his dark hair out of his eyes. "We've got another mission."

Sakay raised an eyebrow. It had been two years since the Razorclaws had attempted anything major—the aftermath of which still stuck in his heart like a large thorn. He wrapped his fingers around the dinosaur tooth that hung from the leather strap around his neck. "I guess I'm not surprised you haven't given up on the cause, but … I don't understand why you're telling *me*. I'm still not ready to have any part in another—"

"This one's different. We already have all the necessary information to head out. And there's no facility to break into, no labyrinthine corridors, no armored gates."

"What is it, then?" Sakay couldn't imagine anything of value that would simply be left out in the open.

"A dominite shipment."

Sakay's pulse kicked up.

Dominite.

When the Razorclaws had first learned of its existence, he hadn't wanted to believe it. After everything the group had done to stop the qhapaq's previous attempt to reunify the Terrains, that tyrant had managed to devise an even more sinister plan. Just thinking of it made Sakay's blood boil.

Kuy continued. "Our insiders got a definitive location as to where it's headed. It should be showing up at a small port in Ika, on Tisqu Isle. We almost snatched a sample before it left the harbor, but we were compromised at the last minute. Now our best chance is to intercept before it moves on after arrival."

"What about guards?"

"We've got that covered. Req cooked up something new. They won't be a problem."

The guards had been the problem last time—not because they were impossible to overcome, but because of special units and the poisoned blades they carried.

"So you're saying you'll just fly over, drop down, pick up the sample, and leave? Without issue?"

"Without issue."

It seemed too easy, but ... Sakay was also well aware of what Req was capable of. Near-silent explosives, incendiary concoctions, light-flash bombs, liquids that could dissolve metal.

"We won't have much time, though," Kuy added. "Req's new 'weapon' is still in progress. Currently it only works for a few minutes at a time. So we'll need several of us to scour the storage bays to find the dominite as quickly as possible. But with all of us working together, I don't anticipate any setbacks."

"Alright," Sakay said numbly. "What do you need from me?"

"A safe haven. You told me once that your uncle has ties with the owner of the Den in Aleta?"

Sakay nodded. The Den was another traders' hub like the Underground, near Tisqu's capital. The two venues had good relations, often transporting their more significant goods back and forth as the markets demanded. "The Den can provide lodging. I'll send a message ahead of you, by flyer. When do you leave?"

"Tomorrow."

"Tomorrow? Well that doesn't give me much time ..."

"Actually," said Kuy, "we were hoping you'd come with us, and vouch for us in person."

Sakay scoffed. "Why would you dare to hope such a thing?"

Kuy took a deep breath and inclined his head closer. "I know how much it pains you. You know I do. But spending your days in this ruckhole, avoiding the crew, isn't going to bring *her* back."

He tensed at the reference. "Neither will fighting for a lost cause."

"The cause is not lost until we concede. That's what she would tell you if she were still with us. You know that." Kuy nodded toward the tooth in Sakay's fist.

Sakay gripped it more tightly.

"What was it she used to say?" Kuy asked.

A sting formed behind Sakay's eyes. He swallowed. "'Always use your teeth.'"

Kuy laid a firm hand on Sakay's shoulder. "Your teeth are going to waste in this place. Don't you think it's time you sink them into something?"

Inhaling deeply, Sakay shook his head. "I don't know, Kuy. We're meddling in something so much bigger than us, against forces we can't possibly match."

"We've succeeded before."

"Success is relative," Sakay argued. "Last time, we cut off the qhapaq's hand, and somehow he managed to grow four more. It's hard enough to live with the consequences of that. Do you really want to tempt fate again?"

"I want to stop a war before it starts. And you should too."

"And how do you plan to get to Tisqu?"

"Wayra bred a swoop of pteranodons up on Mount Qaqra. She lives there now."

Sakay shook his head again. Of course she did. That woman wasn't happy unless she was running with a full gang of velociraptors or nurturing a brood of vicious flyers. "Who'll run this place while I'm gone?"

"Gone where?" Qora said over his shoulder.

Sakay spun around to see her standing behind him. "Nowhere."

She crossed her arms. "I know intrigue when I see it. Speaking of which, someone by the back counter just handed off a sack of aquilops teeth about two minutes ago, and I'm sure they were fake, so you might want to brace yourself for a fight if the buyer figures it out and comes back before you close up."

Kuy and Sakay exchanged a glance.

"I'll be right back," Sakay told the man as he steered Qora into the storeroom.

Shutting the door behind them, Sakay couldn't help but remember the last time he'd been in here with Qora. It was the day Ninan had given Gorgo the beating of his life. The fateful day Qora had brought in the raptoriva, pleading for his help.

"Who was that?" Qora asked. "Where are you thinking of going?"

"It's really better if you don't know," he told her. Not that he'd decided anything officially yet.

"Why? You don't think I can handle it?"

"I know you can handle anything, but that doesn't mean it's a good idea to get mixed up in it."

"Mixed up in *what*?"

"It's more than just trades," he said. "This is a lot bigger than that. It's … rebellion."

Qora frowned. "You think I'm loyal to my qhapaq just because I have to stand on whatever perch he tells me to?"

"No. Gods." He sighed. "I know it's not like that. But … you just got your family in a good place. Everyone's well and thriving."

"I'm *hardly* thriving …"

Sakay knew her victory had been bittersweet, especially once he'd gotten the whole story. The Venture had changed her, turned her into a reluctant killer, and now the qhapaq was forcing her to constantly relive it, to speak about it publicly and stand as an allegorical symbol. Her face appeared on murals throughout the city walls, depicted in action scenes as told by the Venture heralds. And, worse, she'd grown close to Ninan, who had turned out to be the disinherited Third Prince of Sumaq, currently engaged to the island princess and preparing to embark on some pre-wedding tour by ship. He couldn't blame Qora for struggling to come to terms with it all, even if her family was safe in a new home.

"It could definitely be worse," he said.

She acted as though he'd said nothing. "So what is it? A heist? Some kind of revolution?"

He stared at her for a moment, trying to decide whether it would be better to keep resisting, or if it was pointless and he should simply give in right now. Qora wasn't going to let it go—not when she knew there was something he wasn't telling her.

"Fine," he said. "It's a group working against the qhapaq. They call themselves the Razorclaws."

"And … you're one of them?" She narrowed her eyes.

"Yes. No. Not exactly. Not anymore …"

"Since when?"

Since Ramaya, he thought. It was a story he never told anyone, not even Qora, regardless of how close they'd become.

"Two years," he said.

"Two years?" she screeched back.

He shushed her. "Yes, two years. But I haven't gone on any assignments for a long time. Usually I help by providing resources and supplies that would otherwise be difficult to get. *Enhancements*."

By the look on her face, Sakay could tell she knew what he meant. Illegal substances made from certain reptile parts that could affect the mind or body. An enzyme in avimimus hearts could act as a sort of truth serum; pamparaptor liver could cause hallucinations; sinornithosaur venom was a paralytic once it entered the bloodstream; pachyrhinosaur horns, when powdered and ingested, could provide a boost of godlike physical energy; dimetrodon eyeballs could sharply improve mental efficiency, and heal broken minds. And that was to say nothing of other useful substances, like sauropod oils, which could burn for extended periods of time without producing smoke. Some of these things were illegal, or at least very hard to come by, for those without connections. Sakay's connections, however, allowed him access to reptile products as well as weapons, travel supplies, and beyond.

"The Razorclaws are comprised of a core team of skilled individuals," Sakay explained, "supported by insiders who have worked—or still work—close to the qhapaq. Men and women on the crews who have helped build his walls, or those with more advanced positions within his factories, even those who deliver his papyr supplies for correspondence and written orders. It's a growing network to gather intel in hopes of one day deposing the tyrant that oppresses them."

"What have you learned so far?"

"The qhapaq is refining skyrock, for starters. We don't know why, other than the obvious."

"To make reptiles more obedient," Qora said.

"But to what end?" Sakay asked. "That's the question. Better service reptiles, sure, except … Why all the secrecy? Why all the added security? It's not only the plethora of guards outside the refinement facility, but the classified documents concerning it. And to add to that, large shipments of it keep going out to Tisqu, always to different ports."

Qora perked up. "I heard something at Kallpa House today. The qhapaq was talking to the Commander of Watch. He said something about … 'dominionite'?"

"'Dominite,'" Sakay corrected. "Yes. That's the refined skyrock."

"The commander said he was worried about 'enemy attacks.' So, who's the enemy here? The rebel network? Or someone else?"

"We think we're on the brink of war with the other Terrains," Sakay said. "In an effort to take them all back under one empire. That's been an ongoing scheme of the qhapaq's. This is likely the latest iteration."

Qora paled at this information. "And what exactly do the

Razorclaws think they'll be able to do about it?"

"Right now, their main focus is to get a sample of the dominite and figure out what it does, how it works—whether it's just a more potent form of skyrock, or something else entirely. They've also got an elementalist who can break down the sample so we know what's been done to the skyrock, so that we can recreate the formula."

Sakay wasn't sure why he kept saying "we," but he supposed old habits were hard to break.

"So they're going to try and get that sample soon?"

"Yes. They're leaving tomorrow. They want me to go with them."

"Your friend said something about flyers," Qora recalled. "I've been doing pteroflight training for months now. Maybe I could—"

"No." He shook his head. "No, no, absolutely not. You're not coming. You've faced enough danger to last you a lifetime."

The days Qora had been gone during the Venture had been difficult for him. He still would never admit it to her, but he'd waited daily for the heralds' reports, tense and nauseated until he'd finished reading the list of the dead without finding her name. It had been likewise difficult to see the heralds returning with living competitors—those who had surrendered and asked to be removed without completing the race—when she was never among them.

"How are you more resistant to my coming with you on this assignment than you were to my entry in the Venture? Intercepting a shipment can't possibly be more dangerous."

In truth, Sakay thought, Qora did not have the slightest idea how much he'd resisted her entering the Venture. At first, he hadn't taken her seriously. Then, once she'd signed up, he was certain she wouldn't make it past the trials anyway—not because she wasn't capable or tenacious, but because he'd expected the judges to favor much more brutal, male competitors who would put on a "better show." But after she'd been selected to participate, there had been little he could do. Advising her against it would have only spurred her onward. So he'd supported her and encouraged her in whatever way he could, trained her, provided supplies, and hoped for the best. Again, he'd prayed she would come to her senses and back out, or at the very least surrender early on. But she'd persisted. In her absence, he'd tried to set up a few trades that might help her financially, but they'd fallen through, and she'd won the competition shortly thereafter.

Besides, what would he have said, anyway? That she was one of the few important people in his life? That he'd already lost someone a lot like her, and he couldn't bear to lose her too? It would have sounded all wrong, given her the wrong idea entirely.

So he'd kept quiet about the fact that he had often worried for her hunting alone in the woods, that he had always watched the other traders carefully around her to ensure no one tried anything, that she had piqued his curiosity from the first day she'd walked into the Underground at thirteen years old carrying a carcass too big for her shoulders to bear, and that, little by little, he had come to look forward to her visits, to haggling with her, to pretending he wouldn't give in to her prices. He hadn't known just how much he cared until he'd seen her standing on the flats that day at the Venture sendoff—he still hadn't told her he'd been there—and the fear had been all too familiar.

"Sakay." Qora sighed and tucked her hair behind her ear. "I'm tired of just being the Raptoriva. I'm tired of 'waiting' for Ninan. I have a couple weeks' leave from my champion duties. The timing is perfect." She bit her lip. "I … need to feel like

I'm doing something bigger, and more meaningful … and not just moping around while I play dress-up for the qhapaq. And speaking of the qhapaq, I've been working closely with him for a while; maybe something I've overheard could help. I could be useful."

"I have no doubt you'd be useful, *kantuta*. But it's out of the question."

She didn't even bother to argue this time. She just flashed her glossy brown eyes at him, with a desperate need flickering behind them.

Kuy had just guaranteed there would be no issue, Sakay reminded himself. Fly over, drop in, get out. Easy.

Of course, these heists were never easy. Something always went wrong. He'd be a fool to believe they could really pull it off completely "without issue." Still, it seemed far less complicated than anything the Razorclaws had done before, especially if Req had created a way to quickly debilitate any guards.

Like the older brother Qora had lost, Sakay wanted not only to protect her but also to give her what she needed. In this case, she seemed to need an escape, a renewed sense of purpose. He needed that sense of purpose too, he realized. Kuy was right. All former losses would be in vain if he didn't fight now, even though this particular fight was a small one, a starting point. But he had to start somewhere, didn't he?

Finally, he nodded. "Alright. Pack for Tisqu."

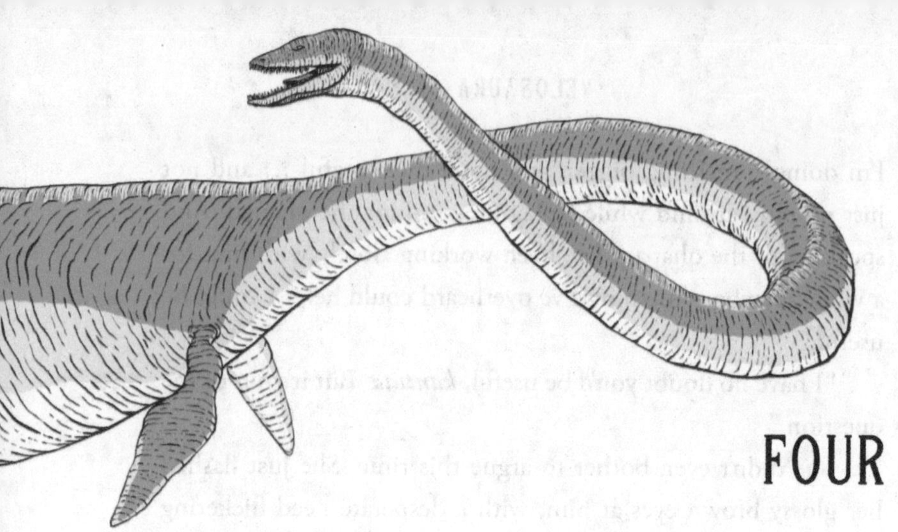

FOUR

NINAN FELT LIKE A FRILL-NECKED DILOPHOSAUR, all strut and show in a dress uniform with a red velvet jacket and brass buttons—a far cry from the simple cotton and wool clothes he'd worn in Thak, and heavy. Even after months of being back at Kallpa House, or at least among highborns, he'd still managed to keep his wardrobe simple—plain tunics with buttons that weren't too shiny, and trousers that were fine-spun but simple. But this was an event that would go down in history; at least that's what his father had told everyone. And so, Ninan had to play the part.

"It's fitting that you're going to be on that particular ship."

He thought of Izhi comparing him to a velosaur. Some velosaur he was, readjusting his uniform jacket like it didn't fit him properly, clenching his toes inside the stiff boots. He was more like that pteromorph, trying to bend and flatten himself into an awkward space where he wasn't meant to fit, shoving tidbits of information under his figurative sceathers in hopes that he might make himself useful.

The pteromorph was still in the cage Izhi had provided, hidden under the bed in Ninan's sleeping cabin. Meanwhile, the microraptors were in the flyer hold—he'd come aboard the ship just after dawn and slipped them inside with the others

32

designated for general correspondence—ready for use.

It was still very early, but already crowds had begun to gather along the city's principal harbor. Many had arrived via sauropod, filling up the extensive seat boxes on the backs of the longneck dinosaurs in groups. The sauropods pulled up to the elevated deboarding structures so that passengers could climb down and join the growing masses.

Other dignitaries—ambassadors and statespeople and governors—arrived on triceratops, making their way to the front for prime viewing.

Officers of the Tisquvian Guard patrolled the viewing zone as well as the ship, wearing plum-colored uniforms and donning sheathed blades.

Eleven Tisquvian flags lined the coast—one for each island—that same plum purple with the nation's liopleurodon-and-shield emblem on the fabric.

Ninan stood amidships with all the royalborns and highborns who had come to socialize and drink and admire the ship before its departure. It was a gala in its own right, with musicians playing bone flutes and dancers in colorful woven garb, and everyone else dressed in their finest, while the royalborns of the Houses of Kallpa and Huapaya greeted their peers and accepted congratulations.

The Huapayas consisted of Qhapaq Achik, his three quyas, and the six children between them all. Paqari was the second born to the first quya. Her position between her twenty-year-old sister (married to the Seafarer's Regent of Suni) and her fifteen-year-old brother (the Heir) made her less important than one might assume, but she maintained her poise and spoke to everyone in dulcet tones. Ninan rolled his eyes, knowing that the instant they were alone, her smile would melt off and her gaze would turn icy. Although she was barely a year older than him, she carried herself as though she thought it were a decade. Today she wore her dark, spiraling curls long down her back, with the front of her hair pinned away from her face by three-pronged gold hairpins shaped like dinosaur claws. Her lavender gown was fitted at the top and flared at the waist, and none of the highborn men could keep their gaze off of her.

As for the Kallpas, Qhapaq Apo had arrived with his three quyas too, along with Ninan's older brothers—Apo-Huk with his two wives, and Apo-Iskay with his one—and of course Ninan himself, who answered only to Apo-Kimsa now.

Qhapaq Izhi was there alone to offer his support, along with the qhapaq of Qolqe.

Izhi caught Ninan's eye and raised a brow. Ninan nodded subtly to let him know everything was in place. They had chosen to keep their interactions few and brief, to avoid any suspicion.

Quya Urpi of Allpa arrived late, alone except for her attendants. Ninan was surprised she had come; the Venture homecoming ceremony had been a rare appearance for her, what with all the scrutiny she faced for ruling her Terrain on her own. According to Qhapaq Apo, Allpa's monarchical methods were "an abomination," and one of the many reasons he sought to reunite the Terrains under one rule—the "correct" rule.

"You've certainly cleaned up," the quya said when she greeted him.

The woman must have been in her thirties by now, Ninan thought, as he marveled at the perfect sheet of shiny black hair that hung to her waist. She wore a draping, ivory gown with red accents, and cuff bracelets, dangling disc earrings, and a wide collar necklace, all made of rose gold.

He bowed. "Your Majesty. Pleasure to see you again."

"What a … joyous event, is it not?" She said this with a slight narrowing of her eyes—a shift so subtle Ninan wasn't sure whether he'd only imagined it.

"Joyous," he repeated. "Of course. What a … privilege to visit a new, beautiful island practically every day."

"That's right," said the quya. "I understand you'll be docking twenty-six times in twenty-eight days? What a schedule …"

Ninan couldn't think on it too long or his chest would get tight. Every stop on the route would require him to perform for elite members of Tisquvian society, to put on his princely face and hold Paqari's hand and pretend he was the luckiest young man alive. Day after day after day.

Most of the island ports required only a few hours of sailing between them, although some required a full day, while a couple of them were far enough apart to require *two* days. After the first few stops along the eastern coasts of Tisqu Isle, the route was a continual zig-zag between the isle of Suni (the second largest island) and the isles around it, working in a sort of drunken circle before returning to Tisqu Isle to skim the remaining ports around its edge. The final stop would be the return to Aleta, Tisqu's capital, from which the *Velosaura* would depart this morning, and where the wedding would take place upon return.

Surely this goodwill tour wasn't *necessary*, but Qhapaq Apo was openly adamant about reinforcing the appearance of Ninan's loyalty after his past treason, and it had the added bonus of keeping Ninan busy and out of the way—possibly for distance from Qora as well—so that he wouldn't have time to get into trouble or disgrace his family again. Meanwhile, the Tisquvian qhapaq would be too distracted with all the excitement surrounding his islands to notice anything sinister in his ally's behavior.

"I've never spent an entire moon away from Sumaq," Ninan admitted to the quya. "I know that my home region is just a lot of mountains and quinoa farms, but …"

The quya's expression brightened. "On the subject of quinoa, I have been very eager to cultivate a particular region of my own lands, but I must say, the process has been difficult. I'm considering an incentive program for agriculturists—land, residence, and generous pay to develop quinoa crops, along with profits for bringing mature seeds to market. I've had success with similar programs, although Allpans don't have the same knack for quinoa as your people do. Our soil is quite different."

"An incentive program would be a fine idea," Ninan said bitterly. "Most in your position would simply lay claim to crops that the farmers are already growing." He pressed his lips together, realizing he shouldn't have said that. But he could only think of Pidru, of the community in Thak, one of many communities beholden to the qhapaq for their yields. "I'm sorry. I didn't meant to—"

"Never apologize for what you really think, Your Highness."

He scoffed. "I thought apologizing for what I think was an obligation of my title. Or better yet, keeping my thoughts to myself in the first place."

"You need not do so in my presence."

As other highborns approached him to offer congratulations, Ninan found himself repeating the same words like a demented macaw. "Thank you kindly," and "what a pleasure," and "so wonderful you could see us off." The morning was wearing on and he wished the High Shaman would come and bless the ship and send them on their way already, but he'd likely have to endure this nonsense a while longer.

Apo-Huk and Apo-Iskay were half drunk, even at this early

hour, and came to offer *their* special brand of congratulations.

"Think you've got enough wind in your sails to navigate a girl like that?" Apo-Huk said with dynamic eyebrows and a pointed glance at the princess.

Apo-Iskay snorted and gave Ninan a shove. "You're assuming he even knows how to 'dock' properly in the first place."

"Probably never 'docked a ship' in his life," said Apo-Huk.

"Probably," Ninan agreed. "But we can't all go around making a *splash* in every port on the coastline, now can we? I'd pity your wives, although I'm sure they must welcome the reprieve—"

Ninan's collar closed up around his neck, the material clenched in Apo-Huk's fist.

"You're lucky we're at a public event," Apo-Huk seethed.

"No, *you're* lucky we're at a public event," Ninan said. "You haven't bested me in a fight since I was thirteen."

"Only because you're a dirty fighter," Apo-Iskay spat.

Ninan shrugged. "Dirty fights for dirty scoundrels."

As Apo-Huk's grip tightened, however, the Tisquvian heralds blasted a fanfare through their brass instruments, calling all attendees to attention.

Ninan's brothers exchanged a glance, during which they seemed to remember they were aboard a royal ship full of refined people, and Apo-Huk released Ninan's collar.

Ninan flashed an artificial smile as he straightened his dress shirt. "It was so *lovely* to see you both today."

When all the Kallpas and Huapayas had assembled, they all faced the crowd that had gathered on the bluffs overlooking the dock where the *Velosaura* waited. Huapaya House, a white-granite castle of random ashlar masonry that sat upon the bluffs' edge, loomed over the ship as well.

Among the other quyas, Ninan found his mother, who slipped her hand into his and whispered, "Everything will be alright." He looked into her hazel eyes, wanting to believe her, but the fact that he'd even reached this point—standing on this deck, waiting to be sent on this engagement tour—made him think otherwise. A pure heart and a good will hadn't saved *her* from an arranged marriage, from being a piece moved about on the political gameboard. What did Ninan even have to offer in exchange for a better fortune? Nothing. All his hopes hung on whether he could help Qhapaq Izhi locate the dinosaur breeding grounds, and even then, he wasn't sure how the subsequent events would play out.

His mother gave his hand a squeeze, as though she knew what he was thinking. He wished he could have had more time with her, but as always, his father had kept him too busy to exchange too many words with her or receive too many of her comforting gestures. For that reason, the serrated-tooth dagger hidden in his boot would have to suffice. It bore the symbols of his Qolqese heritage, not only a physical gift from his mother before the Venture but a spiritual one, carved into its thin-filed blade. This tour was a Venture of its own, and the dagger was the closest he could get to having his mother with him along the way.

Qhapaq Achik and Qhapaq Apo took turns saying a few words, and then the High Shaman of Huapaya House chanted to invoke the water spirits and the wind spirits and the grace of Sky Mother for the journey.

Ninan and Paqari bid their families farewell—stiff embraces and false smiles for everyone on Ninan's part, with the exception of his mother, whom he held onto several beats longer, like he might hold onto the shore as the waves sucked him toward the depths of the sea—and then took their places on the raised command deck at the stern. With a wary gaze, Ninan looked up at the pulley-and-rope system that tied the ship to the dock, and followed it visually to where it met the oversized, golden latch in front of him. The pulleys, designed with brass fittings, were mounted on the taffrail, with ropes tied to cleats.

As soon as all but the crew and passengers had disembarked, the crew retracted the gangway.

The heralds blasted another fanfare, at which point Ninan and Paqari each placed a hand on the latch and, together, disengaged it.

The mechanism gave a creaky, metallic groan, engaging the pulley system and releasing the ropes from the cleats with a clank.

Under the slackened ropes, the ship's stern shifted away from the dock.

The crew unfurled the sails in a single motion, catching the wind all at once. The sails bulged at the force and began to drag the ship out of port.

The captain gripped the helm.

The fanfare continued, with the release of eleven black-and-white feathered rhamphinions that soared majestically over the ship before returning to the shore and perching themselves upon the finials of the eleven flagpoles.

The crowds on the bluffs and around the docks applauded, shrinking in Ninan's view.

As the ship pulled out of the harbor, Ninan stared at the wake lines behind it with a wave of nausea cresting in his belly.

He told himself he was only seasick.

Under skies that roar like a mosasaur
The ship careens and the rain does pour
On waves that heave us far from shore
Heave and ho, heave-ho

At dawn we face the salt and spray
The squall's a-howlin' all the day
We to the water spirits pray
Heave and ho, heave-ho

The longneck monsters pierce the deep
We pray again our limbs to keep
The wild mistress never sleeps
Heave and ho, heave-ho

Drop the anchor, furl the sails
With lines a-stowed we tell our tales
Of reptiles, pirates, and the gales
Heave and ho, heave-ho

Heave and ho, heave-ho

Tisquvian sea shanty

FIVE

IT WAS ALMOST NOON when Qora and Sakay reached the residence and paddocks at Mount Qaqra. It was a remote stretch of hilly terrain at the base of the small mountain covered in golden grasses. A wooden house and dinoshelter stood at the center of a swoop of huge black pteranodons—a striking sight for Qora, who was so used to the pale, albino pteranodons the qhapaq's staff used (bred specifically for the rarity of their whiteness), and which the heralds had also used during the Venture.

Qora and Sakay dismounted the rhabdodons they had ridden to this point, removing their belongings—two traveling packs and a few weapons, including Qora's crossbow.

"Do my eyes deceive me?" said the young woman in charge. She dragged her fingers through her chin-length hair. "Is that … the Venture champion *and* a long-lost Razorclaw?"

Qora frowned at Sakay, still bitter that he'd never mentioned his involvement with a group of renegades before last night. Of course it wasn't the type of thing someone should go around publicizing, but still. She would have thought he trusted her more than that. Looking at him now, and the way he tensed under the woman's gaze, Qora was beginning to think he might have other secrets too.

"Wayra." Sakay extended his hand.

Wayra grasped it but pulled him to her chest and embraced him with several dramatic slaps on the back. "I'm glad you decided to join us." Then she released him and turned on Qora, pulling her in too. "Raptoriva. It's an honor."

Qora squeaked out her thanks.

"Alright, let her breathe," Sakay said.

The woman pulled back but continued to brace Qora by the shoulders, giving her an analytical once-over. "You … are … magnificent."

"I am?" Qora flushed.

"Absolutely. A perfectly ordinary girl who has slain monsters. I can't think of a more magnificent creature." She kissed Qora on the cheek, then patted the spot where her lips had been and turned to Sakay. "Shall we?"

ꝛꝛꝛ

Qora watched Wayra round up the necessary pteranodons and helped her load packs onto the saddles they already wore. From her pteroflight training, Qora had learned that pteranodons remained saddled most of the time, and—at least those bred for transportation—were conditioned to be comfortable with it. Otherwise, saddling and unsaddling such large beasts repeatedly could be cumbersome, what with the complicated system that focused mainly on the base of the neck, due to the large surface area of the wings and the inability to fasten straps directly around the torso.

A few others joined the group: Kuy, the man who had come into the Underground last night; Req, a shorter young man with a rounded face and wild, medium-brown hair; and—Qora blinked hard to make sure she wasn't crazy—Gorgo, the fighter

Ninan had bested during a prizefight.

"The Gorgosaur is a Razorclaw?" She gaped at the towering, burly man with his gruff brown hair and bushy beard. While she'd always assumed him to be in his early thirties, this closer look at him revealed that he was clearly much younger, maybe barely older than Sakay—but his tall, muscular form and shaggy mane and beard contributed to the illusion of age.

"Yes," Sakay confirmed. "That's why I usually bet on him. I've seen him in action enough times to know what he's capable of doing."

Gorgo grunted in Qora's general direction, what she assumed was some sort of greeting.

While Sakay went off with Req to hear about some of his new developments, Kuy approached Qora and introduced himself formally. Apparently he hadn't realized who Qora was, in the dim Underground lighting and without her usual attire. "Apologies for not giving you proper congratulations on the Venture."

"Please, don't apologize. It's not something I like to be reminded of."

"Right." He nodded. "To the audience it's a game; to you, it must have been … quite an experience."

"Anyway," Wayra said, "this is pretty much all of us. The core that runs the network, does the missions and all that. Everyone else just sort of operates in the shadows, supplementing the work, passing along information or donating supplies or sending money."

"'Pretty much' all of you?" Qora asked.

Kuy and Wayra exchanged a doleful look.

"Sometimes we don't all make it out alive," Kuy said.

"But that's not going to happen this time," Wayra assured

her. "We've got a quick mission, and Req has set us up to easily handle anyone who gets in our way."

As if on cue, Req appeared with Sakay, holding a burlap sack and a couple of small powder cannons. He grinned and raised the bag. "We call it hushdust. I cooked it up last week. Toss it in someone's face and it knocks 'em right out."

"You're planning to use it on the dockworkers?" Qora said. "Or the guards?"

"Both."

Wayra gestured at him. "Like I said—easy. Now let's get you on a pteranodon."

꒰꒰꒰

Mounting a pteranodon was second nature to Qora now. She knew how to approach and wait for it to plant its feet and walk itself forward on its wing-claws so that the base of its neck would be low enough to climb onto the saddle. She knew how to balance herself with one foot in the stirrup, bracing the pommel, and throw her other leg over—similar to land-based mounts, except for the saddle shape and size.

Once she was mounted, the pteranodon moved back into its usual waiting position, raising her up as it lifted its neck and waited with tucked wings. Qora's legs dangled around its collar.

Kuy, Wayra, Req, Gorgo, Sakay, and Qora sat on their flyers in a triangular formation. Everyone wore flyer-riding goggles—a necessary accessory on long flights or during heavy wind.

Wayra, raising both hands to her mouth in a sort of cupped shape with some of her fingers interlocked and others sticking out, made a high-pitched, reptilian noise with stunning accuracy.

"What's that for?" Qora whispered to Sakay.

44

"Oh—she does that sometimes. She likes to feel like she's one with the reptiles."

Then Wayra shouted, "Rise!" and took flight.

The others uttered the same command to their pteranodons, each of whom waited for its own rider's word before spreading its wings, which stretched from shoulder to ankle like taut capes.

Qora felt the familiar tug at her navel at the sudden upward motion as the ground dropped away, as those leathery wings gathered more air under them with each flap and then fanned out wide. She tightened her grip on the pommel—her main source of stability during the climb, as the reins were only for changing speed and direction—and sighed as the wind caressed her cheeks.

At the head of the formation, Wayra thrust a fist at the sky, which seemed a deeper blue from this height.

From here, the earth was like a living map, Qora thought, with every swatch of land reduced to its more prominent colors, and sectioned off by trails or streams. She inhaled deeply, savoring the open air, the sun's warmth, and the lack of audience. During her pteroflight training at Kallpa House, she always operated under the critical eye of her instructors; during her arrival at events, she always had to focus on her posture and her timing and her landing; but here, she was free to hunch forward and gawk at the view, to take her time and, when the moment arrived, to land gracelessly in a field below.

Eventually, the group settled into a nice rhythm, loosening formation and riding the invisible streams eastward.

Sakay pulled up alongside Qora and raised his voice so she could hear him over the wind. "You're a natural!"

She scoffed. "You didn't see me when I first started! Couldn't remember to hold the pommel instead of the reins, and then I'd tug the reins by accident and tilt the flyer, which was the worst thing for someone still learning to keep her seat!"

He smiled faintly. "Hey, listen … before we get too far, I just have to ask …"

The tone in his voice told her what was coming. His gaze was full of concern, maybe even pity.

"This isn't about … *him*," Qora said.

"Are you sure?"

"Yes!"

"You're sure this isn't because we're going to Tisqu, specifically—where Ninan is supposed to be?"

"It's not like I'm expecting to *see* him! How would I? We're going to some obscure port, then staying in Aleta. He'll be at sea the entire moon cycle. Besides, I can't imagine how he'd react if he found out what we were trying to do!"

Ninan certainly couldn't be caught associating with anyone who would try to intercept his father's shipments. Last time, his association with traitors (even unwittingly) had cost him his heritage; next time, it would probably cost him his life.

"I'm just worried about your state of mind right now!" Sakay said, angling closer so he wouldn't have to keep shouting. "Sure you can't talk to him, but maybe some part of you just wants to be closer to where he is."

"Honestly, the thought of being near him doesn't help, whether it's within a few miles or within a few feet. At this point, I don't see how he won't end up married in twenty-eight days according to plan." Her stomach went sour as she said it aloud for the first time, voicing the likelihood—the reality of the situation—once and for all. Had she really thought he would escape somehow? With a tyrant like that for a father? With the weight of two Terrains pressing down on him? "He sent me that cordshield because he was fresh off the Venture, still riding the high of how we barely escaped death. He still had some fight left in him then. But a lot of time has passed now. Anyway, I want to do this with you. I want to know what the qhapaq is up to—and even better, I want to stop him if we can."

Sakay nodded. "Alright, *kantuta*. Just be careful. Please. Guard your heart."

"Don't worry." She flicked her riding goggles down over her eyes. Then she clucked at the flyer and nudged it to pick up speed, and called over her shoulder, "It's got iron bars around it!"

SIX

AFTER APPROXIMATELY TEN HOURS of sailing, Ninan still hadn't determined whether his visceral reaction to this trip had more to do with its purpose or more to do with the undulating nature of the ship.

Regardless, he'd spent a lot of those hours back and forth between the gunwale and his bed cabin, trying to decide if he wanted to hurl his breakfast into the waves.

The captain clapped him on the shoulder and said, "Don't worry. You'll get your sea legs in no time."

The dark-skinned woman beamed at him, wearing a plum uniform similar to that of the Tisquvian Guard officers, although hers featured two rows of brass buttons, off-white front panels, and golden flourishes embroidered all over the long sleeves. She adjusted her black feathered bicorne hat over her short sun-bronzed curls.

"Thanks," Ninan muttered.

"I am Captain Yanacha," she told him. "I'm very much looking forward to guiding you and your lovely fiancée on this tour. Might I distract you from your nausea with a brief overview of this glorious vessel?"

He sighed. "I suppose so." A distraction certainly couldn't hurt.

Ninan followed Captain Yanacha to the quarterdeck, where skyrock-tipped tridents were mounted all along the casing of the superstructure.

"We run into pods of elasmosaurians now and then," she explained. "And unlike other species, the ones in this region of the Anqas can actually raise their long necks out of the water and attack."

Ninan hadn't realized he was staring at the tridents so intently.

The captain picked up the one at the end of the row, although this one was tipped with what appeared to be long teeth. "Saberteeth. A gift from the commandant of the Allpan Coast Guard."

Ninan thought of the Allpan competitor in the Venture who had carried the sabertooth spear. As one of the few things sharp enough to cut through the thickest dinosaur skin and scales, no wonder they were so highly revered. He had heard once that Allpa contained large smilodon graveyards in some of the more desolate regions, from which the teeth were harvested.

The captain smiled. "The other tridents will deter any reptile that tries to attack the ship, and sometimes that's enough. If not, I have to come in and finish the job. I don't like to do it, but … it's my responsibility to protect this vessel at all costs."

"Of course."

"It's such a fine ship, after all. It's constructed primarily of ironwood, with copper sheathing on the keel, additional ribs to reinforce the frame, ironbound beams, and twin rudders for precise maneuverability. As you may have seen, below decks are seventeen luxury cabins, the grand suite—which your fiancée will occupy—and two lesser suites, along with a lounge and dining hall. My crew consists of myself, my first officer, eight navigational staff members, thirty deckhands and maintenance workers, and an additional fifty members of culinary, hospitality, and other specialized staff.

"Directly below us is the flyer hold, where we keep messengers and a couple of Huapaya House pteranodons on board at all times, should anyone need to leave the ship quickly for emergencies. I'm sure you saw it from the dock—the caged enclosure that follows the shape of the hull."

"Yes," Ninan said. "That was impressive." The barred gate provided airflow for the flyers, while also keeping them contained. He didn't mention that he'd seen it from the inside as well, when he'd placed the microraptors in their enclosure separate from the slate-purple Tisquvian pteranodons.

"We want to provide the most comfortable and convenient experience for you and the princess. This ship is a Huapaya family heirloom and is known for its extravagant features. For that reason, the princess has insisted that all passengers and crew remain aboard each night."

Ninan had heard all about Paqari's personal suite—sleeping quarters, a dressing room, and a small scriptorium just for her. He had already made himself comfortable in one of the two lesser suites, which had a large canopy bed, a seating area, and a built-in scriptorial nook. While many of the dignitaries located at each stopping point had been more than willing to host the prince and princess, the royalborns would instead be sleeping on the docked Velosaura, as though it were some grand waterborne hotel.

The captain proceeded to share with him the details of each upper deck, complete with historical facts and other tidbits of information, and somehow, after a while, he began to feel a bit better.

The churning in his stomach did not *completely* subside, however, particularly as he thought about the task he would have to complete tonight. He had already worked out the basics of his plan—to excuse himself early from the governor's dinner on the pretense of being tired and retiring early to bed, steal a riding cloak from somewhere on the premises, get to town on foot, hire transportation, and arrive in Ika to plant the tracker. A megaraptor at top speed could get him the necessary eight miles in less than fifteen minutes, although that might be too conspicuous. A rhabdodon would be better, but would take him half an hour. Still, a milder-mannered reptile would draw less attention, and he certainly didn't want any attention on him while he did this.

The most difficult part was figuring out how to bring all necessary items with him when they docked. The *Velosaura* guards wouldn't know he'd excused himself to bed, but they would certainly know if he went back to the ship and left again, so there would be no returning until afterwards. Thus, he had to get the dockworker's uniform to fit under his dress clothes—praying he didn't sweat too much from the extra layers—and then he had to tuck Tuko into the front pocket of his dress jacket that was typically reserved for handkerchiefs. Tuko squawked at first, twisting around until he was comfortable, and then promptly flattened himself as though he had no bones, taking up no more space than the handkerchief that belonged in his place, at least not if the material had been wadded up and shoved inside. But that would have to do. Ninan stuffed a smaller handkerchief loosely on top, making sure to leave room for air.

Ninan and Paqari were paraded from the docks to the governor's estate via the usual ceratopsian seat boxes, pasting on their usual, artificial smiles, and waving mechanically at all those who gathered along the route to see them.

Finally, they reached an enormous stone house surrounded by palm trees, and ascended a grand set of stone steps, where the governor announced them at the top.

A meet-and-greet followed, and then a dinner in the governor's grand hall, where Ninan had his fill of purple corn tamales, yucca fritters with yellow chili sauce, and chicha-spiced dinohyus skewers, making sure to always be eating whenever anyone tried to talk to him so that he wouldn't have to say much, if anything. Tuko twitched in his pocket now and then, but Ninan sneaked tiny pieces of food to him whenever possible, and that seemed to please the flyer.

By nightfall, most of the guests were half drunk, while also engaged in political conversations or dancing to the music provided by the elegant string band. Ninan watched the man who played the charango, the way his fingers moved quickly over the ten strings of the tiny guitar's fat neck. His own fingers twitched, remembering the way it had felt to form those chords.

"I used to play my charango and pretend I was Chaski." He had confessed that to Qora once during the Venture.

"Chaski's Charango" was a children's story about a little boy who couldn't speak, until one day an old man gave him a magical charango that allowed him to communicate through song. Maybe that story had always resonated with Ninan because he often found himself in a position where he couldn't say what he felt. Spirits, he couldn't even say what he *thought*, or *believed*, let alone what he needed, or wanted, or feared. Except in his case it was his status in the political hierarchy that silenced him.

"Apo-Kimsa." The governor approached him with a cup of cocona wine. "Would you be so kind as to favor the guests with a dance?" The governor glanced at Paqari, who stood among a group of young highborn women in colorful dresses, batting a dried palmfan at herself.

Ninan forced his lips into a tight smile and nodded once. "Of course."

Luckily the governor took it upon himself to summon the princess to the center of the tiled floor, where Ninan awaited her. The guests had already cleared a space for the couple, gathering around in a circle, as the musicians finished their piece and began a new, slower rhythm.

Paqari joined Ninan, placing one hand on his shoulder.

They gave each other a shallow bow and then picked up the steps, turning slowly as a unit, like show raptors on display for appraisal. No—more like a carnival spectacle, Ninan thought. Trained animals with their pretty performance, who would return to their respective cages as soon as they'd finished.

"You look … nice," Ninan told her stiffly.

She did look nice. She wore a teal, off-the-shoulder dress corseted through the middle and pleated at the skirt—which hung loosely as she moved but which could fan out wide if she lifted the sides—with geometric patterns embroidered on the fabric. Her black hair was braided into some sort of voluminous mass at the nape of her neck, and her eyes were lined and her lips were stained the color of rumberries.

"They can't hear you," Paqari told him. While her tone was sullen, her expression was as pleasant as a girl discussing a bit of unexpectedly good weather. Formality at its finest.

He wanted to say he hadn't been saying it for show, but he doubted she'd believe him, or care.

They finished the dance without another word, to the applause of everyone watching, then parted ways. Some of the men entangled Ninan in a conversation about the tropical birds and flyers the governor kept on display in the drawing room.

"Nothing like your father's menagerie, of course," the governor prattled, "which I've heard is spectacular."

"Spectacular," Ninan repeated as if in agreement. It wasn't until one of the Unuvian diplomats began to admire a hoatzin—a strange brownish bird with a blue face and red eyes and a crest of spiky feathers—that Ninan was able to transfer the governor's enthusiasm to a new listener and extract himself. He brushed past Paqari and her acquaintances, bidding them a good evening and stating that the day's sail had simply been "too grueling for a mainland-dweller" like himself who had "scarcely set foot on a boat but once before."

Gods, who *was* he? He sounded like the very kind of stuck-up highborn he despised, haughty tone and all.

"Don't tell me you're going to leave me to entertain these guests on my own …" Paqari said with a bat of her lashes. Her eyes bore resentment, even though her smile played it off as a joke.

"Oh, let him rest," one of the other girls said. "Just look at him—all flushed and sweating like that. Poor thing. He's not used to our climate."

Ninan flashed a grin that was both grateful and sheepish. "It *has* been a bit of an adjustment." He brushed his hair off his forehead, simultaneously wiping the mist of sweat that surely glistened there. The extra layers were, in fact, causing his face to flush with heat, and his underarms felt like they had melded to the fabric of the uniform sleeves he concealed. If Tuko was suffering from Ninan's body heat, he didn't react.

Paqari pursed her lips. "Fine, then. Take your rest. Good night, *darling*."

Hesitantly, he pecked her on the cheek. "Good night."

𝔇𝔇𝔇

The second Ninan left the sightlines of the guests, he hurried toward the estate's reptiliary. He wished he could borrow one of the reptiles on the property, but then he'd have to show himself to the workers, who surely would recognize him from his grand entrance on the triceratops. *Stealing* a reptile would be too risky. So he stuck to the plan, snatching a rider's cloak from a row of hooks outside the reptiliary.

The cloak was black, and a size too big, which was perfect for his purposes. He fastened it over his clothes—a third layer now, which was practically unbearable, but he couldn't very well abandon his princely clothes here on the property for someone to find—then put up the hood and disappeared into the night.

When he reached the city buildings, he thought he might suffocate under all this fabric, but he managed to quickly rent a rhabdodon from a dinoshelter next to an inn—transportation for travelers—which required a large fee along with a deposit he would lose should he not return the reptile, and rode toward Ika.

Five minutes out of town, he had to stop and strip down. He shed his dress clothes and draped them over the saddlebag, but replaced the cloak over his uniform, and released Tuko from his jacket pocket, allowing him to ride on his shoulder for the remainder of the trip.

As they approached the port, Ninan dismounted and walked the rhabdodon into some thickets, a place from which he watched dozens of workers unloading crates from a cargo ship and carrying them to a cinderblock storage facility. A foreman directed the workers to secure the crates in specific loading zones, all of which existed behind armored gates. Guards raised and lowered the gates of each zone as needed, using a chain hoist system.

Heart pounding, Ninan tied the rhabdodon to a palm that

was perhaps too spindly to hold it—although the rhabdo was trained for hitching and should have no reason to leave without command, tied or otherwise—then removed his cloak, and transferred Tuko to one of the uniform's front chest pockets. "Sorry, little guy. Just a few more minutes."

He mussed his hair, took a deep breath, and hurried into the midst of the workers as they milled back and forth. He followed another worker to the ship, where someone handed him a shipping crate. Watching the others, he carried the crate to the same loading zone, where he glimpsed the interior—rows and rows of more crates stacked on a flat, wooden bed on wheels, with hookups for ankylosaurs. The far end of the loading zone had another gate, from which he assumed the cargo reptiles would arrive to take the lot away.

It took several minutes and several strategic moves, switching between shipments and zones, checking crates to glimpse their contents. When the other workers would go back for more, Ninan would sneak away from each team and duck behind carts to pry open a crate. After three separate shipments, he had high hopes for the fourth.

It should have been convenient, having a small reptile like Tuko with him, who would react to a skyrock product, except that Qhapaq Apo always lined his containers with thin sheets of lead—which had a blocking effect on whatever energy skyrock seemed to emit—in order to avoid adverse reactions from the reptiles that transported them.

Withdrawing his serrated-tooth dagger from his boot, Ninan slid the blade under the crate lid. Carefully, he pressed down to pry it up, forcing the nails from the wood with a soft squeak. Underneath lay a sheet of lead.

As he lifted the lead, a violet glow escaped into the dim space.

"What in the Five Terrains …" Ninan reached inside, his fingers brushing over what felt like prisms. He pulled one out to examine it.

Tuko peeked out from Ninan's pocket, gaze fixed on the glow of the finger-length object. The pteromorph's reaction—and Ninan's memory of the qhapaq's ring with its purple "stone"—was enough to convince Ninan he'd found the right shipment.

Ninan wasn't sure what he'd expected, but … it hadn't been this. Rocks, perhaps, similar to the skyrock he knew, but polished smooth, or some version of skyrock dust that looked more like silica beads than the usual chalky powder.

"They're … crystals …" he marveled aloud.

And beautiful ones at that.

"Hurry up!" the foreman called to the workers outside. "This needs to leave within the hour!"

Flinching, Ninan returned the crystal, replaced the lead sheet, and closed the lid, using the heels of his hands against the top to force the nails back into their holes. The second he closed off the dominite glow, Tuko seemed to snap back to attention.

Ninan looked at the rows of other crates, trying to determine the best spot to place the pteromorph, where he wouldn't be noticed but likewise wouldn't be crushed. That must be where those durable sceathers came into play, but Ninan hoped Tuko was trained well enough to remove himself from danger among shifting cargo.

Ninan paused, however, remembering what Izhi had said.

"We still have yet to obtain a sample of it. If you're able to do that … it would be immensely advantageous."

Immensely advantageous. Ninan needed every advantage he could get right now. But also, he wouldn't be able to take a sample back to the *Velosaura*. If he was caught with something like that …

He shuddered at the thought.

But I could bury it.

Yes. He could leave it somewhere in the woods, then send word to Izhi and let him know where to find it.

He peered around the cargo at the gate, where two more workers came and went. As he stepped out into view, the sound of several, screeching pteranodons stopped him in his tracks.

His pulse kicked up, filling his veins with dread.

Had the *Velosaura* crew discovered he was missing and sent guards on their flyers? Had he been followed? Gods, he was in for a beating—no, an *execution*—if he was caught here like this, at this dock with all this dominite, in disguise, carrying a *tracking* reptile.

The rhabdodon startled, audible even from here. Wood croaked and snapped. The rhabdodon's cries were long and loud, and then began to fade, along with its heavy tread.

"*No, no, no ...*" Ninan whispered at the wall that separated him from his fleeing transportation.

Further commotion sounded from the docks. Men muttering and panicking and their boots scraping as they scurried.

It was only a matter of minutes—maybe seconds—before the pteranodon riders would discover him.

But there was nowhere to run.

If he left through the open gate, they'd see him in an instant.

Suddenly, the noise died. Ninan strained his ears, but after a series of thunks, the workers seemed to quiet and still. Then it was only pteranodon wingflaps, the whoosh when they tucked in those big wings after landing. A few boots on the ground— riders dismounting.

Then: "Check the cargo bays."

Ninan didn't recognize the man's voice, but he didn't want

to find out if it belonged to anyone he knew. He went to the pulley system for the second gate—the one that wouldn't open until the cargo reptiles arrived—and turned the large wheel that seemed to control it. If he could raise the gate just enough to let himself out—

A shadow blocked the light that had been streaming in from the first gate's opening. "Don't move."

This voice he *did* recognize.

He turned and found himself staring down the barrel of a crossbow.

"Qora?"

Old love and wood will burn
as soon as they get the chance.

Tisquvian proverb

SEVEN

TIME SEEMED TO STAND STILL FOR QORA.

Where was she?

What had she been doing?

Her hands trembled on her weapon, but her aim remained.

She hadn't yet removed her riding goggles, and wondered if there was enough dust on them to alter her vision to the point of delusion.

Ninan was supposed to be on a ship, miles away from here. She'd nearly convinced herself she might never see him again— at least not without a *wife*, and eventually two or three—yet here he was, right in front of her. Alone.

Her pulse was thrumming so fast she couldn't form words. She wanted to punch him—one of those full-body punches he'd taught her to throw when he'd trained her in the woods—and at the same time, she wanted to grab a fistful of his shirt and pull him close and press her lips to his. Instead, she just stood there pointing her crossbow at his head.

With his hands raised, as though she might actually shoot him, Ninan took a few tentative steps toward her.

They stared at one another for what felt like a full minute before he touched one of her crossbow's limbs and gently pressed down, urging her to lower it. Then he reached forward and pushed her goggles off her face.

"Qora …" His fingertips grazed her cheek.

She flinched and stepped back.

"Did you find anything?" Sakay called. A second later, he appeared at the open gate.

Qora kept her eyes locked on Ninan. "You could say that."

EIGHT

"**SWEET SERRATED TEETH …**" Sakay practically recoiled when he realized who he was looking at. "I … I don't understand."

Ninan was standing there in a dockworker's uniform, and Qora looked like she wanted to use every bolt she had to pin him to the wall.

"It's a long story," Ninan told him.

"Well you'd better give us the abridged version—and quick. That hushdust lasts less than twenty minutes."

"Hushdust?"

"Everyone who works here just got an early bedtime. Or … I guess more like a spontaneous nap. No one will be bothering us for a bit."

Kuy came up to the open gate, then Req, then Wayra, then Gorgo looming behind them all.

"Did you find it?" said Kuy.

Ninan drew back at the sight of them.

"They're my friends," Sakay told Ninan. To Kuy, he said, "I think we found the full supply—and a little … bonus, I guess you could say."

"Should I get more hushdust?" Req asked.

Sakay shook his head. "He's—"

"Oh my gods," said Wayra, squinting into the darkness

63

toward Ninan. "You're … You're the …"

Sighing, Ninan came all the way forward so they could see him properly.

"*You* …" Gorgo grunted, clenching his fists.

Sakay grimaced. "Right. I forgot you two already know each other." It had completely slipped his mind, the fact that Ninan had bested Gorgo in a prizefight at the Underground. After having seen Ninan beat a skilled fighter a few days prior to that, Sakay had taken a chance and bet on Ninan instead, despite his usual loyalty to Gorgo—and, unfortunately for Gorgo, that bet had quite literally paid off.

"I'm not here for a brawl," Ninan clarified.

"Then what *are* you here for?" Qora finally said.

Ninan glanced pointedly at everyone else with whom Qora was now clearly associated. "I could ask you the same thing."

"Obviously we're here to steal dominite," Sakay said. "These are the Razorclaws. Qora and I flew in with them earlier."

"Razorclaws?"

"Rebels. Renegades. Anarchists," said Wayra. "At least, that's what we aspire to. There's a whole network—some of whom may have even been at that riot where your father's guards found you drunk before you got your title stripped. That was the gist of how it happened, wasn't it?"

"More or less," Ninan muttered.

Sakay stepped closer, to convey the seriousness of the moment. "The question is … Where do your loyalties lie tonight?"

"Well I'm not here to *protect* this shipment." Ninan gestured at his hair and clothes.

He had a point, Sakay thought. Dressed like that, cowering in dark corners.

"How do you know about dominite?" Ninan added, "What do you want with it?"

"We have a lot of insiders among our ranks," Req said.

"Then you know what it's for? What my father is planning?" Ninan asked.

"We're still gathering information," Kuy admitted. "Req can analyze a sample and give us a better idea. We know it's made from skyrock—only it works differently, and it's stronger."

Ninan scoffed. "To say the least."

"You've seen it in action?" Sakay asked.

"Not to the full extent, but yes," said Ninan. "I don't know how it's made, though; I only know what it's for. My father's breeding a dinosaur army somewhere on Tisqu and he's sending the dominite to train and control them."

Sakay felt himself pale. "'Dinosaur army'?"

Ninan nodded. "Human armies have proven ineffective in reuniting the empire, so now he's working on something unprecedented. Something that can't be matched."

Spirits, Sakay thought. It was even worse than he'd imagined. He'd expected the more obedient reptiles to play a part in the qhapaq's war, but he hadn't expected them to be the *soldiers.* But the more he considered it, the more it made sense.

Men and women took more than a decade to reach an age of maturity, and then required weapons, and constant nourishment—and each came with a conscience. Reptiles, however, matured quickly, were equipped with natural weapons in the form of teeth and claws, could be nourished by an enemy's corpse upon attack, and would experience no remorse for murder. Both humans and dinosaurs could be trained, but with dominite, dinosaurs and other reptiles could be much more easily controlled.

"And if any of the other Terrains *tried* to match it ..." Req speculated.

Nodding again, Ninan said, "He'd take control over those dinosaurs too. That's why he has to be stopped. I've been working with Qhapaq Izhi to find out the location of the base where the dinosaurs are bred and trained, but my father has managed to throw him off the scent every time, with false records, decoy shipments, and killing off any spies who are caught."

Sakay saw a look of understanding pass over Qora's face; this had been part of Ninan's 'plan,' working with the Unuvian qhapaq in hopes of taking down his father. That must have been how he expected to break his arrangement.

"Aren't you supposed to be on the *Velosaura*?" Wayra said. "Won't they notice you're missing?"

"We're docked at Kicai," Ninan explained. "It's just eight miles away. I left after dark and hired a rhabdo. I'm headed back as soon as I do what I came to do."

"You said you're here to 'track' the shipment?" Sakay asked. "How?"

Ninan opened his chest pocket and withdrew a small, gray mass, which then expanded itself, revealing a pointed beak and a pair of wings.

"A pteromorph?" Sakay furrowed his brow.

"Tuko. Apparently he's got eidetic memory and he's trained to follow whatever object I command him to. He'll gather flora from along the way and stuff them into his sceathers, then home back to Unu so Izhi can piece together the trail."

The little flyer wriggled out of Ninan's grasp and flew to Qora's shoulder, sniffing her neck. She looked at him sideways, then reached up and stroked his spine.

"Is there any chance I could get a ride to Kicai?" Ninan

asked, changing the subject. "I'm fairly certain your pteranodons scared off my rhabdo."

ꑺꑺꑺ

Sakay and the Razorclaws watched as Ninan set the pteromorph in between the crates and gave it a command. Then they pried open one of the crates. With the guards and workers knocked unconscious outside, the group had no need to be discreet. And so, when Ninan pulled back the lead sheet and released a brilliant purple glow into the space, everyone gasped.

Wayra picked up one of the crystals and brought it close to her face. "This came from skyrock?"

Req examined one as well. "I never would have imagined the product to be something like this."

"We'll have time to marvel over its properties later," said Kuy. "Right now we need to load up several of these crates."

"Absolutely not," Ninan told him. "It's already bad enough that you've apparently knocked out the workers and guards. If a large piece of the shipment is missing, it could endanger everything I've been working towards."

"Well we can't undo what we've already done," Sakay reasoned. "We had no idea you'd be here—or that you'd be working against your own father."

"It's worse than that," said Ninan. "*I* need a sample too. But when my father finds out about a raid that occurred the same night as this shipment, he's going to get suspicious."

Wayra produced a couple of small canvas bags with drawstrings from the pack she carried on her back. "How about we take two or three crystals from different crates until we have decent samples? Then we can put everything back like it was, so it doesn't look like anything was stolen. Maybe the workers will be too afraid to tell anyone—and even if they do, we can take something else instead as a decoy."

"Steal from another shipment ..." Kuy said.

"Yes. There are at least twenty crates of dried lavacap mushrooms in the next cargo bay. We purge half of that in the water and it'll look like someone was just after a drug supply."

Qora was silent the entire time, and Sakay wondered how she was handling this.

Once everyone at least tacitly agreed to this plan, Qora was the first to leave the loading zone, with the Razorclaws following behind, then Sakay and Ninan.

As they stepped out onto the quay, Ninan's eyes widened at the workers and guards sprawled out in heaps along the ground, their faces dusted with powder.

"Hushdust," Sakay reminded him.

Req's powder had put the workers and guards instantly to sleep, collapsing them where they'd stood. They were sprawled in awkward and in some cases undignified positions. A few of them would have head injuries or sprained wrists, Sakay thought, which was unfortunate, but necessary.

"Does it work on reptiles?" Ninan asked.

"Not yet, although I'm sure it's in the works."

"Where'd you get your hands on something like that?"

Sakay clapped Req on the back. "We have a brilliant elementalist. Probably could have worked for the qhapaq, if he'd been born without a conscience."

"Speaking of elementalists who work for the qhapaq," Ninan said, "I'm going to need to stop somewhere remote and bury my sample for Qhapaq Izhi. He'll want to have it analyzed as well."

Ninan went off for a few minutes to verify that his rhabdodon had indeed fled, and returned with a saddlebag and a riding cloak. "The rhabdo threw my things, at least, when it ran."

"We can ride two to a flyer," Sakay told him, "since it's only a few minutes' ride."

"Alright, everyone," said Kuy, holding one of the canvas bags filled with dominite crystals. "Let's get back to—"

Three pteranodons inched toward him, eyeing the dominite in his hand. Kuy stumbled backward, but the flyers trailed him, fixated. His throat flexed.

"That's why the crates were lined with lead," Ninan noted. "Take my riding cloak and wrap the bags to add extra layers. It won't completely solve the problem, but it'll at least dull the effects."

The group split up to dispose of several crates of the hallucinogenic mushrooms and wrap both bags of crystals in as many spare layers as they had on hand, then began to mount the flyers, all of which were at least moderately distracted by the dominite. Two of them held the dominite within their saddlebags—those belonging to Wayra and Kuy—heading up the group. Qora, Ninan, and two other Razorclaws, had yet to mount.

Sakay was about to tell Ninan to hop on the pteranodon with him when a guard suddenly came at Qora, swinging a regulation baton.

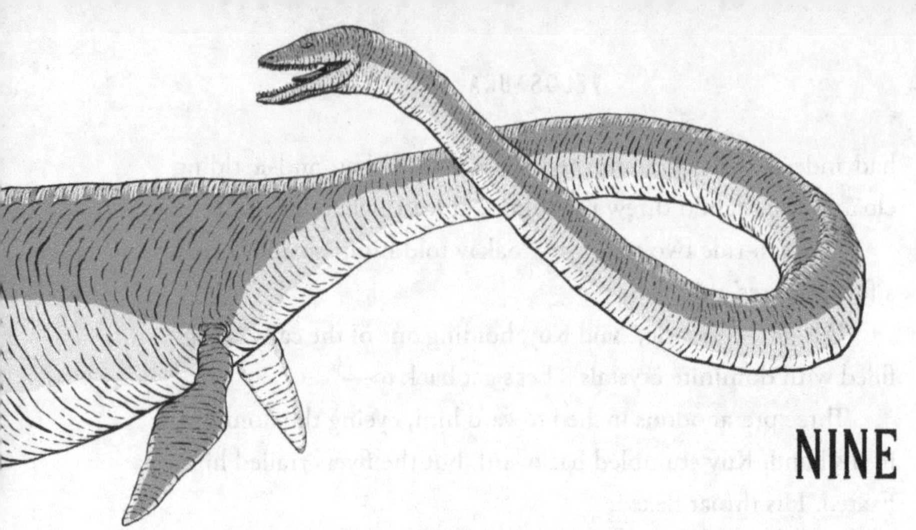

NINE

INSTINCTIVELY, NINAN STEPPED IN FRONT OF QORA, facing her as his ribs took the hit. He bit out a cry of pain, tensing against the baton.

Qora's breath hitched. She stood pressed between Ninan and the pteranodon's side, her chest rising and falling rapidly. She looked so different now, in her dark clothes with her hair tied back in a low knot, and flyer-riding goggles on her head. He didn't even know she'd *trained* on flyers, let alone could fly solo.

They were so close together that his lips nearly brushed hers before he spun and caught the guard by the wrist to block a second strike.

"Go!" he said over his shoulder. He bent the guard's wrist until the man dropped the baton.

Qora scrambled to mount her pteranodon behind Ninan.

Ninan threw an uppercut and then a blow to the jaw that collapsed the guard instantly.

Other guards and dockworkers were waking now too, some of whom had gotten to their feet—albeit stumbling—joined the commotion.

Preparing himself to fight, Ninan planted his feet and counted his opponents.

The Razorclaws kicked up, rising into the night, except for

Sakay and Qora. Qora rode her pteranodon on the ground and pulled up next to Ninan and thrust out her arm.

"Get on!" she told him.

He took one last glance at the approaching guard, then gripped her wrist to wrist—suddenly reminded of when their positions were reversed that day in the jungle as he'd ridden in to extract her from the midst of the wild pterodactyls preying on her—and pulled himself onto the saddle behind her.

The memory of the kiss that had followed that event warmed him even more as he slipped his arms past her to hold onto the pommel. Then his stomach dipped for a different reason as the flyer lurched into the air, carrying them away and leaving several gaping guards and dockworkers behind.

The winged ones do not defy gravity; they merely delay it.

Sumaqi proverb

TEN

QORA TRIED TO KEEP HER MIND on her flight path, but the feeling of Ninan's arms around her made her all too aware of her pulse.

His heartbeat thrummed against her shoulder blades and she wondered if its quick rhythm had anything to do with her, or whether it was only due to the scuffle they'd just left at the docks.

When he inclined his head forward and brushed a few loose strands of hair from the side of her face, she thought she might have her answer.

"I'm sorry," he said against her ear, sending chills down her spine. "I know you must be thinking the worst of me right now."

Ever so slightly, she leaned backward into him, but restrained herself from giving herself fully to his embrace—an embrace that was more necessity than affection, thanks to the cramped saddle space. At this moment, he belonged to someone else, and she knew it was important that she didn't forget that. Whatever his plan was, he was running out of time.

The pteranodon's wings sent air rushing all around them, a cool wind in this humid place. Dark trees sprawled below, mostly palms, as nocturnal dinosaurs milled about between the foliage.

Qora gripped the reins more tightly, fingers clenching the lines to steady herself. She took a deep breath. "If I really thought the worst of you, all of this probably wouldn't hurt so much."

At the front of the pteranodon formation, Kuy signaled for the group to land in a clearing up ahead.

For the last few seconds of their descent, Qora reveled in her closeness to Ninan, soaking it in, pretending he was holding her on purpose, the way she'd wanted him to all this time. And then, as the pteranodon's feet hit the ground and it tucked away its wings, she tucked away her longing too.

꒰꒰꒰

"First and foremost," said Kuy, as the group stood in a circle, each having led their respective pteranodons on foot, "We need to discuss the tyrannosaurus among us." He looked at Ninan.

"Me?" Ninan pointed to himself.

"Of course *you*," Gorgo grunted.

Qora cringed as she remembered their last exchange at the Underground before the Venture, the way Ninan had pinned Gorgo to the ground and cranked back his arm.

"Look," Ninan told him, "I'm sorry I sprained your shoulder, but to be fair, you tried to break my face."

"Give me another chance and maybe I'll just—"

"Okay Gorgo, that's enough," Wayra cut in. "If you can't be a good loser, stop getting in the ring. Better yet, save it for someone who's *not* on our side."

"Well, that's what we have to make sure of," Req said.

Kuy nodded and focused on Ninan. "Our knowledge of your involvement in this is compromising to you. Likewise, *your* knowledge of *our* involvement in this is compromising to *us*. Despite our common goals, we all have to be careful."

"I think it goes without saying," Sakay said, "that Ninan's

secret is safe with us." He glanced around at everyone else. "Right?"

Everyone nodded except Gorgo, who rolled his eyes.

"And yours with me," Ninan replied. "Although I would like to inform Qhapaq Izhi that he has allies within Sumaq's borders."

"Fine," said Kuy. "We'll take whatever support we can get. As long as you keep your father off our trail, we shouldn't have any problems."

"Glad that's settled," said Wayra.

"We should part ways soon," Req suggested. "The dockworkers will eventually report our attack, so it's vital the prince returns before anyone can link him to what we've done."

Ninan crossed his arms. "Agreed. Hopefully if everything *looks* in order upon inspection, my father will at least proceed with the shipment, otherwise I've placed that tracker for nothing."

"But if the tracker is discreet enough," Qora said, "then it might still be able to get to the base, even if Qhapaq Apo reroutes the cargo."

"Let's hope so." Ninan spoke to her as though she were the only one there, locking a gaze on her that seemed to block out everyone else.

Qora shivered but said nothing in response.

"Qora and I can take the prince back to his ship," Sakay announced. "We'll meet you all at the Den afterward."

The Den had been so similar to the Underground when Qora and the Razorclaws had arrived in the early afternoon, Qora had thought it was no wonder they'd asked Sakay to come along. The venue was *above* ground, but with a similar trading counter, mounted dinosaur heads, and gamblers and traders at tables drinking pisco and malt liquors. Not wanting to fly through the night—especially not over water—the Razorclaws would be lodging with Den patrons.

"Sounds good," said Req. "Godspeed."

ꑇꑇꑇ

Ninan rode with Sakay this time, thankfully, although Qora had mixed feelings about it. There was something especially torturous about being physically close to someone from whom she knew she ought to remain emotionally distant.

After Ninan buried his bag of dominite and committed the location to memory for Qhapaq Izhi, the three of them headed back toward Kicai and were now preparing to land outside the city so that Ninan could continue on foot. Approaching the ship with two black pteranodons carrying two additional companions wouldn't exactly imply good faith.

And that plan was all fine and good until they realized Ninan would still have to find a way to sneak back onto the *Velosaura* without any of the guards or crew noticing. It wasn't even late enough that all the passengers would be asleep—but it was certainly late enough that anyone wandering the deck would seem suspicious.

"You can always tell them you were just out drinking," Sakay offered. "In fact, it doesn't even have to be a lie ..."

When Ninan didn't protest, Qora followed as Sakay landed them at a place along the pier, within view of the ship. Ninan ducked behind Sakay's shoulders, but even with the city's lanterns it would have been too dark for any of the *Velosaura* crew to recognize him from here.

They all dismounted. Sakay and Qora led the flyers on foot

and hitched them outside a wood-built, two-story establishment. The windows were open to the air, leaking flame-light and music and the chatter of socializing patrons. A sign above the swinging-door entrance read "Uchu's Kantina."

Qora didn't feel like going inside the kantina, but Sakay insisted they could at least get a good meal here, make sure they were all on the same page as far as information, and take a flight break.

Inside, they found a round table near the front and sat equidistant from one another. Ninan excused himself for a moment so that he could change clothes, not wanting to try to get back on the ship later in a dockworker's uniform. Meanwhile, Sakay ordered a round of chicha and chugged the whole of his glass within ten seconds of receiving it. Qora sipped hers quietly while they waited for their food—troodon stew, ceviche, stuffed peppers, and potatoes huancaína—and Ninan came back in dress trousers and a loosely buttoned, white dress tunic, but carried his formal jacket under one arm as he combed his fingers through his hair, which was a bit shorter now and properly cut. His gaze was shifty, but no one seemed to look twice at him, engaged in their social activities and mostly drunk and not even thinking that a foreign prince could possibly be walking among them at this time of night.

They had to speak loudly to hear one another over the noise, which grated on Qora's ears and was beginning to give her a headache.

"Okay," Sakay said through a mouthful of stew, "Here are our options. One, we wait until dawn and you sneak onto the ship while the crew's distracted getting ready to set sail, and when they see you, you act like you've been there the whole time, but simply fell asleep in your clothes. Two, Qora and I create a diversion by flying over the ship and shouting obscenities while you make your way back to your sleeping cabin as the guards prepare for defense. Three—"

"Maybe I'll just show up and not say anything," said Ninan. "Highborns are expected to do as they please without consequence. I could also say I took a walk and got lost."

Sakay shook his head. "Bad idea. They'll think you've been out at a brothel or something."

"Better that than out committing treason against his Terrain," Qora said before a bite of potatoes.

Ninan raised his voice another notch as the music kicked up. "Either way, the three of us probably shouldn't be seen together after this. There's no good reason for you both to be here."

"He's right," Qora told Sakay. "I'm due back at Kallpa House for the Heritage Festival in two weeks, to fly over the parade. The qhapaq has no idea I left Sumaq."

"Well it's not like you *had* to leave Sumaq," Sakay said. "I told you to stay."

"That was your first mistake." Ninan's mouth quirked ever so slightly. "You know you can't tell her to do anything."

Qora tightened her fingers around her utensil and shot him a glare. "You think I can't do as I'm told?"

"I think most times you *won't*," Ninan replied.

"That's interesting, because I've been letting *your father* tell me what to do since the second I stepped foot out of that gondola after the Venture." Qora's pulse raced and her breathing turned heavy. "Day after day, week after week, I've obeyed. In fact, I've been doing what *everyone* tells me to do." She dropped the utensil and began to gesture wildly. "'Chin up,' 'stand here,' 'sign this,' 'wear that,' 'greet them,' 'get on the pteranodon,' 'try again,' 'one more time until you get it right.' A never-ending string of commands that I follow like a trained reptile. And *you*—you wanted me to *wait*. So I've *been* waiting. All this time. Gods know what for, because from what I've learned tonight, it looks like we're about to enter a full-on war—and despite our best efforts, I don't see how there's any way we can stop it, let alone stop your stupid wedding. So excuse me for not wanting to sit around in Qhusi while the whole world turns upside down and knocks us flat on our asses in the process."

Ninan sat dumbfounded for a moment, like he'd been slapped in the face. When he finally opened his mouth to reply, a burst of the swinging doors cut him off.

The music stopped and the voices around them faded.

Qora, Ninan, and Sakay turned to the entrance, and there—backlit by the moon and the pier lanterns—stood the Tisquvian princess.

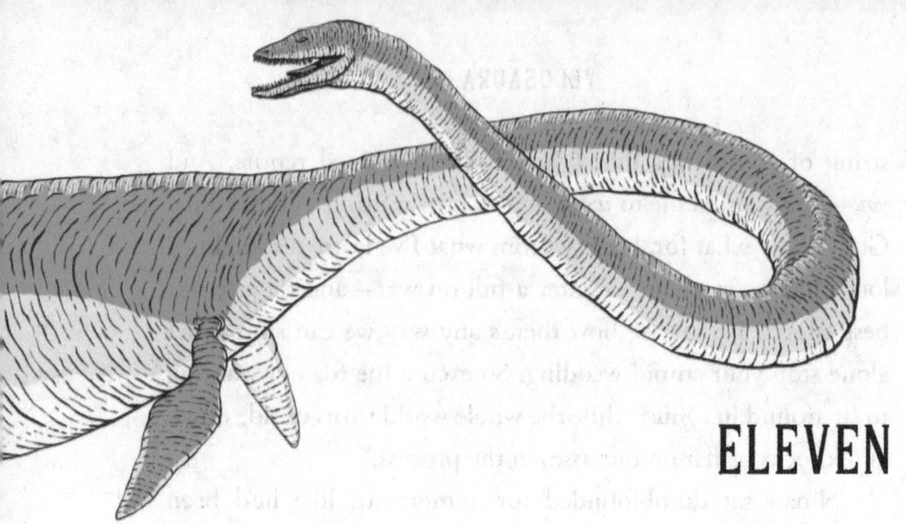

ELEVEN

FOR A MOMENT, SAKAY FOUND HIMSELF short of breath.

The princess was a vision even in her silk nightrobe and modesty cloak, with her hair swept back and her raw-umber eyes piercing as she took in the scene. He'd only seen her at a distance as she'd flown over Qhusi in departure after the Venture homecoming, waving stiffly to all the citizens below.

She approached their table, with several guards around her like a protective swarm of bees. Everyone in the kantina stepped aside to allow them passage, whispering amongst themselves that the princess was in their midst.

Paqari stopped short of the table's edge and looked from Ninan to Qora to Sakay.

"What's going on here?" she asked flatly.

Ninan stood and bowed, and although he and the princess were, for the most part, equals in rank, she did not reciprocate his greeting. "I apologize. I'm sure this must look … confusing. What happened was … um …"

Qora and Sakay stood and bowed as well. Discreetly, Qora stepped closer to Sakay, almost as if to show her distance from Ninan for Paqari's sake.

Gods, what must the princess be thinking right now? Sakay wondered. Would she suspect foul play? Would she eventually link Ninan to the raid in Ika? More pressing, though, was how she knew to find Ninan *here*, at this hour.

Some of the kantina customers made their way closer, trying to get a better look at her.

"Keep everybody back," Paqari ordered the guards.

Sakay didn't think that was much of a "goodwill" attitude, as her tour implied, but he had to admit he liked her feist.

"With all due respect, *darling*," Ninan said, "What are you doing here?"

"I was trying to relax in my suite," Paqari said, tipping her nose up. "I wanted to read in peace. But I found the cacophony emanating from this … *fine* establishment … to be incredibly distracting. So I came to insist that it be shut down for the remainder of my stay in Kicai."

Sakay had to stifle a laugh. Shut down the entire place?

"However," she added, "I most certainly didn't expect to find my betrothed among the brutes who drink here, and even less, the Venture champion."

She pinned her gaze on Qora.

Everyone in the room remained silent, like one collective breath held in suspense. How difficult it must have been for this audience to keep calm when not only were they standing in the presence of their own princess and the Third Prince of Sumaq, but also the newly famed Raptoriva.

Ninan looked like he was trying to work out an explanation, but of course there wasn't much to work with. In what way could this possibly appear *not* to be conspiratorial?

When she'd figured, perhaps, that she'd tortured the room enough, Paqari concluded, "It seems Qhapaq Apo has finally agreed to send the Venture champion to Tisqu."

Sakay caught a glimpse of Ninan releasing a clenched fist.

But then Qora said, "Not exactly."

Ninan shot her a look, as though to say that she was ruining a perfectly good cover story, but Sakay was sure such a lie would have been found out quickly—as soon as word got back to Qhapaq Apo, who had definitely *not* sent Qora—so there wasn't really any point in agreeing with Paqari's assumption.

Qora cleared her throat. "I'm on leave from my champion duties, and I … decided to come on my own. I figured if my qhapaq wouldn't send me, I'd fly out by my own means."

Paqari stared at her for a moment, her scrutiny flicking over Qora's flyer-riding clothes and the goggles on her head. Then she turned on Sakay. "And who's this?"

"He's … my bodyguard," Qora replied. "Leaving the Terrain without the qhapaq's permission, I thought at the very least he would want me to be safe—being a beloved celebrity and all."

Sakay nodded once in support. "We encountered Ninan—I mean, Prince Apo-Kimsa—on his way back to the *Velosaura*, and then came here for a drink to catch up, but I'm afraid we lost track of the hour."

"I assure you," Qora added, "that we had no intention of interfering with your tour."

Her skin was flushed, and the rhythm of her breath—slow, but constrained—told Sakay she was trying to hide her panic. He stood close enough to her that he could subtly place his hand on her back, a gesture of comfort he hoped would calm her.

"That's right," Sakay said. "We were advised that Kicai was the best place to visit first, for the botanical gardens"—This was the city with the botanical gardens, wasn't it? He hoped he wasn't remembering incorrectly—"and assured a warm reception, should the champion like to make an appearance at the city square tomorrow. We weren't aware the *Velosaura* would be here at this time."

Improvising an explanation was a talent Sakay had developed at the Underground. He'd watched his uncle elaborate on the origins of many goods, even after having just received them, to talk them up to potential buyers. Mind-bending elixirs, or rare and colorful dinoleathers. The way his uncle had spoken with such confidence even when most of what he said had been exaggeration or, in some cases, speculation; no one had ever questioned him. Sakay had practically been raised in that place, working to earn extra money as a young child, and then living under his uncle's care exclusively from the time he was nine years old after his mother's death. He'd never known his father, and it was just as well; he was likely better off that way.

With a slow analysis and then a flat smile, Paqari simply said, "I suppose it was fate."

"Fate?" Ninan said.

"Are those your pteranodons outside?" Paqari asked Sakay and Qora. "The black ones?"

"They are," Sakay confirmed.

Paqari clicked her tongue. "What a shame Qhapaq Apo didn't see fit to send you at his expense. He should have provided you a pterobeast and gondola, with a pilot, rather than leaving you to *ride* such a distance on pteranodonback."

Sakay got the sense that she found such transportation not only inconvenient but also distasteful. But he supposed the highborns could be that way. It was all well and good to ride reptiles for *sport*, in parades or for competition, but never on a full journey.

"Where will you be staying?" Paqari asked.

"With a family friend," Sakay told her. "In the capital."

The princess crossed her arms and looked at them each

in turn again. "No. That's unacceptable. You'll stay aboard the *Velosaura* and join us on the tour."

"Oh," said Qora. "I really don't think that's a good—"

"I insist."

Ninan scoffed. "You *insist*? Doesn't having the champion on board detract from the purpose of the tour?"

"Absolutely not. In fact, my people have begun to take offense that the champion has yet to make an appearance on our islands. If your father truly wants to show goodwill and prove his investment in our marital alliance, he will allow the champion to remain with us and attend our events."

"That's very generous of you," Qora said, "but Qhapaq Apo has only given me two weeks' leave. The tour will take *four* weeks … won't it?"

"I'll have my father speak to my future father-in-law and settle the matter tomorrow via messenger. Qhapaq Apo will make an exception."

Qora and Sakay exchanged glances. This would complicate things, but denying the princess would certainly have consequences too. Of course he himself didn't have to stay; there were plenty of guards aboard the *Velosaura*, which made him— or at least his bodyguard persona—redundant. But he couldn't leave her like this, dealing with this awkward situation alone for the next few weeks. He supposed he could find a courier in Kicai before setting sail in the morning, to send a message to the Razorclaws at the Den and let them know he and Qora wouldn't be joining them after all.

Ninan was slowly going pale as the conversation went on. As if it hadn't been bad enough for the poor boy, Sakay thought, playing the part of a willing groom and pretending he wasn't working in rebellion against his own household, now he'd have to spend every day with the girl he wasn't allowed to have—right next to the girl he would be forced to marry. Sakay thanked his lucky star spirits he wasn't in such a predicament. Although, he certainly understood the feeling of longing for someone he couldn't have.

Qora opened her mouth like she might argue, but Paqari raised a hand to silence her.

"Finish your business here," said the princess, "and then I expect to see you all aboard my ship within the hour."

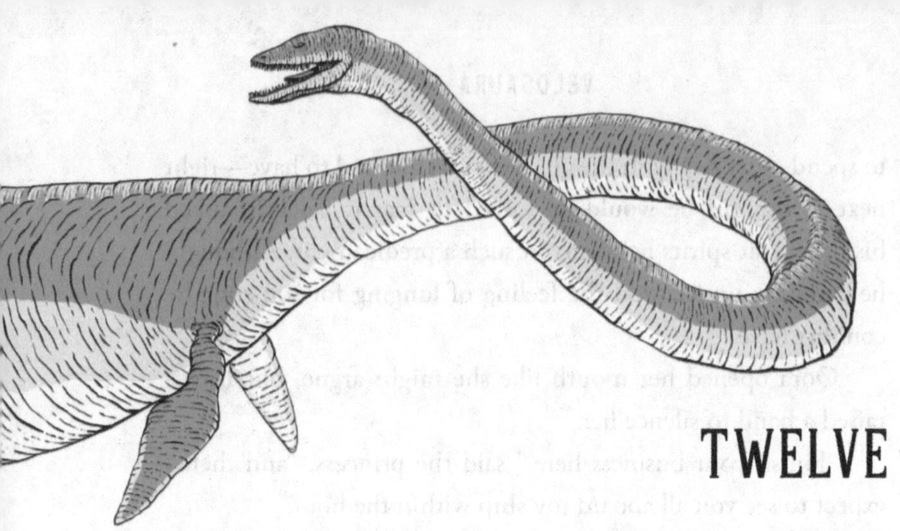

TWELVE

WHILE QORA AND SAKAY GOT SETTLED in the spare sleeping cabins, Ninan stole away to find one of Izhi's microraptors, attaching a small strip of papyr to its leg with an update on his progress, a mention of the rebels who had helped him, the news that the champion would be joining the tour, and the location of the buried dominite.

Down in the flyer hold, *Velosaura* crew members wrangled Sakay's and Qora's pteranodons and urged them in with the other large flyers, providing water and fish. Paqari had insisted on hosting the reptiles in addition to Qora and Sakay, stating that there was "plenty of room" and, after all, Qora was a guest, not a prisoner, who could leave at will, should she need or want to. Ninan had grumbled internally during Paqari's statements, knowing full well that one need not be chained to be a prisoner.

As he watched the microraptor fly off into the night, he heaved a sigh that carried everything from the past several hours, and steadied his hands on the gunwale.

The water churned around the ship, and again, his stomach churned with it. It churned at the movement of the water and it churned at Qora's presence on this vessel with him and it churned at Paqari's suspicious generosity—which he would have to pick apart mentally another time, after he'd had some sleep and a chance for his mind to catch up to the ramifications of all these things—and it churned at the memory of Qora apparently taking comfort in Sakay's hand on her back at the kantina. It churned at the thought of his best friend and adoptive family living under threat of the Guard until Ninan fulfilled his duty that his father had set forth for him. Finally, it churned at what he'd done in Ika and his continued communication with Izhi, a treasonous effort that might very well result in his own death.

He gathered himself, inhaling the sea air so forcefully that the salt burned his nose. It seemed to settle his belly, however, and he hurried off back to the main deck. Focused on his destination, he almost barreled right into his fiancée, who strode across the planks like some eerie nightingale in her silk nightrobe and cloak.

"Apo-Kimsa," she said when he bowed in apology. "I thought you had gone to bed by now." After a pause: "Then again, I thought you'd gone to bed when you left the governor's estate, and I found you two hours later at the kantina on the pier, so…"

"I swear that wasn't part of the plan," he told her. "Believe me, I'd much rather have been in bed than …" He thought of all the places he'd been that night—in town, at the dinoshelter, soaring through the air, at the docks in Ika—and was frankly surprised he hadn't been missed. "Than … out."

She glimpsed him sideways, then sauntered past him and stood with her back to the ocean, resting against elbows on the gunwale. He wasn't sure what to do, but he didn't feel like he could just walk away, so, hesitantly, he joined her.

They didn't speak for several long seconds, until Ninan broke the silence and asked, "You really think this is a good idea? Bringing Qora and Sakay on the tour?"

Paqari shrugged. "Why not? Everyone's eager to see *her*, everyone's eager to see *us* ..."

Ninan couldn't believe how thoughtless Paqari was. She only cared about her audience. He was sure it hadn't occurred to her to even ask whether Qora *wanted* to come aboard and be a part of this whole spectacle; she'd simply commanded her new guests to stay, and that was that.

"Aren't you worried?" Ninan asked.

"Why should I be worried?"

"First of all, because ... she'll ... well, she'll take attention away from you."

"Maybe I don't want attention," Paqari muttered.

Ninan scoffed. "Of course you do. You love the way they look at you, how pleased they are when you give them what they want."

She tucked a bit of windblown hair back into one of its pins. "You don't know anything about what I love."

He raised an eyebrow. "Anyway, there's also the small issue of the time I spent with her during the Venture. People talked about us—a lot. Made up stories. Imagined things between us that ... might not have been there." *Weren't there.* That's what he'd meant to say. But he hadn't been able to make himself say it like that because it would have been a lie.

"You mean the alleged, whirlwind romance in the depths of the grueling jungle as you both fought for your lives among dinosaurs?"

"That's the one," Ninan deadpanned. His father had done what he could to stamp out the rumors, even paid off most of the heralds not to report what they'd seen. But plenty of heralds, along with other competitors, had seen them staying together, watched them fight together and help each other. Ninan's and

Qora's lives and interactions hadn't been their own; they'd been pieces of entertainment.

Paqari turned around and looked down into the water. "I think you both might have felt something due to the circumstances. But ultimately, you know who you are, Apo-Kimsa—and you know what she is."

He clenched his jaw. "What is she?"

"She's no one. Aside from winning the Venture."

Ninan had to quite literally bite his tongue to keep from lashing out. He'd spend his whole life listening to this kind of ruck, about what gave someone any value—blood, gold, heroic feats. And he was sick of it.

Paqari picked at one of her cuticles. "But it's clear there's something between her and her bodyguard now, so ..."

Ninan's stomach churned yet again. He tried to sound casual. "Is there?"

"It's not obvious to you?"

"They're old friends ..."

"Hmm. Well, I could have spotted it a mile away." She sighed. "Anyway. I only came out for a breath of fresh air. I need to get some rest before we leave tomorrow. Good night."

He replied "good night" a beat too late and Paqari was already halfway across the deck.

When she disappeared down the companionway, Ninan gazed up at the stars again, and focused on Astrodon, trying to find all the stars that formed the shape of the mythical sabertooth cat's eyes, ears, and teeth. Legend said it was the ancestor of the smilodon, an avatar from the High World whose saberteeth were made of hot starlight that could cut through any piece of earthly matter. The smilodons that had come after hadn't been nearly as deadly, but even to this day they possessed teeth sharper than the deadliest dinosaurs. If only they, too, had thick scales and enormous bodies; perhaps then *they* would be the rulers of the animal world.

But that was the fate of so many things, wasn't it?

If only.

>>>

After wandering the passageways below decks, Ninan finally located the spare cabins. All the doors were closed but one, which was cracked an inch or so, spilling a flickering light onto the wood. Ninan's heart pinched when Qora's shadow moved over it. He raised his knuckles to the door.

"Hey," came Sakay's voice from somewhere within the cabin. "It's going to be fine. I promise."

A sliver of Qora's form came into view. Sakay put his arms around her and pulled her in.

Ninan dropped his hand, and went back to his own cabin.

"Call it what you will, but the kantuta will always be a kantuta."

Shaman Sisa Achirana

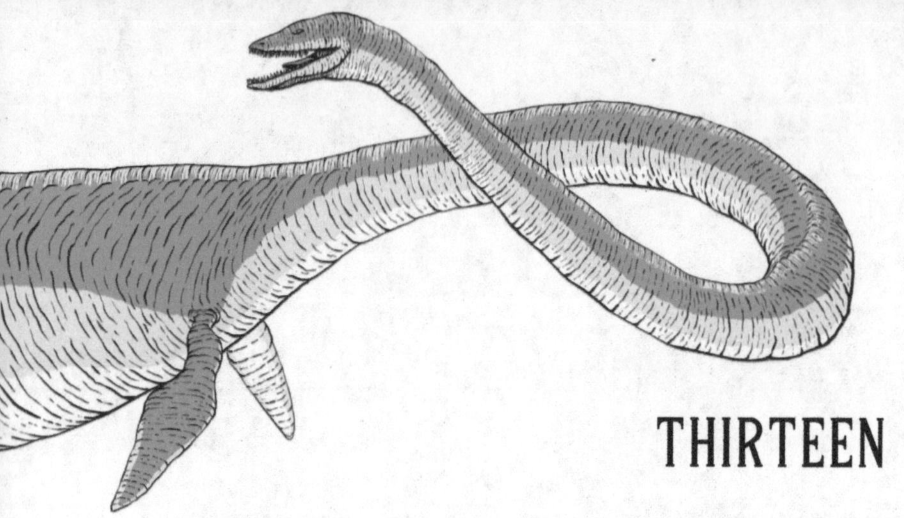

THIRTEEN

QORA WOKE TO A GLIMMERING LIGHT coming through the small window in her sleeping cabin. She wasn't sure when, exactly, she'd fallen asleep; she must have been more tired than she'd realized, to manage sleeping despite all the things that had been plaguing her mind.

She couldn't believe she was really here—not only that she'd run into Ninan, but that she was now part of the grand goodwill tour everyone had been talking about. In a twisted way, it was a wish come true. She only hoped having to watch Ninan and Paqari parade around the port cities in their fine clothes and regal accessories, while she trailed along like an afterthought, wouldn't be the emotional death of her.

The maids had provided her a sleeping gown, a sleeveless white thing that ended at her knees, which was a welcome change to the riding gear that stifled her in this climate. It was nice to let her skin breathe. Unfortunately, she'd have to put the thick pants and long-sleeved shirt back on now that she was awake.

The sounds of crew members moving over the decks crept into the room, while their muffled voices were audible through the windowglass. They'd be preparing to set sail by now, Qora thought—tweaking the rigging and soon to draw up the anchor. She quickly dressed, grabbed her crossbow, and went to Sakay's cabin, but it seemed he'd already gone to the courier. He'd promised to send word not only to the Razorclaws but also to Qora's family, to let everyone know they wouldn't be returning to Qhusi for a while.

When Qora emerged above decks, several of the crew greeted her and welcomed her aboard, followed by a dark-skinned woman with short, spiraling hair, in a seafaring uniform.

"Captain Yanacha," said the woman, extending a hand. "It's a great pleasure."

Qora accepted the gesture. "Qora Kanchaya."

"I was very pleased to hear the news that you're going to be joining us."

"Well, I'm sure a Venture champion doesn't seem that exciting when you're transporting a *princess*," Qora replied.

"On the contrary. I like passengers who aren't afraid to get their hands dirty—especially if they can wield a weapon."

Qora adjusted her crossbow strap across her chest, which allowed the weapon to hang at her hip, and also had a small quiver attached. It was silly to carry it around this well-armed ship, but she also didn't quite know how to be without it. While she was more at ease than she had been before the Venture—in terms of always having to have the crossbow on her person—it was so much a part of her *persona* now that that affected her use of it too. "I don't imagine I'll need it with all these guards."

"You never know what we might encounter." She indicated a supply of tridents.

Of course there were plenty of reptiles living in the water, Qora thought, with even more space to grow and prowl than the ones on land. "Is it dangerous out here?"

Captain Yanacha lifted one shoulder. "Most marine reptiles hunt below the surface. We're probably more susceptible to the wild flyers than anything, but those tend to keep to the shoreline."

"Well," said Qora, "After what I've seen, I'd like to think I'm prepared for just about anything."

Captain Yanacha patted Qora's arm. "That's what I like to hear."

Qora glanced around and spotted a small belfry, which housed a shiny brass bell, on the forecastle superstructure. "Is that some kind of warning system?"

"It has multiple functions," said the captain. "We use it to mark the hour—but only every three hours, dividing the waking day into quarters—as well as to signal distress. One chime for each division of the day, or a repeated steady rhythm for distress. Or, on occasion, we use it to announce the aerial arrival of a royalborn, highborn, or dignitary, in which case you will hear three chimes repeated thrice."

Suddenly the captain turned to one side and stood at attention, then lowered her head in a bow.

Qora turned as well—to see the princess approaching—and bowed like the captain.

"Good morning, Captain." Paqari wore a pink dress with a large emerald dangling around her neck. "Good morning, champion."

"Good morning, Your Highness." As Qora said this, it occurred to her that she probably ought to address Ninan the same way when she saw him next—a strange concept after all they'd been through. "You can just call me Qora." The princess's use of the word *champion* as a sort of title only reminded Qora of Qhapaq Apo, and while being aboard this ship came with its own drawbacks, Qora wanted to take advantage of the distance between herself and her snide benefactor.

Paqari stared at her for what felt like a beat too long, and then said, "We'll be setting sail soon, but please do make yourself at home. However, our next stop is quite close and only takes about an hour to arrive." She looked Qora over with a roving, analytical gaze. "I don't suppose you've brought anything different to wear?"

Qora glanced down at her clothing. "No, I haven't. I wasn't planning on a long stay. Just a few appearances. And this is what's most practical for flying."

"Well, it's hardly appropriate for a visit to the magistrate's manor in Rikracha. We'll have to get you into something better. Follow me."

Paqari had already turned on her heel, as if expecting that Qora would be close behind. Hesitantly, Qora followed the princess across the deck, down the companionway, through several passageways, and finally to the entrance of what appeared to be a suite, complete with polished-wood furniture, lush area rugs, mirrors in gilded frames, and a canopy bed.

She didn't realize she was gaping at the whole of it until Paqari snapped her fingers. "This way."

There was a shelf full of dinoleatherbound fiction books—with titles like *Phantom in the Seastorm* and *Blood of Lost Thieves* and *The Woman Who Lay Dead*—as well as a wooden puzzle box, a magnifying glass with a pearly handle, and a cipher cylinder with letters from one of the ancient alphabets. The walls bore charts that detailed constellations, Tisquvian botanicals, and ocean tides.

"Spirits, this is incredible," Qora said.

"Isn't it? Many of these things belonged to my paternal grandmother. My oldest sister said it was a lot of old clutter, so I thankfully had the privilege to inherit them. I'm the only one in the family who appreciates them anyway. Priceless literature and fascinating antiques. I thought it would be fitting to keep them with me during the tour, since the ship was my grandmother's as well—a gift from my grandfather while he was qhapaq. He commissioned it for her and spared no expense."

"I can see that."

"He also gave her this." Paqari touched the gem around her neck, pausing pensively. "People say he actually *loved* her, if you can imagine that."

"That must have been ... difficult," Qora said. For all her feelings about Qhapaq Apo, and qhapaqs in general, it hadn't ever occurred to her to wonder what the quyas felt. Three to a qhapaq, only there to produce one potential heir apiece. Paqari was right; how could there be any room for love in a marriage like that? And while Ninan would never be qhapaq, the same was expected of him, for tradition's sake—for the emulation of the sacred trio. If this marriage was allowed to happen, Paqari wouldn't be his only wife. Qora had known that, but as Paqari stroked the heirloom with her thumb, Qora felt a growing ache in her chest.

"Anyway," Paqari said, "Enough talk. We have work to do."

Paqari led her to an enormous wardrobe, with at least a hundred articles of clothing dangling from a rack, and began to rifle through everything. "Let's see ... This one's a little too bold ... No ... Not interesting enough ... Blue isn't really your color ..."

Qora tried to chime in, but the princess was too engrossed in her task to take notice.

"Too plain ... Too elaborate ... Hmm, maybe for one of our appearances on Suni, but not today ... Ah!" She withdrew a simple, red dress with white flowers embroidered onto it.

"That's gorgeous," Qora said. "But … Qhapaq Apo doesn't really want me wearing anything like that. I'm only supposed to wear the types of things I would have worn during the Venture. I should at least be seen in something practical."

Once again, Paqari stared as though Qora were speaking utter nonsense. "Qhapaq Apo isn't here. And this is *my* tour. So if I say you can wear this, you can. Understood?"

It didn't seem so much "can" as it did "will," but Qora nodded once as Paqari handed her the dress.

"You can use my dressing screen over there. I'll be back in five minutes with a beautician to deal with the rest of you."

"The rest of me?" Qora held the dress against herself and frowned.

Paqari only smiled condescendingly before she stepped out of the suite and closed the door.

❩❩❩

Sometime during the styling session—in which a very serious and reserved woman manicured Qora's fingernails, put a light amount of cosmetics on her face, and arranged her hair in long waves with a side part—the ship had taken off. Qora hoped Sakay had made it back on time.

When the beautician left, Qora looked at her reflection in one of Paqari's elaborate mirrors, running her fingers over the embroidered flowers on the dress. It had a square neckline, with the majority of the flowers covering the bodice, and wide sleeves that fell three-quarters of the way down her arms. The skirt was loose and flowing, and came down to her ankles. In these clothes, with her hair like this, she almost looked like she belonged with the kinds of people she would be forced to associate with on this tour. She thought briefly that if Ninan were to stand beside her, she almost looked like she could belong with *him*, too. Almost. The thought that it was his fiancée's dress put a sour taste in her mouth, however, and then she wanted to tear the whole thing off, no matter how the color set off the bronze tone of her skin.

She flexed her toes against the soft rug and immediately realized she needed shoes. She peered into the wardrobe, where an entire row of shoes lined the inner wall—sandals with dinoleather straps and wooden heels, platforms with jute-fiber soles and woven uppers, dainty boots with pointy toes. Her own boots—the boots that Kallpa House had recreated for her—sat next to the pile of her regular clothes, looking bulky by comparison. But Paqari hadn't offered her anything in the way of footwear, and she didn't know when the princess would return, so, for the moment, she slipped her feet into the boots she knew so well and figured the dress was long enough that no one would notice.

Above decks, Kicai had already begun to grow smaller with the distance. Paqari and Ninan stood together at the stern of the ship, waving to the crowds that had come to see them off.

Qora set her crossbow on one of the pitch barrels clustered around the mainmast, well aware that the weapon did not complement her ensemble.

"Wow," Sakay said in Qora's periphery.

She turned to see him leaning back with his elbows on the gunwale, standing between two cabinmaids, one of whom was smiling as she brushed her fingers over his elbow. He said something to them and then came over to Qora.

Qora fanned out the skirt a little. "The princess insisted."

"Well, she has good taste." Sakay took her hand and raised it, drawing her into a spin.

The length of the dress, paired with the clunkiness of her boots caused her to stumble and she let out a little yelp. Thankfully, Sakay caught her before she fell face-first on the deck, but once she'd regained her balance, she locked eyes with Ninan, who had glanced over his shoulder at her commotion.

"Thanks." Qora cleared her throat as Sakay released her. "This might be a bit of an adjustment."

"It might help if you had the right shoes."

When the ship had sailed far enough from the port for the prince and princess to stop waving, they relaxed their painted-on smiles and came amidships, where Qora and Sakay were observing the scene.

"Sleep well?" Sakay asked Ninan.

Ninan was combed and dressed to a princely standard again, but somehow there was something ruffled about his appearance.

"As well as I was able. Still working on those sea legs." He flicked a glance at Qora, showing no acknowledgment of her appearance other than a subtle flex of his jaw before clearing his throat. "I hope you both found your cabins comfortable."

Paqari approached Qora and straightened out the hem of one of the dress sleeves for her. "Well, I think you're finally looking adequate, champion. It might be a few more years before you're able to completely fill out a bodice like that, but it's a *vast* improvement from before. Except"—The princess widened her eyes in horror at Qora's feet—"dear gods, why are you wearing *those*?"

Qora lifted the skirt a few inches, revealing her costumed hunting boots. "They're all I have with me. I'm sorry—are these not 'adequate'?" She suppressed the smug expression that threatened to creep onto her lips.

Paqari clutched the gem around her neck and stepped back

as though the visual discord were contagious. "I'll get you into something nicer before we dock."

At this point, Qora figured she'd already tainted Paqari's vision of the dress on her, so she went ahead and slipped her crossbow strap back around her body. *An accessory*, she thought. Not exactly a gem, but at least it was useful.

Paqari scowled.

Behind her, a few of the crew stopped what they were doing and went to the starboard side, lining up along the gunwale. Other crew soon did the same. They all stood rigid, each with their right fist on their chest.

"What's going on?" Qora asked.

Paqari went to stand at the end of the line. Ninan, Sakay, and Qora trailed her.

Sakay shrugged at Qora, but as they looked out over the water, some eight or nine marine reptiles pierced the waves, swimming in formation and making shallow leaps above the surface as they moved past the ship. They were each the length of three men laid head to toe, and the width of four stacked belly to back.

Qora recognized the shapes—the flipper limbs, the snubbed tails, and heads that were similar to a spinosaur's but which merged with thick necks and short bodies. Their sleek, black skin and white spots were unmistakable.

"Liopleurodons," she said through a breath.

The princess put a fist to her chest as the crew did. "They rarely come up to the surface. When they do, we show them due respect."

Qora glanced at the ensign attached to the stern, the banner with Tisqu's liopleurodon-and-shield.

As soon as the liopleurodons disappeared, everyone returned

to work. Paqari excused herself. Ninan hesitated, like he might stay and socialize, but of course he had already compromised his mission and his good standing by associating with Qora and Sakay the previous night, and so, after an awkward pause, he excused himself as well.

Once Ninan was out of earshot, Sakay flashed Qora a sympathetic smile and said, "Think you'll be able to handle four weeks of this?"

She rolled her eyes. "You know we're not staying here for four weeks. You can't be away from the Underground that long, and the qhapaq will have a fit when he finds out I'm here and demand I go back to Sumaq."

A knot formed in Qora's belly when she thought about how the qhapaq would respond. Technically she hadn't disobeyed him—at least, not yet. If she stayed too long and missed the next event, sure. But he'd given her no direct orders to steer clear of Ninan. It was obvious he *wanted* her to, but for now she could plead ignorance. And the princess had insisted … so, there was that.

"Yeah. Probably."

"Anyway," Qora said, looking over her shoulder at the cabinmaids as they watched her and Sakay and whispered to one another, "you seem to have made yourself … comfortable."

He shrugged. "Gotta entertain myself somehow."

"I understand 'opportunity cost' is important in business, but they're people, Sakay. Can't you ever just settle on one woman?" Her tone implied a playful annoyance, although when she considered her own words, she did find herself more annoyed than playful. His playboy behavior was so oddly … *unlike* him. Which wasn't to say she'd ever known him to be much different—she hadn't known him well until the past year—but something about the way he flirted and flitted around didn't fall in line with his otherwise loyal tendencies.

Sakay's cocky expression faded. He held his tooth necklace in a fist.

"Sorry. Did I say something wrong?"

"No."

"You sure?"

"I'm sure."

She analyzed him, looking for a break in his defenses. What Wayra had said at Mount Qaqra made her wonder now.

"Sometimes we don't all make it out alive."

Did that have something to do with Sakay's reaction? Or with his initial reluctance to join the Razorclaws on their quest for dominite?

Qora was trying to decide how to phrase her next question when something in the distance caught her attention.

Winged creatures on the horizon.

Dark brown.

A swoop of ten or eleven.

While the similarities were only basic, Qora couldn't ignore the urge to take cover—couldn't shake the memory of giant blue pterodactyls racing toward her with dagger-claws angled for snatching. Her heart pounded at the thought of leathery wings engulfing her, toothy beaks slashing at her arms and face.

These didn't look exactly the same, but she wasn't familiar with the different species that might live around the islands.

Sakay followed her gaze to the flyers and seemed to immediately understand. He draped an arm around her shoulders. "I'm sure they won't bother us. We're not causing a ruckus. And the ocean's not like the inland waters; there are plenty of fish out here, so pterodactyls wouldn't need to go looking for mammals to supplement their diet."

"We're probably more susceptible to the wild flyers than anything," the captain had said.

Still, something didn't seem quite right. It was hard to tell from this distance, but they looked … bigger. In fact, they were looking bigger by the second, getting closer and closer like they were heading straight for the ship. And—were those *riders* on their backs?

Perhaps they were visitors, or wardens of the sea. But the aggressive pace at which they approached did not bode well.

"Sakay …"

Sakay squinted, pausing for several seconds before a look of dread came over him. "I may have spoken too soon."

The brass bell chimed a staccato rhythm as someone screamed, "Pirates!"

The pirate ship must have been far off, Qora thought, because the seas were clear in all directions for what she could see. But for pirates who could afford flyers, it was a logical method—keep their ship at a safe distance while they pillaged and plundered.

Sakay grabbed her by the arm and pulled her toward the companionway.

The guards began to shout, "Everyone below decks!" repeatedly, as they physically urged all passengers out of harm's way, along with any crew that weren't strictly necessary.

Paqari was heading amidships, with guards racing to meet her when one of the oncoming flyers swooped low, angling sideways. Its rider—a man with salt-corroded skin, in tattered dinoleather riding gear—gripped the saddle with muscular legs as he reached out and snatched the necklace Paqari wore, tearing it from her body.

Other riders landed on the deck, drawing blades and

swinging at the guards that blocked the entry points to the ship's interior.

The flyers in the flyer hold screeched and squawked in response to the sound of intruders.

Paqari cried out as the flying pirate soared across the water and circled the ship looking for other easy targets, while his comrades worked to gain access to the lower decks. Sakay tugged Qora along, with the companionway mere yards from them, but she watched the airborne pirate with his smug expression and posture, and a fire began to burn in her chest.

"Qora—come on!"

Additional guards forced Paqari down the opposite stairwell, while she kicked and protested, lamenting the loss of her gem.

"People say he actually loved *her, if you can imagine that."*

Maybe that gem wasn't worth the effort, Qora thought, but after taking down a spinosaurus with a machete, this scraggly man on a pteranodon didn't seem so daunting. She wrenched out of Sakay's grasp and ran for the lower starboard shroud attached to the foremast, her boots thunking on the deck as her dress billowed around her legs. She grabbed hold of the ratlines, climbing over the gunwale and down the hull. Ninan caught her eye before she'd fully descended, having shucked off his dress jacket and begun to grapple with one of the pirates. Her heart leapt at his skill—as it always did—even in the midst of such a brutal situation.

But there was no time to admire him. She dropped level with the flyer hold from its open side, slipped between the cage bars, and tugged on the chain to raise the gate. Then she located the pteranodon she'd flown in on and unhooked its leash. Her dress was excessive for this, but she bunched it up around her thighs and climbed into the saddle. "Rise!" she told the pteranodon.

The pteranodon, already eager to enter the mayhem, shot out like a cannon.

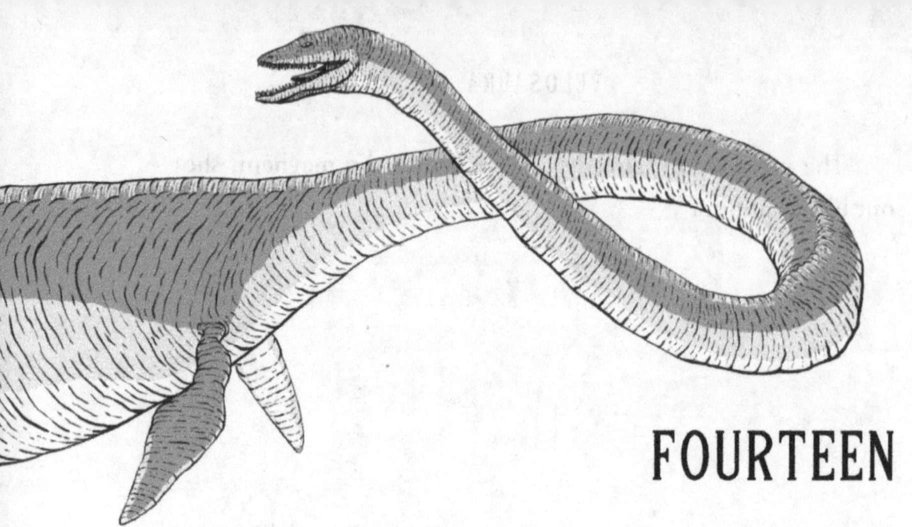

FOURTEEN

NINAN WAS SO DISTRACTED when he saw Qora take off, he took a blow to the jaw. He grunted, grabbing the pirate by the scruff of his shirt, dragging him close and thrusting a knee into his gut. Then he twisted back the pirate's arm and forced him to the ground, where he held him in place with his boot.

Meanwhile, Qora and the airborne pirate circled one another. While Qora balanced herself precariously on her saddle—as she'd let go of the pommel to load her crossbow—the pirate charged at her with a cutlass.

Ninan cringed.

Qora dropped her loaded weapon and let it dangle by its strap while she clutched the pommel and ducked, but the pirate still managed to slice one of her sleeves on her way down. The shredded material fluttered as she turned her pteranodon into an ascent, climbing after the pirate, who still clasped Paqari's gem.

Aboard the *Velosaura*, another pirate came to defend the one that Ninan still had pressed face-down on the deck, but Ninan knocked the blade from the woman's grasp, slipped to the side to avoid her fist-strike, then clinched her by the middle and flung her over the gunwale into the sea.

Sakay was working his way to the ratlines, but the guards and pirates cluttered the deck, blocking him from getting to the flyer hold for his pteranodon.

Panting, Ninan watched Qora aim her crossbow and shoot her opponent's raised arm. The pirate's cutlass plummeted and splashed. Qora spanned, loaded, and shot again, sinking a bolt into the pirate's other arm. As the pirate pitched forward, shrieking in pain and struggling to remain seated, Qora positioned herself above him and flew her pteranodon parallel to his, slightly offset. When she began to climb out of her saddle, Ninan forgot all about the pirates on board and rushed to the gunwale.

"Qora, no!"

Qora dropped onto the pirate's saddle, landing behind him. He flailed his elbows, but she only pressed one of the sunken bolts deeper into his flesh and he let up enough for her to lift Paqari's necklace. Her pteranodon continued to fly without her alongside the pirate's, but Ninan was at a complete loss as to how she planned to get back onto it.

Spirits, what is she thinking?

He had to tear himself away again when another pirate came at him with a knife. But he gave this pirate the same treatment as the other, snatching the blade and hurling him overboard.

The guards managed to subdue the other seven or so pirates between them, although not without injury, while Captain Yanacha and her crew kept the foreign flyers under control with their tridents.

All pirates seemed to be accounted for, except one—who had evaded capture and taken to the air, and was quickly catching up to Qora.

Now everyone watched the skies as Qora pushed herself to standing on the pirate's saddle, using the pirate's shoulders for balance and apparently unaware that a second airborne pirate was closing in.

Paqari had forced her way back up from below decks to see the spectacle, with attendants insisting she stay out of this chaos, but she shrugged them off and hurried to Ninan's side. "The champion can't be serious …"

"I wish I could say she wasn't." Ninan gripped the nearest backstay and held his breath. He had to do something. There were flyers all around; he could mount one of them and go after her—

But it was too late. The second pirate slashed at Qora.

Sakay joined Ninan, gaping.

In some instinctive move, Qora threw out the skirt of the dress she'd been struggling to hold away from her legs, catching the pirate's blade and twisting it away. The dress took several cuts, and the maneuver cost Qora her balance.

She plunged into the water.

"Retrieve!" Ninan and Sakay shouted in unison at her pteranodon.

Ninan held his breath again. Gods, he hoped that the pteranodon was trained to retrieve its rider when commanded. It was the standard, in Sumaq, for a good riding flyer.

The pteranodon swooped over the area where Qora paddled in the waves. It scooped her up with its long, toothless beak and carried her laterally, face down.

Stunned and dripping wet, Qora still wriggled her weapon into position and shouted "Rise!"

Again, the pteranodon obeyed, holding her so that she was in line with the second pirate. The pirate kicked his own flyer and darted away, but Qora shot him fast between the shoulder blades, unseating him instantly. She took another shot at the first pirate, who had been barely holding on as it was, leaving them both to the water for the *Velosaura* guards to apprehend.

She then commanded her pteranodon to touch down, where it tilted at a diagonal to turn her upright, and she landed in a crouch on the deck once it released her. Slowly, she rose to standing, heaving to catch her breath.

Ninan hurried toward her, but stopped short when he remembered that Paqari and at least two dozen other Tisquvians were watching. It took everything not to pull her into him and crush her against his body.

Paqari approached with cautious steps, at which point Qora withdrew the necklace and extended it to the princess.

Speechless, Paqari accepted it, staring at Qora with a furrowed brow.

Qora swiped a mass of wet hair off her cheek. "Sorry about your dress."

🌙🌙🌙

Over the course of the next half hour that remained before reaching Rikracha, the guards fished out the four pirates they hadn't already apprehended—the two Qora had shot down and the two Ninan had ejected—and coaxed the riderless flyers from the air down to the deck, all to be turned over to the government upon docking. The girls had been whisked below decks, both with severe reprimanding from the attendants and maids for not following safety instructions, and Ninan had been taken to the on-board physician for an examination, with praise for his bravery in fighting the pirates hand to hand.

"I'm not really the one who deserves your commendations," Ninan muttered. "*I* didn't tackle pirates from the sky ..."

The physician cleaned one of Ninan's facial nicks with a stinging antiseptic.

Ninan hissed at the pain but said nothing. He wondered if the general response to these feats would have been different if Ninan and Qora had been in opposite places during the conflict.

＊＊＊

The *Velosaura* remained at port for an additional hour while Ninan, Paqari, Qora, and Sakay got cleaned up. Ninan didn't see any of them until the triceratops arrived to carry them into the city.

Sakay came across the gangway in a pair of fitted dress trousers, polished black dress boots, and a light-blue tunic that was perhaps a size too small but which revealed the shape of his muscular arms. He was at least two inches taller than Ninan, and he exuded the kind of rugged charm that made even proper ladies swoon—the type of devilish rogue women liked to be "corrupted" by. It had been bad enough in Sakay's usual, lowly state, but now that he'd seen a bath and a comb, it was somehow even more severe. None of this would have necessarily stoked the coals of Ninan's envy, if it hadn't been for Qora emerging just after, and the particular way Sakay glanced over his shoulder to grin at her.

"I expect you'll have that thing torn up before sundown," Sakay said of her dress—yet another piece of fabric stitched in such a way that Ninan was beginning to think it had been designed specifically to torture him. The phrase "torn up" didn't help either, even if Sakay was only referring to Qora's rogue behavior.

This dress was sleeveless and green, with some sort of wrapping feature that draped from one shoulder and came to a tie at her waist on the opposite side. The skirt didn't flare, but rather hung straight and grazed the ground with its hem. Qora had to lift it to walk, revealing that she'd finally abandoned her boots for delicate dinoleather sandals. She also wore her hair long and loose again, along with dangling pearl-bead earrings.

Paqari stepped out behind her, wearing the Tisquvian purple she often favored, bare-shouldered to show off the gem Qora had retrieved for her, and gold bracelets to match the necklace chain.

This is going to be a long afternoon, Ninan thought.

When they arrived at the magistrate's property, the triceratops had to traverse a long lead-up to the manor—a stone-paved boulevard lined with yarina palms. The large manor at the end had a fine plaster coating, washed in white, and the veranda opened into a series of arches.

The servants attended to the group, escorting them inside where the magistrate greeted them.

She was a graceful, middle-aged woman in a yellow and crimson robe-dress with flowing sleeves and a wide, dinoleather belt. Her head bore a delicate headpiece made of bronze, with a rosinqa stone at the center, and a row of short velociraptor feathers splayed across the top edge.

"Welcome, welcome!" She extended her decorated arms, bangle bracelets jangling.

Paqari and Ninan went first, thanking her for her hospitality and remarking on what a lovely manor she possessed, and then Paqari presented Qora.

"What a surprise! I'm afraid I was unable to attend the Venture homecoming ceremony but I've heard such incredible stories about you!"

Qora smiled politely, but Ninan knew she wouldn't be looking forward to recounting the details that the magistrate would most certainly be asking for later. To everyone else, what had happened during the Venture was a tale of bravery and enthralling escapades. To those who actually participated, it was the stuff of their nightmares. Ninan could count the days on one hand that had passed since he'd dreamt of one of those blistering hot nights in the jungle, during which a gang of atrociraptors might have eaten him alive. The memory of Takan restraining and beating him still haunted him.

The magistrate and her attendants led the group on a tour of the manor, with polished tile floors in alternating color patterns, and curling wooden staircases, and enormous windows with sheer curtains. Behind the manor, a terrace sprawled for at least a hundred yards, hosting a long outdoor banquet table surrounded by several smaller tables laid out with tablecloths and fine tableware. Servants were already carrying silver vessels laden with food, whose scents wafted out enticingly.

Ninan realized that, in all the chaos of the morning, he'd eaten nothing, and was quite hungry.

While everyone waited for the finishing touches on the food, Ninan was forced to socialize again, as guests approached him and congratulated him on the upcoming wedding, indelicately brought up the topic of his disinheritance and subsequent reinstatement, and asked him about his experience with the Venture.

Paqari dragged Qora around and introduced her to many of the young ladies, several of whom Paqari seemed to already know—important society girls, apparently, who would be traveling to some of these same events by air, when their schedules permitted. "Can you believe it?" Paqari said to a group of the girls. "The champion, aboard *my ship*."

Qora played along like a little pet, and Ninan wondered what was going through her mind, how she felt about all this.

He wondered whether it was better than making appearances in Qhusi with his father. At least she didn't have to wear the same clothes all the time here. He was certain she hated that. The Venture heralds had made caricatures of all the competitors—except that most of the others had returned to their normal lives afterward. The ones who had lived, at least.

Any young ladies not gawking at Paqari and interrogating Qora were hovering around Sakay, who had pushed the sleeves of his tunic up to his elbows and unwittingly—or perhaps wittingly, Ninan wasn't sure—displayed the muscles of his forearms, a feature that was not lost on his audience.

When everyone finally sat down to eat, Ninan was seated next to Paqari, but directly across from Qora, while Sakay sat to Qora's side.

The servants placed plates of food in front of them, featuring oviraptor steaks, steaming yuca root puree, and a salad of amaranth greens.

Once everyone had had a few mouthfuls, the magistrate looked at Paqari and said, "I heard you had quite a scuffle this morning. I trust that everyone isn't too rattled?"

Ninan wondered whether the attendants had been gossiping with the magistrate's staff, or if word had gotten back from the port authorities so quickly.

Paqari dabbed the corners of her mouth with a cloth napkin, although there was no food residue to be seen there, cleared her throat, and said, "Yes, I'm afraid there were a few pirates who chanced a raid. Unlucky for them, my guards managed to apprehend them all."

"Thank the gods," said the magistrate.

"The prince also fought rather bravely," Paqari added. "I knew he'd done well during the Venture, but I had yet to see him in action. The pirates were no match for him."

"I am highly trained at hand-to-hand," Ninan reminded her. "But thank you."

The princess pursed her lips. "In any case, it seems I'm surrounded by heroes. Even the champion came to my rescue this morning." Paqari glanced down at the gem around her neck. "When one of the pirates tried to make off with my grandmother's necklace, our very own Raptoriva chased him down and took it back."

The magistrate pressed a palm to her chest. "Really?"

Qora's face pinkened at the remark, and an expression of horror overcame her as she looked down at her food. Ninan figured she should be used to this kind of attention by now. Then again, he supposed large and faceless crowds were different than this direct attention, in a more intimate setting.

Turning to Ninan, the magistrate said, "I can see why you chose to ally yourself with such a girl. There were so many tales of her bravery, but to think another such event happened so close to my own shores. How wonderful!"

"Wonderful," Paqari agreed before taking a sip of coconut wine.

Qora took a drink of her own wine—a longer, thirstier sip—then set down the glass with more force than Ninan thought necessary.

He watched her, all finely dressed and made up, remembering how she'd looked coming back out of the water in her pteranodon's grasp, all tangled and soaked and limp from the impact.

What had she been thinking?

If he knew her at all, she probably thought she was giving those bastard pirates what they deserved. She probably saw them as no different than the majority of the men in the Venture, taking whatever they pleased and caring for no one. She must have thought it impossible—unreasonable, even—to simply watch it happen from the deck. And there would have been no convincing her to get *below* decks. No, that would have been out of the question. But still. In the Venture, it had been necessary, but this was a different situation. There were guards here to protect her; she should have allowed them to do their duty.

"She's brave, yes, but she can be reckless at times," Ninan blurted. He shot her a pointed look, although no one else seemed to notice.

She narrowed her eyes at him, curling her lips in disgust—as if to say he'd done no better.

It was true; he hadn't exactly kept *himself* out of harm's way either. But he didn't value his own life as much as he valued hers. And he knew the full extent of his own limits and skills; he hadn't even known Qora could *fly* until yesterday, let alone practically perform acrobatics from the air.

"How *did* the two of you manage to become allies, by the way," the magistrate asked, "during an event in which you were destined to be enemies? I've been dying to know."

Ninan could only think that it had been too easy, really.

Easy as breathing.

He'd had to fight to keep himself *away* from her, in fact. Her tenacity, and her beautiful fury—even when she'd directed it at him individually—had been like dominite, and he like a reptile.

"I guess you could say that we … built a … mutual respect," Ninan said. "From early on, I found her integrity impressive— along with her skill."

"Yes," Qora said with a bit too much enthusiasm to be sincere. "He didn't expect me to be so *competent*. It must have been a shock when he discovered I even stood a chance."

Really? She still hasn't let this go? Ninan took a subtle breath to calm himself.

"Well"—he forced a chuckle—"I think I was just caught off guard by the fact that you were so young."

"Of course. The *one* year between us does make such a difference."

Paqari glimpsed Qora sideways, raising one eyebrow.

"Young compared to most of the other competitors," he clarified. "And there's also your size. That was somewhat deceiving as well."

"I'm average for a girl my age."

Okay, fair point …

"I admit, I made assumptions—not unlike *you* did …" He tried to keep his tone playful, but he knew a venomous tinge had seeped into it.

"Did you suspect his true identity?" The magistrate asked Qora.

Ninan answered before she could reply: "She accused me of setting those traps on the way to Lake Waylla."

"Only because I found evidence to support my theory," Qora argued.

"*Circumstantial* evidence," Ninan bit out.

"Well, I knew you were hiding *something*. Your behavior was suspicious from the beginning. And then you turned out to be Sumaq's Third Prince, so … apparently my instincts were good."

The magistrate sipped her wine and smiled. "It seems you still have a bit of a rivalry, doesn't it?"

Neither of them replied.

Several of the young ladies in attendance began to drown Paqari in questions about the wedding, particularly about her dress and which of the old ballads would be played at the end of the ceremony and who would be in attendance. For the remainder of the meal, most conversations remained between those seated beside one another while Ninan avoided eye contact with Qora.

After servants cleared the tables, guests moved freely around the terrace, beginning new conversations. Qora was once again swept up by Paqari and the other young ladies, while Ninan stood with Sakay drinking in silence.

The chatter around them faded gradually, however, as a new guest appeared at the back doors of the manor leading out to where the crowd mingled.

Ninan recognized the man instantly.

"May I present," said one of the magistrate's attendants, "Thalu Machaqway, beloved competitor of the thirteenth quinquennial Runaqan Venture."

Even though Ninan had only been eight years old at the time of that Venture, he would never forget having seen Thalu Machaqway in person at the Venture homecoming ceremony in Qolqe. The man had recently turned twenty at the time, and while he had not won the Venture, he had survived to the end, returning to much praise and admiration—a hero in his own right, possibly receiving more attention than the champion himself, who had unintentionally sacrificed an arm to a colony of vicious pterodaustro in Huandoy.

The young ladies flocked to Thalu, whose posture spoke of bravery and prowess. He wore a familiar ensemble—familiar in that Ninan had seen this specific ensemble before, but also familiar in that it was a repeated, caricatural style used for celebrity recognition, like Qora's green jacket and hunting boots. It was the same billowing off-white shirt and woven vest he'd been known for—but in finer fabrics, of course—to make himself recognizable, even though it had been ten years since he'd earned his celebrity status.

"Apologies for my late arrival," he said.

The magistrate greeted the former competitor, and then Ninan and Paqari went forward as the guests of honor. Thalu bowed to them both.

"Please allow me," Paqari said, "to introduce you to the Raptoriva." She gestured for Qora to join her.

Thalu took her hand at the introduction. "Qora Kanchaya. What a privilege."

She accepted his hand—the hand that had fearsomely gripped his famed whipsword—and … blushed? Was she *blushing*?

Gods. Thalu wasn't even particularly good looking, Ninan thought, just built strong and rugged, with a manicured beard and a confident swagger. He wore his Venture persona well, sure, but he'd been maintaining it for more than a decade, continuing this show into full adulthood and parading around on the glory of a long-gone period of time.

The more Ninan looked at him, the more his admiration began to fade.

"The privilege is mine," Qora said.

She has to say that, Ninan reminded himself. That's what was expected of her in a setting like this, with these kinds of people.

"Your Venture performance was quite impressive," Thalu told her. "I think it even puts mine to shame."

Qora smiled flatly.

Yes. There it is. She could see past that strange magnetism. She had to.

Was this man's pride even *warranted*? Considering he'd

spent most of his Venture in disguise, devising clever ambush attacks and building camouflaged hideouts. From what Ninan remembered, Thalu had survived by keeping out of the way, mostly. Ninan had had to do the same, of course, and so had Qora, but it was strange that everyone found it so impressive.

"You flatter me," Qora told Thalu in a dulcet tone similar to Paqari's—although Ninan thought it carried a hint of sarcasm. "The jungle is nothing compared to the icy peaks you had to ascend."

"Well, I won't say it was easy." Thalu grinned.

"Will you be attending any of the other events on the tour?" Paqari asked.

"I plan on it, yes," Thalu replied. "I'm looking forward to visiting Count Kisqa in particular. I do love a good sport—but I suppose everyone here already knows that." He winked at Qora.

Ninan rolled his eyes.

After that, the conversation gained more participants and drifted to topics of weather (a storm expected within the next week along the northeast region of the islands) and politics (a scandal with the vice chancellor that might threaten his position in office) and soon everyone began to break off into smaller groups following different subtopics.

Ninan, however, found himself a part of the group that included Qora, as Qora was Paqari's special guest, and while he and Paqari were naturally the main focus of the magistrate's attention.

"We're all so very pleased at your engagement," the magistrate told them. "The alliance between Sumaq and Tisqu is a godsend. You have no idea how it calms the fears among the islanders, especially with the events of late."

"Events?" Qora asked. "What events?"

"Well, the attacks, of course. Several villages have been victim to dinosaur attacks," the magistrate explained. "Specifically dinosaurs that are not native to the islands."

Ninan felt a sudden squirming sensation in his gut. He stole a glance at Qora, whose complexion paled.

Just like the sailbeast, Ninan thought. More of his father's experiments wreaking havoc on innocent bystanders.

"We fear it may be a type of biological warfare," the magistrate continued. "It's happened between other continents, on which the nations from one to the other are attempting conquest. They've introduced non-native species—depositing eggs or hatchlings on foreign shores—to weaken the population prior to attacks. It hasn't always been very effective in *those* lands, but our Terrain is small and vulnerable. For that reason, we welcome the alliance with Sumaq."

Ninan, Qora, and Sakay all exchanged troubled looks, and Ninan knew they were sharing a thought: Those dinosaurs had nothing to do with extracontinental warfare.

"Did these attacks happen in any particular region?" Qora asked.

"Six non-native dinosaurs were caught terrorizing some of the villages along the western coast of Phapa."

The *Velosaura* wouldn't reach Phapa for a week.

But Ninan could get a message to Izhi tonight. Izhi could begin investigations immediately.

FIFTEEN

RED COVE GREETED THE *VELOSAURA* with a series of wave-cut caves and rocky headlands, with many of the city's stacked-stone and cinderblock buildings standing as close to the edge as they could get without falling off. Count Kisqa's mansion was built in grand tiers and lengthy staircases that led straight down to the sand, and the whole structure was coated with a pinkish plaster that stood out against the island greenery and the bright blue sky.

Crowds were already gathered across the shoreline and along the pier, while dozens of gray-blue plesiosaurs—with riders on their backs—swam in the shallows, weaving around buoys painted red. The plesiosaurs had tapered bodies with backs at least fifteen feet in length, and long snaking necks that extended another ten or so feet more. They each had two fore-flippers and two hind-flippers and short inflexible tails.

Qora took in the scene, never having seen anything quite like this before.

Paqari came to where Qora stood. "Magnificent, aren't they?"

"Yes," Qora replied.

"They're not actually dinosaurs; they're sauropterygians," the princess informed her. "And most of their species can't raise their necks above the water—they don't have the strength—but this subspecies is unique to the Tisquvian isles, similar to their local elasmosaurian cousins that can be quite terrifying if you spot one in the middle of the sea. Like the towering, aquatic monsters from children's stories." She beamed at the creatures with admiration. "They're quite graceful. You'll see what I mean when you ride one."

Qora jerked her head to look at Paqari. "*Ride* one?"

Paqari nodded. "Of course. The count expects it. He's obsessed with the sport."

"What sport?"

"The races?" Paqari said this as if Qora should have known. "That's what the buoys are for. It's part of the racecourse." She narrowed her eyes. "Don't tell me that intimidates you. Not after you went after a pirate on pteranodonback ..."

"That was different. I'm not trained on water reptiles."

"It can't be worse than falling to your death from the air. Worst case scenario, you slide off into the water. Don't worry; you'll love it."

Qora shuddered at the thought. It was one thing to leisurely take a ride on a new animal; it was a different thing entirely to *race* one.

When the ship docked, the passengers didn't have to bother with any triceratops, since they wouldn't be going inland. The count himself arrived at the end of the gangway to greet them.

He was probably in his early thirties, wearing a belted, one-piece article of clothing. The dark blue material bared his muscular arms at the top, and merged to pant-legs that were loose around the thighs but which ended mid-calf in a snug hem. His feet were bare, certainly not what Qora would have expected from a count, and his dark hair swooped low on his forehead.

Paqari linked arms with Qora and whispered, "He'll be racing, too."

The count, flashing a toothy grin with symmetrical dimples, said, "Gods and spirits, how did I get so lucky? The princess *and* the Venture champion?" He kissed Paqari's hand, then Qora's, and then as if shaking himself from a daze, added, "And of course Sumaq's Third Prince!" He greeted Ninan with a handshake and a half-bow.

"So pleased to see you again," said Paqari.

"Pleased to meet you," Qora said.

Ninan said nothing.

"And who's this?" The count indicated Sakay, who was observing the plesiosaurs with rapt attention.

"The champion's bodyguard," Paqari explained.

Sakay greeted the count as well, and said, "Such fascinating creatures. Do you breed them yourself?"

"Some," said the count. "A few of the competitors bring their own to the races, but many of them come from my collection. Do you ride?"

"Only rhabdos and pteranodons," Sakay told him. "Although I have to admit, I'd love to try one of these."

"Well you must join us then! I always insist that my guests participate."

"He's not really a guest," said Paqari.

"Anyone with an interest in reptiles is welcome," the count insisted. "The trained plesies are quite docile, and they love the exercise. Besides, this is a *friendly* race. Anyone can do it. Come! Let me show you around and then I'll let you all dress for the race." He gestured at his own clothing.

The group toured the mansion, with the same tile floors and sheer curtains as the other highborn homes, along with indoor tropical plants, jute rugs, and wood-carved art. The servants provided light refreshments in the form of shrimp cocktails, tiny maize cakes, gallimimus meatballs, and melon water, while the group met and mingled with other high-class guests. Most guests were dressed in fine cottons, in the form of sleeveless dresses or tunics or robes, some with short pants that bared parts of their legs, and open-toed dinoleather shoes. Then the count made good on his promise and provided them with one-piece articles of clothing like his own, which he referred to as a "tide suit."

Everyone received a different color tide suit, so as to be more distinguishable to those watching the race. Paqari wore her usual purple, while Ninan wore Sumaqi red, Sakay wore a sort of rusty brown color, and Qora wore forest green. "Ever the Raptoriva," the count said to Qora. Qora forced a smile and adjusted the fit of the lightweight material, feeling somewhat naked in the sleeveless top and shorter pant-legs.

A few other participants came to meet them—two young ladies that Paqari seemed to know from other social events, the Tisquvian ambassador's son, three performers from the Suni Carnival of Reptilian Wonders, and the Aletan Theater's lead female player, along with Thalu Machaqway and a handful of commoners who, through some regular contest, had won the privilege to join them, making for a total of around twenty racers.

Thalu winked at Qora and Paqari just before he dipped his finger into a small container of pachyrhine and snorted it with a cheery jitter. Qora wondered how much a stash like that had cost him, and if he even had much money left from the Venture after all these years or was only putting on a show.

She caught Ninan glowering at Thalu, although Thalu didn't notice. It had been Ninan's apparent displeasure with Thalu yesterday that had made Qora behave more friendly toward the former competitor, a way to ruffle Ninan's feathers even though she knew it was childish. In any case, she couldn't deny that Thalu had a certain magnetism about him whenever he arrived somewhere, but it faded as soon as he spoke or made flirtatious gestures.

The other highborns wore colors too, while the middleborns and lowborns all wore the same gray. Everyone wore goggles, just like the ones for flyer-riding, this time to keep the water from splashing into their eyes.

The count went over a map of the race course, explaining that they would be racing ten miles across the strait until they reached South Ridge, the southernmost village on Suni—which was the neighboring isle, and the second-largest of *all* Tisquvian isles—before doubling back. The first to make it back to the starting point, which would then become the finish line, would be the winner. "Watch out for the sea stacks when you approach South Ridge, though," he warned. "They're closer together there, and there's more of them. It's easy to lose sight of the other racers that way, which makes it harder to know your position among them."

After some introductions to the crowd, provided by an announcer using a large funnel to amplify his voice, each racer prepared to mount a plesiosaur. Qora glanced at Ninan as her plesiosaur swam up to the dock, positioning itself so that she could climb onto its back.

Ninan nodded once at her, but she didn't know what to make of it. A truce, for the moment? A reassurance that this race was not a matter of concern? Not that she needed—or wanted—reassurance from him.

She swung her leg over, and shivered as her feet slid into the water. Her toes found the stirrups, which were angled slightly backward compared to the ones on a megaraptor or a rhabdo, or even on a pteranodon. In this case, a rider had to keep their feet from interfering with the movement of the flippers. This position forced her to lean further forward than she was used to on a reptile, but this saddle also came up higher on the base of the plesiosaur's neck, almost like a collar, and had three pommels—one in the center and another to the right and left—allowing her a good grip. There were no reins, however.

Paqari had already mounted and maneuvered her plesiosaur away from the dock, moving through the water with ease. "You just add pressure on the pommels," she told Qora. "Right pommel for a right turn, left pommel for a left turn, both at the same time to go forward. Pull back gently on the center pommel to slow down, or pull back abruptly to stop. The plesies are very sensitive to touch and will respond accordingly."

"Thank you." Qora took a deep breath.

The plesiosaur twisted its neck and turned its face to look at her, emitting a soft clicking sound. Qora reached forward cautiously until her fingers touched the reptile's short, slick snout. Its eyes were like giant teal marbles, with black dots at the center that stared at her. "Hi," she whispered. "You won't drown me, right?" The plesiosaur blinked a couple of times, then turned its head away. Qora ran her gaze down its neck covered in faint spots, all shiny and wet, muscles flexing under the skin like a serpentosaurid. It was, indeed, a fascinating creature.

Ninan seemed to adapt quickly to his plesiosaur, which was no surprise after all his highborn training with reptiles, and Sakay settled into the bucking rhythm.

The count balanced himself into a standing position and waved to the crowd. The people cheered.

Qora thought she saw Ninan roll his eyes before he gripped both pommels and moved toward the buoys that marked the starting line.

Following Paqari's instructions, Qora led her plesiosaur to the starting line as well, and waited for everyone else to gather. Soon, the announcer was at the voice funnel again, calling out the names of all the racers, each of which received a different volume of applause from the audience. When Qora's name came up, the people chanted *rap-to-ri-va*, *rap-to-ri-va*, *rap-to-ri-va* as they had when she'd returned from the Venture, and even though she tensed at the familiar sound, she also had to remind herself that these people felt inspired by her—another reason, she realized, that she tolerated the persona the qhapaq had set up for her, because she had given people hope … and hope was important. This volume was exceeded only by that for the count, whose grandstanding apparently knew no bounds. He pounded his own chest with his fists, and cried out at the same time, matching the energy, still standing on his plesiosaur's back.

Qora wondered if he was going to perform the entire race like that, but when the announcer pulled the sparkcord on the large firestick whose colorful blast of light set the racers in motion, the count dropped into the saddle and charged forward.

She pressed both side pommels so that her plesiosaur did the same. The other racers took off too, all spread out at first and then slowly passing one another or cutting in front and behind.

Qora gripped the pommels and pressed herself flat against the place where plesiosaur's back curved to meet its neck, so that her upper body didn't thrash with the movement. Riding this reptile was similar to riding a raptor, with a type of galloping motion that rocked her, except that it was more forceful against the resistance of the water. The sea sprayed up with each flap of the plesiosaur's flippers, dotting Qora's goggles.

The strait was a little over ten miles across, and the count had told her the plesiosaurs could swim up to thirty miles per hour, which should make this race approximately forty minutes round trip. Even though Qora didn't really know what she was doing, her plesiosaur did, following the buoys and turning with the curves. It was fast, and seemed to have a competitive spirit among its own kind.

After the first few minutes, Qora's stomach roiled at the persistent up-and-down—an effect so much more severe than the sway of the *Velosaura*—and she wished she could slow down, but at this moment she was keeping a good pace and remaining ahead of many of the racers. Being a "champion," she didn't want to come in last; even if her pride were to allow it, she didn't imagine the qhapaq would appreciate the embarrassment when word got back to him—and it *would* get back to him eventually. Qora hardly knew whether she wanted that or dreaded it; if the qhapaq insisted she go back to Qhusi, it would be both a burden and a relief.

The count was far ahead, as to be expected, with Thalu Machaqway and one of the carnival performers close behind, and then Paqari and two skilled middleborns. Ninan, Sakay, and Qora weren't far from one another, with additional racers on both sides and the rest trailing them. Somewhere between the plesiosaur's agility and Qora's training on other reptiles— allowing her the strength and endurance to hold on at high speed—she was able to put on a good show, doing her best not to give away the fact that she was on the brink of hurling up her shrimp cocktail.

If she didn't think about the motion, she did like the way the speed over the water had a cooling effect on her skin, a refreshing chill against the heat.

When she felt confident enough to look around, she gazed up at the rocky sea stacks, towering over her like otherworldly giants of nature. Something that might look like a mythical monster in the dark, but which, in the bright sunlight of the late morning revealed textured layers of the earth piling up over millennia and eroding.

For a few miles the sea stacks were sporadic, but as Qora approached South Ridge, they came shorter and closer together.

Before Qora knew it, the first half of the course finished and the racers began to turn back for Red Cove, plesiosaur heads bobbing to regain speed after redirection.

The count remained at the head of the group with more or less the same order of racers at his back. He punched a fist in the air and hollered his excitement for reaching the halfway point.

As Qora carefully turned her plesiosaur with pressure on one of the side pommels, she glanced around at the rocky headlands of the South Ridge coastline and the village beyond it, where stone houses dotted the landscape. She was about to turn her attention back to the race when a flyer in the distance caught her eye. A white one.

She flinched at the sight of it, pressing too hard on the opposite pommel. The plesiosaur wavered, losing speed in its confusion. Despite being at Qora's command, the plesiosaur seemed to want to resist her now that her instruction deviated from its knowledge of the course. But Qora couldn't focus. She couldn't take her eyes off that flyer.

In a matter of seconds she was dead last, with the final few racers moving ahead of her. She wrestled with the plesiosaur, steering it toward one of the sea stacks.

I have to get a better view.

Reluctantly, the plesiosaur obeyed, bringing her to the base of a shorter sea stack with a series of jutting nodes that looked relatively easy to scale. Qora slid off the saddle and onto the rocks, grabbing hold of different parts of the protruding surface and pulling herself quickly up to the top. Her hands and feet were slick and she lost purchase several times, scraping her shins and forearms, but when she reached the top, the flyer remained within her view—just barely.

The white flyer grew tiny in the eastern sky before descending toward the nearest land mass. The island of Sut'u.

Qora didn't know if it meant anything that someone on one of the qhapaq's albino pteranodons apparently had some business there, but it was certainly worth mentioning to Izhi and the Razorclaws.

When she lost sight of it, she suddenly remembered where she was, and where she was supposed to be.

She would never catch up to the racers within any reasonable timeframe now. And she had no explanation for why she had fallen so far behind.

UNAY: Did the gods drop the rocks from the sky as a gift, or were they simply trying to strike us?

CHUWI: I do not believe it was to strike us, for if that were the intent, we would be dead. After all, gods do not fail in their aim.

UNAY: Then perhaps we have been struck with a curse instead— the curse of greed and contention. Wherever there is power to be possessed, humankind will seek it, covet it … and kill for it.

Echoes in the Void, Act II, Scene VII

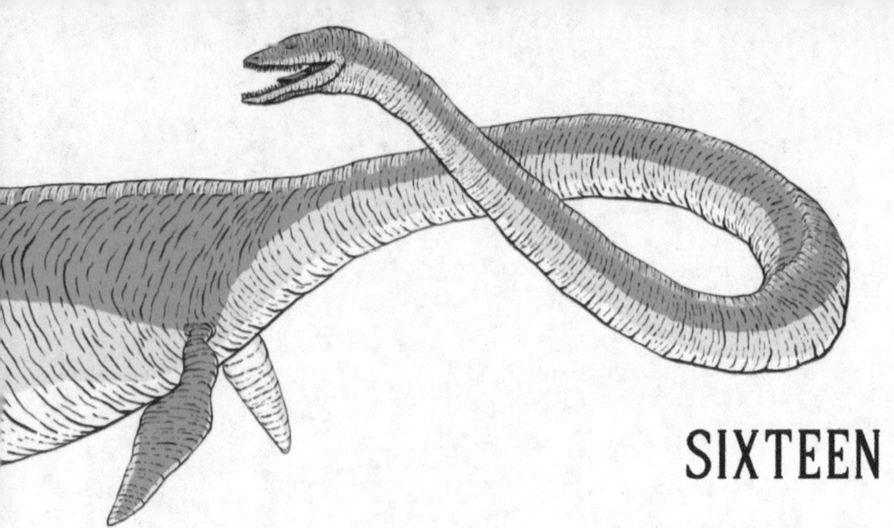

SIXTEEN

THE RACE WAS EXHILARATING. Sakay breathed in the salty air, savored the rush of it over his bare arms. The plesiosaur was one with the water, cutting through it like the sharpest of blades, and carrying him across the ethereally blue surface. The plesiosaur wove between sea stacks, eager to keep up with the others. Sakay leaned into the movements, angling for speed as he worked to stay ahead. He and Ninan had been neck and neck for several miles, and he'd finally managed to pass him, but now Ninan had fallen so far behind Sakay had to pause and look back.

What is she doing?

Ninan was near the back of the group now, with most of the gray-clad racers passing him. Sakay slowed his plesiosaur and fell back too, until he and Ninan were level.

"I don't see Qora." Ninan glanced around.

Sakay realized he hadn't seen her for several minutes either—not since before the turnaround at South Ridge. He'd been so focused on gaining on his opponents, he hadn't been looking out for her.

His stomach sank.

Suddenly he imagined her buried in the waves and struggling to reach the surface. If the plesiosaur had thrown her, or if she'd strayed into more dangerous waters …

Gods, no …

Sakay turned the plesiosaur around as the last of the racers skimmed past.

The boys backtracked over the course, navigating the passages between sea stacks with difficulty.

"They all look the same," Sakay growled.

"I'll take right, you take left," Ninan told him.

Sakay nodded and the two of them split up, scouring the sea stacks. They were almost all the way back to South Ridge before Sakay spotted Qora halfway down one of the sea stacks' rocky sides—with blood on her forearms. Her plesiosaur waited below, clicking in distress.

"Over here!" Sakay called to Ninan.

Within a few seconds, Ninan had circled around to where Sakay was. "Are you alright?!" he asked Qora.

"Yes," she replied through gritted teeth. "I'm fi—"

Her foot slipped.

She scrambled to regain her grip on the rocks.

Sakay and Ninan rushed to the base of the sea stack to dismount, but Qora lost footing again and plummeted toward the water.

Qora's plesiosaur dipped its head under the surface, slithering into the zone where Qora had fallen, and brought her up in the curve of its neck.

Together, Sakay and Ninan managed to hoist Qora back onto her saddle.

"What were you doing?" Sakay demanded.

Spirits, this girl was going to be the death of him.

Ninan gripped his pommels and panted, with a look on his face that bordered on furious.

"There was"—Qora panted too, and lay forward on her

plesiosaur, hugging its neck—"I saw a … a white pteranodon. That way." She pointed weakly to the east. "I needed … a better look." She sighed, with her face pressed up against the plesiosaur's wet skin.

"You're sure?" Sakay said.

She nodded.

Ninan frowned, "Did you see it land?"

"It descended on Sut'u," she told him. "I'm certain."

〉〉〉

Sakay, Qora, and Ninan passed the finish line a good five minutes after everyone else. The count, along with Paqari, Thalu, and a few of the other more distinguished racers, greeted them with worried faces and persistent questions.

What happened? Are you all okay? Why are you bleeding?

Sakay turned on his charm and regaled them all with an improvised story of a pod of vicious saltwater hyphalosaurs— slimy long-necked sea lizards the size of compies—that had spooked Qora's plesiosaur and sent her crashing into the rocks. Noticing she'd been missing from the group, he and Ninan had gone back for her, just as a small ichthyosaur had intercepted, scattering the hyphalosaurs and allowing Qora to speedily escape. It was a tall tale if he ever told one, but it worked.

Once everyone had calmed down, the attendants took Qora inside to treat her scrapes, while the rest of them enjoyed another round of drinks, and dino meat on sticks to facilitate mobile socializing. Despite the racers having splashed (or, in Qora's case, fully submerged) their tide suits, the heat and the breeze left them all dry again in less than an hour.

Later, Sakay found Ninan brooding on the balcony, while

sheer curtains ballooned gently in the sea breeze at the opening. He sat down on the wooden bench beside him, and handed him a meat morsel. Ninan accepted it but didn't take a bite.

"Only three days in and already so many close calls," Sakay muttered.

He couldn't even fully blame the Razorclaws for all of them. The mission to steal dominite had been successful, and with almost no negative consequence. Everything else had been the result of his and Qora's separate associations with the Third Prince. And something told him this was only the beginning.

Would there ever be a moment of relief?

It was difficult to say whether he truly wanted one. While the past couple of years had been relatively quiet—at least until the Venture—he couldn't say that spending his days at the Underground was especially meaningful. On the other hand, participating in anything "meaningful" so often seemed to mean risk and danger and … loss.

"You were really worried about her," Ninan said quietly, picking at the meat.

"Of course I was. She only came to Tisqu because of me—because I was stupid enough to talk within earshot about what the Razorclaws were doing, and there was no way she wouldn't have wanted to be involved. I'm responsible for her."

"That makes sense … I guess."

"What about you? You seem a little rattled yourself. Not to mention a little … lost."

"Lost? Me?" Ninan chuckled bitterly. "Haven't you heard? I'm right where I'm supposed to be. A once-wayward son, now returned to his rightful place, fulfilling his duty. The pride of Kallpa House."

Sakay shook his head and scoffed. "Sometimes I don't get

you. I understand you're in a tough spot—'duty' and all that—but this isn't the version of you I met at the Underground before the Venture. This isn't the guy who *survived* the Venture and won back a royalborn title."

"It's hard to maintain a fighting spirit when your father has control over an entire Terrain. When he can hold anything and anyone hostage if you don't behave as he wishes."

"Sure. But you're a prizefighter. You know how to feint and slip a punch and come out of nowhere to hit where it hurts. You've dealt with bigger, badder fighters before. You don't wait for permission to strike."

"Yeah, well, maybe this time I'm in a no-win situation."

Sakay didn't know how to convey the gravity of what he'd experienced, but he knew Ninan needed to snap out of it. "I don't have a solution for you, but … that's simply not true. I've seen a no-win situation—and this isn't it."

Ninan sat up straighter. "Be honest with me. Is there something between you and Qora? Something … beyond friendship?"

Sakay analyzed Ninan, the boyish lack of confidence, the look of heartache on his face. With dramatic pause, Sakay leaned forward with his elbows on his knees. "There … is …" He took a deep breath. "… Nothing of the sort."

Ninan exhaled forcefully like he'd been holding it. "You're such an ass."

Sakay grinned. "I know."

"Paqari seems to think you and Qora are close."

"We are. But not like that."

"You've honestly never even *thought*—"

"She was only thirteen when we met, and I was sixteen. I'd be lying if I said it hadn't crossed my mind that I might come to feel something for her once we were older, but ... honestly, I've only ever felt for her like a sister. Someone to look out for. Someone who'll call me out on my ruck. I understand why you're devastated not to have her, but, rest assured ... I won't be the one to try and take her from you."

"Not that it matters." Ninan scoffed. "My circumstances have taken her already."

"I understand that. More than you could know. In fact, that may be the very reason I'll never see Qora—or anyone else, for that matter—as someone to give myself over to in any sort of permanent way."

"What do you mean?"

"I mean ... There was a girl who was everything to me, once. And circumstances ... took her." He ran his fingers absentmindedly along the patterns shaved into his hair. "There is no replacement. There never will be."

"Gods." Ninan's throat flexed. "I'm sorry."

"Nothing to be sorry for. But just know ... it's not over for you. Not as long as you're both living and breathing." A pang seized Sakay's chest.

Ninan narrowed his eyes, furrowed his brow.

Sakay sensed Ninan might have more questions, but this was a day of sunshine and sport, not a day to wallow in the past. He'd let the conversation take too dark a turn, and now quickly lightened his tone. "I envy your skill with your fists, but I certainly don't envy you this situation." He forced a laugh. "Although, it could be worse than being a prince on a fancy ship with a feisty princess and a sweet—but sometimes scaly—Venture champion who's been missing you like crazy."

Ninan raised his chin a little. "You think she missed me?"

Sakay chewed his dino meat and swallowed. "I know she did."

"Well, now she only seems annoyed. You heard her at the magistrate's luncheon."

"You two have spent too much time apart. You forget how she is."

"Insufferable?"

"Mmhmm," Sakay mumbled through another mouthful of food.

"And clever. And a force to be reckoned with."

"You should probably have a more serious conversation with her. Without an audience."

"Not sure how I'd accomplish a thing like that." Ninan picked a piece of meat off the stick and chewed it pensively. "I barely managed to sneak out of the parlor to get a moment alone out here. And I have no idea where she is."

"She's down at the caves."

"Caves?"

"I distracted the count and some of the socialites while she slipped away. Now's your chance." Sakay clapped Ninan on the back and stood to leave. "Don't waste it."

SEVENTEEN

NINAN MARVELED AT THE ROCKY STAIRCASE with its individual steps that led down to the caves within the base of the headland.

Inside one of the smaller caves, Qora sat on the ground with her feet in the water and her head resting on her knees, her tide suit dry now with a salty residue on the green material. She startled when Ninan blocked the light at the entrance.

Sighing as she recognized him, she said, "If you're here to lecture me about being 'reckless,' then don't bother. I've learned my lesson."

"I'm not. But while we're on the subject, I'd appreciate it if you tried a little harder to keep your life." He raked his fingers through his wet hair, still not used to the fact that there wasn't as much of it anymore.

"I'm trying to make myself useful. Otherwise I'll go crazy spending all month on that boat." She pointed her head in the vague direction of the *Velosaura* where it was currently docked. "And *I* would appreciate it if you didn't treat me like a little girl."

"That's not what it's about ..."

Qora picked up a stray rock and tossed it into the shallow pool at her feet, where it plunked and sent out little ripples. "What's it about, then?"

"It's …" he huffed and pinched the bridge of his nose.

I don't want to lose you, is what he wanted to say. But it would have sounded ridiculous—because, in a way, he'd already lost her. Hadn't he? What good did it do to tell her to protect herself because of what he felt for her, when what he felt for her didn't change the situation they were in? He could beg her to stay alive, to stay *in his life*, but she couldn't be in his life. Not if he married Paqari. Not unless he wanted to be like his father, and all the other highborns, with their extramarital affairs. He feared what the future held for him, for whomever he'd have to take to wife after the island princess, for the rules that would follow the birth of his heirs, and the royalborn culture that would try to steer him toward a parade of mistresses.

Suddenly he felt nauseated. It wasn't this singular wedding that was the worst of it; it was everything this wedding would set in motion. In this moment, he could do nothing to stop it.

Meanwhile, Qora had been sitting here alone, in a cave, with nothing but her wasted affection for him.

"I know this isn't easy for you," she said.

"I know it's not easy for you either. Like an idiot, I asked you to wait for me, and then you heard nothing for months. I should have tried to send you another message. I wanted to, believe me. But every day that passed without progress, the less I believed I'd be able to give you any reason to keep hoping."

To that, she said nothing, just tossed another rock into the water.

This time, Ninan watched the ripples more closely, feeling like a stone in the water himself, with no power to do anything but sink, while his position disrupted everything around him. "Gods … I wish we could just run away."

Qora pushed herself up off the ground and dusted off her

hands. "We both know that was never an option. Not when there are people we love and care about who would be left behind to take punishment for our rebellion."

Yes, Qora had her mamáy and her brothers to worry about. And Ninan had his own mother, and of course Pidru and Tamya—and then, all of Thak. Qora didn't know about that part.

But she seemed to sense the way her words had affected him.

"What's wrong?" she asked. "Besides the obvious …"

He shook his head. "Nothing. It's difficult. That's all. Talking about it just makes me think about it, and thinking about it, well …" He turned and looked out at the waves, the worst of which always managed to die down before ever reaching the shore, blending into smooth waters that slid calmly over the sand. His thoughts could be the same—turbulent when he got into the depths of them, tamer if he only remained in the shallows.

Qora crossed her arms. "I don't believe you."

Her loose hair fluttered across her cheeks, so wild compared to when he'd known her during the Venture. The events that forced her to become the champion had set her likewise loose, broken her open and made *her* wilder too. Out of necessity. Gods, she was stunning. Like a thunderstorm. Like the vines and brambles of the sprawling jungle. Like the roar of a dinosaur.

"My father," Ninan conceded, "has guards occupying Thak's perimeter." His shoulders sank. It felt good to tell someone, especially Qora, although saying it out loud for the first time seemed to make it more real, more severe.

Qora looked up at him, brow furrowed. "He's holding your family hostage …"

The fact that she had said "family" told him she knew him better than anyone, even for how relatively little time they had spent together.

Ninan nodded. "He'll kill them all, if I don't cooperate."

"Spirits …" she breathed. "I'm so sorry." Her arm twitched, like she might reach out to him, but if that was her intent, she restrained herself.

Her restraint spurred an ache inside of him. He wanted her to reach out, so badly.

But … if she wouldn't … *he* could.

He bracketed her against the inner wall of the cave, so closely that his chest collided with hers each time he inhaled. Whatever control his father had over him, that tyrant wasn't here now. No one else was either. Just himself and Qora. In this moment, he could pretend he was free to act as he wished.

"What are you doing?" Qora's face was flushed pink, and her eyes pleaded with him.

She put both hands against him, almost in position to push him away, but with no force behind them. He put one of his own hands on top of hers and threaded his fingers through her fingers. She didn't protest.

His heart pounded.

This is dangerous.

Gently, she pulled her hand away. "We can't."

"Can't what?"

"You know what."

"I don't know how to properly be around you," he admitted. "Not like this—under these circumstances, with highborns watching our every move." Tentatively, he cupped her face, running his thumb across her bottom lip, wanting so badly to taste it. He felt her shiver beneath his touch, a sensation that sent his blood rushing. "But … I need you." All he had to do was lean in another inch.

It was like the lava flows all over again, touching her, having her within reach—and yet, despite everything in him wanting to give in, everything around him seemed to deny him the privilege. The situation, the risks, the impossibility of the future he so desperately wanted to see.

I can't pull away this time. I won't.

Except, he had to.

Qora's eyes welled and her jaw trembled.

Maybe she was thinking of that night right now too, how much it had hurt when he'd stopped. Only now she must know it wasn't because he wanted to.

"It doesn't matter what you need," she choked out. "Or what *I* need. Or what the princess needs, or what Sakay needs, or what your friends in Thak need. We're all just pieces in your father's game—and there's nothing we can do about it."

He stroked her hair and fought the sting growing behind his own eyes. "There has to be *something*—"

"There's not. We might get Izhi enough information to delay an attack, but as far as your wedding is concerned …"

"*No.*" Ninan struck the cave wall with the flat of his hand, making Qora flinch at the sharp echo. "I refuse to accept that!" He winced as pain spidered down his wrist.

Qora ducked under his arm but he caught her around the waist. "Please. I'm sorry. I'm just—" He clenched his teeth. "I didn't mean to—"

A tear slipped down Qora's cheek and she shook her head. "Just … let me go. Please."

With Ninan lost in his hesitance, Qora slipped out of his grasp, and for now, he reluctantly allowed it.

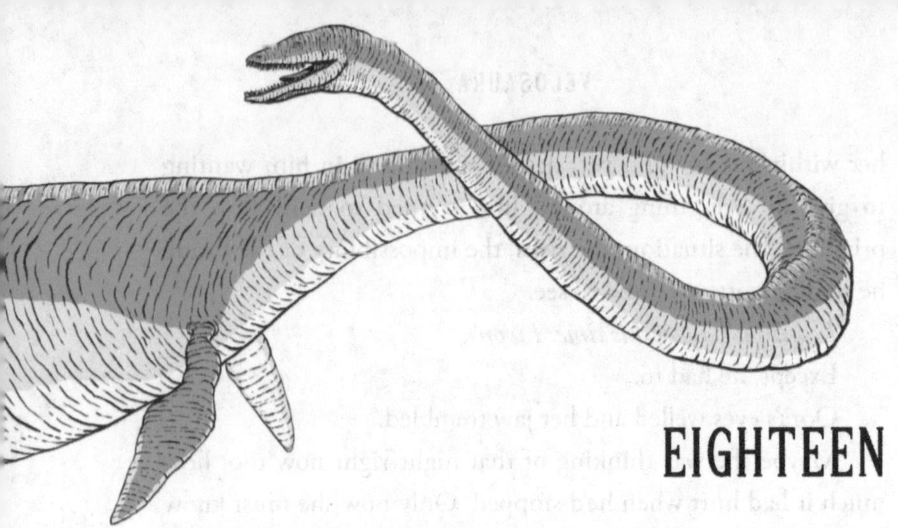

WHEN QORA HAD SURFACED at the count's mansion, some of the socialites had swarmed her with questions about the plesiosaur race, and then about the Venture, and then the count had emerged from the mansion with widely open arms and a "There you are!" and additional questions of concern before he insisted she come inside to get her fill of meat and melon water. And then finally, as the day grew late, it was time to return to the ship, so that all passengers would be aboard when the crew set sail at dawn. Qora had been so tired, she'd fallen right to sleep, with no idea whether Ninan had boarded before her or after, and it was just as well since she'd hardly had a clue what to say to him.

The next day, the group had gone on to the trademaster's banquet in Payllay, where Paqari must have introduced Qora to at least a hundred people, while several of the high-ranking men whisked away Ninan and Sakay to a men's lounge for most of the evening.

Now the *Velosaura* was nearly to Sillu, and since Qora had been on the ship long enough to get settled, she requested a consultation with one of the on-board tailors to provide her some more practical clothing. She didn't mind the fine fabrics, or even a few ruffles or embroidered details, but should the ship encounter any other unexpected guests or situations that required her to run or jump or take flight, she wanted to be able to move properly.

"Some fitted trousers," she suggested, "that taper to the ankle and can tuck into a pair of boots."

She went on to select two pairs of feminine boots, with soles more narrow and uppers much more delicate than the heavy hunting boots she was used to. None of these boots would have lasted long in the jungle, but she wondered about the advantages of their lightweight composition.

Finally, she chose a number of blouses—mostly off-white cottons with embroidered flowers, and a few jewel-toned satins—to go with her dainty trousers and boots, and left the tailor feeling like a brand new girl.

With several hours of sailing to go, Qora had gone above decks for some fresh air, feeling that her cabin below was too stuffy. But of course feeling like she couldn't breathe may have had more to do with Ninan, and being the Raptoriva, and all the espionage, than it did with the ship's confinements. Either way, the salty air was a refuge, and the way it seemed to cleanse her lungs also cleared her mind a bit, at least for small moments at a time. Not unlike the waves, her conversation with Ninan kept flowing back to her, trying to drag her out with it.

She tilted her head back and inhaled deeply.

Sky. Air. Waves.

Clear head. Clear heart.

Ninan's thumb brushing her lip.

No—

Air. Salt. Water.

More air.

His hands in her hair.

Breathe.

Skin. Fingers. Lips.

Ugh.

She kicked one of the barrels on the deck and turned to take a walk along the foredeck but a tiny squawk halted her. She looked toward the sound—something lost among the barrels—and then she spotted a dress jacket thrown over one of them.

Qora stepped closer.

It was Ninan's jacket. He'd cast it aside when the pirates had landed—the narrow fit would have inhibited his fighting movements—and must have forgotten it.

Peeking out from between the sleeve and the front panel was a tiny gray beak.

What in the Five Terrains?

It couldn't be the same one, could it?

Slowly, Qora approached.

"Tuko?" she said.

The pteromorph crawled out of the fabric, with his sceathers all ruffled and full of organic debris. He cocked his tiny head and stared at her. She extended her index finger and allowed him to analyze her scent. Immediately he squawked again and flitted onto her outstretched hand, sniffing her other fingers and following some invisible scent trail all the way up her arm and onto her shoulder, then into her hair.

He smells Ninan on me.

Of course he did. After what had happened in the caves, Ninan's scent was practically everywhere. An ache filled her when she thought of everywhere his hands had been, his arm around her waist, his—

"Spirits," she said, swallowing hard to shake the memory.

After Tuko had thoroughly analyzed her, he flitted back down to her open palm, turned his back to her, and flapped his tail, as if in demonstration of his collection of leaves and petals.

"You were supposed to take those to Unu," she whispered. "Why are you here?"

He squawked again.

Qora sighed and rolled her eyes, then darted a glance around. She'd have to take him to Ninan. "You also have terrible timing." How could she deal with Ninan right now, with how they'd left things?

She hurried across the deck and toward the stairwell. One of the guards stood nearby, chatting with a maid, and Qora took a sharp turn to avoid them both. Although it wasn't likely that either of them would notice the pteromorph, or care, Tuko's particular role in all this made Qora slightly paranoid. Not paranoid enough, however, to avoid barreling right into Paqari as she came up the stairwell.

Qora's shoulder collided with the princess.

"Oh my gods, I'm so sorry—" Qora stumbled and lost her hold on Tuko, who squawked and flapped until he found purchase on her arm again and quickly clambered to where he could perch back on her shoulder.

Paqari pressed a flat hand to her own chest and huffed, then turned her gaze on the pteromorph. "What is is *that*?"

"This?" Qora glanced at Tuko and cleared her throat. "Oh. Um. Nothing? He's just a … a pet. Sort of."

"A pet?" the princess spat. "You didn't have a pet before."

"Right. Well, that's because he … um … leaves, and comes back. So he hasn't been with me. Until now."

"So he's a messenger …"

"Not exactly."

Paqari wrinkled her nose. "What's in his sceathers?"

"Just things he picks up when he's out."

"How did he find you? Flyers are only trained to return to a stationary place."

"He's got eidetic memory." That wasn't a sufficient explanation, though, and Qora knew it. Eidetic memory only meant he could remember very precisely where he'd already been and what he'd already seen; it didn't mean he could find someone who had traveled beyond that. Unless Tuko's memory had given him a perfect mental picture of the ship and he'd simply scoured the sea within a few miles of the coastline, flying around until he'd found it. But that would also mean he'd abandoned his original master, seeking out Ninan specifically.

Paqari crossed her arms. "I don't understand. What would be the purpose of such a pet?"

Ruck. This was awful. Why couldn't Qora have reached the stairwell a minute later? She had to think on her feet. "It's a ... *recreational* pet."

The princess jutted her chin. "Recreational?"

"Yes. It's a new curiosity in Qhusi. It's like ... a game. A puzzle. You send out your pteromorph and when it returns, you're supposed to spread out all the things it's gathered and use them as clues to where it's been."

No, that was too close to the truth, Qora lamented internally.

And what was she thinking, anyway? She wanted to throw Paqari *off* the scent, not intrigue her; this was a girl with a shelf full of enigmatic literature and brain-bending artifacts.

But it was too late now. Qora had already spoken her explanation. She embellished it with, "I thought he was lost in Kicai. I never should have let him go out, but of course I was expecting to stay on land; I didn't know I'd be sailing with you until after I sent him. It's a miracle that he found me." That last part was sincere, and she stared at Tuko meaningfully. She didn't like to lie, but protecting the pteromorph's motives was a matter of people's lives; if Izhi's efforts were discovered this early, there might be no hope to stop the reptile army before it grew too big for anyone to control.

"That hardly seems like fun for you when you wouldn't know the flora here well enough—or the regions—to solve such a puzzle." Turning up her nose, she plucked out one of the leaves tucked between Tuko's sceathers and inspected it. "For example. Do you even know what plant this belongs to?"

It looked like a piece of monstera, only the holes were so big it was more of a greenish skeleton. Qora shook her head.

"Monstera obliqua. It's a decorative status plant because it's typically hard to find in the wild anywhere outside of Emberview. And this one"—she plucked out a wilted, orange flower petal—"is from an inqa-lilly, probably from Pasto. Inqa-lillies grow all over Kunka too, but assuming the pteromorph traveled north from Kicai—based on the monstera obliqua— Emberview would make the most sense."

"You're right," Qora said. "This wouldn't have been a fun game for me."

Paqari plucked another bit of debris from Tuko's sceathers, a piece of something that looked a bit like monkeybrush but purple. "I do see the appeal, though, for someone with the appropriate knowledge. A very interesting concept."

"Thanks?" Qora tried to commit the first two items to memory, because she would want to relay that information to Ninan and Sakay—if she could get away from Paqari unscathed.

"Bring your pteromorph to the front room of my suite," Paqari told her.

Qora bit the inside of her cheek. *What could the princess possibly want with Tuko?*

"Why?"

Paqari was already halfway down the companionway steps when she cast a bemused look over her shoulder. "So we can finish the game …"

Oh, it was a game alright, Qora thought. Just not the one Paqari thought it was. And it was much more dangerous than Qora wanted to admit.

〰〰〰

In the suite, Paqari went to a large table at the center and extended her hand. It took a second for Qora to understand that the princess wanted the pteromorph. She eased her fingers under him and lifted him carefully. He twisted his head back and squawked at her, but ultimately allowed her to transfer him to Paqari, who accepted him like she would a clod of dirt—pinched delicately between two fingers and held as far away as possible until she set him down in front of her.

"Let's see …" She leaned over him and continued to pluck other plants from his stash, laying them down one by one. "That's feathergrass … that's a bit of lobelia … that looks like it's from a palm frond, probably dinoheart palm … a few strands of suka string moss … some babytail clover … and this last one's another type of feathergrass that only grows in our more arid soils."

Now that she had finished removing everything, Tuko roused his feathers, dropping a bit of sand onto the table. He must have landed on the beach several times to rest, Qora thought, while he'd been searching for the ship. She couldn't imagine how tired he must be, being so small, and after all that flying.

Qora watched Paqari lining up the flora. The princess rearranged a few pieces, stopped to stare at her work, and then

150

pulled a rolled-up map off one of her shelves and spread it out. After some thought, she rearranged another couple of pieces and went for a third, but checked the map again and apparently decided she'd been right the first time.

"Okay," said Paqari, "I think this is it."

"Really?" Qora leaned over the map.

"The lobelia and clover would be found closest to Kicai, around Blue Falls, so it does appear your flyer went north. Then the inqa-lilly, as I said, probably came from Pasto, which is north of Blue Falls. Then there's the suka string moss, which hangs on most of the trees around Karu, and violet monkeybrush, which is very common on the outskirts of Rumipuka. But Rumipuka is almost directly west of Karu, so at that point he changed direction a bit."

Paqari pointed to each new location as she said it, while Qora looked on with fascination. This girl was brilliant; it was a shame the Razorclaws and Qhapaq Izhi couldn't rely on her as a part of their efforts to gain intel.

"Again, he would have had to find the monstera," the princess continued, flicking the skeletal leaf, "in Emberview, continuing to move west, and then shifting north again—northeast, maybe— where he would have found the feathergrasses throughout Aqu Aqu and its surrounding villages, coming upon the ordinary feathergrass first and then gradually moving into the sprawl of ch'aki feathergrass, which is more hardy."

"What about the dinoheart palm frond?" Qora asked.

"That's the only thing I can't account for. But, realistically, it could be from any of these places. Everyone plants those palms for extra shade. I wouldn't factor it into the puzzle; it's inconsequential."

"So he finished in Aqu Aqu?"

"That's what it looks like. Odd place to stop and turn around. Does the game really just depend on his whims?"

Qora nodded. "If there was any rhyme or reason to his path, it might be predictable. Right? And where's the fun in that?"

Paqari cocked a brow but didn't question her further. "Well, thank you for this brief diversion, champion. I do enjoy learning about all the unique ways that lowborns spend their time."

"… You're welcome."

"Now," Paqari said, "if you wouldn't mind removing this mess from my suite, I'd like to be alone."

Smiling her sweetest smile, Qora scooped up the plants and then the pteromorph, her heart skittering at the valuable information she now possessed, and left the princess, who was none the wiser to the fact that she had just assisted with a major breakthrough.

Qora hurried through the passageways until she reached Ninan's cabin and had just raised her fist to knock on the door when the above-decks bell rang out three times. She paused, turning her head toward the sound.

Three chimes more.

Then, three chimes again.

Three chimes repeated thrice. To announce the arrival of a royalborn.

Then a muffled voice came down from the main deck— from one of the crew—shouting at the others. "It's the Sumaqi qhapaq!"

NINETEEN

NINAN—WHO HAD BEEN PORING OVER A MAP of the islands at his desk and trying to figure out what features of Sut'u might appeal to his father in terms of reptile breeding—flinched at the sound of the bell.

The muffled voices of the crew shouting that Qhapaq Apo was approaching the ship were enough to spur him onto his feet. He flung open the door to find Qora standing there—with Tuko.

"What in the—"

Qora shoved the pteromorph at him. "Hide this. I'll explain later."

He nodded and put Tuko inside one of the desk drawers, cracked open just enough to give him some air.

Qora was already partway down the passageway when the echo of the bell dissipated, and Ninan followed her at speed. They ran into Sakay in the companionway and exchanged glances of concern.

"You'd better stay down here," Qora told Sakay. "We can try to explain my being here, but explaining *you* might be a little more difficult. I don't think the qhapaq would appreciate some strange rogue on board."

Sakay chuckled. "'Strange rogue'?"

"You know what I mean," said Qora.

"Fine by me." Sakay shrugged. "I'll be in my cabin."

Above decks, Paqari and Captain Yanacha waited on the forecastle, gazing up at the enormous flyer and gondola that approached the ship.

Ninan took the same composed stance beside Paqari that he usually did during public appearances, and Qora seemed to specifically *not* be standing near him, standing on Paqari's side and keeping a few respectful feet of space between them.

The pterobeast descended, creating enough wind with its wings that Ninan almost thought it would catch in the sails and throw the *Velosaura* off course. It lowered the gondola onto the deck but flapped to keep itself airborne, only allowing the qhapaq to exit with two attendants before it took off again. Even a ship as grand as the *Velosaura* couldn't accommodate such a large flyer comfortably; it was already a stretch with the pteranodons in the flyer hold. The pterobeast circled widely in the air around the ship as the qhapaq stepped forward.

Every member of the crew stopped what they were doing and took a knee.

Paqari bowed and said, "Qhapaq Apo, what a lovely surprise."

Ninan, Qora, and Captain Yanacha bowed as well, but remained silent.

The qhapaq kissed Paqari's hand and replied, "Imagine *my* surprise at finding my champion here with the happy couple."

Right to the point ...

Ninan tried not to roll his eyes at his father's rhetoric. "Surprise" nothing. The qhapaq had surely received word about Qora at least two days ago, whenever the ship's microraptor with Paqari's message to her own father had been relayed from Aleta to Qhusi. But of course the qhapaq's grandiosity wasn't limited to majestic speeches; he often spoke the same way in a room alone with Ninan.

"Yes, I insisted," Paqari told him.

"How, may I ask, did she come to find herself on the *Velosaura*?"

Qora and Ninan looked to one another to determine who would try to field the question, but Paqari spoke again before either of them could muster an excuse.

"I sent for her myself."

What? Ninan fought to keep his facial expression neutral.

"A last-minute request," Paqari explained. "I took it upon myself to share her with Tisqu, to finally bring the Raptoriva onto our own soil. I assure you that my father is pleased."

Why would the princess lie? Ninan could think of no reasonable motive, other than she simply wanted the extra attention and admiration that might come from keeping Qora as her guest—in such a way that Qora might even appear to be a close, personal friend. Or, perhaps Paqari was genuine in wanting her people to meet the champion, and she knew it was much less likely the qhapaq would let Qora stay if it appeared that the invitation aboard had come *after* Qora's arrival in Kicai.

The qhapaq flashed a condescending grin. "Your father doesn't know the lengths I've gone to, to preserve the sanctity of your union to my son." He then turned a sharp gaze on Ninan. "His alliance with the champion could affect your image in a very negative way."

"With all due respect," Paqari said, "I'm not concerned. It is a much greater gesture to the Tisquvians to send your champion to them, than it is to preserve some ideal of highborn matrimony."

Ninan turned to her with a deeply furrowed brow, both confused and impressed by her boldness. Not only did Paqari not shrink in the presence of Qhapaq Apo, she was forthright enough to give her opinion. Sure, she was a princess, but she wasn't an heir, and was daughter to a qhapaq who was basically at the mercy of this one.

Captain Yanacha came forward and bowed again. "Your Majesty, it is a great honor to receive you aboard the *Velosaura*. And, if I may … I would like to assure you that Apo-Kimsa has behaved with all the dignity of his class and position."

Ninan locked eyes with his father, observing the doubt and disbelief on the man's face. For an instant, he thought his father could read his thoughts, see right through his stony stare into the memories of his finger's sliding between Qora's, to his desperate thoughts of longing. But even with dominite, the qhapaq was just a man. Ninan reminded himself of this over and over as his pulse beat heavily.

"I would expect nothing less," said Qhapaq Apo. "But people do talk."

"The people have received the three of us well," said Paqari. "With nothing but joy and admiration. And you assured the House of Huapaya that there was no issue, that Apo-Kimsa's integrity was beyond reproach. Unless there *is* something that should concern us …" She raised a challenging brow.

The qhapaq pursed his lips and narrowed his eyes at her. He gave a forced smile. "Of course not. But, as you well know by now, reputation is often the result of perception, not fact."

"I appreciate your efforts to protect my reputation, and certainly yours as well, but public perception is no concern of mine—unless, however, my people should believe Sumaq is not a true enough ally to lend us their champion for a few weeks."

Qora stepped forward. "Your Majesty, I've explained to the princess that I am due for multiple engagements with you in Qhusi soon, the Heritage Festival in particular, and that I couldn't possibly—"

"You *could* possibly." Paqari raised her hand in a command for silence, then turned her gaze back on the qhapaq. "Surely you could spare her for the rest of the tour, Your Majesty. She has already been attending your events several times a month, has she not?"

"She has," he replied.

"So there has been plenty of opportunity for the Sumaqi people—and I dare say for Unuvians, Allpans, and the Qolqese— to see her in person. But not for the Tisquvians. Even if she has to miss your Heritage Festival, it's only fair."

Qhapaq Apo kept his eyes fixed on Paqari, his face a mask of inscrutable calm until a flicker of calculation passed over him. His jaw tightened in a subtle flex. After a long pause that Ninan was sure was deliberate, he broke his silence.

"Fine," he said tightly. "I will allow this to continue. But should I catch word of any problems, you will return my champion at once."

"Absolutely, Your Majesty. I appreciate your generosity on this matter. I believe my father will be pleased with the response from those over which he rules."

The qhapaq turned to Qora. "You will return two days before the equinox, to prepare for your appearance at the Revelry."

Ninan's pulse quickened. *He's going to make Qora attend the Revelry?* He'd almost forgotten about Revelry—a tradition that always occurred the day following a royal wedding, in which highborns gathered in a sort of matchmaking, marriage-market social event to take advantage of what they liked to call "the spirit of unity," which they believed to be abundant in the wake of marriage between those with divinely sanctioned blood. If Ninan ended up having to go through with this, the last thing he wanted was for Qora to have to be stuck *celebrating* it as a famed guest.

Qora paled at the request, but bowed nonetheless. "I promise I won't be late."

"I will send a pterobeast for you at afternoon's Fourth Bell, as usual, on that day."

As if the pterobeast pilot could read the qhapaq's body language from afar, the enormous flyer swept downward and lowered the gondola with perfect timing, at which point the qhapaq stepped inside and was carried away.

꩜ ꩜ ꩜

After yet another banquet, Ninan, Qora, and Sakay gathered in Sakay's cabin, and Qora emptied Tuko's findings from her pockets onto the desk. It wasn't nearly as big as Ninan's desk, but it was enough to analyze the materials. Ninan unrolled a small map and set Tuko down beside it.

Tuko nipped at the corners of the map papyr.

"Aqu Aqu?" Ninan asked.

Qora nodded. "That's what Paqari said."

"You're sure she didn't suspect anything?" Sakay asked.

"I'm not *sure*, but she didn't react in any way that leads me to believe she thinks we're up to something. I mean, I wasn't exactly eloquent with my lies, but I think they were good enough. And she seems to like puzzles, so …"

"Well finding that base has definitely been a puzzle." Ninan picked up the orange flower petal and inspected it.

"Anyway," Qora said, "I think she said the clover came from right outside Kicai, and the inqa-lilly is from Pasto, and the moss is from Karu, so that shows a northward trail. And then after that, Tuko went west to Emberview—that's where this sad-looking monstera comes from—and then back north where he got the feathergrass."

Ninan stroked his chin and sighed. "Aqu Aqu isn't a remote city or anything. I would have thought my father would hide his activities on one of the smaller islands, or at least somewhere less populated. But I guess that's the whole point, right? To not be obvious?"

"Don't forget the pteranodon going to Sut'u," said Sakay. "That could still be something."

"Right." Ninan tried to pull the map away from Tuko, but the pteromorph shredded the papyr with his little teeth and pinned it down with his claws. "Another pressing question: Why would Tuko come here instead of going back to Izhi?"

"He likes you for some reason," Qora said.

"A lot of dinosaurs can pick up a scent trail from several miles away," Sakay offered.

Ninan shook his head. "But that's not what he was trained to do. He's not a hunter, or even a seeker. It's like he just sort of … went rogue."

Qora offered Tuko her palm and he jumped into it, particularly focused on the space between her fingers. "He would have had to *look* for you."

"He does know the ship. But that's a lot of effort."

"No offense, but why does he like Qora so much, though?" Sakay asked.

Ninan's and Qora's eyes met for an instant and her cheeks flushed.

Shrugging, Ninan said, "I'm sure he just … senses … that I trust her." *With no regard whatsoever for my scent on her skin.* "Who knows?" But the flyer did seem to have his own sense of loyalty to whomever he chose, regardless of who had trained him. "His instincts are … interesting, to say the least."

"We can speculate about this later," Qora said. "The bigger issue is that we won't get anywhere close to Aqu Aqu for at least two weeks. Not until we've stopped at all the islands surrounding Suni and circled back to Tisqu Isle."

"When we reach Qaqakuna." Ninan put a finger to the map. Qaqakuna was still forty miles from Aqu Aqu, one to two hours by land depending on which reptile, half an hour by flyer if he could manage to sneak a flyer off the ship without anyone noticing.

"So what?" said Sakay. "Izhi's people can go, can't they?"

"They can," Ninan agreed. "I'd just … really like to check it out myself. I hate leaving everything to Izhi." It wasn't that he didn't *trust* Izhi, exactly, but, he had no reason to put his full trust in *any* qhapaq. Even with the best of intentions, no highborn leader with that much power could have truly pure motives.

"Doesn't seem like we have much of a choice, though, does it?" Qora said.

Ninan pinched his lips together. The only thing to do would be to get another messenger flyer out as soon as possible. "We never do."

🌙🌙🌙

The next four days and the next four stops were more or less the same. The *Velosaura* docked at Uya, Mat'i, Rakisqa, and finally Masi, each with visits to large estates by triceratops, each with lavish dinners and a social hour with whichever dignitaries were in attendance. Ninan managed to keep his wits about him, even as Qora kept her distance and stuck close to Sakay. The distance was necessary, Ninan told himself; as much as he resented his father's concerns about Qora coming along on this trip, those concerns were valid as far as protecting Ninan's ability to continue gleaning information. Anything that might draw attention to his connection with Qora—rumors, speculation, questions—could put the whole thing at risk, which meant putting *everyone* at risk, at the mercy of a reptile army controlled by one man determined to reunite the Terrains by force.

He took comfort in Tuko's company, keeping the little flyer in his desk drawer and bringing him scraps from the kitchen to eat, letting him flit around the cabin whenever he was in there.

By now, Izhi had certainly received his most recent message, explaining that Tuko had returned to the ship rather than to Unu, but that the pteromorph had done his job and given them enough clues to search Aqu Aqu for evidence of the reptile base. Ninan also mentioned Qora's sighting of the white pteranodon flying toward Sut'u, in case Izhi had enough additional information to make sense of it, and the attacks on Phapa that the magistrate had told them about. Soon, Ninan would know whether Izhi had pieced anything new together, as the *Velosaura* was less than a day's journey from K'iti, to which Izhi would fly out to attend the governor's masquerade ball where Ninan, Qora, and Sakay would be.

For the moment, Ninan tried to breathe more easily. If the rest of the trip could continue as it had the last few days, he might be able to survive it. He chose not to focus on the idea of seeing it through to the *end*, however, but rather tried to believe that speaking to Izhi in K'iti would grant some unforeseen hope that might change his circumstances.

He strolled the quarterdeck and shivered as the clouds thickened above him, which carried a chill with the graying sky. Qora and Sakay were off among those clouds, exercising their pteranodons.

Ninan fidgeted with the serrated-tooth dagger from his mother so that he could feel close to her, Ninan wondered what she might tell him if she were here right now. Would she still tell him everything was going to be alright? Had she said that before because she truly believed these circumstances would somehow play out in his favor, or only because she believed her son was capable of enduring them regardless of the outcome? Knowing her, Ninan worried it was the latter. While he'd once admired that kind of faith—the faith that the gods might spare a sailor from the wrath of a storm, rather than dispelling the storm itself—because of what it implied about the strength of the human spirit, he didn't feel strong enough to swim in the waves of his own life right now.

Captain Yanacha stood on the bridge holding a brass spyglass to her right eye.

Ninan tried to see what she was observing, but it all looked grayish blue to him, and increasingly hazy. "Everything alright?"

The captain collapsed her spyglass with a snap. "Unfortunately, no."

In the midst of the waves up ahead, Ninan finally spotted something—dark, rounded things—emerging from the depths. "What is it, Captain?"

She snatched up her sabertooth trident and spun it once, catching it upright in a tight grip. "Terminonatators."

TERMINONATATOR *(tur-mih-noh-NAH-tuh-tor)*

Clade: Sauropterygia **Length:** 150 ft **Weight:** 8-10 tons

Enormous, long-necked water reptile with a streamlined body, four paddle-limbs, short tail, and small triangular head. Teeth are slender, conical, and recurved to interlock and trap prey.

The Runaqan Compendium of Reptiles

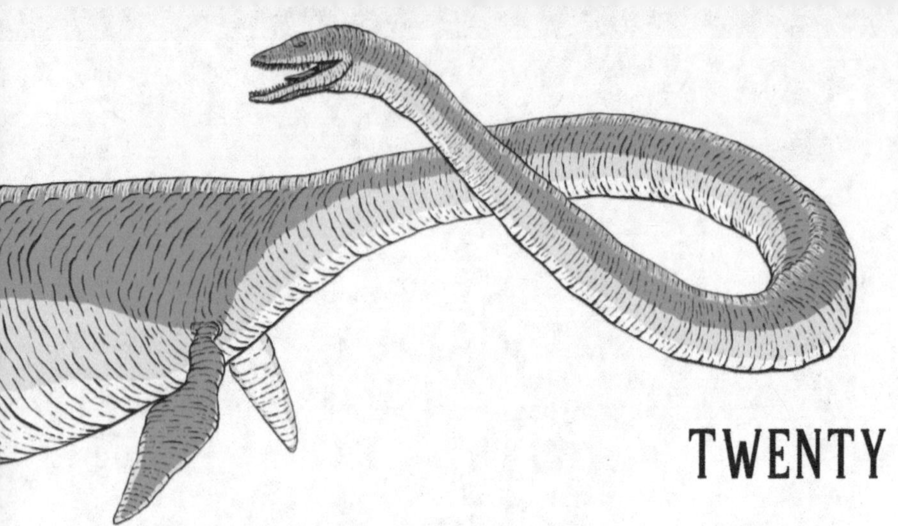

TWENTY

QORA LEANED INTO THE PTERANODON as it spread its wings and glided through the air, circling the *Velosaura* from at least a hundred feet above. She went wide into the grayed-out distance as a spatter of rain hit her cheek. She knew she probably ought to bring the flyer down, but something about the cool mist beckoned her, a reminder of the cool mists of Qhusi, of home—a blanket of vapor to hide behind.

Committing to one final lap, Qora gripped the saddle with her thighs and raised her arms, soaking up a new spatter of fine rain and breathing deeply to savor its scent.

Thunder rumbled as the clouds continued to darken.

Sakay dipped under Qora with his own pteranodon and hollered with a pumping fist.

Laughing, Qora took the reins again, and shouted, "We should probably head back!"

He nodded.

Qora let the pteranodon glide into a turn, catching the heavy wind that had begun to swell through the region, and prepared to drop, when she spotted a long neck stretching up out of the water.

Then another.

And finally, a third.

"Sakay!" she called. "Do you see that?"

He slowed his flyer and angled for a better look.

More plesiosaurs? Qora thought.

But … wait …

Qora volleyed a glance between the creatures and the ship, visually calculating the distance that set them apart and comparing their size to the ship's hull.

No. Not plesiosaurs.

"That doesn't look good!" Sakay called back.

The reptiles were too big to be plesiosaurs.

Much too big.

"Elasmosaurian cousins … quite terrifying if you spot one in the middle of the sea … towering, aquatic monsters."

Paqari had mentioned this, but it hadn't seemed as though it were a possibility to actually see one on the tour—let alone three.

It was hard to be sure from this vantage point, but Qora thought the reptiles' necks must be as long as the *Velosaura* was tall—masts included.

Thankfully she had her crossbow. She'd resolved never to leave the ship without it after the pirates. For now, being airborne, she and Sakay were easily out of reach for the monsters below.

But Ninan was still down there.

The distress bell rang out for several seconds. Already, it seemed that the crew was working to alter the direction of the ship to avoid the monsters.

Nudging the pteranodon, she shouted, "Descend!" and braced herself to plummet. Sakay followed. They both swooped closer, until they reached the height of the sails, which flapped as the pteranodons flapped, wild movements to keep everyone and everything upright.

"What's the protocol for this?!" Sakay called down.

"Stay where you are!" Captain Yanacha told him. "You two are safer up there! We'll do what we can from down here!"

Ninan pocketed the tooth dagger he'd apparently brought with him, and accepted a trident from Captain Yanacha, while some of the crew stood in formation readying their own tridents and the rest manipulated the rigging and reefed or furled the sails to accommodate the growing storm. Many of the guards had taken up tridents too, in addition to their blades, and prepared for what was to come.

Qora's initial thought was that her crossbow likely wouldn't be enough to take down a reptile that size—but then she remembered the spinosaur.

It's just a matter of finding the weakness.

At least these reptiles weren't covered in thick scales. Their slick skin might not be that hard to pierce, if it came down to it. But they were huge, and they roared among the waves with a territorial tone.

"Will they attack?" Qora shouted as the reptiles approached the ship. It seemed like a stupid question, given their position, but maybe they would just be curious, investigate the strange human vessel in their midst, and then move along. Some reptiles were gentle giants—like the long-necked sauropods on land. But even after the ship redirected, these reptiles continued to close the distance.

Captain Yanacha returned to the helm and called back, "Not usually! But a storm can drive them to the surface during a hunt! They'll seek other food sources when the turbulence scatters their prey under water!"

"Looks like our timing is perfect!" Sakay said sardonically.

Several of the guards tried to insist that the prince go below decks, but Ninan ignored them.

"Let him be useful!" Captain Yanacha said. "We need all the help we can get!"

The captain shouted more directions at the crew and the guards, but the reptiles continued to close in on the ship, dispersing and surrounding it.

One of the reptiles curved its neck like a great serpent, head cocked, and came at the deck with a snap. Crew members scattered to avoid the open mouth that struck the decking, then swarmed it with trident prongs. The creature hissed and reared its head, then pulled back to strike again.

The other two reptiles came in to strike too.

The deck creaked and cracked under the force of each one. They struck and snapped their jaws and roared when the trident prongs came against their skin.

Qora and Sakay continued to circle above, neither of them sure whether to interfere, whether an attack from above would only anger the reptiles more and further endanger the crew.

Sakay withdrew a hunting knife and held it at the ready, although Qora shuddered to think how close he'd have to get to use it. Maybe if he swooped in from behind and went for a neck, but those necks were so thick and muscular and flailing.

Qora gripped her loaded crossbow in one hand and her saddle pommel in the other. Raindrops cascaded down her goggles now, and her body heat was starting to fog the lenses, to the point where she had to push them off her face to see.

Captain Yanacha held back her own trident, instructing the crew to continue deterring the reptiles, but the reptiles struck again and again and again, unintimidated by the skyrock prongs.

It probably wasn't enough skyrock, Qora thought. Maybe

if there had only been one of these monsters. Maybe if they weren't so hungry, and if there wasn't a storm stirring up the waters where their usual prey would be. Still, they seemed too eager. Surely the captain would give Qora the go-ahead to start shooting any minute now, as it quickly became clear that the reptiles weren't going to back down.

One of them narrowly missed a crew member's outstretched arm, instead cutting into the ratlines with its fangs.

Ninan charged at another one, angling his trident to insert the prongs into both nostrils at once.

Yes! Qora thought. The closer to its senses, the better.

But the reptile reared back and bared its fangs in an ear-splitting roar—before driving back down toward Ninan.

"Ninan!" Qora screamed.

Ninan dropped the trident and threw himself into a roll just before the reptile would have cut him in half, but struck his head on a barrel as his body came to a stop on the slick deck.

No, no, no …

He wasn't moving—and the reptile was poised to strike again.

TWENTY-ONE

NINAN GROANED AS STARS FLASHED around his vision. For a few seconds, he was too disoriented to move. By the time he got his wits about him enough to push himself up off the deck, a wide jaw with enormous teeth came at him. Before he could cover his head, a crossbow bolt streaked through the air and pierced the terminonatator's neck below the jaw, forcing the beast backward.

While the terminonatator snapped its teeth in Qora's general direction—and she, thankfully, flew out of reach—Ninan got to his feet and retrieved his trident.

As he readied himself to fight again, shouts from the companionway drew his attention. Despite attendants struggling against the princess and shouting at her to get back below decks, Paqari surfaced. With ever-widening eyes, she gaped up at the three beasts for several seconds before she fetched a trident, prodding and poking along with everyone else to try and force the terminonatators back into the water. With no hint of her usual grace, she struck with a fury and a desperation Ninan never imagined he'd see from her.

The guards shouted at her to get back to safety, but they were too distracted fighting to physically escort her away. Some of them did manage to block her from participating.

Ninan continued to work on the one in front of him, fighting alongside other guards and crew, and aiming for the nostrils with each strike. From above, Qora and Sakay did their best to distract the terminonatators, swooping in and out of range to encourage them to change position so that the fighters below could get a better angle at them. The skin at their throats seemed to be the most sensitive, but there was so much neck twisting around that it was difficult to get to it. In between strikes, Ninan caught a glimpse of Paqari thrusting her trident prongs straight into the deck and abandoning the weapon upright before she ran to an arrangement of barrels and began dragging one out of place.

What the hell is she doing?

The crew that weren't fighting were up in the rigging, trying to furl the sails in all this wind. The force of the terminonatators slamming into the deck and taking chunks out of the gunwale wasn't especially helpful in keeping the ship from capsizing. One of the crew was just a young boy, maybe fourteen, although his small size and agility made him a quick climber.

Qora was conservative with her bolts, taking a few calculated shots, while Sakay kept swooping in from behind and slashing.

Captain Yanacha held back and waited for an opportune moment to stab her sabertooth trident, causing one terminonatator to rear back, howling in pain. It lagged for several seconds, enough that the guards and crew surrounding it almost seemed to relax, perhaps thinking that they'd finally persuaded it to cease its pursuit of them. But then it shot forward with a fury, whipping its neck and coming down on the captain.

The captain twisted out of the way, and had nearly achieved a good position to strike back when the terminonatator's jaws snapped shut on her lower leg.

Ninan gasped.

The crew shouted curses as two of them rushed to her side. There were only seconds to spare before they'd be needed again, and they each got under one arm to hoist her up.

But—wait. Why wasn't she screaming in pain? And … where was the blood?

The terminonatator chomped several times, emitting a wood-splitting sound from its mouth, before spitting the leg into the sea. A solid, dark object in the shape of a human shin.

A prosthetic?

Ninan couldn't believe it. This whole time?

Captain Yanacha allowed the crew to haul her to a standing position, then screamed at them all to focus. She used her trident as a support to rebalance herself, and approached the chewed-up gunwale where she continued to strike from one leg.

Paqari finished her arrangement of the barrels, and then ran to the belfry. She yanked the rope, forcing the bell to ring out long and loud, a clanking sound so sharp even the wind and thunder couldn't muffle it. She pulled it over and over, with guards yelling at her to stop, but soon she caught one of the terminonatator's attention. Lifting the hem of her dress, she climbed on top of one of the barrels and waved her arms, calling out to the monster. It inclined its neck toward her, slamming its head forward, teeth bared.

She launched herself off the barrel as the teeth closed around the space where she'd been. The terminonatator crushed and bent the metal hoops of the barrel, bursting the pressure within, while the staves cracked and splintered.

And then came a viscous flood of pitch.

The pitch oozed into the terminonatator's mouth and dripped down its jaw.

The terminonatator gagged and sputtered, rearing and

flailing and tossing barrel debris in all directions.

Despite the thick coating of pitch on its tongue and teeth, it let out a stifled roar, and finally—spirits, *finally*—drew back, and slipped down into the water.

The crew and guards cheered.

Ninan hurried to Paqari to help her up, as they both gaped at the terminonatator's head disappearing into the waves. He didn't know what to say, other than, "Brilliant …"

Panting, the princess grinned and nodded at the other barrels. "Let's give the others the same treatment."

The available crew had already had the same idea and worked to set up additional pitch barrels in strategic locations, dragging them to where the two remaining terminonatators were attacking.

Ninan nodded at Qora and Sakay, who each took charge of a separate terminonatator and circled its head to keep it distracted long enough for the guards to get situated.

Qora and Sakay dipped and soared and climbed and dipped in dizzying swirls. While Qora worked on the starboard side, Sakay worked on the portside. The starboard-side terminonatator, however, was quicker, and nipped far too close to Qora's pteranodon for Ninan's liking—not that he liked her up there at *all*, or even within a mile of that thing. But Qora dodged and maneuvered each time. She had to keep close, otherwise the terminonatator would lose interest and attack the deck again.

"Ready!" Captain Yanacha said from below.

The barrels were in position, with several in a row along both sides of the deck, and a guard standing behind each one as bait—multiple opportunities for the terminonatators to come down.

At the command, Qora and Sakay both swooped out of the

way and everyone below braced for impact.

Except … the terminonatator on Qora's side wasn't falling for it. It was entirely focused on Qora, stretching and craning to get at her. Not having realized immediately that she was in danger, Qora had to fly in between the sails for safety. The terminonatator snapped at her pteranodon's tail, narrowly missing, and instead clamped its teeth over the topmast studding sail as the ship careened on the turbulent waters.

The crew member manning that sail cried out in the chaos. It was the agile boy, Ninan realized—but that agility might not be enough to save him now.

The damaged rope snapped and set the sail loose.

The wind whipped the wet canvas over the boy, trapping him inside.

Ruck, Ninan thought. With the way the rain came down in sheets, that was going to feel like being waterboarded. And the boy now had the terminonatator's full attention, while the barrels on the starboard side of the deck lay untouched.

In the midst of all the screaming and flailing and roaring, along with persistent thunderclaps, Qora's pteranodon went wild. Qora pulled at the reins and called for it to slow, but she could scarcely control it, squinting into the rainwater. She wouldn't be able to help the boy even though she was closest to him.

Meanwhile, Sakay tried to control his own pteranodon, but the wind seemed to make it difficult for him to stay airborne without flailing, and he swiped his hands over his face like the rain was stinging his eyes.

Ninan climbed the ratlines to get to the boy. As he worked his way up, the portside terminonatator chased the moving guards and crew below and came down on one of the barrels and picked it up, but dropped it before crushing the staves.

Above, the crew boy struggled under the loose sail, while the other terminonatator chomped at the edge of the canvas trying to get to him. Ninan reached him with difficulty, still holding his trident in one hand—he wasn't about to go up near the terminonatator's teeth unarmed—but he stuck the trident into the ratlines to hold it in place while he withdrew his tooth dagger.

He slashed at the canvas.

The terminonatator slashed its fangs at him.

He ducked out of the way, but the terminonatator came again.

Qora wrestled her pteranodon to cooperate behind them and managed to aim her crossbow, at which point she sent several unsteady bolts at the terminonatator. She had to do it at close range, though, due to the wind and the unwieldy beast she sat on. But with every cut of the sail, Ninan pulled its attention back to him, and with every shot Qora pulled it back to her, and they did this like a dance—just like they'd done with the spinosaur at the ruins of Utula—working together to keep this monster from finishing off either one of them or the boy. The bolts stuck well enough until the terminonatator bent and curved its neck, and then they all sprung out and fell into the waves that crashed up high enough to go over the gunwale and spill water onto the deck surface.

The other terminonatator came down on a second barrel now, and crushed it until it oozed pitch like the first time. Paqari was still somewhere down there, although Ninan didn't know where; probably being held back by whatever guards could be spared to deal with her. And again, the pitch worked wonders as a deterrent. The terminonatator moaned and twisted, and the pitch stuck to its teeth, and slowly but surely the beast relented and returned to the sea.

Finally, Ninan cut the last of the sail fabric that clung to the boy, releasing him to breathe freely again. The boy gasped and panted.

But that still didn't solve the problem of the raging terminonatator that remained. Ninan would have to get himself and the boy down to the deck, and maybe then the terminonatator would return its attention to the pitch barrels. But Qora probably wouldn't be able to distract it long enough for them to get down. She had to be nearly out of bolts by now.

There were milliseconds to decide—but that was enough. Ninan thought of the boy practically smothered in the sail, the canvas that Ninan still held onto after having scrunched and gathered it under his arm to pull it back. He climbed higher on the ratlines and threaded his legs through for stability so that he could use both arms, and just as the terminonatator darted its head forward again, Ninan unfurled the canvas, catching the wind perfectly to cover the terminonatator's eyes and snout.

The terminonatator inhaled, sucking the canvas painfully against its nostrils.

Its mouth stretched wide in a wail.

Ninan removed his trident from the ratlines and stabbed it up into the terminonatator's soft palate. He yanked it out and thrust it back in again, and again, and again, until blood began to spill.

He wasn't close enough—not fully inside the mouth, as Qora had been with the spinosaur—and the prongs didn't go deep enough to kill it, but the injury was enough to force the creature to recoil in a way that it had not done before. Moaning, the terminonatator sank down, gradually drifting from the

Velosaura, neck wavering, and slipped back to the depths of the ocean, leaving the canvas floating on the surface, a pale marker on the inky blue.

)))

Breathless, Ninan clung to the ratlines while the waves died down—not so turbulent now that there weren't three enormous beasts stirring up the already storm-tossed waters—and looked on as Qora and Sakay landed their flyers.

Ninan wanted to go to Qora, as always, but as soon as she dismounted, Sakay had already taken her into his arms, crushing her with some sort of exhausted relief that made Ninan's stomach sour.

She's not mine, he reminded himself. If anything, he really ought to see to his fiancée.

The rain kept pouring and the winds were still a bit rough, but the crew pulled together to patch whatever damage they could in the moment (the rest would have to wait until they reached K'iti) while also seeing to everyone's wounds. Captain Yanacha hobbled around on a crutch but was no less commanding without her lower leg; of course, she'd been without it all this time, Ninan simply hadn't known.

Regardless of the victory, Ninan still felt defeated as he climbed down and found Paqari with several attendants assessing her for injuries and once again insisting she get below decks.

He was worried for her too, he had to admit. The second she'd started ringing the bell, he wasn't sure she'd make it off the ship alive. But she'd done well. They'd all still be fighting the terminonatators—and maybe losing, by now—if it hadn't been for her competence.

When he approached, she threw side-eyed glances at her attendants and, reading her, they dispersed. She and Ninan stared at each other for a few seconds, both soaked to the bone and still dripping with new rain, before he told her, "Thank you."

She averted her gaze. "It was the least I could do."

"No, the least you could do would have been nothing. To stay below decks in your cabin and let the professionals take care of this." He said it almost scoldingly, but he couldn't keep the admiration out of his tone.

She raised her chin defiantly, but said nothing.

Then he added, "But I'm glad you were here."

"And you as well," she replied, with a subtle glance at the damaged sail.

"Are you alright?"

"I'm fine."

Another few seconds of staring. Many people were watching them, and they both knew it. He inched toward her and extended his arms, and she hesitantly stepped into him, allowing a chaste embrace.

Over her shoulder, Ninan caught sight of Qora while Sakay inspected one of her palms—probably for friction burns from the pteranodon's reins—and, for an instant, Qora looked toward him.

They locked eyes.

Her mouth twitched into a flat, grateful smile, albeit a sad one too.

Ninan ached all over, outside and in. But, as usual, he'd simply have to bear it.

TWENTY-TWO

THE LOUNGE BELOW DECKS smelled of dinofire ointment and placodus oil and antiseptics. No one had been severely injured, but many had gashes on their forearms and shoulders, while a few had sprained ankles or wrists. Qora had been lucky to make out with nothing but rein friction burns—because she'd foolishly forgotten her riding gloves—and mild whiplash. Her head throbbed and her muscles were sore, but otherwise, she was fine. Mentally and emotionally, well … that was a problem for another time.

Captain Yanacha apparently had another prosthetic leg in her cabin, although it was a more rudimentary version and she would need to order a better replacement once they made port. Qora still couldn't believe the captain had been walking around on a piece of wood all this time; the woman's strut had been flawless.

It took another hour or so for the storm to die down—or for the *Velosaura* to sail out of it, Qora wasn't sure. The guards prepared for another attack, keeping the pitch barrels close to the gunwale, but no other large reptiles saw fit to harm them. Qora still didn't understand why the terminonatators (she'd learned that's what they were called and struggled to say the long name properly) had been so persistent.

Tur-mih-noh-NAH-tuh-tors.

Reptiles that size might not be deterred by small amounts of skyrock, but surely between that and persistent prodding by sharp prongs they would have given up much sooner and sought out an easier meal elsewhere. But maybe the scent of so many human prey had been too enticing? And worth the pain?

Qora was glad Paqari had thought to use the pitch. It was the kind of resourceful strategy Qora wished she'd thought of herself. Like sinorn venom on her bolts. She lamented the fact that Paqari was not only stunningly beautiful, but clever and brave as well. Her chest burned at the memory of Ninan embracing the princess. Maybe he didn't love Paqari right this minute, but Qora didn't see how he wouldn't come to eventually.

🌙🌙🌙

When they arrived at port in K'iti, Qora was glad that a maintenance crew came shortly to get started on repairs. Paqari also ordered a full careening of the ship—which would involve removing all loose furniture and cargo, and tilting the ship onto its side to inspect, clean, and re-tar the hull (all but the copper bottom, of course). Captain Yanacha said it wasn't necessary, but Paqari insisted on leaving nothing to chance when it came to everyone's safety. With an abnormally large crew and all the efficiency Paqari's money could buy, they'd have it ready again in record time, quickly enough to continue the tour on schedule after the masquerade ball. Maintenance would empty the ship as soon as all passengers had disembarked for the event.

Qora had hoped to get ready on her own, without much fuss, but it was only a few minutes after the announcement that Paqari sent one of the attendants to fetch her.

"I wanted to thank you," Paqari said as she flipped through her clothing rack full of gowns, "for your help earlier. It was so fortunate that you and Sakay were airborne—and your technique was excellent." She held up a beaded blue dress in front of Qora and cocked her head.

"I'm glad I could help. You were brilliant, though. You could have stayed safe down here, but you protected your ship and crew instead."

"My *family's* ship," Paqari reminded her.

"Still."

Paqari pursed her lips and held up another gown, this one silken and red. She laid the bodice against Qora's chest and fluffed out the skirt over Qora's hips.

"You're not thinking of that for *me* ... are you?" Qora asked.

The princess flicked her eyes upward at Qora's. "Why not? Don't you like it?"

"It's lovely, but ... I thought I was supposed to wear green. I assumed I'd wear a green gown, and a raptoriva-head mask."

Scoffing, Paqari tossed the dress onto the bed and returned to the rack. "Not this time, champion. The masquerade—at least as far as the governor is concerned—is not a place to stand out. Not as yourself, at least. He likes his guests to be ostentatious, sure. Dazzling. Gorgeous. But the point of a *masquerade* is to pretend to be someone you're not for the night."

"But, aren't we guests of honor? Doesn't it defy the purpose of inviting celebrities if you can't tell who they are?"

"Of course, of course." Paqari swatted the air. "We'll arrive bare faced at first, but in cloaks." She pulled two black velvety cloaks from the far side of the rack—full-length, long-sleeved, hooded things—and raised them in demonstration. "The governor will introduce us, and we'll make our remarks and greet important people for an hour or so. But *then* we'll go to private dressing rooms, remove our cloaks, and don our masks—*not* modeled after our own terrenal reptiles or, in your case, that which denotes your reputation, but something different. Anything you like."

Qora's initial instinct was to reject this idea, although she couldn't say why. Maybe it had been all those months working with the qhapaq, and all the times he'd drilled into her the idea of maintaining her persona. Maybe it was the fear that she'd be recognized regardless, that no amount of disguise could truly set her free from the way people knew her now—or the fact that *people knew her now.* But the more she thought about it, the more it sounded … nice.

"Alright, but why the cloaks?" Qora asked.

"To preserve the mystery. It's a game. For those who arrive with companions, they're supposed to try and find one another without knowing what costume to look for. For those without companions, it's a night of intrigue where one might fall in love or have a wild affair with a mysterious stranger. And for those who aren't partial to such things, they can simply seek out their friends or acquaintances. Fun for all."

Qora didn't love the idea of having to play games, but she had to admit, it sounded interesting.

Several beauticians came in and helped both girls climb into elaborate underdresses, with fabric cut and sewn specifically to emphasize or "compensate" where it was "needed." Then the girls sat while the beauticians powdered and bronzed and lined different parts of their faces, and brushed and arranged their hair. Meanwhile, Paqari had some of her attendants bring in a selection of gowns specifically for Qora, ordered from the city's finest shop. "I've asked for your size specifically. You're a little shorter than I am," Paqari explained, "and not so …" She made vague gestures at her chest area.

"'Filled out'?" Qora suggested.

"Exactly."

When the beauticians had gone, Paqari told Qora to pick whichever gown she liked.

The selection contained every possible color. There were some with wide skirts and others with fitted shapes all the way down, and some with off-the-shoulder sleeves and others with no sleeves or straps, and some had embroidered patterns on them while others were made of solid fabrics sewn into ruffles or pleats. Qora ran her fingers over the rack until she landed on a magenta gown. It had an empire waist and a slight flare to the skirt—a subtle A-line—and a v-neck with short sleeves sewn at a diagonal seam directly to the collar, and a wide band of fabric where the bodice met the skirt.

"Yes," Paqari said over Qora's shoulder. "That suits you. Put it on this instant."

Before Qora could protest, Paqari had it off the rack and was guiding it over Qora's head, and then began to adjust the material on top of the underdress. Qora shifted until the skirt lay correctly, while Paqari rummaged through a trunk with several layers and divided compartments until she withdrew two gold cuff bracelets, narrow jade drop earrings, and a gold collar necklace with jade stones embedded in the metal.

"Just a *little* bit of green," Paqari said of the stones as she laid the necklace on Qora. "You are still the Raptoriva, after all."

The princess added the cuffs and earrings, too, then turned Qora toward the mirror—and Qora almost fainted. She looked like a princess herself. Her heart clenched at the sight of her body in the deep pink gown, almost a full color opposite to the green jacket that had become her self image. Her hair shone in long, loose curls, and her eyes were lined and shadowed in a sultry and menacing way. Her skin practically sparkled with bronze powder.

"Still the Raptoriva," Paqari repeated, "and now you shimmer like one, too."

ꕔꕔꕔ

Qora had donned her cloak, fixing the clasp at her neck and pulling up the hood to cover her hair, as Paqari had instructed. She arrived at her cabin and adjusted the hood so that her hair and earrings wouldn't show, to "preserve the mystery," Paqari had said. A few minutes later, Sakay knocked on her door, wearing a matching black cloak.

"I'm here to escort you to the masquerade, miss." He took her hand with a sarcastic flourish and kissed her knuckles. "And might I say, you look lovely in your … tent."

"You look very handsome yourself," she told him. "I'm sure you'll still manage to get lots of attention tonight, even before you reveal what's underneath."

He stepped in front of her mirror and flexed his biceps, which were lost under the loose, long sleeves of the cloak. "You think so?"

Qora rolled her eyes.

They would be receiving their masks at the mansion, according to Paqari, so for now, they only needed to be dressed, and to take the triceratops that awaited them. As far as Qora understood, Paqari and Ninan would go ahead on a separate triceratops, while Qora and Sakay would take the next one, and all other dignitaries from the *Velosaura* (such as Captain Yanacha and any high-ranking attendants) would follow.

The governor's mansion was a series of white-washed cylindrical towers with reddish clay tiles on the conical roofs. Spiral staircases wrapped each tower, and wide bridges spanned the distance between them. A massive courtyard stretched out below, with a maze of tall hedges sprawling from its sides.

As with most of these places, palm trees lined the pavingstone path leading up to the gate, a huge set of iron-bar doors that matched the palisade surrounding the property.

All guests arrived in similar dark cloaks that hid all signs of their attire and stylings, like they were all a part of some cultish rite. Hopefully the whole thing wasn't just a ruse to get everyone here for human sacrifice, Qora mused. Surprisingly, Qora found herself eager to see what everyone was really wearing, the colors and the masks.

Paqari quickly took Qora's arm and introduced her to the governor, an older man with angular features and deep forehead wrinkles. It was impressive, Qora realized, just how difficult it was to get a first impression of someone without seeing the style of their clothing or the color of their hair. This was the same for the governor's wife, the councilmen and councilwomen, and the Countess of Phapa, all of whom Qora met within the next few minutes. Bare faces in a sea of black velvet. She only caught a glimpse of Ninan, her heart pinching at the sight of his "Kallpa nose" in profile. Sakay quickly amassed an audience of young women even without baring his arms or the rugged cut of his hair, as though he had some aura that simply drew them in—his own form of dominite for these reptilian beauties—and was forced to regale them with thrilling but fictitious tales of defending "the champion" from danger. When he saw Qora watching, he grinned and gave a little shrug.

The guests ate from trays passed around by servants, who stood out in their loose white shirts and purple vests. Most of the food was from the sea—grilled ammonites and seaweed wraps and a smaller species of spiral-toothed helicoprion fish with a delicately fried breading—and of course there were fruit wines and juice cocktails.

Qora met governors that were visiting from the other Tisquvian isles, city councilors from just about every city on the isle of Phapa, several debutantes, directors of architecture, military leaders, sculptors, musicians, and more. But there was no sign of Qhapaq Izhi anywhere. She imagined someone of his position might get a special announcement, but she could also imagine Izhi slithering in like a snake in the night and not wanting to draw attention to himself, especially under the circumstances of his espionage. Either way, she was eager to know what he'd learned about Aqu Aqu, and if his elementalists had been able to break down the sample of dominite.

After a while wandering the courtyard and the corridors, with someone stopping her every minute or so to introduce themselves and rave about the Venture stories that had enraptured them, Qora spotted Paqari with a few young women that must have been local socialites.

Paqari looked up and gasped. "There you are!" She turned to her group and said, "Ladies, you *must* meet the Raptoriva."

Qora stepped forward and the girls separated to allow her a place in their conversation. The princess then proceeded to introduce Qora to one of her own distant cousins, then to the governor's niece, the much-too-young wife of one of the isle's military generals, and the daughter of some famed Tisquvian cartographer Qora hadn't heard of.

Each of the girls had painted lips and darkened eyelashes

and the subtle glimmer of expensive earrings dangling from deep within their hoods.

"This must be your first masquerade," said the governor's daughter.

"Yes, I'm afraid so." Qora sipped her luq'usti, mango, and pineapple cocktail, and tried to look more confident than she actually felt.

"You'll love it," said the general's wife, who looked to be the same age as Qora, if not a bit younger. "It's strange, at first, but you never know who you'll end up dancing with. I actually met my husband here last year. Of course, this time I'll be trying to find *him* in near darkness, rather than some handsome stranger, but the intrigue is still fun."

"Is it really that difficult to recognize your escort?" Qora asked. Everyone had their own body language, their own sense of style, and mannerisms that might easily give them away.

"You'd be surprised," said Paqari's cousin. "With the very dim lighting and the elaborate masks …"

"I'm sure you'll have no problem locating Sakay," Paqari told her. She held a flat hand to the edge of her mouth and whispered, "I think he'll be wearing a dracovenator mask." Then she winked.

Well there goes the mystery.

"Oh yes, I've heard your bodyguard is quite charming," the general's wife remarked. "Surely once he sheds the cloak he'll be easy to spot." She lowered her voice. "But, he's not really *only* your bodyguard …"

"I'm afraid so," Qora replied with sarcastic gravity.

Paqari and the general's wife exchanged disbelieving glances, but Qora didn't bother to argue with them.

They chatted about a few mindless things, from the state

of the avocado groves to the useless efforts of urbanizing the Aquchay desert region to the popularity of cochineal as a lip coloring, and then the governor called for everyone to gather for the official start of the masquerade.

"Welcome, welcome!" he said with a grand gesturing of his hands. "It is such an honor to have you all here tonight—and even more so that we can celebrate the impending union of our princess with the Third Prince of Sumaq!"

Paqari found Ninan and took his arm near the front of the large crowd of guests, and together they turned to look at everyone with gracious smiles at the surge of applause.

"Furthermore, we are lucky to also have the Raptoriva, our most recent Venture champion, with us as well." The governor waved Qora forward, and she did as Paqari had done, facing the guests with a nod and a smile. "Bonus points if you can find any of these three guests of honor in the dark!"

Soft laughter rumbled through the mass.

"Now, if you're not familiar with our rules," the governor continued, "you will be allowed to wander the courtyard, the corridors, and the gardens and maze as you please, but you must not speak to one another. First we'll dim the sconces, and then my attendants will select a few of you at a time—discreetly, and at random—to go to the dressing rooms and perfect your costumes, and then release you into the gardens in a steady flow, where you'll find a place to wait until the music begins. When everyone's ready, the musicians will signal the official start, and from there you may move freely and interact in silence. Use your sense of smell, your sense of touch ..." He winked and induced more laughter. "To ask for a dance, simply extend your *right* hand to someone. Alternatively, extend your *left* hand if you would like to invite someone for a 'private audience.' You may take that to mean whatever you wish. After you've interacted sufficiently in silence, some of you might like to make an educated guess as to whom you've invited to follow you, and then you may both unmask in the courtyard to discover whether you were correct; others might find it more amusing to interact anonymously, and leave your dalliances behind when you leave my home. These interactions are the best part of the game, to better determine who's who—or even meet someone new! Now, please, enjoy yourselves ... and no cheating!"

The guests applauded once more and the servants dispersed to dim the sconces. With the low, flickering lights, and everyone in black, Qora felt an eerie tension in her chest—eerie, but somehow exciting too. Everyone mingled again, but now spoke in whispers, as though lower light required lower volume.

Qora wove through the guests and ducked to avoid the high councilman who had cornered her earlier and asked far too many questions about skinning reptiles. At least, she was fairly certain it was him. Already the darkness was playing tricks on her eyes, and no one even had their masks on yet. She thought she caught a glimpse of Thalu Machaqway as well, speaking to a woman she didn't recognize with a hand pressed to the small of her back.

The same group of young ladies that Paqari had introduced Qora to were gathered again—evident because of their collective, gossipy energy—although this time without Paqari herself. Paqari was several feet away, with her back to them, whispering emphatically to the Countess of Phapa.

Paqari's cousin leaned closer to her group and darted a sideways glance at the princess.

"Ugh," said the girl. "How mortifying ..."

The governor's niece nodded. "This whole tour ... all to make the marriage seem more legitimate ..."

"Wait, what do you mean?" asked the general's wife. "It's not legitimate?"

"It's *legitimate*," Paqari's cousin confirmed. "But my uncle had a very hard time finding her a match."

"Why?"

The governor's niece lowered her voice again, testing Qora's hearing. "Because of the princess's involvement with that watchman. You didn't hear about it?"

The general's wife shook her head.

"Oh, it was a huge scandal," said the governor's niece. "They tried to pass it off as a rumor, but the princess *sullied* herself with some middleborn watchman after he started working at Huapaya House. She was caught sneaking around with him— on multiple occasions."

"Normally after something like that," the cousin added, "even a first-quya princess wouldn't be suitable to marry a qhapaq's son. My uncle considered himself lucky that the offer came through from Sumaq. A formerly disinherited prince is better than no prince at all. As it was, he was going to have a hard time even getting a count or a governor to agree."

The cartographer's daughter huffed. "Now she saunters around like she's practically a quya herself and she's not even married yet."

The girls all leaned in closer together and continued to whisper.

Then, in Qora's periphery, Paqari's face flashed a hard expression—and Qora turned to see the princess disappear into one of the corridors.

In the full courtyard with guests slowly filtering out to the dressing rooms, Qora figured there would be a few minutes before she and Paqari would be dismissed, and slipped out to follow her.

She found Paqari slowly pacing one end of a small drawing room.

Not knowing what to say, Qora stood there watching her for a moment, unsure whether Paqari had noticed her.

Finally, Paqari paused and looked up. "Aren't you going to ask if it's true?"

"That … hadn't actually occurred to me," Qora admitted. "But that doesn't really matter. They shouldn't be talking about you like that."

"What—you're too good for gossip?"

"I can be critical of others," Qora told her. "Although I've had a taste of what it's like to have a qhapaq determining my every move. Whatever you did, I'm sure anyone who knew the full story wouldn't blame you."

Paqari seemed to consider these words for a moment, then draped herself over a chaise lounge and raised her chin. "Anyway, it *is* true."

Qora sat delicately on an adjacent chair. She wasn't sure why she'd followed the princess; maybe it had been the way Paqari had looked at the other girls after hearing them, the evidence of a tiny fracture in her otherwise-perfect facade.

It was easy to think that being a lowborn forced into unwanted fame was the worse of their two fates, especially when it carried the added humility of caring for a prince who was now engaged to someone else. But Qora knew enough about the highborn world now to understand that Paqari's life was likely much more complicated than that. And, despite the adoring crowds and doting attendants, Paqari seemed … alone. It wasn't lost on Qora that no one else had seen the princess slip away—or perhaps seen and not cared.

"What happened to him?" Qora asked. "The watchman …"

The princess unfastened the clasp at the top of her cloak, then refastened it. Her voice came out tight—almost choked. "He was sent away."

Qora pressed her lips together, thinking of the night she'd returned to Qhusi with Ninan after slaying the spinosaur, the way Ninan had gone with his father so solemnly as though the flanking guards had been marching him off to prison. In a way, they had been. No matter how many times Qora had returned to Kallpa House, the qhapaq had ensured she and Ninan never saw one another. When a qhapaq wanted to separate two people, they might as well have been dead to one another.

Paqari's eyes turned glossy but she maintained composure. She cleared her throat. "When my father found out about us, he spared him—a rare mercy—but stationed him far away. By the time I learned where, it was too late. He was married, and my father was preparing to engage me to Apo-Kimsa." She poked at the corners of her eyes before any tears could fall.

"You must have really loved him."

The princess cleared her throat again. "I think I did. Although I'm not completely sure what that means, to be honest. It's never been a part of my future." She laughed bitterly. "I only know about romantic love from the stories my nursemaid used to tell me."

"That's why your grandmother's gem was so important to you," Qora inferred.

"It's silly, I know. It wasn't even as though she was my grandfather's singular love; he still had his other quyas—and his mistresses. But I'm a fool for fiction, I suppose."

"It's not fiction," Qora told her. "I've seen it. Before my papáy died. It's a choice, sometimes, to love like that, to love someone when they're at their worst. It requires humility, and forgiveness. And it's agony because you've split your heart in two, but one half lives in someone else, whom you can't always be with … or protect."

"That must be why I feel I've lost some sense of myself." The princess said this matter-of-factly, rather than in a self-deprecating way.

"Your father used you as a bargaining chip. And worse, your family and friends seem to treat you as though you're a chip lacking in *value*."

"Well, I don't know why I've ever expected anything more," said Paqari. "I'm not the heir—not even a spare, and never could be."

Qora frowned. "Our systems are highly flawed. Just look at Quya Urpi of Allpa; she rules her Terrain with no issue—aside from all the qhapaqs complaining about it."

Paqari shrugged. "A man can plant his seed in many women and secure his line several times over with little effort. That's a power no quya can match—especially not without a husband."

"Sometimes men are a bit like reptiles, I think," said Qora.

"Vicious animals?"

"Intimidating. Cunning. Thick exteriors. Thicker *heads*," Qora mused. "And like humans in the face of those reptiles, women tend to be smaller, thinner skinned, vulnerable."

Paqari flashed a dark gaze. "Penetrable."

Qora didn't want to dwell on the implications of that. "Except … we're also smart. That's why they've tried to keep us ignorant, for fear of losing their ground. We have resources that they don't. 'Weapons' they can't get their claws around." She thought of luring the spinosaur across the waterfall pool, and trapping him in a sinking pit. "Powerful men may get the better of us, sure. But in the end, we'll just have to find a way to make them sorry they did."

Paqari raised an eyebrow and said, "I like the way you think, champion."

Qora smiled. "The Allpan quya also told me something once that I can't seem to get off my mind. When I was fresh off the Venture, feeling defeated—even though, ironically, I'd just been the one to *defeat* that monster—she laid her medal on me and said, 'My name is refuge.' I haven't spoken to her since, but those words gave me a bit of strength, like maybe she knew something of what I felt at that moment. I guess … what I'm trying to say is … you're not alone."

"Thank you." Paqari folded her hands in her lap and pursed her lips. "I suppose you truly are a champion … in more ways than one."

TWENTY-THREE

NINAN ADJUSTED HIS MASK, a full facial recreation of a dracovenator with dark metal scales layered onto the surface in realistic detail. It wasn't so different from a raptor head, except that two jade-green crests ran parallel to the snout, from the tops of the eye sockets down to the nostrils. From the front, the crests were angled in a v shape. The eye holes were inaccurate, of course, since dinosaurs tended to have their eyes on the sides of their heads, rather than pointed forward, but they allowed Ninan to see—not all that well, but some—and still gave the general idea of the dinosaur.

He wore gray pants and black dress boots, and a white shirt with mother-of-pearl buttons. He brushed off the lapels of his dress jacket, which was a velvety material similar to that of the cloak, only in a green that matched the head-crests of his mask. Even though he was dressed as a dracovenator, he still couldn't help but think that he was more or less wearing Qora's raptoriva color. The thought comforted him as much as it made him ache.

The attendants sent him off to the hedge maze, which featured hedges as tall as he was. He wandered through the dark passages with nothing but the almost-full moon's light gleaming and casting shadows everywhere. There were other guests scattered throughout, wearing an array of formal clothing and all manner of dinosaur likenesses on their heads. Paqari had cheated and told him she'd be wearing an ankylosaurus mask, although he'd seen two such masks already—one on a man, and another on a woman too stout to be the princess—so maybe knowing this wouldn't be that much of an advantage anyway.

He picked a spot at a dead end among the maze and waited for several minutes until, finally, the music swelled from the courtyard. It was slow and ominous, with bone flutes playing low notes and guitars plucking individual strings. Everyone began to move and interact, mostly approaching one another with curious head-tilts and analytical gazes. A few extended their right hands quickly in a request to dance, and then made their way to the courtyard where they'd be closer to the music and have space to sway and perform the steps together. Others extended their left hands and disappeared deeper into the hedges or into some of the darker corridors.

Ninan had been sure this game wouldn't be difficult, as he was familiar enough with Paqari's shape and posture—he wasn't blind—to pick her out among others. But in this dimness, and with so many gowns covered in ruffles and beads or fluffed out with underlayers, and among so many young women of status and upbringing who carried themselves similarly, he worried it just might take him all night. It was equally unhelpful that most of the people of Runaqa shared darker hair, typically ranging from medium brown to black. Other continents, he'd heard, were home to people with hair as light as maize, and skin like cream—which would be dead giveaways here.

Tucked away in different corners of the hedge maze were guests wearing masks that resembled the heads of parasaurs with backward-sweeping cranial crests, pachycephalosaurs with dome-shaped crowns circled in bony knobs, point-crested pteranodons, frill-necked dilophosaurs, triceratops, the more elaborate kosmoceratops and chasmosaur and styracosaur, and theropods that were mostly indistinguishable except for scale colors that did not reflect any particular dinosaur but were simply for coordinating with clothing. Most masks had elements that were gold or silver plated, studded with precious stones or gems, and decorated with feathers.

Eventually Ninan's attention landed on a girl in a pinkish-red gown—a color Paqari might have called something like "magenta" or "cerise"—wearing jade earrings and gold bracelets and a gold collar necklace. Her ankylosaur mask was pebbled with additional jade, and the four diagonal horns—two pointing up from the crown of the head and two pointing down from the cheekbones—along with a small pointed beak, were gilded. Squinting, he thought there was a strong possibility that he was looking at his fiancée. He also thought Paqari might be slightly taller than this young woman, but then he remembered the higher-heeled shoes she sometimes wore and it occurred to him he might be conflating her natural height with those. Additionally, the mask and its horns added some height, so it was hard to say. Regardless, he was tired of this game already, and he'd spent at least a half hour searching.

He approached her and extended his right hand. She looked up at him, although her eyes were hard to see from within her mask, save for a slight shimmer. She seemed to analyze him, hesitating, but then dropped her hand into his. He tried to decide if it felt like Paqari's hand—he'd held it enough during events and greetings—but everything about this night was eerie and confusing. Surely he was overthinking this.

When they arrived in the courtyard, the young woman brought both arms to his shoulders and let her hands fall relaxed behind his neck, while he held her by the waist.

The bone flutes emitted a breathy, resonant melody, while the guitars echoed with each pluck of the strings. Ninan swayed with his partner, and together they turned slowly amid other pairings. He glanced around at the others—a typical formal scene except for the strange addition of decorated reptilian faces, all bizarre and unnatural. Then he turned back to the young woman, and strained his eyes to better take in her appearance.

What do I do now? he wondered. *Just keep dancing and see if I can figure it out?*

He wasn't certain enough to unmask them both and risk embarrassing himself in front of all these people.

But then he had to ask himself *why* he wasn't certain. What about this girl didn't leave him fully believing she was Paqari? She had the ankylosaur mask. She was close enough to the right size (although, again, these gowns minimized or added to the wearer's shape, like some strange witchcraft). He didn't know much about the nuances of women's fashion, but he did sense that what this girl was wearing had some of Paqari's personality in it; in fact, he was positive he'd seen her wear these exact jade earrings (he'd noticed them because the straight, narrow shape had reminded him of blades of grass). So, what was missing?

Ninan raised his left hand and brought it to the back of his partner's right hand draped over him, and gently slid his fingers between hers, curling his fingertips just enough to get underneath and feel her skin above the first joint.

He sucked in a breath at the feel of the thickened skin there.

Calluses—right where a crossbow huntress would have them.

If I could not see your face,
I would know you by the shadows that you cast.

If I could not feel your skin,
I would know you by the way your form shifts the air.

If I could not hear your voice,
I would know you by the sound of your heartbeat.

Llariku Qumir, Qolqese poet

TWENTY-FOUR

QORA GASPED. The way he'd slipped his fingers in between hers from behind—it was all too familiar. Just like in the caves.

She'd just been trying to figure out a way to slide her hands down to his biceps and give them a subtle squeeze, to determine whether the bulk there was genuine, or only the result of the thick sleeves of his dress jacket. Otherwise, this young man (she'd *assumed* he was young, at least) was barely tall enough to be Sakay, but now that she thought about it, those head crests added several inches to his height that didn't truly belong to him.

As he ran his fingertips along her calluses—the ones she'd earned from years of spanning her crossbow—her pulse quickened and she stepped back from him.

They stared at one another, stagnant in the sea of moving bodies with their reptilian heads.

She knew it was him. And he knew it was her.

Now what?

They seemed to silently agree that they must not unmask themselves, because of course everyone would see that they were together, and that they had made a grave error in selecting one another. And yet, it appeared that neither of them was going to leave.

As the music played and their eyes met, Ninan slowly

extended his hand to her again—this time, his *left* hand.

Qora looked at it, pressing her lips together from behind that gilded ankylosaur beak.

"Extend your left hand if you would like to invite someone for a 'private audience.'"

This was a bad idea. Obviously. But still, she reached out and accepted it, and allowed Ninan to lead her away.

They wove between couples, and then between pillars, and then between hedges, until they were deep into the maze, passing guests who hadn't yet found their partners, and other "private audiences" of a more sensual nature that made Qora blush behind her mask. One couple seemed to have no sense of their lack of privacy—some man in a silver troodon mask and a woman in a crimson parasaur mask and matching gown with one sleeve falling halfway down her arm. Qora averted her eyes.

Her pulse raced with each step, as she thought about what might happen here, as Ninan continued to run his fingertips over hers—over the calluses, as she wondered about Paqari and Sakay who were still wandering around looking for them (and much less likely to find them while they were out here alone together).

Then Ninan pulled her into a corner and drew her into him in a tight, desperate embrace. His heartbeat pounded through him so hard she could feel it, almost matching her own but a fraction of a second offset. His breath was heavy and so was hers, and she longed for the fresh air she might be able to inhale were she not inhibited by this stupid mask.

The embrace contained the longing of all the months they'd been apart. It held the yearning of two people whose positions in life simply couldn't allow them to be together. It held the fright and the anguish and the relief that came with the dangers they'd faced and survived thus far on the *Velosaura*. She wrapped her arms around his body and soaked in his essence, his scent—the human scent that was unique to him, the kind without description, the kind that underlay his added highborn fragrances of balsam and muña.

She grasped at the fabric of his jacket, and he pressed his hands into her back before wrapping a wide section of her hair around his knuckles. How strange they must have looked, she thought—part human, part animal, like hybrid creatures of fiction, twined together like this. She reached up to his face and dragged her thumb along his jawline under the edge of his mask, and before she could stop herself, she was pushing it up and off of his face. And then he was removing hers, too. Both masks clattered on the stone pathway and she pressed her lips to the same place where her thumb had been, so close to his mouth but not daring to touch it. Likewise, he kissed the side of her forehead and down to her cheekbone. This, of course, was not any less of a betrayal to Ninan's engagement, but they both knew there would be no coming back from a true kiss.

Qora buried her face in his neck, tucking her head between his chin and his collarbone. She closed her eyes, willing herself not to cry, wrinkling his shirt as she clutched the material. He gripped her waist and kissed her hair, making her pulse thicken through every part of her.

No—she couldn't do this. It ached so badly and she never wanted to leave his arms, but this wasn't the type of person she wanted to be. Someone without honor. Someone with no respect for the consequences of her selfish behavior.

She remembered her conversation with Paqari, about the way of things, about the obligations and the punishment she'd endured. Whatever the princess was or wasn't, that girl didn't deserve what had happened to her, or the shame that would come with whatever scandal Qora's closeness to Ninan would bring about if anyone were to find them like this.

Qora stepped back, shrugging off Ninan's embrace. "I'm sorry. I—"

She flinched at the sound of rapid footsteps on the pathway, growing louder. She and Ninan exchanged a look, and both reached down to pick up their masks, but neither managed to replace their disguise before someone appeared at the junction: a man, in a maroon dress jacket and carnotaur mask, which he promptly removed when he saw them.

"Sakay," Qora breathed.

He darted a glance from one to the other, raising an eyebrow. Surely he'd been looking for Qora; Ninan must have been quite the additional surprise. Qora's face heated; she imagined it must be the color of her dress.

"Is everything alright?" Ninan asked.

Sakay nodded once. "Izhi's here."

TWENTY-FIVE

SPIRITS, THESE TWO ARE GOING TO *get themselves killed,* Sakay thought.

All evening, he'd struggled to find Qora, and finally given up after the sixth or seventh glamorous young woman had approached him extending a left hand. So off to one of the dark corridors they'd gone. While it had been difficult to enjoy themselves in such ostentatious masks, they had just begun to figure out a strategy when echoing applause from the courtyard had drawn his attention. The gasps and remarks from the guests implied that someone of great importance had arrived, and Sakay hadn't been able to help but think this might be exactly what he and his friends were waiting for.

Surely enough, he'd raced to the courtyard to see Qhapaq Izhi, along with one of his quyas, surrounded by bowing guests. Under his arm, Izhi had held a triceratops mask pebbled in blue opals and sprouting three gilded horns. Sakay had wondered how long the qhapaq had been among them, waiting for a good opportunity for this grand reveal. The mask should have given him away, for all its national symbolism, but since, presumably, the idea was to choose a reptile and color of mystery, Sakay supposed people might not have expected the obvious tribute. And of course there were other Unuvian diplomats among the guests.

In any case, he'd scoured the property looking for Qora, and now he'd found her. With Ninan.

"Let's go." Ninan squeezed Qora's fingers once before releasing her.

〉〉〉

The group hadn't been in the courtyard three seconds before Sakay spotted a servant slipping a strip of papyr into Ninan's hand.

After reading it, Ninan said, "He wants us to meet him at the top of the east structure."

Sakay took the lead, trudging up the staircase that wrapped around the cylindrical tower, huffing when he reached the top. "It had to be all the way up here?"

Izhi was already inside when they entered, standing with his back to them, hands clasped behind himself as he stared out the window. He turned as they unmasked themselves. "Apo-Kimsa. Raptoriva. And … a rebel friend, I presume?"

Sakay nodded.

"You received all my messages?" Ninan asked.

"Yes," Izhi replied, "Although I can't say I was pleased to learn that my tracker had deserted me."

"He provided the necessary information," Qora said firmly. "That's all that matters, isn't it?"

"I suppose," said Izhi.

Ninan's gaze shifted. He glanced over his shoulder, then lowered his voice. "You're sure this location is secure?"

"Absolutely."

"How do you know?" Sakay crossed his arms.

"Because the governor is with us in this matter. He's highly opposed to Qhapaq Achik's collusion—he knows that's what it really is—with Qhapaq Apo, and he's agreed to help our cause in any way he can."

"Fine." Ninan narrowed his eyes but didn't question the man further.

Qora gripped two of the horns on her mask. "So, were you able to find anything in Aqu Aqu?"

Izhi's jaw flexed. "No."

"No?" Ninan said.

"I dispatched a team of investigators as soon as you sent me word. They found nothing. No trace of any kind of base or facility. No remnants of dominite or skyrock. No evidence of dinosaur breeding or feeding. It was a dead end."

"How can that be?" Qora asked. "Tuko's scraps created a clear trail in one direction, and that's where it stopped."

"I am displeased, to say the least."

Qora furrowed her brow. "Alright, then. What about Sut'u? Ninan said he would inform you that I saw a white pteranodon descending on its shores. There has to be something *there*, at least."

"I've conducted an aerial investigation and found no further evidence of Qhapaq Apo's presence there."

Ruck, Sakay thought. He knew that had to have been a clue; Apo wouldn't have someone land there for nothing. But the likelihood of getting more information was slim. If Izhi couldn't figure it out, he wasn't sure how Ninan or the Razorclaws would.

"And the 'foreign' dinosaur attacks on the west coast of this very isle?" asked Sakay. "You should have received word of that too ..."

"I've had people scouring this isle for the past two days. Nothing yet."

"Well what about the dominite?" said Ninan. "You retrieved the sample I buried, didn't you?"

"My elementalists are still analyzing it. No progress yet. Where is that useless tracker?"

"In my cabin," Ninan told him.

"Dispose of him as you see fit."

Sakay caught Ninan's eye, and saw the subtle, defiant head shake.

"In the meantime," Izhi added, "please continue to keep your eyes and ears open for other leads, and message me promptly. I will continue to utilize additional sources of intelligence, but I've been apprised of the remaining stops on your tour should I need to fly out and meet with you again. Unless circumstances change, we can convene once more at the gala in Port Waqta. Now, you three are to return to the masquerade, and several minutes later I will follow and make another appearance. However, we will not speak again tonight."

❱❱❱

Masked once again and sweeping separately back into the courtyard with Qora on his arm, Sakay wished Ninan good luck on locating the princess.

Many people were unmasked now, but Qora had suggested she and Sakay dance for a few minutes and make a show of revealing themselves together. At least that way it would look like they had guessed correctly.

While they danced, a man dressed like a silver troodon revealed himself to be Thalu Machaqway, along with his partner—a romantic partner, according to what Sakay had overheard while waiting to enter the dressing rooms—who had now removed her indigo pachycephalosaur mask and kissed Thalu for an applauding crowd.

A look of confusion passed over Qora's face. Sakay wondered if she, too, had seen that same silver troodon with his hands all over a crimson parasaur in the hedges less than thirty minutes ago. But he also wondered whether Qora had been about to tangle herself up in a similar scandal when he'd found her with Ninan.

"So," Sakay said, leaning his carnotaur snout between the two side horns at the left of her mask so she could hear him better. "Are you going to tell me what I walked up to earlier?"

"I don't want to talk about it."

"Yes, I guess it should be clear that you think *talking* is overrated."

She smacked him on the arm. "You have no idea what this is like."

Sakay scoffed. "No idea?"

No idea what it was like to long for someone he couldn't have? No idea what it was like to have an aching emptiness that could never be filled? The thought that Qora could be so out of touch was becoming an irritant too obnoxious to bear. She'd pined for Ninan for months, and now she was traveling alongside him, attending masquerade balls and lavish dinners, and sure, he was promised to someone else, someone more powerful than her, with little hope of ever being free to be with Qora, but at least she'd been able to steal a few moments alone with him, to *touch* him. What Sakay wouldn't give for one more touch, one more moment. At least Qora could speak to Ninan whenever she wanted. "At least Ninan is *alive*," Sakay bit out.

Qora frowned. "What's that supposed to mean?"

The heat of this climate had been tolerable, for the most

part, but the sweat building up behind Sakay's mask was quickly starting to feel suffocating. As the memories of his past swelled within him, his breaths turned shallow and cumbersome. He pushed off the mask, drawing looks from everyone around them. He paused, having forgotten, for an instant, that he was part of a game.

After a quick glance at the onlookers, Qora removed her mask as well, and those who recognized her and her "bodyguard" applauded. Sakay and Qora each gave a little bow, and then he brought her close to him again to resume the dance.

"What aren't you telling me?" Qora whispered in his ear.

"Never mind."

"No. You're not doing that. You brought this up. Tell me." She looked him over with a searching gaze. "Does it have something to do with the sixth Razorclaw?"

Sakay's heart pinched at the mention, however vague. He was keenly aware of how awkward it was to dance while holding a mask, and now his jacket had become too hot as well. His eyes stung, and he could scarcely contain the force building behind them. "Can we ... get out of here?"

⟩⟩⟩⟩

They found a bench at the edge of the garden. Sakay removed his jacket before taking a seat, then rested his elbows on his knees, and rubbed the back of his neck. He hadn't thought about her in so long—*really* thought about her. *Glimpses* of her memory, of the loss of her, yes, but the mission that had brought him here—seeing the Razorclaws again—had somehow primed him for reliving it, and now, seeing Qora so distraught over Ninan, who was still living and breathing, and walking around on the same property, it was … too much.

Qora sat beside him, quietly at first. But eventually, she asked, "Will you tell me her name?"

He hesitated. How long had it been since he'd spoken it? "Ramaya."

"When …" Qora paused. "I mean, how long ago did she …"

"Two years."

She covered her mouth for a moment, eyes averted in thought. "Oh, gods. Sakay. I … I remember. You were gone for weeks. I had to haggle with your uncle once, and he was so intimidating I didn't go back to the Underground for a long while. Then when I did, when I saw you were there again, you were … quiet. You didn't argue with me that time."

"Sounds about right."

"But I never imagined …"

"You couldn't have known. I didn't *want* you to know." He let his spine come up against the backrest of the bench, and looked up at the night sky all speckled and clear.

"I guess there's a lot I don't know about you. Although I guess there isn't really a good reason for you to share those things with me."

Without looking at her, he took one of her hands and held onto it. "You … have become … important to me. Despite how tough I was on you in the beginning—even until recently. Despite my best efforts to distance myself from … basically everyone."

Her fingers twitched in his grasp. "You're important to me, too."

"You remind me of her. A little." He huffed. "In a more … sisterly way."

She smiled softly.

"Ramaya was ... a force," he continued. "She came into the Underground to make a trade—of something she'd stolen, no doubt; she was stealthy, and cunning, and incredibly well trained. And when the other traders tried to take advantage of her, she ... well, she made them regret it."

"Is she the reason you joined the Razorclaws?" Qora asked.

Sakay nodded. "I never thought I'd see her again after that first night, but ... we seemed to keep finding each other. She ended up back at the Underground when the others recruited her for an assignment. They needed a thief to help them steal from the qhapaq."

"Steal what?"

"That's another story for another time. Long enough to fill a small novel, surely." He wasn't quite ready to provide those kinds of details yet anyway. He didn't know if she'd ever be able to look at him the same way if she knew that the very war that threatened them today was a direct consequence of that mission.

"Well, did you at least succeed? Can you tell me that much?"

"Yes and no." Sakay wiped a mist of sweat from his forehead. "Sometimes you can succeed in the moment, but your true losses don't become apparent until later. We did what we set out to do. But Ramaya ... she ..." He shook his head. "She was wounded. We thought she was alright. But a few months later ... the poison took her." A tear broke loose from one of his eyes, and this time, he let it fall. No matter how much he told himself that his own wounds had closed, it always seemed something simple that could make them bleed again.

Qora scooted closer and slipped her arms around him, resting her head on his shoulder. For several minutes, he allowed her to hold him, allowed her to transfer her warmth—not the warmth of her body, as there was already so much bodily warmth here, but the warmth of her spirit, the warmth that had drawn him to her from the beginning despite her otherwise often scaly demeanor. In a way, she had given him purpose these past few years; even though he'd only seen her maybe once or twice each week, he'd made a point of looking out for her, and after Ramaya when he thought he'd be numb and internally dead forever, Qora had continued to come into the Underground with a scowl and a ferocity that made him smile.

There he'd been, the only child of a disturbed woman who had died before he was ten years old, raised by his uncle among rough and rowdy men, with no future but to continue with the business of the Underground. And then, having lost the one person who had made him feel as though he were worth something, he wasn't sure he had much to live for—had even pondered releasing himself from this cruel world—but Qora, so young and lonely, and with no older brother to keep her from trouble, gave him something to tend, and visits to look forward to. While a meager consolation, it had been enough for him to keep up with his day-to-day grind. That, along with the occasional thrill of winning bets and making good deals, and whatever opportunities for dalliances and distractions, which were always as fleeting as the elation that came with them.

He didn't want Qora to know his pain, in any capacity. But as with anything involving the qhapaq (or, in this case, the qhapaq's son) there were likely to be casualties—if not literal deaths, then at least the death of one's hope.

"I told you to guard your heart, *kantuta*," he reminded her. "Maybe now you can better understand why."

TWENTY-SIX

JUST AS NINAN WAS ABOUT TO GIVE UP and unmask himself publicly, regardless of not having found Paqari, someone tapped his shoulder: a girl in a purple gown wearing a kosmoceratops mask. The kosmoceratops likeness had the same three horns as a triceratops, but with a taller bony frill that sprouted a row of small, forward-hooking horns along its top edge—one of the more ostentatious ceratopsians in nature, and even more so here begemmed in amethyst.

"That had better be you," Ninan said through his own mask.

"Yes, Apo-Kimsa." Sure enough, Paqari's voice.

He didn't bother to take her hand; he just started walking toward the center of the courtyard. Thankfully, she followed, and then they stood facing one another over an embossment of flourishes on the floor.

Ninan removed his mask. Paqari did the same. Everyone turned to look, and quickly began to applaud. They both forced their usual smiles, and then Ninan swept her into a dance.

"It certainly took you long enough to find me," Paqari told him once the other guests had returned to their own interactions.

"You told me you'd be wearing an ankylosaur mask."

Paqari gasped. "Oh, gods ..." She looked up at him with horrified eyes. "I did, didn't I? I'm so sorry." She shook her head.

"That was my intention, but at the last minute I changed my gown, and of course I realized this color wasn't suited to the ankylo, so I switched it, and I completely forgot to inform you."

"Well, now you know why I didn't find you. Although you certainly found me."

"I ran into the champion and her bodyguard after they'd unmasked," Paqari confessed. "They told me what to look for. I do hope you can forgive me. This game is ridiculous, and now I'm horribly embarrassed, and I'd really just like to forget the whole thing."

Ninan was angry, to be certain, but his mind was far from that anger, or the concept of forgiveness. His thoughts were rather occupied with the memory of Qora's lips along his jaw, and his hands in her hair, and the darkness of the hedges where they'd been able to pretend for a moment that nothing outside of them mattered. And so, with his mind lost in such chaos, all he managed to say in response to the princess was, "It's forgotten."

⫸⫷

After the masquerade, everyone from the *Velosaura* traveled back to the ship and went to their separate cabins without conversing.

Ninan was at a loss after the night's events, his time with Qora having stoked his desire to the point of catching fire all over again, while Izhi's news of the dead-end location felt like a bucket of water on whatever flames of hope he'd maintained for success against his father.

Regardless, he quickly fell into a slumber, although a restless one, and once again joined the group aboard the ship first thing in the morning.

The next three days of the journey took them to the tiny Kiru Islets in the north—Llullu, Ch'iñi, and Ichik. Each was known for maintaining its pre-modern cultures as a sort of novelty, preserving the old-style villages along with the old ways, even among the highborn families who governed there. All three were more or less the same, hosting grand beach-side bonfire festivals in honor of Ninan and Paqari (and of course Qora, who was a pleasing addition as always).

The guests at these events were more pleasant to talk to, Ninan discovered. Rather than being forced to endure endless political discussions, he found himself learning of the history of Tisqu, the way some of the islands had been formed from the remnants of an ancient shield volcano, and how the volcano Molten Fang had formed on top of it. He learned of the silverleaf plants native only to the islands, adapted to high humidity and harsh volcanic environments, with a silvery sheen that reflected the sun in order to conserve its own moisture. And then of the local compies with their multicolored specks and feathered forelimbs. The people here held a deep affinity for their land, for the fascinating qualities of nature, less concerned with modernization and more concerned with Sky Mother's blessings.

Despite the antiquity of the structures on the islets, the dignitaries' homes were vast, made from sturdy native hardwood frames and thatched with intricately woven leaves. The roofs were steeply pitched, with large overhangs for shade. They had multiple rooms and platforms arranged around central gathering zones, and were decorated with detailed wood carvings and feather collections and colorful tapestries. But still, these particular highborns seemed to value the open air the most, marking off areas of beach with wooden poles and suspending ropes between them, from which dozens of flickering lanterns hung.

They were also quite proud of their food, which they cooked over the open flames in grand displays. Llullu was known for its roast dinohyus, while Ch'iñi and Ichik each boasted distinct variations of entelodon magnus, presented with roasted fruits like pacay and lucuma. Many of the more haughty dignitaries and socialites who had been present at the masquerade and Count Kisqa's mansion and the magistrate's luncheon were curiously absent from the islets' sandaled gatherings upon the sand, and for that Ninan was grateful, as he enjoyed the change of pace—especially with the more relaxed dress code that allowed guests to wear lighter-weight, simpler clothing.

These islets seemed to extend an invitation to all, as colorful flyers—many species Ninan was not familiar with, but which were iridescent and lovely—came to perch on every surface, with no one shooing them away, while little cartorhynchus came ashore and beached themselves nearby, scooting on their bellies, propelled by their flippers as their tails drew serpentine shapes in the sand behind them.

Ninan drank purple chicha and listened to stories of old sea battles against the great mosasaurs that inhabited the region, some of whose bones formed decorative tunnels leading to and from the more prominent beach sites.

Sakay continued his effortless flirtation and was either chatting with some woman or had disappeared entirely.

Paqari spent most of her time with the highborn young women of the islets, apparently discussing the ways in which they extracted perfume scents from the local flowers, or the way they cultivated the sweetest honey, or their methods for creating the deepest hues in their dyes.

When it came to dyes, Qora seemed to have many questions too, reminding Ninan of the story Qora had told him about picking mora berries with her brothers during the summer—one of the many sources of their mother's pigments.

Between the performance dancers that twirled flaming bolas, and the musicians with their woodbox drums and pan pipes, and the distribution of dinohyus and entelodon meats, and the cultural conversations, Ninan and Qora managed to avoid one another on all three islets.

Qora frequently drew the attention of older children, particularly girls, who wanted to know the tales of how she'd survived in the jungle. Some of the girls had even commissioned their own small crossbows and begged her for spontaneous shooting lessons by firelight.

Meanwhile, Ninan stuck close to the dignitaries, especially those who might provide insights on any of Tisqu's island landscapes and unwittingly give him clues as to the best location for his father's reptile breeding. All he'd gathered so far was that Sut'u was best known for its striped geological formations and its aquafern plants, that Qhapaq Achik wanted to urbanize the desert regions in order to take advantage of potential salt and metal resources, that the citizens of the isle of Phapa had recently grown fond of placodonts as a meat source and were unfortunately hunting them to near extinction, and that a new trend in jewelry was driving up the price of topaz. It was the closest to political talk that he'd been able to steer any of them into—reluctantly, but he needed information—and all topics only concerned natural resources, which he had to admit made sense after his few days among them.

By late evening on the islet of Ichik, the last of the Kirus, Ninan was ready to return to his cabin and curl up alone, defeated. Tuko would appreciate the scraps of food, as he did every night, and Ninan would close his eyes on another failure of a day.

As he prepared to make his excuses to everyone and bid them good night, an older woman approached him.

"Your Highness," she said with a bow. "I am Lady Munay. We met once, a long time ago, in Sumaq."

He tried to place her, to think when he would have seen her, but he came up blank. "I'm sorry, I don't think I …"

"Of course you won't remember me." She swatted the air. "You were only a young boy. Seven or eight, perhaps. But I remember that little folk song you used to perform …"

"Folk song?" Ninan said.

"On the charango. You used to play for all the guests at Kallpa House—or so I was told. I only attended once. How did it go again? Let me see?" She put a finger to her chin. "'Swift as a raptor, she captured my gaze …'"

A beautiful captor—the gold in the maize.

The melody came to his mind in an instant. The pattern of the strum against the strings. A simple tune with quaint lyrics, something a child could easily learn to play—the very first thing, and one of few things, he *had* learned to play. At that age, he hadn't considered that it was a love song, only concerned with his ability to entice a pleasant sound from the instrument for the rare attention it afforded him. He'd soon learned not all attention was good, however, when Apo-Iskay had smashed the charango on the cliffs.

"You have a good memory," Ninan told the woman. "That was a long time ago."

"A few years is not so long ago when you're my age. Do you still play?"

"Oh, gods no. I mean, I'm sure if I were to try, some of it might come back to me, but I guarantee I've forgotten the whole third verse and I barely remember the chords."

"I think you're too modest, Your Highness. You really ought to favor us with the tune. I'm sure one of the players here wouldn't mind lending you an instrument."

The charango player looked up and nodded.

The few people who had overheard began to coo at the idea, murmuring small encouragements. Ninan shook his head, face flushing. How he'd ever yearned for such attention was beyond him now. Now he just wanted to bury himself in the sand.

Then Paqari seemed to catch word of this idea too. "You never told me you were a musician, Apo-Kimsa. Please do not hide your talent. I'm sure everyone would love to hear."

Again, Ninan tried to decline, but the excitement only grew. "Please?"

"He's just being coy."

"Come, now, you can't deny your own fiancée. A princess!"

Next thing he knew, someone was pressing a charango into his hands and urging him to the forefront of the gathering space. He stood facing the guests, with the other musicians behind him. He glanced back as though they might be able to help him avoid this, but the pan flautist only shrugged and offered a vague expression of sympathy.

Ninan placed his fingertips onto the fretboard, holding down what he was only partially certain were the correct strings. He glanced outward, catching sight of Qora, her cheeks painted gold in the flickering firelight as she watched curiously. Shakily, he strummed once, and cringed in anticipation of a discordant sound, but the instrument was perfectly tuned. The chord was pleasant, evoking instant smiles from his audience.

He strummed again, slowly picking up the rhythm, teasing it out of the depths of his memory. Then, the words flowed to his tongue.

Swift as a raptor,
She captured my gaze.
A beautiful captor—
The gold in the maize.

Like mist on the mountains,
I found, then, you'd gone,
And all but lost count when
I numbered the dawns.

Then on the horizon,
The skies spun a view,
So much like a prize won,
Because I saw you.

Till my bones turn to fossil,
My cause will be this:
Each day to be lost still
In love's sweet abyss.

As he finished the strum pattern, he thought he saw a tear slip down Qora's cheek, but like the girl in the song, she seemed to have disappeared, in her case among the other guests, and Ninan brought the song to its closing cadence. The guests clapped, and he took a bow before handing the charango back to its owner. As his fingers brushed the neck one final time, he suddenly felt a pang in his chest at letting it go. How strange, the way painful memories were so intertwined with the good ones.

〉〉〉

When Ninan arrived back on the ship, Captain Yanacha was leaning on the gunwale, smoking a pipe carved into the shape of a terminonatator—a long neck forming the stem, and a flippered body forming the stummel, with a glowing hole in its spine. When she drew from it, she looked like she was kissing the reptile's tiny mouth.

Ninan scoffed a laugh.

The captain turned to look at him and raised the pipe. "You like it? I had it made in Llullu. A little memento of our encounter on the way to K'iti."

"It's magnificent." He paused and glanced over at the bonfire down on the beach, whose flames were dying as everything wrapped up, while the guests lingered and chatted. Then he turned back to the captain. "You're not tired of the ship? Don't you want a break from it?"

She shrugged. "I'm her steward. It's my job to stay close to her. Besides, if there's anything I need a break from, it's *highborns*."

"In that case, I'll leave you to it …"

"I'm not talking about you," she clarified with a low chuckle.

"Why should I be the exception?"

"You don't belong with them, and you know it."

Ninan raised an eyebrow, then slowly approached the gunwale beside her and rested his elbows on it. "Why do you say that?"

"Nature always has its flaws. A runt in the litter, congenital abnormalities, mutations, stress factors that influence development—children who don't seem to belong to those among whom they were born."

"I'm a mutation …"

The captain released a puff of smoke. "Of sorts."

"Well that explains a lot." It explained why his brothers had always treated him like ruck on their shoes, why his father had so easily thrown him to the reptiles of the wilderness as punishment.

"There are also hierarchies within hierarchies," she told him. "I'm guessing you landed at the bottom of yours."

"You guessed right."

"That's afforded you a level of understanding when it comes to the 'lesser' of us. You know what it is to be stepped on, to be outcast. That's why the people of Runaqa have welcomed you back to your position. Even though you're not one of them, they assume they have your empathy—or at least your sympathy."

"They assume I can do anything about their condition. But I can't." It was something he hadn't had the chance to think on properly, but it was certainly a problem lurking in the back of his mind. Another concept tearing him in two. He'd been doing his best, working with Izhi, expecting that he might be able to gather adequate information to help keep the citizens of all Five Terrains safe from war, but he had yet to succeed. As far as holding any power to change the legal situations that kept people of Sumaq bound to the qhapaq's purposes, Ninan had made no progress.

"Who's to say you can't?"

"You know who. I may be a prince, but like you said, within the hierarchy of Kallpa House, I'm the *least* of them."

"Yes, but within the forces of nature, you're as powerful as anything."

He rolled his eyes. "More nature talk? I suppose you're going to expand on the Kiruvian ideals of the sea spirits whose divine energy gravitates toward the 'noble of heart'?"

She huffed. "No. I'm not much for spiritual things. I much prefer the physical." She took another drag on the pipe and blew it out in a quick stream. "Are you familiar with *rapapapay*?"

Ninan shook his head.

"It's onomatopoeic. A word that describes the sound of flapping—as in wings of a flyer, or ship sails in the wind—and lapping, like water against the sides of a boat. It's a common word for seafarers, for obvious reasons. It represents movement that creates waves, a force that creates a disturbance. As a metaphorical concept, it represents the way we each affect the space around us, the impact we have on matter, and how it can reflect back to us. Ripples we send through the cosmic fluid of our lives. Nothing without consequence. It has spiritual undertones, but it's scientifically based as well."

"Every action produces a reaction, yes." Ninan sighed.

"I don't mean to belittle your intelligence, Your Highness. What I'm trying to say is … You are no less capable of 'making waves' than anyone else. Certainly if you were to wave your arms around this very minute, you would not produce a hurricane. But any well-timed and well-placed motion can make a difference. Metaphorically *or* physically."

"How about waving a flag of surrender?" That was easy enough, and all he felt like doing anyway.

"Or you could continue waving your *fists* around. You're pretty good with those."

"Sure, I can defend myself, and maybe a few others in my immediate surroundings. But … in the grander scheme of things?"

The captain smiled wanly and patted Ninan on the back. "In the grander scheme of things … I think you just need to figure out a few new ways to punch."

꒰꒰꒰

Back in his sleeping cabin, Ninan pulled off his shirt and turned down his bed. Footfalls bounced off the deck above him, signaling that the others were returning too.

Next to the lantern on Ninan's nightstand, Tuko nibbled at a nugget of entelodon meat. Ninan sat heavily on the bed and watched the little reptile, who paused to look up at him, cocking his head to the side.

Ninan pondered, as he had for so many nights now, what had gone wrong with the shipment Tuko had been tracking, or whether Tuko had purposely led them astray—and if so, why? Of course it could have been another decoy, except that Ninan had verified for himself that the contents were dominite, and the reaction of the Razorclaws' pteranodons had supported this. Surely Tuko was not so easy to fool, with his memory and his strong sense of smell.

Ninan stroked Tuko's beak with one finger and sighed. "What are you up to?"

Armed with the charango guitar, Chaski began to sing the words that he had not had the power to speak.

From "Chaski's Charango"

TWENTY-SEVEN

IT TOOK THE *VELOSAURA* TWO DAYS to get to Phapa City, but when they made port, Qora found the first opportunity to slip away. It would be hours before the minister's banquet, and she needed a break from pretending she wasn't slowly shriveling from the inside out.

During their journey, Ninan and Paqari had kept to themselves, while Sakay had continued his on-board social life among the cabinmaids and any female crew that caught his attention.

Qora had spent time studying maps of the islands, along with a few books on Tisqu's history in hopes of gathering additional clues that might lead to an answer about Qhapaq Apo's activities, but to no avail. She'd been expecting to find something about Sut'u's potential significance to the qhapaq— why he would send someone there—but the most interesting thing she'd learned was that the isle was home to a plethora of aquafern plants, which contained a gel within their leaves, and that ingesting that gel could allow someone to remain hydrated for extended periods of time, even in extremely hot climates. Apparently the Qolqese government had tried to bully Tisqu into exporting it to their desert regions, but it became a protected resource with strict limitations on its use. Maybe the qhapaq was trying to win favor with Qolqe, the way he had with Tisqu, by mediating the aquafern trade?

Now she wandered Phapa City's main streets, coming upon the day market, which wasn't so different from the one in Qhusi but for the colorful little flyers that flitted to spilled grain, the floral stands, and the tropical fruits. Qora wore the same hooded cloak she'd flown over in, keeping herself obscure, although she didn't expect anyone here would recognize her as quickly as the people in Sumaq might. After all, there were no banners or murals here with her face on them.

She stopped to pet a stray bagaceratops, then purchased a carton of magmaberries, a sunstone melon, and a few pterofruits. As she went to head back to the ship, she came across a carpenter displaying wooden musical instruments. When she spotted a charango, she stopped.

"See something you like?" the woman asked. "I make everything here myself."

Qora nodded and pointed to the charango, whose mouth—the sound hole in the body behind the strings—was lined with pearloid teeth. The sound box was domed at the back, and carved with a scaly texture stained green under the finish.

"It's gorgeous," Qora said when the carpenter handed it to her.

"The tuning pegs are made of sauropod bone," said the carpenter, "and the mouth details are mother-of-pearl."

Qora ran her fingers over the different parts, and found herself smiling. "How much?"

☽☽☽

Since she'd overheard Paqari tell Ninan that he would require a fitting for a new dress jacket for the upcoming banquet—

because "the people in this city favor patterned fabrics"—Qora took the opportunity to sneak into Ninan's suite while he was gone, and laid the charango on his pillow. Tuko was perched in the rounded window beside the bed, and he squawked in her general direction.

"Sorry you can't go out more often," Qora told him. "But you nearly got us in trouble already and we don't need a second incident." She dropped a few magmaberries on the nightstand for him, and he flitted over immediately to nip at them. "See you later."

The banquet was indeed crawling with people who favored patterns, with floral gowns and jackets sporting the tiny geometric shapes of the Old Empire. On one hand, it was beautiful; on another, it was practically an assault on the senses.

Qora managed to keep her wits about her, even as Ninan and Paqari held hands for the minister's benefit, and tried to make conversation with some of the highborn ladies, keeping to simple topics like the style of their gowns and the quality of the food.

Then it was back to the ship once more, hopping over to the city of K'uchu on the isle of Q'umir, and then to Llawt'u back on the isle of Suni, where Molten Fang could be seen from its opposite side oozing lava in a steady stream through a channel that fed straight to the sea—as it apparently did in several locations surrounding the mountain.

The *Velosaura* was docked with a prime view. Qora stood on the quarterdeck and watched the orange glowing liquid pour and strike the water, which spewed violent clouds of steam flecked with black as the lava cooled and hardened on contact. The scent of acid and minerals tinged the air, although the ship was a safe distance from danger.

Several of the crew also watched, perched on the yardarms or leaning over the railing of the forecastle, but here Qora was mostly alone.

Or so she'd thought.

She flinched at the sound of Ninan's familiar tread. She didn't know when she'd memorized it, or how one set of footfalls could differ so much from another, but when she glanced over her shoulder, he was there.

He came and stood beside her, staring out at the lava. They watched in silence for several minutes before he said, "I don't suppose you're thinking the same thing I am …"

The last time they'd basked in the warmth and the glow of lava together, he'd almost kissed her. He'd taken her hands in his, and told her not to fear the monsters. She'd learned that monsters and men weren't so different sometimes. But Ninan, at least, was gentle, and an ache spread through her body when she remembered.

She worried the inside of her cheek. "I might be."

"I'm still sorry," Ninan told her. "For not …" He held his breath for a few seconds, then released it abruptly and shook his head.

Qora knew it was better that he didn't say that out loud. "My mamáy likes to tell me, 'The wild ones don't wallow, so neither should we.' Self-pity is primarily a human trait, and an unproductive one at that."

"Good advice, I guess. Not so easy to take it."

"Sometimes I wonder," Qora said, "if it was only the fear and the fighting that bonded us. Whether we really felt what we thought we did, or if we just—"

"No." Ninan leaned closer to her and whispered it. "Don't say that. Please don't say that. You have no idea what you meant to me then—what you still do now—"

She drew back slowly. It was what she wanted to hear—of course it was—but the timing was torturous. Why did it have to be like this? Why did they have to have met the way they had? Among monsters and lies, amid political turmoil, both of them entangled in the qhapaq's agenda. "I wish I was the nobody I used to be, instead of a champion," she admitted. "And I wish you were the nobody you *pretended* to be when I met you. Maybe it could have been different. Maybe we would have seen each other at a countryside courting festival. And you would have asked me to dance. And you would have twirled me around in my red skirts and …"

Ninan flinched toward her, almost taking her hand from where she'd placed it on the rail, but catching himself. He cast a look around them, a necessary caution, and Qora did the same, verifying that no one had seen.

Now he only let his smallest finger graze hers. "I know it was you."

"I don't know what you mean."

"The charango."

"What charango?" Her face warmed at the lie.

"That's exactly why I … why you're …" He huffed, and dragged both hands backward through his hair.

"You don't have to say anything," she told him. "I just wanted you to have it. That's all. It's nothing."

"It's not nothing," he argued. "It's not nothing, because it's from you. And you're … everything."

"I'm really not."

"Your effect on me, it's … *rapapapay*," Ninan said.

"What?"

"The sound of beating wings, or lapping water. The result of a disturbance in the fluids of nature. Qora, you … *disturb* me. You have interfered with everything around me, sent waves in all directions that have struck my heart and soul. From the moment I met you, those waves have pulled me in, tossed me back and forth, tugged me deeper and deeper, and I've been floating on them ever since. Sometimes I think I'm drowning, but … then I think, maybe I'd rather not breathe anyway."

Qora's eyes welled and her lips parted, but she said nothing. What *could* she say? When Ninan was a prince, with a fiancée, and meanwhile somewhere an army of dinosaurs was growing and thriving under the relentless control of someone who refused to be stopped.

"Ninan …" She looked at him through watery eyes.

"You two aren't exactly being subtle," Sakay said as if from nowhere.

Just like the lava hitting the sea, the heat between them evaporated in a violent cloud.

Swiping at her eyes, Qora recomposed herself. "Sakay. How long have you been there?"

He raised an eyebrow. "Not long. But I was hoping to find you both. So, once again, thank you for saving me some time."

Qora's face warmed yet again when she thought of Sakay finding her and Ninan together in the hedge maze.

"Is everything alright?" Ninan said.

"Yes," Sakay replied, "but I've decided to fly back to Sumaq."

"What? Why?" Qora tensed. Being stuck on this ship without Sakay? For almost another two weeks? At the very least, he'd been a buffer. But mostly, he'd been her refuge.

"I need to see to things at the Underground. And I'm sure the Razorclaws have returned as well; they'll want updates on everything we've learned. If Izhi's going to sit on his ass, I want to see what progress we can make without him. I'm sure you both want that too."

After what he'd confessed the other night, Qora wondered if the potential to work with the Razorclaws again was igniting old flames in his heart—a burning for revenge. When it came to the qhapaq, and the way his ripples tended to spread wide and destroy the ones people like Qora and Sakay loved most, she knew that feeling well.

Ninan nodded once. "We do."

"But you're my 'bodyguard.'"

"There are more than enough guards here."

"Will you be back?" she asked.

"I don't know. I guess it depends."

Qora didn't want to think about what that meant. Instead, she wrapped her arms around him and pressed her cheek to his chest. "Please be safe."

When she released him, Ninan took a turn to embrace him as well—the sturdy kind of embrace between two men determined to keep emotions brief, with a couple of brusque pats to the shoulder blades to dispel any suspicion that they might actually care for one another.

"We'll see each other again soon," Sakay told them. "I promise."

TWENTY-EIGHT

THE *VELOSAURA'S* STOP AT KUMKA was uneventful, and Ninan felt a strong itching in his bones to move on, to get to Qaqakuna, the first city back on the main island in two weeks— and the first city back on the main island since Izhi had given him the news that Aqu Aqu was a dead end. Poring over the island maps, however, told Ninan that Qaqakuna was just forty miles from Aqu Aqu, a journey that would take him around forty minutes with the mile-a-minute pteranodons that the crew kept in the flyer hold.

But of course it was ridiculous to be doing that math when he knew full well he couldn't take one of those pteranodons without someone noticing. It was the same issue he'd had in Kicai. And besides, why should he bother to go to Aqu Aqu when Qhapaq Izhi had made it clear there was nothing there? Still, Ninan couldn't ignore the drive to see for himself.

Qaqakuna was visible from Kumka, being a mere thirteen miles across the strait, with elevations that protruded like beacons despite the distance and the curve of the earth. As the ship approached, it grew larger in Ninan's view, just as the desire to reach it grew in his mind.

He was forced to endure another banquet, this time at the Qaqakuna mayor's manor, which sat atop another rocky coast similar to Count Kisqa's in Red Cove, which was to be expected considering they shared a coastline along the northeast edge of the island.

The scenery surrounding the manor was verdant, although it appeared to require much irrigation and landscaping, as the city neared the east side of Tisqu Isle's desert zone.

While some of the guests lingered at the manor once the meal had ended, most of the *Velosaura* passengers went to return to the ship, having grown weary of so many events and likely finding them underwhelming now, as Ninan did.

Ninan hadn't seen Qora for at least half an hour, so he guessed she must have gone back early.

Paqari complained of aching feet and was eager for a bath in the "glorious copper tub" within her on-board suite and wished to make the acquaintance of the manor guests no longer.

Still not having put the idea out of his mind that he might sneak off, Ninan realized he now had the perfect opportunity to do it.

"I think I'll stay a while longer," Ninan told Paqari. "I didn't have a chance to talk long with the barterlord and I'd really like to ask him more about his plans to allocate crimson salt to the Sunfire Basin region."

Paqari sighed and waved him off. "Do as you like."

Gods, this is too easy. Ninan grinned.

When most of the *Velosaura* guests had gone, he slipped away to the manor's reptiliary and once again snatched a riding cape, only this time he wouldn't need to carry a dockworker's uniform. In anticipation of this similar situation, he'd worn his lightest-weight dress shirt and trousers, and purposely avoided a dress jacket. With the added heat, many of the other men had also foregone jackets this time, so he didn't appear too out of place anyway. He'd even slipped his serrated-tooth dagger into one of his boots, just in case he needed something extra for defense. And once again, he prepared to walk to the city to hire transportation.

"What do you think you're doing?" Qora whispered sharply.

Ninan clutched his chest and spun to face her. "Great ceratopsian skulls …"

She peered into the dinoshelter's entrance. "You're lucky it's me and not your fiancée. Or one of the guards. Where are you going?"

He put the hood up on the cloak. "Aqu Aqu."

She furrowed her brows. "That's at least forty miles."

Clearly she'd been studying the maps too, which gave Ninan a strange little jolt of admiration.

"Anyway, there's nothing there," she added.

"Says Izhi."

"You don't believe him?"

Ninan shook his head. "I don't know. But all of this doesn't add up. I have to see it with my own eyes."

"And what exactly are you expecting to see in the *dark*?"

"There's a waning crescent, at least. And besides, dark is the best time to look for clues. If the training grounds are hidden, there may be lanterns or torches that would give them away easily at night. Whoever my father's got manning that place can't operate in complete obscurity. And darkness has the added benefit of keeping *me* hidden; I can't just fly over some military base in the daylight without being spotted—and possibly shot down."

She put her hands on her hips and analyzed him. "Fine. I'm going with you."

His instinct was to tell her no, but he was certain Sakay had denied her request to accompany him to Tisqu in the first place, and yet here she was. So, what difference would it make? And it wasn't like he *didn't* want her company.

He did, however, give her lavender dress a pointed once-over, scanning the material that—while lightweight enough for an excursion—hung all the way to her ankles. Her sandals, at least, were flat-heeled, with thick straps, but still not ideal footwear for flying.

She huffed and stepped close to him, bent down, and slid her fingers into his left boot. He shivered at the touch, but it was brief. When she came up empty, she went for the right boot instead.

Ninan squirmed. "How did you know——"

"I could tell by the way you were walking earlier. I just forgot which side it was on."

After she removed the dagger, she hunched over and stabbed its blade into the skirt of her dress. She worked it sideways and twisted behind herself and maneuvered it again until the new length of the skirt ended just above the knee, and discarded the excess fabric. Then she made several vertical cuts that divided the remaining skirt into wide strips to allow her legs more mobility.

Ninan made a point to turn his gaze elsewhere, blushing.

She pinched the blade and handed the dagger back to him, hilt first. "Also, I'm going to need a ranged weapon."

ꙫ ꙫ ꙫ

It had been an unanticipated additional risk to sneak into the manor's armory, Ninan thought, and a likewise unanticipated disappointment to find no crossbows there, but as he well knew, Qora refused to go out into the night unarmed—she lamented that she'd arrived at the manor that way, but it would have been impossible to bring her own weapon to the banquet—so Ninan had conceded to the risk and Qora had conceded to carry one of the longbows that were available.

"It's not what I'm used to," she admitted, "but I see no reason I can't work with it just fine."

They grabbed a riding cloak for her as well, and made their way into the city.

Renting a pair of pteranodons cost a full sack of silvers and a hefty deposit, but Ninan was prepared. He paid the handler, who kept staring at Qora throughout the transaction process—taking down Ninan's false information, selecting the fastest flyers from the shelter, discussion of price and terms—and Ninan had begun to think better about having brought her. She was probably more interterrenally recognizable than he was, having so recently won a competition between all Five Terrains. The handler could simply be admiring her, maybe have caught a glimpse of her shredded dress beneath her cloak, but regardless Ninan didn't care for the intensity of the man's gaze.

"Come on." He steered Qora away the second he could reasonably do so.

They might have been able to get by with just one flyer, but in case something happened to it—like the way he'd lost his transportation in Ika—he didn't want to end up stranded.

They stopped to buy a couple of lanterns as well, as the waning crescent moon would be too dim to see by between cities and villages, then mounted and took flight.

The glow of the lights below was more concentrated back toward the city center, with illumination growing more sparse at the edges, and only a few sporadic lights on the coast. Ninan and Qora flew southward in a tense silence, with little more than a whistle of wind and the flap of the pteranodons' wings to punctuate it.

Rapapapay, Ninan thought. He wondered how nature could function properly with everything making waves in all directions, in constant contradiction of each other—waves of sound, waves of light, waves of raw energy, moving through air and water and earth. He wondered how pure chaos didn't reign supreme, how anything could maintain form or structure or rhythm. As he watched the wind blow through Qora's hair, he knew those waves could be beautiful, of course, but he also knew that that same wind could destroy entire buildings and cities when it grew violent. The worst part was that he could never predict which kind he would have to face.

Ninan and Qora probably hadn't even made it a full two miles from the city when a harsh, reptilian cry pierced the calm. The pteranodons trilled in response. The source of the cry had come from several hundred yards to the west.

"What was that?" Qora asked.

"It sounded like …"

Distant screams followed, and then another shrieking roar, and then more screams.

Ninan and Qora exchanged glances.

This wasn't some large, wild reptile hunting in the woods. For one thing, there were no woods here to speak of. And, the sounds of sheer terror from one of these villages foretold something much more sinister.

Without any discussion, Ninan and Qora turned their flyers and descended toward the commotion. Amid the screams, wood splintered and glass shattered, and the small flames of the village lanterns spread to a large, beckoning blaze.

The vague silhouette of some large theropod darkened the

otherwise glowing streets. Most citizens scattered, while a few remained outdoors with weapons or tools at the ready.

Several homes had caught fire, flames billowing in the dry wind and lapping at nearby structures threatening to catch onto those too.

The people in the street slashed at the dinosaur with long blades, and fired arrows in its direction.

Qora clenched her nearly-bare thighs around the saddle and nocked an arrow onto her stolen bow, angling it laterally—so that it took the shape of a crossbow—and drawing back. She fired from the air, striking the back of the reptile's head.

The arrow stuck for half a second before the movement of the reptile's flexing muscles ejected it.

As Ninan and Qora flew closer, the species of the reptile became more clear.

"It's an irritator," Ninan said. "Or … something like it."

It was a type of spinosaurian but in place of a sail, a row of conical spikes lined its back, from the crown of its head to the tip of its tail, each extending several inches. Its skin was a mottle of yellow and brown. It stood twice as high as a fully grown man, and its snout was long and finely tapered.

On pteranodonback, Ninan and Qora circled the creature, trying to draw its attention away from the people in the street. Qora took another two shots, a bit unsteadily as she wasn't used to this bow, aiming at the underbelly, but every one of her arrows bounced.

This has to be one of my father's, Ninan thought. It only made him more certain that the qhapaq did have a facility nearby; he had to, because it was clear this creature wasn't native to these lands. If it were, the people would have encountered one before, and perhaps known how to defend themselves against it. Furthermore, there was no natural habitat for such a thing in this region. Spinosaurians were semiaquatic, while freshwater would be scarce here.

"You know what you have to do," Ninan told Qora.

She grimaced, but nodded.

While the irritator raged below, snapping its jaws at the people surrounding it, arrows and throwing blades struck its scales, again tossed aside the second it took a step in any direction.

Ninan swooped low on his flyer, so low and close to the irritator that Qora gasped.

When the irritator opened its mouth to snap at him, Qora fired into its throat.

Its roar went high pitched for an instant before cutting to complete silence.

Qora's arrow tip emerged from the back of the irritator's head.

The irritator wavered, then collapsed in a large, scaly heap.

꩜꩜꩜

From the ground, the irritator seemed much larger. Having landed the pteranodons, Ninan and Qora helped put out the fires with the other citizens who had come forth once it was clear that the irritator would no longer be a threat. This took about an hour, and then it was time to tend to the injured and assess the damage to buildings.

"It was only a matter of time before it happened to us," said a woman who clutched a small child to her chest.

"What do you mean?" Qora asked.

"Surely you've heard about the other attacks …"

Qora glanced at Ninan. She must have been thinking these were the same attacks they had discussed back in Rikracha.

"Several villages have been victim to dinosaur attacks—specifically dinosaurs that are not native to the islands. We fear it may be a type of biological warfare."

That's what the qhapaq would want them to think. But this was no escape of specimen, as the sailbeast had been—or, at least, that's what he'd *thought* the sailbeast had been. Ninan was certain the irritator, and any other reptiles attacking villages throughout the islands, was released on purpose as a sort of … test.

Two younger men inspected the irritator carcass.

One of them wrung his hands, a sour look on his face. He whispered to the other: "This is our fault."

Ninan hesitated, not wanting to be rude and reveal that he'd overheard, but he had to know. "*Your* fault? How?"

The other young man shot his companion a warning look.

"We found the reptile a few miles south of here, a few days ago. We used skyrock to drive it into a cave. It wasn't that hard; we had a lot of weapons, and there were more of us …"

Were.

"We thought we'd trapped it securely—piled heavy rocks at the entrance—but somehow it escaped. My brother and I followed its tracks here, except … we were too late."

Ninan clenched his fists. He glanced around at the injured; no one had died, apparently, but many were bloodied and some would likely bear scars for the rest of their lives. Some of the people who had been helping these young men *had* died, it seemed, and many more could have died tonight. This was only the beginning if nobody stopped the qhapaq.

He scoffed and stalked off.

He didn't know where was going, but he needed to get away from everyone else. The heat and his dress shirt and the thought of an indeterminate amount of loose killer reptiles seemed to be restricting his airway. From back at the attack site, Qora's voice barely reached his ears now, as she told the young man, "It's not your fault … I know you were just trying to …" fading behind him as he continued to walk.

Ninan walked for several minutes beyond the homes, and finally stopped to pace a clearing of sparse, brown grass, pulling at his hair.

How many other villages were facing monsters like the irritator? How had Izhi not been able to find the base yet? Time was running out—Ninan could feel it. Somehow, he sensed that the days leading up to his wedding were very close in number to the days leading up to whenever his father would begin a sincere effort to take back the empire. Of course this wasn't certain; maybe it was only paranoia. But the qhapaq rarely did anything without planning it down to the details. Throwing Ninan to the wilderness after his disinheritance had been one of the few rash and uncalculated decisions the qhapaq had ever made, as far as Ninan could remember, but the qhapaq had rectified it quickly and methodically with the Venture, and with the arranged marriage to Paqari, and by threatening Pidru and everyone in Thak.

The timing of this tour and these attacks could not have been an accident. Although surely his father hadn't expected him and Qora to be flying over this village at the very moment they had, or for those young men to have tried to trap the irritator days ago, inadvertently setting it on a rampage that ended here tonight. That had been lucky. It had been a good thing that Ninan wasn't giving up, that he relentlessly sought information;

otherwise, he would not have been here to witness this. But the benefit of that knowledge didn't make it any less distressing.

With heavy footsteps, he headed back to the village, where he swept past Qora as she finished wrapping up a little girl's burnt arm. She looked up as he approached his pteranodon.

"There you go," she said to the girl. "Try to get some rest."

Ninan mounted the flyer.

Qora came after him. "Are you leaving?"

"I still have to try to get to Aqu Aqu tonight. Are you coming?"

She glanced back at the villagers, and then up at him again. "Ninan, you can't still think it's a good idea to go. It was a flimsy idea to begin with—and that was before we spent more than an hour dealing with all of *this*."

"I have to go. Come or don't come. But I'm going." He kicked his heels and commanded the pteranodon to rise.

Qora muttered something to the villagers, some form of apology and well wishes that he couldn't make out once the wind got into his ears, but a minute later she and her flyer eased into his periphery.

"Ninan!" she called. "Don't do this! You need to land. Right now. It's late ... and you're angry. We've already risked too much being out here this long. Please touch down!"

He ignored her.

"Ninan!" she called again.

Again, he ignored her. He couldn't argue with her right now. It was hard enough to hear each other, and anyway, he couldn't allow her voice to try and calm him. Calm was the last thing he needed. He needed to ride out this anger and let it lead him somewhere productive. He couldn't keep sitting back and doing nothing—especially not after what he'd just seen in that village.

For a long moment Qora continued to fly with him in resigned silence, hanging back as if in hopes that he would slow down, but he only leaned into the flight, urging the pteranodon faster.

Then: "*Apo-Kimsa Kallpa.*"

Ninan cast a sharp look at her, blood pulsing through his veins like a drum. He wouldn't have expected such a visceral reaction to his own name, but coming from *her* …

The pteranodon wavered under his distracted control. Clenching his jaw, nostrils flared, he swooped into a descent over one of several mesas beneath them.

He landed with Qora right behind. They both dismounted abruptly and came toward one another.

"How dare you call me that," he snapped. "You know better than anyone how much I *hate*—"

"How dare you *force* me to call you that? How dare you force me to remind you who you are. Even if you don't like it, you still have to—"

"I can be who and what I choose."

"Can you, though?"

"I can try. I can keep trying to be more than a useless highborn who does whatever the qhapaq says. Not just my father, but *any* qhapaq. Izhi. Achik. Someone has to actually *do* something about these monsters my father has already begun unleashing on innocent people. And if Aqu Aqu really isn't the site, I need to know for certain."

"So you'll get there and … do what? It's the dead of night. I'm sure you only vaguely know the way from the maps. You could end up lost. Or worse, caught. If you get caught, there won't be a second chance to redeem you this time, no Venture or noble feat you can use to get you back in good standing. Your father will have you *killed*."

He threw up his hands and turned on his heel. "So be it, then!"

She followed him and shouted at his back. "Open rebellion from anyone in a position like yours never ends well. You have to keep playing the game. Working the system. You have to stick to the plan and watch from the inside. *Quietly*. You can't go around acting like a Razorclaw!"

Ninan reached up for his pteranodon's saddle pommel. "Yes, I know I'll never be like Sakay. Thanks for the reminder."

Before he could step into the stirrup, however, to pull himself up, Qora hooked her fingers around his bicep and tugged him backward.

He shrugged her off but faced her again, fuming. "Can't you ever just—"

"I don't want or expect you to be like Sakay," she told him. "But I do expect you to appreciate your unique position and its value—and not compromise it all in a fit of blind rage."

"My rage is not blind. I can see *very* clearly."

"I don't think you can. I think you're throwing your fists like you always do, but the heat and the pain of the fight are getting to you. The sweat and the blood are dripping into your eyes, and you're starting to falter. I know you're tired of pretending, tired of trying to keep your wits about you. Don't you think I understand that? Don't you think I'm tired too? And *furious*? But maybe people like us—princes and champions—don't get to be who we want, or have what we want. Maybe that's just the sacrifice we have to make, to tamp down the raging fires we hold inside, so that the ones with less power can rise up around us— *because* of us. If there's any hope of saving this continent from war, our best chance is to play our parts. To let go of that urge to fight and defy. To accept that no one can win every battle." Her eyes welled and her voice began to break. "We've both already won more than we deserve."

The sight of her emerging tears only fanned the flames of Ninan's fury. "There are too many battles at once! On one front, I'm fighting to find the growing source of my father's power. On another, I'm fighting the guilt of all of my failures—the failure that allowed my friends to live in fear under my father's guards. And on another front, I'm fighting everything I'm feeling for ..." His breaths turned shallow as he looked at her, as her head gave a little shake like she didn't want him to say it. He took a step toward her. "For ..."

"Ninan ..."

He framed her face in his hands. "You want me to stop fighting? Stop defying? Fine. *This* battle, against myself, against what I want whenever I'm standing next to you ... I give up. I surrender."

His lips met hers in a reckless collision.

He held this fierce and desperate kiss. He allowed for only the tiniest release before he kissed her again.

A soft whimper escaped her throat as she seized the fabric of his shirt and pulled him closer, drawing him closer. She slid her hands up his back and gently clawed at his shoulder blades.

Ninan's whole body relaxed. Qora was an oasis in this desert, after having taunted him for weeks like a mirage—but now he was fully in her midst and she was real and tangible, quenching him.

The give and take between them became almost rhythmic. She combed her fingers through his hair, and then he found her lips again, and with each kiss he fell deeper and faster, as though he'd jumped from a cliff and was becoming more lost to gravity with every passing second, and he knew he might end up crushed and broken at the bottom of a canyon but he didn't care.

It would be worth it.

TWENTY-NINE

THERE WAS NO ONE ELSE IN THE WORLD besides the two of them for those several minutes, standing there on the mesa in the middle of the desert under stars, the hot wind meandering around them. Even though this place was dry as bones, and would be insufferable for any extended period of time, Qora wished she never had to leave that spot, or Ninan's embrace.

But at some point, she pulled back for air, and touched her forehead to his and whispered, "We have to go."

Wordlessly, he nodded, and they parted to fly back to the city.

〉〉〉

They returned the pteranodons, and walked to the manor holding hands with fingers intertwined, with a melancholy between them. Ninan left his cloak and the longbow at the edge of the property—perhaps the staff would blame the items on some drunken guest—while Qora kept her own cloak to hide her cut-up dress.

Back near the ship, Ninan kissed her in the shadows once more before ascending the gangway, reluctant to let go of her hand. She insisted he go on ahead of her, and that she would board several minutes later to avoid any suspicion that they'd been together this entire time.

The guards regarded Qora solemnly as she boarded and made her way back to her sleeping cabin. She raised her lantern and passed through the quiet passageway until she found her door, and when she did, Ninan was waiting for her.

She couldn't help but smile a little, still not fully allowing herself to think of the consequences of where they'd been and what they'd been doing. "You know this sort of defeats the purpose of coming in separately ..."

"Not entirely," he whispered.

They'd at least fooled the guards well enough—Qora hoped—along with any other potential witnesses.

Qora slipped between Ninan and her cabin door, facing him. "You know we can't let this happen again." She trembled as he slipped his hands under her cloak and trailed his fingertips along her bare arms.

"I know. I just ..." He closed his eyes and took a deep breath. "I'm not ready to say good night. I can't. Not yet."

Her chin quivered. "You have to."

He steadied her chin with one finger and drew her mouth up to his. He murmured against her lips, "I will—eventually."

Gods, she loved the taste of him. The feel of the tip of his tongue. His rough fingers on her skin.

Allowing him to start this up again—the kinds of touches they'd left behind at the end of the Venture—had been a grave mistake, because she knew now that pretending she didn't feel this would be so much more difficult. She ached deeply just *thinking* about it; how would she cope when she actually had to endure it?

"We have to stop"—she drew back just enough to allow herself to speak, panting—"before this gets us both into trouble we can't recover from."

"Too late," said a voice at the end of the passageway.

Qora's throat went thick as Ninan turned away from her.

Paqari.

🌒🌒🌒

Qora had expected Ninan to extract himself from proximity to her, but he didn't. He held her, almost proudly, although not without a hint of shame for his own lack of control.

Paqari didn't say anything for several agonizing seconds. She seemed to be warring within herself over something, but Qora for the life of her could not guess what. Were her pursed lips and tight glare only the result of a blow to her pride, or was there something more? Even though she had loved and lost someone else, did she actually care for Ninan now?

"Your Highness ..." Qora pled. She slowly forced Ninan to release her, taking a step toward the princess.

The princess held up one hand. "Don't."

A tightness built in Qora's chest. Paqari was already subject to traditions that would leave her on the fringes of her own marriage as time went on; she didn't need Qora making a fool of her this way before vows had even been exchanged. Qora couldn't say the princess was her friend, but under different circumstances, she might have been.

"I'm sorry," Qora told her.

"You're not."

"She is," Ninan argued. "This was entirely my fault. She begged me to stay away from her, but I wouldn't."

"Yes, it was clear she wants *nothing* to do with you ..." Paqari crossed her arms and narrowed her eyes.

"You're the one who brought her on board," Ninan argued.

249

"Oh, so it's *my* fault you've degraded our match. Of course. How could I possibly blame you for making *your own choices* in the matter?"

"That's not what I meant. I just meant that—"

"Actually," Paqari said, "you're right. It *was* my fault. I was aware of the rumors. I even sensed there might be some truth to them, with the way the two of you often seemed to find and be near one another—or involved in tense cross-conversations. I even imagined longing looks across the deck. But I told myself I was paranoid. I told myself surely I was letting idle speculation among lowborns get the better of me."

It was ridiculous, Qora thought, for a young woman with so much beauty and power to appear so … helpless. But Qora sensed it had to do with the lover she lost, and to the inevitable future that awaited her no matter whom she married. It was lucky for Paqari that she would marry Ninan, however; he was kind and caring, and he would be good to her in whatever way he could despite the expectations put upon them. Despite not loving her. He might even be capable of *growing* to love her. Not like many sons of qhapaqs who only saw their first wife as a means to an heir. The princess had the opportunity for a better marriage than most in her situation … but Qora was making a mess of that right now. She wrung her hands. "Paqari, I really am—"

"I don't care for the pity in your eyes, champion. I don't want it and I don't need it. But honestly, your part in this is the worst of all. I expected this sort of thing from *him*." She shot Ninan a seething glare. "Not from you. While I never liked your style and I found your manners untamed, I did at least respect you."

Did.

That was like a bolt to the chest.

Ninan came forward. "I told you it's not her fault. Please don't be angry with her. I made her promises I couldn't possibly have kept. And then I couldn't leave her alone."

Paqari's chest rose and fell heavily. "It doesn't matter. I'm too angry to keep standing here and discussing this. Do as you wish, but I beg you to at least have the decency not to get caught by anyone else." She turned on her heel and thundered down the passageway, disappearing around the turn.

Qora and Ninan exchanged glances. Qora felt like she was sinking to the bottom of the sea, all life force having drained from her body as her lungs filled and her last breath bubbled to the surface without her.

"Go to her," Qora choked.

He stared at her with a pleading expression.

"It's not over yet," she insisted. "Play your part. *Go*."

Now it was Ninan's turn for his eyes to well. He cupped her face but didn't kiss her this time. "I'm sorry."

And then he went.

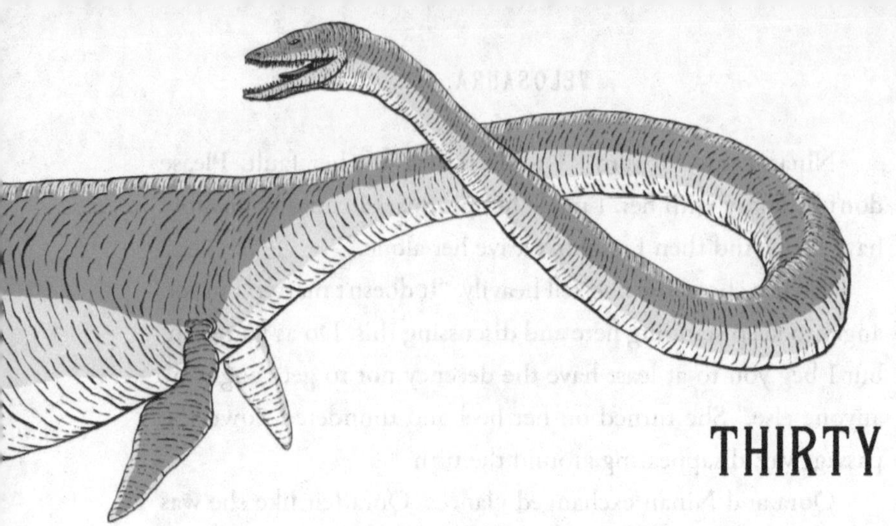

THIRTY

NINAN CAUGHT UP WITH PAQARI just as she'd stormed into her suite. She was about to swing the double doors shut simultaneously on his face when he stuck the toe of his boot a few inches inside, stopping the doors before they came together.

He winced when they crushed his foot between them.

Paqari gasped. "Spirits. What are you doing?"

"Please talk to me." Ninan forced his way through the opening.

The princess glared at the intrusion. "I will not."

"Look, I know you might not be able to understand—and I'm not trying to make excuses—but at least tell me ... what happens next."

He hated the idea that he was at her mercy, but he was. If she revealed what he'd done, he could be severely punished. His own father might not punish him for "dalliances" provided no one else knew, but Qhapaq Achik might consider it a great dishonor and break the arrangement, and *that* would definitely evoke some kind of punishment—with Achik's cooperation and provision of island property for the reptile army likely being contingent on the arrangement. Even though Ninan was actively trying to sabotage his father's plans, his father obviously wasn't meant to *know* about it.

"What happens *next*? What—" she pinched the bridge of her nose and took a deep, heavy breath before she relaxed—a semblance of tranquility but with a fiery sense of loathing—and looked him in the eyes. "Obviously I'm going to tell my father! His agreement with Qhapaq Apo was based on the idea that you had redeemed yourself from your old ways. But this … This just shows me that you're as much of a traitor as you ever were!"

His heart thundered. "Paqari …"

"I mean, sure I will fully expect you to do this sort of thing once I've produced your first heir for you. You're only doing what all highborn men do. But, *right now* …" Her eyes burned with disgust.

That's really how she saw him? Like other highborn men? Like his father?

"I … never wanted to be like them," he said.

She raised her chin. "It's in your blood, Apo-Kimsa."

He stepped deeper into the room and sharpened his tone. "It's in these traditions, too. In the way people like you and I are forced into arrangements for political gain. I don't know about you but I was coerced and manipulated and threatened into this engagement. Is that what you want to hear?"

Paqari flinched but didn't say anything. A flicker of understanding passed over her countenance, although Ninan wasn't sure to what extent she might have understood his pain points.

"A year ago," Ninan continued, "I was getting blisters on my hands cutting quinoa—poorly, I might add—with no hope of ever returning to this kind of life. Like an idiot, I still thought I was missing something. Despite my father's abuse, I still wanted to earn his respect. I didn't know how good I had it, in isolation, living like a lowly but at least normal human being. And then the man dragged me back to Kallpa House and insisted I compete in the Venture—led me to believe it was my own choice, when the entire time he had elaborate plans to get me to do what he wanted so that I could be worthy to be engaged to you, to travel on this cursed ship, for no other reason than to win favor with Tisqu. You can draw your own conclusions as to why that is.

"But I never expected Qora to affect my behavior within the competition; I never expected to feel *anything* for her, let alone *everything*. It was impractical, and inconvenient, and most definitely not inconsequential. So forgive me if I've found it difficult to break a bond forged in the fires of life and death, when I never asked to be born as prince, never asked to be cast out, never asked to be brought back, and sure as the Grave World never asked to fight monsters and men for the right to stand before you tonight trying to explain myself when I'm frankly still trying to figure out the very essence of who and what I'm supposed to be—with no success, I might add."

Again, Paqari didn't speak. She stared at him, her chest rising and falling slowly and meaningfully.

Ninan held up both hands as if in surrender. "For what it's worth, I *am* sorry for disrespecting our marriage. Even though neither of us had any choice in the arrangement, you don't deserve the disgrace I've brought on you and your family. For that, I do sincerely apologize."

After a moment, the princess put her palm on his chest and gently pushed him backward until he stepped out of her suite, and said, "Don't let me catch you with her again."

Then she closed the door.

ꓽꓽꓽ

Sleep for Ninan had been as turbulent as the waves that rocked the boat. He felt somehow that he had lost consciousness for periods of time, although he felt like he'd been awake for hours too. At twilight, he was up and dressing himself, and then he'd sat on the bed with his knees up, entertaining Tuko with a strip of papyr.

As the first sounds of waking passengers reached his ears, he emerged from his suite.

He wondered if Qora had already gone above decks. As he passed her cabin, her open door caught his attention and, despite his better judgment, he peered inside.

The room was empty.

But not just empty of Qora; all her things were missing.

The only thing that remained was a bundle of knotted strings on her desk. A quipu. Or the semblance of a quipu, made from the fabric of the dress she'd cut the night before, cut further into narrow strips.

The code within the knots read: I'M SORRY

His pulse kicked up and he raced to the flyer hold, boots thundering on the wood as he went. Several of the crew paused at his haste, but he didn't care how ridiculous he must have looked. He burst into the hold and surveyed the swoop, but there were only two slate-purple pteranodons left—the two with which the *Velosaura* had set sail, which belonged to the Huapayas.

Qora's flyer was gone. And so was she.

Fire, water, and air remind us
that not all things are meant to be
fully grasped in the hands.
Some things must flicker
and flow of their own accord.

Allpan proverb

THIRTY-ONE

EVEN WITH THE FLYER-RIDING GOGGLES to shield against the sharp wind, Qora's eyes burned. Lack of sleep, paired with intermittent tears throughout the night, had left her weary and vulnerable. At least she had the riding cloak she'd stolen from the mayor's manor to keep her warm as the air turned cold upon nearing the Runaqan mainland. Even in the warmer winds, it had kept her skin from chafing.

When the mist-shrouded mountains of Qhusi appeared in the distance, Qora felt as though she'd been everywhere in the world these past weeks, as the scent of the crisp air welcomed her home. She soared over and around the perimeter of the large peaks, and then over the foothills, scanning the landscape for the meadow and the particular trees that marked her property until her two-story stone house appeared.

For once she could traverse the skies without recognition, a cloaked rider on a dark flyer with no distinguishable features. In peace, she descended on the grounds surrounding her home, clinging to the pteranodon's pommel for a moment as she released a sigh of relief before she dismounted.

She'd half expected her mamáy or one of her brothers to come out and greet her—or to already be outside tending to something—but the house and the yard were empty and quiet but for the compies scuttling about and the alpacas bleating from behind their enclosure.

Inside, the house was empty as well, and Qora stood for a moment in the entryway, unsure how to conduct herself.

The Heritage Festival, she thought suddenly.

It was today.

The qhapaq had expected her to fly over in the midday parade, before Paqari had insisted Qora extend her leave for the *Velosaura* tour.

Qora imagined her mamáy would be selling yarns among the vendors in the city, and the boys would be assisting—or enjoying the festivities.

She glanced at the green jacket that still hung on the hook by the doorway, right where she'd left it the night before she'd flown off for Tisqu with Sakay. After the lecture she'd given Ninan about sacrifice and playing his part, she couldn't rightly ignore what the jacket stood for, what it meant for her in this moment. Now that she was home, it didn't make sense for her to hide here alone. She had a part to play as well.

The consequences of getting caught with Ninan were uncertain at this point, but she could at least try to please the qhapaq—distract him, if nothing else. Her departure from the ship would also allow her not to worsen the problem.

She took a deep breath before she approached the jacket, running her fingers over the stiff material. Slowly, she removed her riding cloak, then took the jacket off its hook and slipped her arms inside one by one. She gave herself a moment to accept it on her body before she went to her room to look for bands to tie her hair. Twisting her hair into those two braids was like a strange farewell ritual to whatever freedom—if being trapped in a cage of her own feelings could be considered freedom—she'd possessed on the *Velosaura*, but she did her best to complete it with dignity.

She swapped her feminine boots for the costumed hunting boots, her real crossbow for her show crossbow, and took to the skies once again. Of course the qhapaq might not appreciate her arrival on a black pteranodon instead of one of his, but she hoped he would at least appreciate her appearance.

This time rather than circumventing the city, Qora flew directly between the outer mountains to where the heart of Qhusi was nestled, and swooped down to the domed mountain at the center that was lined with roads and buildings and the connecting bridges and stairways.

Street music rang out, with the drumbeats reaching her ears first, and then came the uptempo melody of horns and bone flutes.

The midday parade had already begun, with rows of dinosaurs marching side by side and in a long queue, decorated with caparisons in the terrenal colors.

Pageant wagons were interspersed throughout the queue, carrying costumed actors that represented historical figures or characters from beloved stories.

Traditional dancers moved uniformly in groups while onlookers waved banners and miniature terrenal flags with the spinosaur-and-shield emblem.

Highborns and celebrities rode through in their seat-boxed triceratops as usual but today were draped in red silk and black tassels, while a manually borne float with a large black-and-red spinosaur figure made of gypsum plaster headed the whole thing.

Qora soared lower and steered her pteranodon into a flight path that aligned with the parade, coming up on the tail end, where she slowed and eased over the route.

Spectators and parade-participants alike gazed up to where she flew, quickly recognizing her and cheering.

She held onto the pommel with one hand and raised the other in a slow wave, and even managed a smile as she turned to each side of the street in greeting. Among the cheers and chatter, she caught a few of their comments while she passed.

"It's the Raptoriva!"

"She's back!"

"Oh, she looks majestic!"

"What a beautiful black pteranodon!"

"Raptoriva!"

"Where's she been?

"Qora Kanchaya!"

Qora continued to smile, particularly as she reached the city square, where Qhapaq Apo was seated in a comfortable, tented display with his quyas and Ninan's brothers. The qhapaq actually stood when he caught sight of her, his brows furrowing. She threw him an apologetic look as she dipped her head in as much of a bow as she could manage from her saddled position in the air, and soared onward.

As the market vendors came into view, Qora couldn't possibly have missed the glorious new stand she'd purchased for her mamáy, with its mahogany poles and bleached canvas tenting that allowed the yarns to stand out in a spectral pattern. Hundreds of skeins of alpaca yarn filled baskets across the table and all around the base while customers rifled through and made their purchases. Qora's mamáy was busy enough that both boys were helping her rearrange the skeins and make calculations. She looked up and gasped as Qora swept past.

Qora waved, but the expression on her mamáy's face caught her off guard. She couldn't describe the feeling it gave her. It was as though her mamáy had seen a ghost—but it wasn't as though Qora had been gone such a long time.

She's just surprised.

After a rough night, and then a wearying, four-hour flight from the islands, it wasn't unreasonable that Qora was simply imagining things. Her eyes still burned, and her head ached, and she was certain if she were to lie down she could fall asleep on the spot. In fact, once she was finished here, she thought she just might try that; she could certainly use the rest.

When she reached the head of the parade, she performed several flying loops—sweeping up and around in tight curves that threatened to unseat her before everyone. The cheers that she received in response sent her twirling in another round, until she was too dizzy to continue and thus gave a final gesture of appreciation before flying off.

She landed at the hitching grounds west of the city center, where a vast lot full of spaced posts served as a place to station reptiles. It was nearly full, but she located a spot and, with a bowline knot, tied her pteranodon and hurried to the market to meet her family.

As she neared the streets, spectators spilled into every crevice of the city, crammed between buildings and into alleyways, cluttering the sidewalks and even stepping into the gutters. The aroma of smoke and roast dinosaur meats caught in her nose, along with the faint odor of ruck. She'd have to make her way up three—or was it four?—blocks to get to her mamáy's stand.

Children clamored for a better view of the parade, and mobile food vendors shouted the items on their menus, and parade musicians' music grated against the music of the sidewalk performers. Qora put up her hood and joined the chaos, anticipating that everyone would be too caught up to pay attention to her conspicuous clothing. After all, they'd seen her in the sky only minutes ago, and might not expect that she'd be among them on the ground now.

Qora kept to the edges, inching her way up the street. Still dizzy from her wild flying, the din and the crowd overwhelmed her, and she hurried on in hopes of reaching a respite more quickly. She'd just stepped off the curb toward the next block, however, when the profile of a young man up ahead instantly shot a sensation of ice through her veins. As though this were literally true, she froze in place, causing several other pedestrians to crash into her. But she made no apologies, nor did she move out of the way while she strained her vision to make out whether what she was seeing was genuine.

And then the man turned his head and Qora's only view of him was from behind.

But there was something familiar in his stride, in the way he held his shoulders.

Qora's feet seemed to move independently of her now, picking up speed, weaving through the mass of people. She nudged between them and pushed with as much force as was polite while verging on aggression. Her pulse pounded and the noise around her seemed to muffle.

She had to get to him.

What am I doing?

This was crazy. What did she expect would happen? She knew that once—*if*—she could see his face, she would be instantly reassured that she had hallucinated. She would see a stranger, and he would think she was a deranged girl, and she would completely embarrass herself.

It just wasn't possible. She *knew* that.

And yet, something deep in her core urged her to keep going, held her in a vise grip of desperation, would not let her stop.

She could almost get to him. He was within arm's reach.

She stretched out to touch his elbow.

Her fingers caught his sleeve.

He stopped. Turned.

His eyes locked on hers.

Spirits, it was those same eyes—she knew them so well.

Or, *had known* them, once.

She choked out a sob.

Recognition filled his gaze.

The whole world seemed to fall out from under her.

Before her vision went blank, she managed a single word.

"Ollan."

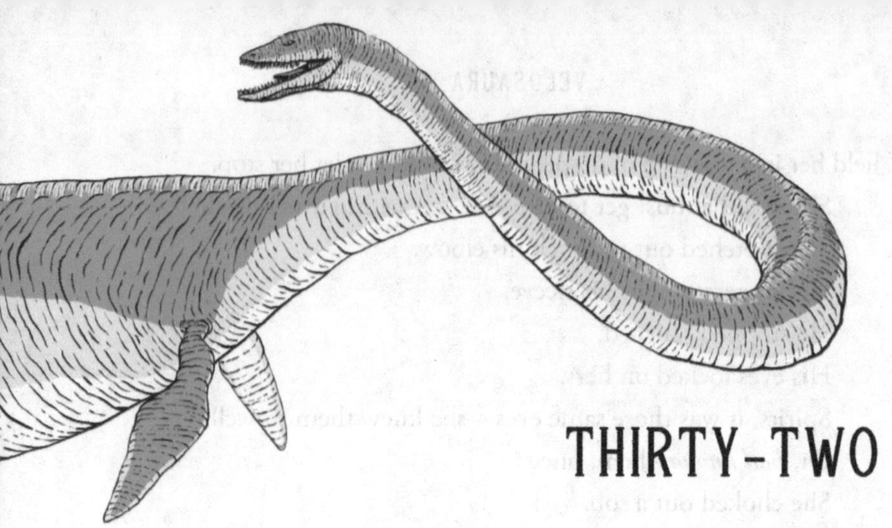

"YOU MUST BE JOKING," SAKAY SAID. "Three hundred silvers?"

The trader on the opposite side of the counter pushed the leathers forward. "That's being generous. This is genuine aquilops hide."

Sakay scoffed and leaned in with a sharp gaze. "Do you honestly think I can't spot a fake?" He pushed the leathers back at the trader.

"You're making a mistake."

"I'm not." He crossed his arms and waited as the trader hesitated, then picked up the leathers and left.

I don't have time for this, Sakay thought, returning to the task of sorting through his inventory.

In his absence, the workers he'd left in charge had nearly run the place into the ground. They'd accepted several questionable trades—which he was parsing right now to ensure they hadn't paid for counterfeits—everything from rare teeth to medicinal bone powders to special "foreign" liquors. They'd also allowed a black market deal to take place at the Underground, which had started a brawl that drew authorities directly to the establishment, but thankfully there was no evidence when they arrived, and none of the witnesses had been willing to talk.

It was lucky he'd returned when he had, before anything more chaotic had happened, but he'd spent the past few days trying to get things back on track.

He was in the middle of analyzing the authenticity of a raw emerald when a messenger approached him at the counter. The messenger presented a folded papyr.

"Thank you," he told the woman.

Sakay flipped open the flaps to read the words at the center.

COME TO MOUNT QAQRA AS SOON AS YOU CAN.

〰〰〰

When Sakay arrived at Mount Qaqra, the grounds were crawling with additional dinosaurs. Not only had Wayra retained her swoop of pteranodons, but apparently she'd also adopted ten rust-feathered hypsilophodons (herbivorous ornithopods that stood waist high), a skitter of exotic long-fingered compsognathus (all of whom were very dextrous and grabby), and several microceratus (bipedal ceratopsians not much bigger than the compies).

The new dinosaurs wandered in relative proximity to one another, every so often lending their attention to the house, as though it contained some particularly alluring food source.

"Long time no see," Wayra said as she came to greet him.

Sakay looked over the new acquisitions, raising an eyebrow at the way they waited. "It looks like you've been busy the last few weeks. Although, I have to say … I'm a little confused."

Kuy and Gorgo were apparently off tending to other things, but a few seconds later, Req emerged from the stone house. His hair was mussed and sweaty, and he panted with each step.

"Sakay. Glad you could make it."

"Thanks. Is everything alright?"

"Not exactly." Req glanced at the dinosaurs.

"Dominite?" Sakay guessed. "You must have had time to work on the sample by now."

Req nodded. "I have."

"He's cluttered half my house with his experiments," said Wayra. "A necessary evil, I suppose, to be able to test his findings on my reptiles."

"So you know what it's made of, then?" Sakay asked.

"As we assumed," Req told him, "it's a refined form of skyrock, boiled down to its purest elements. What I did not expect, however, was that it contained no *additional* elements. Instead, it appears to remain isolated—but it has been chemically restructured in such a way as to change its properties and effects."

"What does that mean, 'chemically restructured'?" Sakay asked.

Req bent down and gathered four stones in one hand and two sticks in the other. "Skyrock is a compound called nebulon sauride, which means it contains the elements nebulum"—he held up the stones—"and saurigon"—he held up the sticks—"in a specific combination." He laid the items in an arrangement: two stones and one stick together, then another two stones and one stick together. "The dominite, however, is not a different substance, nor is it nebulon sauride chemically bonded with a new element, which I thought it might be. Instead, it's the *same* elements, and the same amount of both, but in a *new* combination. An isomer." He rearranged the items so that all four stones were piled together, with the two sticks side by side.

Sakay looked at Wayra, then back at Req. "That's good news, then, isn't it? We don't have to look for some other substance. We have all the material in the sample."

Req shook his head.

"Why not? Can't you just … recombine those elements as Qhapaq Apo has done? Repeat the process?"

"Unfortunately, no. With this particular isomer, it seems we need a catalyst," Req explained. When Sakay just blinked at him, he added, "Something that spurs the change. Another element perhaps, or a particular condition such as heat or pressure, that can bring about the rearrangement."

"But he doesn't know what it is," said Wayra.

Sakay frowned. "I see."

"In the meantime," Wayra told him, "we've also learned a few things about dominite. Things that are a bit … disturbing."

"Disturbing?" It was disturbing enough, Sakay thought, to see how the reptiles hovered in proximity, the obsession in their behavior.

"Let us show you," said Req.

⟫⟫⟫

"We'll demonstrate first with the hypsilophodons only," said Req.

Once Wayra had sheltered the other dinosaurs, she brought out one of the crystals, its purple glow vibrant. Immediately all the hypsilophodons approached her, similar to the way the pteranodons had approached when the Razorclaws had first taken the sample from the docks in Ika. This time, however, in the light of day and without the panic of guards attacking, Sakay noticed the ordered way in which these reptiles surrounded Wayra, in a circular fashion with equal space between them.

Almost like … soldiers. Sakay shuddered.

"Position," Wayra told the reptiles.

All at once, the reptiles raised themselves to full height and lifted their heads to attention. They stared at the crystal, unblinking and unflinching, as though they were in the presence of some divine being.

Wayra then extended the crystal toward Sakay, who stood several feet from the group. But—no—she wasn't gesturing for him to take it from her—she was *pointing* it at him.

"Target!" she commanded.

The reptiles jerked their heads in his direction and hyperfocused on him, snarling.

He flinched. "Sweet serrated *teeth*, Wayra! What are you doing?"

All she'd have to do was say the word "assail" and they'd shred him to pieces in an instant.

Calmly, she replied, "This is what we're dealing with. This is the power of the dominite." She lowered the crystal, and the dinosaurs followed it with their eyes. "At ease," she told them.

They relaxed back into their previous trance, awaiting her next command.

"As you can see, under such an influence," Wayra said, "the reptiles are highly susceptible to suggestion. That, paired with the fact that they are already trained to be loyal to a specific person—in this case, me—they will then basically be beholden to that person's will and follow any command given."

"*Any* command," Req emphasized. He gestured for Sakay to follow him. "I have something else to show you."

Sakay trailed Req further up the mountain, into a sprawl of forest where the trees grew dense. Wayra was close behind.

"So it's clear the crystals emit some kind of energy—as skyrock does—that captivates reptiles in particular, when they are in proximity to it," said Sakay.

"Yes," Req agreed. "The stronger the energy, and the closer they are to it, the more overcome the reptiles will be."

"But it can be blocked, it seems," Sakay added. "Certain materials seem to dampen the effect—like lead."

"Not entirely," said Wayra, "but that's correct."

"And where are we going now?" Sakay asked.

"I performed a few experiments," Req told him. "I wanted to see what would happen if I were to leave crystals out at different times of day, in different lighting conditions, at different temperatures, in different types of soil, and so forth. I also wanted to see how many reptiles each crystal would draw, and what sort of range it might have. There's one particular crystal site I'd like you to see."

Sakay narrowed his eyes. "What have you concluded from the experiments thus far?"

"The crystals tend to perform the same under most conditions," said Req. "At their size, they seem to attract any reptiles within a few yards, regardless of placement. However, they appear to be susceptible to photodegradation. In other words, when exposed to light for too long, their violet color fades—and so does their energy. The crystals become chemically inert."

"So their power is limited," Sakay said, "assuming the user takes advantage of them during daylight hours."

Req nodded, then reached a point within the woods and stopped. "I'm going to need you to brace yourself for what you're about to see."

"Alright." Sakay swallowed.

Wayra grimaced, which didn't make Sakay feel any less uneasy, considering she must have known exactly what they were going to look at.

"Bear in mind," Req said, "that this was not intentional. I kept thorough records of my experiment sites. However, I've been awake at all hours, exhausted—"

"Refusing to eat," Wayra cut in. "Delirious. Delusional."

"I failed to retrieve one of the crystals," Req admitted.

Wayra's expression turned grave and sullen. "For an entire week."

Sakay raised an eyebrow. He didn't immediately understand where this was going. *They'll follow any command. Brace yourself. A crystal left in the woods for an entire week.* Just as he slowly began to put the pieces together, Req stepped aside, revealing a circle of rhamphorhynchus carcasses up ahead.

Bile rose in Sakay's throat. He covered his nose and mouth.

The rhamphorhynchuses appeared to have collapsed on the spot, gathered around the place where the crystal had been— which Req had since retrieved, no doubt—in a formation similar to the one Wayra had induced a few minutes ago. Their carcasses were piled amid their own ruck, which emanated a deathly scent along with whatever their rotting flesh produced.

"They will ignore their own hunger," Wayra choked out, "their own bowels, their entire sense of survival ... just to be near the energy of these crystals."

Req took a deep, shuddering breath. "We, and the Unuvian qhapaq, only possess a small sample of this power—half of which I have lost to light exposure, thanks to my experiments and my former ignorance on the matter. Qhapaq Izhi may have already ruined his own sample, not knowing what we now know. And neither of us knows how to recreate it. Meanwhile, Qhapaq Apo has the ability to create a limitless supply, and has trained an army whose size we cannot guess, but regardless, you can see that he has the power to make them do anything he wants.

They will not falter for hunger, for thirst, for fatigue. They will not question or resist or even hesitate, as some do under the influence of skyrock."

"And unless we can find a way to match that power …" Wayra said.

Suddenly Sakay thought he might vomit. Not for the ruck and the rotting, but for what had caused it. "Unless we can find a way to match that power … We're doomed."

"When facing the trials of this world, it is best to think like an alchemist: With the right approach, you may transform the materials set before you into something more desirable. But also remember that even the best minds of the century cannot make treasure of lead."

The High Shaman of Kallpa House

THIRTY-THREE

AFTER LEAVING CHINCHA POINTE, the land only turned more barren. The entire isle of Qallu—at least as far as Ninan could see from the port cities of Uma, K'antiy, and Muyuchisqa—was nothing but a stretch of desert surrounded by the sea. The parched earth, with its unrelenting heat and lack of vegetation, felt all too parallel to the blistering emptiness he'd felt since Qora's departure four days ago.

Although the *Velosaura* would once again be docking back on the main island—the final zag before keeping to the edges of Tisqu Isle for the remaining few stops—Ninan would have to endure one last desert city called Ñan.

The activities within these cities and among the highborns there were slow paced, as though the residents and guests had resigned themselves to baking in the heat. Then again, Ninan thought, perhaps the pace had more to do with the fact that even the smallest physical exertion would provoke a sweat, and thus, sitting still was the best way to endure.

Uma was a city of tall adobe buildings plastered with rich clay, while K'antiy was home to lavish tent palaces with fabrics woven in status colors of red, purple, and yellow, and Muyuchisqa featured stone castles along the coast with open windows placed to capture the slightly cooler breezes brought on by the water.

Ninan and Paqari greeted the people who had braved a journey under the unencumbered sun to come and see them in person, and then attended the lazy gatherings that followed, where servants fanned the guests with enormous, dried fronds (clearly sourced from some other place where plants grew without the force of a human hand) and feasted on platters of fruit and large portions of dinosaur meat.

Paqari did not speak to Ninan beyond what was strictly necessary, but all events went forward as planned, and so it seemed she had no intention of revealing Ninan's betrayal.

As usual, Ninan made small talk with governors and councilpeople and socialites, and answered questions about the Venture, and accepted congratulations for his engagement. But with conversations as dry as the landscape, he'd taken to sneaking Tuko into his trouser pocket—an impressive feat for the pteromorph—and slipping him small pieces of fruit. He'd asked Paqari's on-board tailor to make him a looser pair of trousers, under the pretense that he needed "more room to 'breathe' in this climate," which wasn't untrue, but it also made more room for the pteromorph, especially since Ninan wouldn't be able to get away with hiding him in a jacket anymore (not unless he wanted them both to die of heatstroke). It was tempting, though, not to command him to fly out and bite the more obnoxious dignitaries.

"Just command him to 'sting.'"

By the time the *Velosaura* reached Ñan, Ninan had begun to fully relish having the pteromorph with him. Without Qora, or even Sakay, to dampen the agony of playing this role of "esteemed highborn prince anticipating his wedding to the island princess," he had little refuge. After another social hour and an especially boring conversation with the chief hydrographer about water rights (apparently Ñan and its neighboring city were in a constant battle over access to the Cerulean Thread that flowed between them), Ninan managed to escape to the roof of the chancellor's vast, six-story, adobe-brick mansion, where the sun beat down with a fury in the lack of shade, but at least there was a view.

The mansion was located on a relatively isolated stretch of land away from the city center, which would have been impractical due to the lack of water resources, but of course money was no object for the chancellor, and thus, several wells were distributed around the property that must have had to reach extreme depths. And of course local hydrologists were working on improved means for desalination, seeing as there was in fact a great deal of water surrounding the entire isle, if only it were potable.

But this location, and this specific vantage point from six stories high, afforded residents the ability to see one of many grand designs etched into the desert floor, the outline of a shape made by scraping away the top few inches of the ground to reveal the lighter-colored sands below. It took Ninan a while to catch his breath after climbing all the stairs, and he would have regretted it for the sweat marks that extended from his armpits to his waist, were it not for the solitude he'd achieved upon arrival.

The geoglyph visible from here was called Screeching Velociraptor, and the chancellor had told of many more that existed further inland, all of which were hundreds of feet wide and showed the images of different creatures and objects, such as Ceiba Tree, Attacking Mosasaurus, The Furious Diabloceratops, Orchid Blossom, and Tarantula. The chancellor had even suggested a flight tour of the geoglyphs, as they were scattered over a span of around two dozen miles toward the Volcano Emberdome, but Paqari had apparently already seen them the last time she'd visited the region, and other guests (most of whom had also seen them before) remarked that today was one of the hottest days of the year and perhaps another time would be better. After all, flying directly under the sun for such a stretch, with no shady stops, would be grueling. Ninan was told that he could—and should—return during the "cold" season, which, according to description, still sounded warmer than a spring day in Qhusi.

And so, Ninan let Tuko loose on the roof's ledge, and looked at Roaring Velociraptor, and wondered how much more of this he could take. He would have *preferred*, in fact, to fly into the open desert and see the geoglyphs, even in the torturous heat, rather than remain at the mansion.

Still stuck on the mystery of the reptile base, Ninan also carried one of the maps with him, folded up small in the pocket opposite Tuko, and he now withdrew it and spread flat over the ledge where Tuko seemed to have spotted a spider and gone hopping off to catch it.

Ninan located the geoglyphs on the map, although they were faint, as if in attempt to mimic the light color they truly were, and dragged his finger along their sequence. When he ended at the Tarantula mark, his gaze fell a short distance toward the eastern region, where the name AQU AQU caught his eye. He leaned closer, mentally gauging the miles between the two places, and narrowed his eyes. "That's got to be less than twenty …"

Tuko snapped his beak a few feet away and crunched the spider's exoskeleton between his teeth.

Ninan looked up at Tuko and something suddenly clicked in his mind. *What an idiot I am …*

Qora had been right. It would have been pointless to go to Aqu Aqu before—at night, and worse, without a guide. But

Tuko could have been their guide. Why hadn't Ninan thought to take the pteromorph before? Tuko would remember every place he'd been, and then when they reached the alleged "dead end," he could lead them to whatever more specific place Izhi surely must have missed when he'd sent his spies to investigate.

It wasn't too late, though. Here in Ñan, Ninan was as close to Aqu Aqu as he had been in Qaqakuna, maybe even a few miles closer. And this time, he wouldn't need to sneak out under the cover of dark. He could take a *Velosaura* flyer in broad daylight—because now he had the perfect excuse to take a short trip out: a solo tour of the geoglyphs.

THIRTY-FOUR

FOUR YEARS AND SEVERAL MONTHS AGO

OLLAN ARCHED HIS BACK as the three-fingered claw pierced his flesh.

He thrashed against it, as saliva dripped from the black mouth above him. This reptile was like a small spinosaur—small only by comparison, as its spinal sail rose still several feet higher than Ollan was tall.

What was it? How was it here in these woods?

His heart pounded so fast he thought it might explode. Blood seeped from his side, soaking his shirt.

Somewhere around him, his thirteen-year-old sister scrambled to retrieve one of the bolts she'd shot a minute before. He wanted to scream at her to leave it, to get somewhere else, but the teeth closing over his shoulder stole his breath.

"Ollan!" Qora screamed.

A bolt soared past the reptile.

"Qora—run!" Ollan managed.

She hesitated.

What is she doing? She needs to get out of here.

Ollan tried to wriggle free but his movements only seemed to sink the reptile's claws deeper.

He choked out the word "Run!" once more.

His thoughts were a blur.

Everything in view was chaos—gnashing teeth, the shimmer of the sun through the trees reflecting off obsidian scales, underbrush swaying and snapping, flashes of Qora.

In all that, he barely made out that Qora had found a tree and begun to climb.

Yes, he thought. *Get up high. Out of reach.*

As reptilian teeth cut into his arm, his mouth tried to cry out but the sound was muffled, unintelligible.

The forest floor scraped his back as the view above him shifted. The reptile dragged his body.

He tried to flip over, to grab hold of ferns or exposed roots, fingernails clawing the dirt seeking purchase. But a streak of blood trailed behind him.

His energy waned.

In less than a minute he found himself deeper into the woods, somewhere he didn't recognize. He managed to snatch a branch that had snapped, either from wind or a flyer too large having perched there, with a split and pointed end. As the reptile opened its mouth for attack, Ollan thrust the point at the hard ridge behind its teeth, drawing blood instantly.

The reptile snarled and flailed, and in those brief seconds, Ollan spotted a formation of rocks, with a crevice between them just large enough to hold him. He slipped free and pushed himself onto his hands and launched himself forward, lodging his body into the crevice.

The reptile was at his back and slammed its face at him, but came up short when the width of the space would not permit it to pass through. Ollan flinched at the abrupt motion, inadvertently throwing his head back against the rocks, sending a crack of pain through his skull and skitter of stars across his vision.

The reptile roared and struck again several times, but Ollan slid to the ground and shrank into himself, clutching the larger wound at his side before he slowly drifted out of consciousness.

$$\mathcal{DDD}$$

What followed came in flashes. Two vague figures—a man and a woman—armed—shouting—arguing.

"Capture" was the only word that reached Ollan clearly. Whatever weapons they possessed seemed to intimidate the reptile.

Skyrock, Ollan thought.

But in the end, the reptile disappeared swiftly into the forest.

When the next clear words struck his ears—"kill him"—he sensed they weren't meant for the dinosaur. He tried to sit up, tried to speak, but he couldn't form words to explain himself. And then he lost consciousness once more.

$$\mathcal{DDD}$$

Ollan woke on a bedmat. Not his own bedmat, as it did not smell like his own, and not in his own house, because the light was different—in this case, firelight. Although, he couldn't conjure the full memory of "home," even though he knew this wasn't it. Someone had wrapped his body, treated his wounds. Suddenly the memory of how he'd achieved the wounds was increasingly hazy. His head throbbed, with an ache that spread across his face and behind his eyes.

A woman appeared at his side. She must have been almost thirty, with dark hair tied in a knot at the nape of her neck. She wore a woven poncho and fitted pants, and boots that looked almost military, and extended a cup of hot, maroon liquid.

"You …" Ollan croaked. "You were … there …"

"Don't talk if it's too painful," she told him, kneeling beside the bedmat.

"Where am I?"

"I was supposed to kill you, but I couldn't," she said softly.

Ollan didn't understand how that explained his location. He tried to sit up but the movement made his skin pull, and sent a tearing sensation along his side crossing his ribs. He sucked in a sharp breath.

"I stopped the bleeding in time," said the woman, "but you still need to rest. This is for the pain." She tipped the cup to his lips and helped him drink.

It tasted metallic, with a salted, vegetal undertone, although diluted and possibly sweetened with cane sugar to make it more palatable.

She grimaced a little as she watched his reaction. "It's a dilution of aquilops blood—a controversial but effective painkiller and anti-inflammatory."

He tried not to regurgitate that liquid as he thought about its contents. After an effortful swallow, he said, "Why were you supposed to kill me?"

"I work for the qhapaq," she explained. "And as soon as my superiors find out that I didn't kill you …"

Ollan relaxed his head against the pillow behind him and released a defeated sigh. "They're after you now too."

"This is a good hiding place."

Looking around, the place appeared to be some kind of hunting shack, made of wood and stocked with a few weapons, several ceramic jugs of what Ollan assumed was water, medical supplies, a corner chair, and a stone fireplace with a kettle over dwindling flames. The whole thing was the size of a single, small room, with one window and a weathered door. A rhabdodon was hitched outside.

"Who are you?" Ollan asked.

"The better question is, who are *you*?"

"I'm …" He furrowed his brow.

What had happened before this? He'd been in the woods. But why? Hunting? Traveling? He remembered hiding among the rocky formations. The face of a black and red theropod gnashing its teeth. It must have attacked him, although the details of such an attack escaped him. His consciousness had come and gone in waves.

"I tried to ask you your name when I first brought you here," the woman told him. "You opened your eyes for a moment and I thought you were awake. You said, 'I don't know.' Then you closed your eyes again, and you've been asleep until now."

"You brought me here on your own?"

"My partner left me to track down the sailbeast. You were delirious, but with my help, you were able to stand for a few seconds at a time. I managed to get you onto my rhabdodon, who carried you until we arrived."

"'Sailbeast'?"

"That thing that attacked you. It's a hybrid—an experiment of the qhapaq's. His handlers bred an entire pack, but this particular species has been difficult to contain. My unit was tasked with recovering those that escaped. My partner and I received a tip that one was loose in the area where we found you, so we tracked it down. We didn't expect survivors."

"You mean witnesses."

"Exactly." She made him drink again.

After he'd forced himself to finish the contents in the cup, he wiped his lips on his sleeve, although even lifting his arm to bring his hand to his face was painful.

"If you can't remember who you are, it's going to be very hard for me to get you back home."

"Yes, I can see how that would be a problem." Gods. How could he not remember? It was like trying to catch smoke in his hands, grasping at a swirling mass of particles that appeared to be tangible but which only wafted away when he got close. The knowledge was there, though, thinly and vaguely.

The woman nodded. "Try to get some more rest. Maybe it will come to you."

⫸

Ollan wasn't sure when he'd drifted off again, but this time he woke to the woman jostling him. Darkness had fallen over the room but for bright moonlight and the dwindling embers of the fire.

"We have to go," she said. "Members of my unit are approaching this part of the woods now. I've heard their rhabdodons. There's not much time."

With difficulty, Ollan climbed back onto her rhabdodon, realizing quickly that such large wounds scabbing over were almost worse than fresh ones. At least shock and adrenaline had dampened them initially.

She climbed up in front of him and took them deeper into the woods. The moon was full enough to see by, so they didn't risk lighting a lantern.

As they put distance between themselves and their pursuers, Ollan couldn't help but feel as though he were leaving something important behind. Some*one*, maybe. But of course it didn't matter right now, not when he could be killed, not when the woman who had saved him—his only potential link to what had happened to him—could be killed as well.

"Where are we going?" he asked.

"There's a copper mining town a few miles west. I think you'll be safe there until you can remember where you come from."

"What will you do? Won't the unit keep pursuing you?"

"They will. But I've got a cousin in Unu. I'll probably try to make it there. It's quite a journey, but the unit will have a harder time tracking me down once I've crossed the border."

They rode for what felt like hours. Ollan had no idea what time it was, but he sensed light creeping in on the horizon. When they stopped at the stream to let the rhabdodon drink and rest, the woman said, "I'm going to walk a while. The rhabdo can't take two riders for this long."

"I can walk," Ollan insisted. The aquilops-blood concoction was beginning to wear off, but it had helped his pain substantially and kept it at bay. He might be able to go a ways on foot.

"Your condition is delicate," she told him. "You've already lost a lot of blood, injured your head apparently, and I'm sure you'll be slow as a grazing stegosaur. You're better off on the rhabdo, and I can keep a good pace leading you from the ground."

As Ollan suspected, however, even at the woman's near-athletic pace, walking slowed them too much. It wasn't long before other dinosaur footfalls became audible, crunching leaves on the forest floor.

"They're gaining on us," Ollan said.

The woman stopped to assess. She looked like she was straining her ears, trying to determine the distance and direction from which the sounds came.

Ollan shook his head. "Why are you doing all this for me? You don't even know me. You've risked your position in your unit, and worse, your life. I'm grateful, but … it doesn't make any sense."

"There was a time when I *would* have killed to protect myself." A darkness came over her and she lowered her eyes. "A time … when I did." When she flicked her gaze back up at him, she seemed to be asking him whether he understood her meaning.

"You're looking for redemption …"

She picked up her pace, tugging the rhabdodon's reins behind her. "There's no redemption for me. But I refuse to do the qhapaq's bidding any longer."

They hurried for another half mile or so, but the sounds of the pursuing unit only grew louder.

"You have to ride again," Ollan told the woman.

She shot him a panicked look, but finally nodded and positioned herself to climb back onto the saddle.

Before she could, a man swept into view—the same man she'd referred to as her "partner." The man who had left her to kill Ollan and gone in pursuit of the rogue sailbeast. That much Ollan remembered.

The man approached, aiming a compact crossbow at the woman. "I'll give you one last chance. Kill him and give yourself up, or I'll kill you both right now."

Ollan's fingers itched for a weapon, despite the fact that he couldn't recall whether he even knew how to use one. He *must* have known, or his instincts wouldn't be so strong. Regardless, there was nothing to aid him in this moment.

When the woman hesitated, her partner shifted his aim at Ollan. Before he could trigger, she lunged at him, tugging his rhabdodon off course and deterring his shot. His bolt zipped past Ollan.

The woman withdrew a knife as the man dismounted.

Ollan dismounted as well, but stumbled as soon as his feet hit the ground. He landed on all fours, pain searing his side again.

The man withdrew his own knife—the same kind, perhaps part of their unit's standard weaponry—and he and the woman circled one another, slashing and grappling. Within a minute, the man had seized the woman and turned her so that her back was to his chest. He raised his knife, ready to slice her throat, but she angled her matching knife backward and plunged it into his gut. With a final fury, he dragged his blade along her neck before he himself collapsed.

No!

Ollan crawled to where the woman lay. He pressed his fingers to the cut as blood trickled out.

The man had compromised her artery.

"You … have to … go …" she strained. "There's money … and s-s-supplies … on the … rhabdo. Get …"

"I'm not leaving you here," Ollan insisted. "Not after you helped me."

"Get … to … safety."

"No, I—"

Her complexion was sallowing quickly. Her breaths began to still. Blood continued to seep past Ollan's fingers, even as he pressed harder to stifle its flow.

"Please," she whispered with her last breath.

And then she was gone.

The other members of the unit were closing in.

Resigned, Ollan forced himself back onto the rhabdodon

and raced onward. By the time the sun had risen, he no longer heard the sounds of anyone at his back. His pursuers must have found the woman dead, he thought, along with the man, and considered this the end of their task. After all, they hadn't known Ollan had been with her—not for certain, at least. She had been their primary target, for her refusal to obey orders.

When the mining town came into view, Ollan stared at the wooden buildings and the unpaved streets, with a few citizens staggering off to their early morning tasks in the dim sunrise.

"Until you can remember where you come from."

He didn't know how long it would be until he could remember. But even though he had no recollection of anything that might give his life meaning, the natural urge to survive persisted in his mind. And so he rode into the town and entered the first inn he came across. He took the sack of coppers the woman had packed, and laid several on the counter for the innkeeper.

When the innkeeper asked for a name, Ollan replied, "Give me the first one that comes to mind."

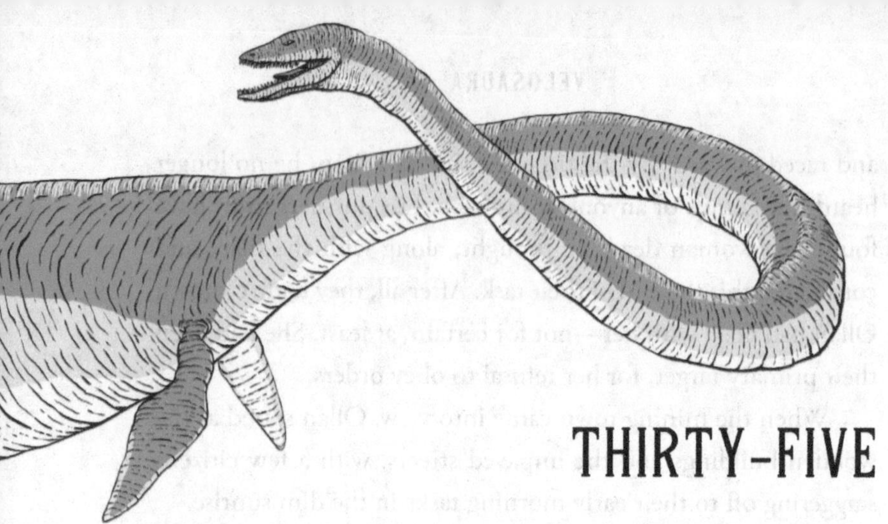

THIRTY-FIVE

QORA SAT ON THE FRONT STEPS of the house and tossed expired food scraps at the compies, just like she was always telling Hakan and Rimaq not to do. "You'll spoil them," she would say, "and then they won't eat the rodents." But there was something satisfying in drawing them close to her, in pleasing the little reptiles.

"Hungry?" Ollan said from the doorway, holding two bowls of something that smelled sweet. He didn't wait for her to answer; he came and sat beside her and handed her a bowl.

She inhaled deeply to ground herself in the moment, still not sure her mind wasn't playing tricks on her. "I've missed your rafañote. Mamáy uses half as much cinnamon."

"You could have made it my way anytime." He took a bite.

"It's not the same."

Their mamáy and the other boys had gone to the market early to take advantage of the lingering traffic from the Heritage Festival, which always seemed to keep people in a shopping mood for several days after. Even with Qora's Venture prize money, their mamáy didn't want Hakan and Rimaq to lose their work ethic, nor did she want to be dependent on Qora for everything—or *anything*, if she could help it. But she'd also insisted Qora get some rest—Qora's passing out on the street had put her mamáy on edge—and thus Qora had remained at home every day since, with Ollan keeping an eye on her.

And Qora wouldn't have had it any other way.

In the four days since the Heritage Festival, she had soaked up every second with her oldest brother. He'd been the one to catch her when she'd passed out on the street, and then she'd woken in his arms, to his glorious, scarred face looming over her—and nearly passed out again. It had taken hours for the truth of him to sink in. She'd hugged him so tightly and sobbed enough to fill the well outside with tears that were a cocktail of rage and guilt and joy and overwhelm.

They'd had to return for the pteranodon she'd left at the hitching grounds in the city, and then Qhapaq Apo had of course interrupted her after the parade by summoning her to Kallpa House to discuss her unexpected arrival. She'd assured the qhapaq that all had been well aboard the *Velosaura*, but that she'd found the repetition of the tour to be tiresome, and the princess had graciously allowed her to return home earlier than planned. And how fortuitous! Just in time for her to appear during a citywide gathering! The qhapaq had met her feigned enthusiasm with a dull glare, but dismissed her with no further questions or commands, only reminding her that she was due back in two days to prepare for the Revelry. With that, she'd hurried back to Ollan without another thought.

Ollan's story was surreal, everything from his survival to his rescue and memory loss to the simple life he'd led as a miner. He'd explained how he'd had flickers of recollection now and then, a face or an event, brought on by a scent or a phrase. How the stories of the Venture had captivated him, particularly those involving "the girl with the crossbow," as the idea had struck something deep in his mind. How images of Qora's face had felt so familiar. How Qora's visit to the nearby city of Anta, where Ollan had happened to be in person that day, had made him all the more desperate to remember, driving him to a mysticary who had prescribed a dimetrodon eyeball, which had healed his mind sufficiently to bring him back to himself. But by then, Qora had gone to Tisqu, and so Ollan had instead shocked their mamáy alone at the house, causing her to fall down and weep uncontrollably, unable to bear the emotion of her lost child standing before her. But he had held her until she could grasp the reality of his reappearance, and Hakan and Rimaq had arrived shortly thereafter to learn the news.

His scars were thick and prominent. Any deeper and he would have bled to death. Qora still couldn't fathom how he was alright, how he was real, how much more of a man he'd become, and that he was sitting beside her right now.

"You're doing it again," he said when he caught her staring.

She shook herself out of her daze and brought a spoonful of the nutty bread pudding to her lips. "Sorry. I just don't think I'll ever get used to it. After all these years of thinking I'd never see you again. Missing you. Blaming myself…"

He put an arm around her shoulders. "I know you're not going to listen to me, but I'll say it a million times: You did what you knew best to do, and so did I. We can't change anything now, but … we can be glad we're finally together again."

She let herself sink into him, savoring his presence and his warmth and his smell. "You're right."

In some ways, he was like a complete stranger, but in other ways, it was as though he hadn't ever left.

They sat in silence a while and then finished the rafañote, and then Ollan said, "We've been at the house all week. Why don't we do something different today?"

"Like what?"

"Like … face one of our demons."

⊃⊃⊃

It was baffling how alike Ollan was to Sakay.

"You have to deal with your demons one way or another, kantuta."

Qora knew they were both right, but that didn't make it any less difficult.

As many times as Qora had been in these woods since Ollan's death—no, not his death, not anymore—going into them *with* him stirred a new emotion. It was like a reenactment. An uncanny semblance of the last time she'd seen him before he'd disappeared.

It was chilly, and she hadn't wanted to wear either of her green jackets, so she wore the riding cloak from Tisqu, and carried the crossbow Ollan had left behind.

"I can't believe you kept it."

"How could I not?"

He smiled. "I'm glad you didn't stop practicing. Especially after what happened to me. You faced *that* demon well."

"It was vengeance, not bravery."

Having had a few days together now, with nothing to do but catch up, she'd told him everything that had happened leading up to and during the Venture—well, *mostly* everything—as well as all that had happened since. He now knew that she had killed the sailbeast, tried to trade the raptoriva and been caught, and entered the Venture to save Rimaq, as well as what Ninan meant to her, what the qhapaq was working on, that the Razorclaws and Izhi were working against Apo, and why she'd returned from

Tisqu earlier than planned.

It was a relief to confide all these things, especially in him, in the person she'd wanted to talk to for so long.

"It's hard for me to see you as a young woman," he admitted. "I still remember that little girl. Thirteen, so eager to grow up, but just a kid."

"Don't worry. I got plenty of your same lectures from Sakay."

He chuckled. "I'm glad he's been looking out for you. Doing what I couldn't."

In the depths of the wooded lands near the property, they walked.

"You're going to stay here, aren't you?" she asked.

"Of course. Now that I've managed to find my way back, I don't see any sense in ever leaving."

"Good."

She wondered whether he would return to the Guard, after all this. After years as a miner. Would his absence be considered desertion? Did it matter now that, as far as records were concerned, he was technically dead? Certainly his loyalties lay elsewhere since the very organization meant to protect him had tried to kill him to cover up Qhapaq Apo's experiments. But there would be time to discuss all that later. Even the vague idea of these topics gave Qora a sinking feeling she wasn't ready to address.

"What about you?" Ollan asked. "Is the qhapaq expecting you for more appearances abroad?"

"I think my celebrity status is winding down," Qora said. "I'm hoping there won't be much more for me to do. I imagine people will be tired of me soon. But I haven't really thought about what I'll do when it's all finished."

"You don't need to hunt anymore, at least."

"I think the best thing for me to do is join the Razorclaws."

Ollan stopped walking.

Qora paused too, and turned back to where he stood. "I know what you're thinking. It's too dangerous. Too risky. And after our family is finally back together—all but Papáy, may he rest in peace—it's ridiculous for me to tempt fate."

"Go on …"

"Except that a war could tear apart not only our family but so many others too, and I'm one of the few people in a position to do anything about it."

He didn't argue with her. He took a deep breath and seemed to be analyzing her. Like he'd said, in his mind she was still thirteen. Even with the added four years and a few months, she still couldn't say she was an adult. Her experiences, however, had given her skills and knowledge that would aid her.

"You could join me," she added. "We could work together. With your military training …"

A flicker of buried rage passed over his face.

Yes, she thought. He was angry too. The qhapaq had stolen several years of his life. Despite their happy reunion, it would be impossible to let that go.

"I want to tell you it's a bad idea," he admitted. "But … you're right. You are in a unique position. You know and understand what most people don't. And you've been connected to Kallpa House in a way most people never could be."

Qora slipped her hands into her cloak pocket. "If we can just figure out—" She scowled as grains of sand lodged under her fingernails.

"What is it?" Ollan said.

She turned the pockets inside out, scattering sand on the ground.

"From the coast?" he asked.

"No," she said. "From the desert."

From that night with the irritator.

It had been windy, blowing sand everywhere. Into her eyes, apparently into the folds of the clothes she'd worn. She gave the material an extra shake for good measure.

Suddenly the memory of Tuko shaking out his sceathers flashed through her mind—the sand that had fallen out after she and Paqari had removed the plant samples. Qora had assumed it had come from the beach, where Tuko might have stopped to rest, perhaps nipping at sandworms, on his journey to follow Ninan.

"Spirits," she whispered. "I know why Aqu Aqu was a dead end."

Ollan raised a brow. "Why?"

"Because it wasn't the *end*."

THIRTY-SIX

SAKAY HAD MEANT TO TAKE a few hours' leave in the morning to see the Razorclaws again, but the Underground had still been cluttered with extra traders who remained in the city after the Heritage Festival.

He'd hoped by now that the traffic would have died down, but the plethora of new, exotic goods on his shelves and in his storeroom proved otherwise. Not that he dared to complain about all the new things he had to trade—maguey ale from Kantuta Bay, dracovenator fangs, epidexipteryx feather quills, and blue Weqese peppers that could practically burn the skin off one's tongue, to name a few.

Regardless, he managed to reach a point in the day when the other workers could handle most of it, with the majority of the more interesting traders having begun to head back to wherever they'd come from, and so took the opportunity to slip out.

He was headed for the dinoshelter attached to the main-level building above the Underground's entrance when a middle-aged trader approached him.

"Raphu ..." Sakay said as the man intercepted his path.

"I didn't realize you'd be leaving so early—but I'm glad I caught you."

Sakay halted and reluctantly shook Raphu's hand. "It's been

a while." *Not long enough, though*, he thought.

This man had come in plenty of times before, trying to trade scavenged jewelry and other accessories. Some had been good enough to earn Raphu a deal, but Sakay always suspected that many, if not most, of these items were stolen, although he'd never had any proof. Sometimes Sakay kept them in the back for a while before laying them out for sale, in case someone came looking for any of them.

"I'd like to test your expertise." Raphu withdrew a corked glass vial from his coat pocket.

Sakay observed the particles within the vial—a collection of what appeared to be alluvial silver. "You want me to tell you if it's authentic?"

"I already know whether it's authentic. I want to know if you're capable of discerning it as well."

"Alright." Sakay accepted the container and opened it. Inside, there were a variety of shapes and forms of silvery metal, from flakes to large grains to tiny nuggets. He plucked out one of the nuggets.

It had a bright, metallic luster with a whitish color tone, which meant that it must have been recently exposed (otherwise it would have a dull patina on the surface or show signs of tarnish). A pinch told him it was the correct density—or close to it, at least. He pressed his thumbnail into the surface, leaving a faint line across the metal. Finally, he gripped it tightly in a fist and held it there for half a minute. When he opened his fist, he rolled the nugget between his fingers. "Interesting ..."

Raphu curled his lips. "I knew you were a clever young man. What have you noticed?"

"It's still mostly cool to the touch. Even though it should have warmed quickly in the heat of my hand."

"But otherwise, it's a very convincing imitation, don't you think?"

Sakay dropped the nugget back into the vial, replaced the cork, and returned it to Raphu. "Sure. What's your point?"

"A fool's silver. There's a rexload of it in Qolqe, at a channel branching off the Kawsay River in the Searing Sands. Some of my guys traced the alluvial metal back to the source, an enrichment zone in the middle of nowhere. Not known to anyone. No competition. We're currently in the process of collecting it in shipments."

"You're going to try and sell it?"

"Why not? It's close enough. Gods know the likes of us could use the financial uplift. I thought you'd want in on it. That's why I brought it to you."

Sakay scoffed. While he was no stranger to using special tactics to make a sale or a better trade—creating false scarcity, anchoring prices, or simply bluffing about value—he wasn't in the business of counterfeit goods. "I'm not interested."

He stepped past Raphu to get to the dinoshelter.

Raphu grabbed his sleeve. "But this could make us a fortune. I'll supply everything; you only have to prime the traders."

Sakay pulled himself free. "It's bad business. I don't recommend that you pursue this any further."

The trader followed him all the way into the dinoshelter. "Will you at least … take the sample?"

"To what end?" Sakay unhitched the rhabdo and climbed onto its saddle.

"I don't know," Raphu said from below. "Just to … think about it?"

"There's nothing to think about. It's a scam, and I want nothing to do with it."

"Alright, then. Take it anyway, and think on its potential for something better. Something more … ethical. Hmm?"

He sighed as he picked up the reins. "Like what?"

Raphu shrugged. "Like I said, you're clever. You can figure something out." He extended the vial.

Sakay paused for a moment, staring at the glittery offering, then rolled his eyes and snatched it from him. "No promises." He gave it a jostle and tucked it into his saddlebag. "I better not catch you trying to trade this stuff at the Underground."

"No sir," said Raphu. "You have my word."

ↈↈↈ

Sakay reached Mount Qaqra with all the requested supplies—silica powder (a hushdust ingredient), magnesium ribbons, hadrosaurus dinoleather riding gloves (because Wayra had said the iguanodon dinoleather cracked too easily after a long ride), and an assortment of the Underground's best spicy ornithomimid jerky. He threw in some honey rum, a loaf of sweet anise bread, and strings of eoraptor tooth beads he thought Wayra might like to make bracelets out of.

Wayra was apparently out trying to break a new megaraptor, and Gorgo was off on a bounty hunt to earn some extra silvers, so Sakay stood and watched while Req and Kuy rifled through the saddlebag to see what he'd brought them. The exotic, long-fingered compies scampered around their feet while they withdrew each item, hopping up and down trying to snatch bits of anise bread or anything that dangled.

"Little thieves." Req nudged them away with the toe of his boot and held up the glass vial of silvery particles. "What's this?"

"'Fool's silver,' apparently," Sakay replied. "A guy named

298

Raphu discovered it in southeast Qolqe and wants to defraud the masses with it."

"Qolqe of all places," Kuy remarked bitterly. "I hear Silver City is struggling to mine the real thing …"

"Just the high-grade deposits," Req said. "When those are depleted, they'll still have lower-grade ores. It's more costly to extract, sure, but it's not *nothing*."

"I suppose it makes sense why Raphu might see a potential market for it," said Sakay, "if newly mined silver will be scarce. But I make a point not to outright lie to people—even if I do skew the truth a bit now and then."

Req uncorked the vial and removed a nugget, holding it on his fingertip, and examined it. "*Looks* authentic." Then he bit it gently.

"It doesn't conduct heat very quickly," Sakay informed him.

"Agh," Req said with a grimace. He stuck out and withdrew his tongue quickly like a serpent. "Tastes funny too." In his distraction, one of the compies leapt onto his chest, clawing into his clothes to maintain position, and snatched the vial in its claws. "Hey!"

The compy squeaked and hopped down, running off before anyone could catch it. It jumped up and took position on the edge of the megaraptors' water trough and tried to shove its snout into the vial's opening.

"Don't worry about it," Sakay told Req. "The stuff's useless."

"Good thing," Kuy said as the compy tipped it upside down and spilled half of it into the water.

After Req and Kuy gathered their items from the saddlebag and set aside the rest for Wayra and Gorgo, Sakay said, "How's it going with the dominite?"

"Same as before," Req confessed. "I took a break to work

on extending the effects of the hushdust instead; it lasts almost a full hour now."

Sakay raised his brows. "Impressive."

"Not that we need that long for most drop-ins, but … it's reassuring to know it gives us more time."

A moment later, Wayra came riding in on a young megaraptor, a dark red one that reared its head as it slowed. She tugged the reins gently. "There now … That wasn't so bad, was it?" She slid from the saddle and led it to the trough where it gulped greedily, stirring the water with its massive tongue."

"Seems like the raptor had a lovely time," Req teased.

Wayra cocked her head and flashed him a not-amused smile. "She's strong willed, but shows a lot of promise."

"Should've used the dominite," said Kuy.

"Sure, and the second I don't have it, she'll be right back to her usual spite."

Req fished around under the collar of his shirt and pulled out a dominite crystal he'd apparently strung around his neck. Its glow was strong and colorful—not one of his light-depleted samples. "At least try it out." He went over to where the raptor drank and held it next to her. "Hey raptor-raptor …"

A low growl preceded the raptor's defeating roar.

Sakay and Kuy flinched.

The raptor snapped her jaw so fast Req would have lost his head if he hadn't ducked.

Wayra tightened her grip on the reins and pulled the raptor away.

"Gods of nature …" Req murmured.

"I don't understand," Sakay said. "You're holding dominite. Why didn't she respond like—" Suddenly he caught sight of the alluvial fool's silver tumbling around in the trough, sinking slowly after the raptor's turbulent lapping. "Wait a second ..." He sifted out one of the tiny nuggets at the bottom with his fingers and displayed it for the others.

"She swallowed that stuff ..." Req said, following Sakay's line of thought.

"You put something in my raptor's water?" Wayra demanded.

"Technically your long-fingered compies did," Kuy clarified. "But it might have been just what we needed. Maybe Req can't recreate the dominite yet, but now we might have a resource for keeping our own reptiles resistant to it."

〉〉〉

The group tested the fool's silver on four other dinosaurs before running out of flakes and nuggets, some of which Sakay had had to pull out of the grass where the compies had spilled the other half of the vial.

"Incredible," said Wayra as she waved a fully powered crystal at a hypsilophodon and it merely cocked its head in curiosity.

The compy test subject came up to her and tried to bite the crystal as it would most other small and easily snatchable goods, but otherwise showed no signs of attraction to it, no trance-like gaze, no lack of individual will. When Wayra held it high out of the compy's reach, the compy squawked angrily and scampered away.

"I can't believe I'm saying this," Sakay told her, "but I'm going to have to ask Raphu for a full shipment of that stuff. I'm obviously not going to tell him *why*, but ..."

Everyone turned their heads at the sight of a black pteranodon swooping down at full speed.

Sakay squinted at the figures on its back: a young woman

and a man, who quickly came into focus.

Qora?

Why wasn't she on the *Velosaura?*

He almost thought he recognized the man, although he couldn't think where from. His pulse quickened as he went out to meet them.

"Is everything alright?" Sakay asked as Qora slowed the pteranodon to a halt upon landing.

"Yes," she breathed. "Yes, I'm fine. Everyone else is fine—as far as I know." She dismounted, followed by her companion.

Kuy, Req, and Wayra joined them and gathered around, exchanging confused glances.

"Good." Sakay let his shoulders relax. "Then, what's going on? Why are you back so early?"

Qora shook her head. "Why I came back isn't important. What's important is that I realized something: Tuko didn't get it wrong. Aqu Aqu wasn't the end of his journey. When we removed the scraps, he shook out his sceathers and dropped sand onto the table. I thought it was just from all those beaches—but what if it was sand from the *desert?*"

Sakay raised an eyebrow. "So what if it was?" He thought about it for a moment. Aqu Aqu was at the *edge* of the desert, close enough that the sand might blow into the city. He imagined Tuko gathering clues from Ika all the way there, and then imagined what would have happened if the shipment had gone *further*, past the city and somewhere inside the Aquchay. No one lived out there, besides perhaps nomadic psychopaths, nor did anything grow in such a desolate place. There would be nothing for Tuko to gather at that point. Nothing except—

He gasped and repeated himself. "Yes. What if it *was?*"

"Tuko collected sand on purpose," Qora said. "That was

the final piece of the puzzle, we just didn't understand. Paqari also mentioned dinoheart palm, that it could be from anywhere because it's grown specifically for shade. Which means that Tuko might have eventually found some at the site, after traveling through long sandy stretches of land, but it wouldn't have been traceable to any specific region, so we never would have been able to guess anyway."

"Spirits …" Sakay whispered.

"And I also realized that the albino pteranodon headed for Sut'u was flying over from a northwestern direction—not from the south, as it would have been if it had come straight from Sumaq. In fact, if it *had* come from the south, I never would have seen it at all." She dug around in her saddlebag to remove a map, which she unrolled, and angled it so that Sakay could see it.

The Razorclaws looked over Sakay's shoulders.

Qora traced her finger along a hand-drawn line that extended from the center of Sut'u to South Ridge, right where she had stopped during the plesiosaur race to climb the sea stack and get a better view of the pteranodon's direction. "Following the path between these two points"—she continued tracing the line beyond South Ridge, westward and slightly northward—"that gives us evidence of a flight that would have taken off from somewhere right around *here* …"

"Right in the heart of the Aquchay Desert," Sakay said.

"What does this mean?" asked Wayra. "Do we know the site location now?"

"Not precisely," said Qora. "But this gets us close."

"So what's the deal with Sut'u, then?" said Sakay. "What would Qhapaq Apo want with that isle?"

"Aquafern," Qora told him.

Wayra frowned. "Is that the plant with the gel inside?"

"Yes," said Req. "It helps with water retention. The Qolqese used to import it but now they're looking into growing their own after some conflict over its scarcity."

"I thought maybe the qhapaq was having someone negotiate something," Qora said, "trying to get other Terrains on his side like he did with Tisqu, but I've recently realized it makes a lot more sense that he's—"

"Using it to hydrate the dinosaurs," Sakay finished.

Qora nodded. "The man on the pteranodon that I saw that day must have been checking on the aquafern resources. And it's lucky, because otherwise we'd have nothing to go on."

Sakay breathed a sigh of relief. "But now we know where to start. For certain."

"We don't have any time to waste," Qora said. "The three of you need to get packed up. My brother and I are leaving immediately—and we want you all with us."

"Brother?" Sakay said.

He sized up the man who stood behind her, who had been waiting patiently while she had explained all these things. Now that Sakay really looked at him, he supposed he could see the resemblance, but …

Sakay's vague recognition of the man slowly turned more clear. *Of course.* He'd never formally met him, but he'd seen him at the Underground before, with other young military officers. Except … it wasn't possible for him to be here now.

Qora grimaced. "Right. I almost forgot. This is Ollan. Yes— *the* Ollan."

Though two rivers may be separate,
they will always find their way to the same sea.

Sumaqi proverb

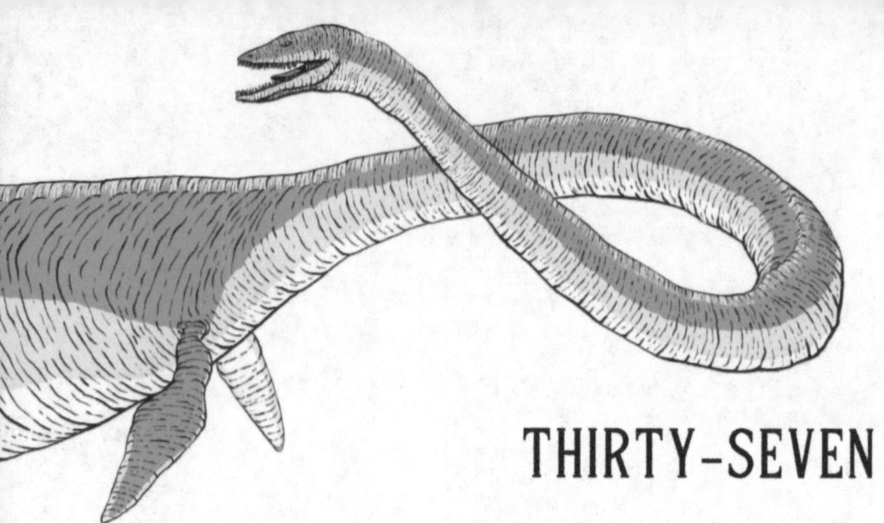

THIRTY-SEVEN

NINAN HAD TO ALTERNATE BETWEEN using the flyer-riding goggles and not using them. Hot wind and blown grains of sand stung his eyes, but sweat dripped from his hairline and got caught along the rims while the humidity leaching from his skin fogged his view. Tuko had ridden on his shoulder, digging in his tiny claws to remain upright.

It had been a grueling half hour, although Ninan suspected it might have taken longer than projected, with the dark-scaled pteranodon struggling in the heat as much as he was—and at least he himself didn't have to carry anyone on his back.

He hadn't told anyone he was planning to tour the geoglyphs, other than the guards who watched him return to the *Velosaura* and take the pteranodon, lest one of the guests offer to accompany him. This way he could go alone, but he also had a pretext if anyone should later ask where he'd been all this time.

After reaching Aqu Aqu, Ninan allowed himself and the flyers a short break for some water and rest, and then Tuko began to squawk and flit so energetically it was clear they wouldn't be able to remain still a moment longer. He must have recognized this area, having passed through with the shipment he'd tracked weeks ago.

Incredible, Ninan thought.

At first, Ninan led the pteranodon on foot so that it could continue to rest its wings, and they walked in relative shade following Tuko. The city was behind them, and so they traversed the rural outskirts until they came to a place where the trees began to thin out to nothing.

Ninan stopped and stared out at another stretch of desert, not directly back the way they'd come but some forty-five degrees easterly of that path. Tuko continued to fly out, but Ninan still waited, calculating, not sure whether he dared to venture to whatever mysterious location the little flyer was headed for.

Of course, he hadn't come this far to quit now. If only the desert didn't look so menacing. If only he hadn't just braved a stretch of it and grown so weary of looking at sand and cracked earth and plateaus. If only his shirt wasn't already soaked with sweat.

Tuko flew back to Ninan and the pteranodon, squawked at them, and flew out again. The pteromorph went back and forth at least three times, beckoning, before Ninan finally sighed and said, "Alright. Show the way."

It was impossible to follow Tuko efficiently by air, with his wings being so much smaller than the pteranodon's, so once Ninan got a sense of the general direction, he flew out with Tuko on his shoulder again. As they got closer to the intended destination, Tuko occasionally took flight and redirected them before returning to his perching place.

Ninan hadn't expected it to be this far. If he'd known, he wouldn't have gone to Aqu Aqu first, as it was probably a shorter flight to the site. But of course Tuko could only remember the route based on a starting point, so, unfortunately, it had been necessary to add the extra miles.

After around twenty minutes, Tuko squawked again, leaving

Ninan's shoulder and dropping down to indicate that they should land. Up ahead was another section of plateaus and a couple of mesas, but nothing that might indicate a reptile training base.

Following Tuko's lead, Ninan urged the pteranodon to drop too, easing toward the closest rock formation where the vertical side met an angled slope. Some of the rock here had eroded into pinnacles, creating multiple breaks through which the land on the opposite side was visible. Tuko selected the area with the largest gap and seemed to indicate that Ninan should land there, and so he did. Ninan then continued to ride the pteranodon and commanded it to walk far enough in between two pinnacles to get a view of what lay beyond.

But it wasn't the roaring of juvenile dinosaurs that struck him first, or the commanding voices of trainers, or the movement of carts pulled by chasmosaurs—five-horned ceratopsians with triangular fenestrae in their bony frills—carrying mysterious cargo, or the lines of guards protecting and directing it all.

It was the group of seven—five male and two female—who were already tucked into the gap with their own flyers observing the same scene.

Qora flinched when Tuko landed on her shoulder, then abruptly turned to see Ninan, clutching her chest.

Ninan stared in disbelief at Qora, Sakay, Req, Kuy, Gorgo, Wayra, and some other man he didn't know.

Releasing a frustrated breath, Qora said, "We've really got to stop meeting like this."

THIRTY-EIGHT

QORA WAITED FOR THE HAMMERING OF HER HEART to die down. She and Ollan and the Razorclaws could have been caught by one of Qhapaq Apo's guards—and she could only imagine what the qhapaq would have had to say about it, or what he would have done to her. While she was relieved that it had been Ninan instead … it was *Ninan*. Again.

"How did you know to come here?" Ninan dismounted his pteranodon and approached the group.

She shared a glance with Ollan, who didn't know the *full* extent of her feelings for Ninan, although she'd told him enough to give him a good idea.

It was awful that her brother's reappearance had coincided with such turbulent events. There was very little time to properly introduce him or to explain what had happened. Sakay had received the condensed version of everything while the Razorclaws had prepared to leave (Ollan thankfully had some basic pteroflight training from his military experience, which had allowed him to accompany them). But now the group had run into Ninan while they were smack in the middle of reconnaissance.

"I had an epiphany." Qora silently acknowledged the pteromorph on her shoulder, who tilted his head to meet her fingers. "Tuko had sand in his sceathers when he found us on the *Velosaura*. I thought it was from traveling along the coastline, but then I realized—"

"How did *you* know to come here?" Gorgo flipped the inquiry on Ninan, who scowled back at him.

"Or maybe the better question is," Sakay said, "how did you sneak away from all the highborns?"

"I'm on 'an aerial tour of the geoglyphs,'" Ninan explained. "I thought if I took Tuko to Aqu Aqu, he could guide me to a more precise location. I didn't expect it to be this far out, though."

Req frowned. "But there are miles of plateau out here. How did you know exactly where *we* would be?"

"Tuko can pick up a familiar scent from miles away." Ninan glanced pointedly at where the pteromorph sat.

The pteromorph nuzzled Qora's chin.

Ollan stepped forward, bowed his head at Ninan, and extended his hand. "It's an honor, Your Highness."

Ninan accepted the gesture. "Thank you. Please just call me Ninan. Welcome to the Razorclaws ..." He raised both eyebrows as though he were waiting for Ollan to fill in the blank.

"Ollan," Qora's brother supplied his own name. He fixed Ninan with a warning stare.

"Ollan." Ninan analyzed him for a moment, then abruptly looked to Qora for an explanation.

"Kanchaya," Ollan clarified.

Qora didn't know why, but Ninan's quizzical look was almost physically painful. Maybe it was because she was still trying to process Ollan's state of being, and because it was difficult enough to explain it to herself let alone to everyone else.

"But ..." Ninan's mouth hung open. "I thought ..."

"He survived," Qora told him. "The attack damaged his mind. A mysticary helped restore his memory."

"I'm afraid I gave Qora quite a startle when she got back to Qhusi a few days ago," Ollan said. "But, I'm here because I want to help, if I can. I served a year in the Sumaqi Guard … before the incident."

"It doesn't really matter how we all got here," Kuy reasoned. "What matters is, what do we do now that we finally have a location for the base?"

Qora, Ollan, and Ninan held a tense silence between them, but for the time being, they would have to set it aside and discuss everything later. It would be dangerous for them to linger here too long, in case they were spotted.

Everyone took a moment to gaze outward.

Below and in the distance, several one-story mudbrick buildings and enclosed outdoor zones sprawled across the desert flats. Dinoheart palm trees shaded the guards around the perimeter.

"Everyone plants those palms for extra shade. I wouldn't factor it into the puzzle; it's inconsequential."

Additional shading stretched along the inner sides of the walls in the form of thatched awnings that covered troughs filled with meat and something that should have been water but didn't look quite right from here.

Within the outdoor zones, uniformed trainers wielded purple dominite crystals and commanded large groups of dinosaurs—what looked like small pyroraptors, dracorexes, and maybe … scutellosaurs?—separated by species. It was difficult to tell for certain, but Qora recognized the feathered silhouettes unique to a pyroraptor (except these were not as fiery in color as others she'd seen) and the distinct arrangement of dracorex horns. The others seemed to have the appropriate bony scutellosaur knobs all over their backs, although she wasn't sure why the qhapaq would bother to breed an herbivore, unless he'd managed to breed it with a more useful mutation.

Each species was subdivided into uniform groups—maybe based on when they were hatched, Qora guessed. But within each group, their size, coloring, and other features were the same, like they had come out of a factory. They assembled themselves in rows.

The vibrance of the trainers' crystals appeared to vary, perhaps depending on how long they'd been using each one.

That's why they need so many, Qora thought, *and why the shipments are so frequent.*

Qora focused on another zone with a fourth species. She had to squint to get a sense of their sort of mottled yellow-and-brown pattern. But the long tapered snouts and the conical spikes down their backs were clear. "Are those …?"

"Irritators," Ninan bit out.

Qora clenched her teeth, fixating on the spinosaurians that didn't seem to be as large as the one she and Ninan had seen near Qaqakuna, but which were equally menacing. The other must have escaped from here. It could have been wandering for months, surviving on whatever smaller dinosaurs it had found and growing in the desert until its size had required more sustenance and driven it toward places where humans were gathered as easy prey. Except—could it have really grown *that* fast? Bigger dinosaurs took longer to reach full size, sometimes several years depending on the breed.

Wayra answered the question Qora hadn't asked aloud. "If Qhapaq Apo is planning on using any of these dinosaurs anytime soon, there's got to be something accelerating their growth—far beyond what's natural. These are all juveniles and younger."

An eerie feeling spiraled up Qora's spine. It was such unnatural behavior for dinosaurs, especially young ones, to be orderly. She thought of the compies at home, how chaotically they behaved even as adults, darting around without any sort of formation among them. The only exception was when theropods hunted in packs, but still they were not so perfectly coordinated like these—hundreds upon hundreds of them lined up like soldiers, watching their commander as though they were possessed by an all-powerful spirit.

Qora had seen people train reptiles before, the same way one could train any other animal. Animals could associate command words with behavior, and would come to easily repeat that behavior when rewarded. Here, however, it seemed the reptiles did not require a tangible reward. Being near the energy of the dominite was more than enough.

"And it looks like they don't stick around for long." Req indicated a row of carts, which handlers were loading with cages full of little reptiles. Some of the carts pulled by chasmosaurs were already making their way westward on faint trails that served as a roadway. "They must train them quickly in batches, then truck them off somewhere. Probably to the coastal ports, and then who knows after that."

Ninan scoffed. "Great. Another location we'll need to figure out."

Gorgo grunted in what sounded like reluctant agreement.

This was only one moment in the history of this base, Qora realized. Who could say how many dinosaurs had already come through? Who could say how frequently they were hatched and dispatched elsewhere *each day*? Who could say how many more species could be trained and distributed before the Razorclaws could get a message to Ihzi, and before Izhi could formulate any kind of plan to put a stop to it? And if, potentially, they were somehow growing to full size in a matter of months …

Kuy withdrew a notebook and a stick of charcoal and frantically sketched an outline of the base, complete with notes about each section.

"This location actually makes a lot of sense," said Wayra. "Most dinosaur eggs thrive in this kind of temperature. Usually the mothers have to maintain it with their body heat and take advantage of seasonal warmth, but here, Qhapaq Apo could probably hatch hundreds of thousands of eggs consistently, year-round, without the assistance of any adult dinosaurs after fertilization—the desert as an incubator."

Other things the group had learned were beginning to make sense too. Qhapaq Achik supposedly "urbanizing" some of the Aquchay must have been a cover for sending more resources to the base.

As a few trainers commanded dinosaurs to break formation and line up along the troughs under the thatched awning instead, Qora squinted at the strange liquid and gasped. "That's the aquafern gel …"

The reason she'd seen someone from Sumaq flying to Sut'u.

Now the only thing lacking in explanation was the mention of dinosaur attacks on other isles—the six sightings on Phapa that the magistrate had mentioned at the start of the *Velosaura* tour. It wasn't likely that any of these dinosaurs had escaped and made it that far on their own, as the irritator might have done. But it wasn't too far a stretch to think that Qhapaq Apo had planted them elsewhere as a distraction, or that Qhapaq Achik had allowed Qhapaq Apo to outright *stage* the attacks to instill fear of extracontinental enemies so that the island people would be more likely to support reunification later on.

Sakay squinted, scanning the base and pointing at a uniformed man. "Look at him. The one on the far right. His hand. Does it look …?"

"Black," Qora breathed, marveling at the dark tone of that hand in contrast to the rest of his skin.

"I've seen a hand like that before," Sakay said. "On a guy who came into the Underground last year. Said he'd been bitten by a venenovenator. Their particular venom will do that to flesh. If you get antivenom in you fast enough, you can stop it from finishing you off, but you'll be left with some nasty side effects at the bite site."

A microraptor flapped into the enclosure where the black-handed man observed the training. He accepted it, removing something from its leg before releasing it to one of the handlers.

"I think that's the beastlord," Wayra told them.

"Beastlord?" Ninan asked.

"That's what the head of the dinorider units in the militaries are called," Ollan confirmed. "I imagine it's the same for units made up entirely of dinosaur soldiers. Although this is the first I've seen of such a thing."

Wayra folded her arms. "He *must* be in charge if he's the one receiving messages—orders, probably. And from the look of his hand, he's had a lot of experience with deadly reptiles. Enough to earn him a high rank over them."

The man slipped what might have been a papyr into the front of his uniform.

"Can't we just follow one of the microraptors out of here?" Gorgo asked. "Wouldn't that lead to something useful?"

"Probably not," Ollan said. "All military correspondence will be routed through the capital. It would only lead us back to

Aleta and then we'd still have nothing real to go on."

"Where do you think the qhapaq is sending the dinosaurs?" Req asked Ollan.

Ollan shrugged. "Hard to say. Depends on his strategy. If I had to make an educated guess, I'd say he would have camps set up throughout the mainland, in locations closest to where he thinks he'll need them. While I was in the Guard, he always kept military reserves stationed near points of potential conflict. Of course this time he'll be the one *creating* the conflict, and his reserves will be more ... reptilian ... but, I'm sure his thinking is the same."

"So he's probably divvying them up among the camps," Qora concluded.

Ollan nodded. "And he's probably looking to create conflict where it will do the most damage. Rival capitals or other major cities, or sources of revenue—mines, quarries, cash crops. But he can't keep camps on foreign soil, so most of them are going to be right at the border, with the most direct routes to his attack points."

"But Qolqe probably won't put up much of a fight," said Kuy, "and Allpa lies beyond Unu, so a direct path to that capital would be difficult. Which means Unu should be the qhapaq's first target, shouldn't it?"

"I'd say so," said Ollan. "I'd bet that at least one of the camps is located at the border near Yupa. Maybe another one parallel to Huandoy. If he can advance on those and manage to occupy either of them, he could set up subsequent camps on Unuvian soil and position himself to threaten Allpa."

They all kept quiet for a few minutes and let these speculations sink in. For many, many months the rumors of this war had been just that—rumors. There had been evidence, to be sure, but witnessing it up close was something else entirely. The reality of impending, deadly conflict seemed to be expanding before their very eyes.

"So, what do we do with this information?" Req said.

"I hate to say it," Ninan replied, "but I think the obvious answer is to tell Izhi."

Kuy shook his head. "There's a *reason* you hate to say it. There's no telling what ulterior motives he has. We shouldn't involve him this time. We've got other people willing to help the Razorclaws—a good network we could pull from. Maybe we can handle it ourselves."

"How?" Wayra said. "Even with everyone we could gather, I'm sure it won't be enough if Qhapaq Apo uses all his resources to fight back. And it's not like we can take advantage of the dominite; we just barely got our hands on a sample and we still don't know how to replicate it. I can train a lot of reptiles, but not *that* many." She pointed at the base.

"Izhi isn't my favorite choice either," Req admitted, "but … what else are we going to do? He's our only high-powered connection."

"Couldn't we take it to another terrenal leader?" Wayra suggested.

"Who else?" Kuy said. "Tisqu's clearly not our ally. Qhapaq Apo has had Qolqe in his pocket ever since he married his third quya"—he threw a glance at Ninan—"No offense."

"What about Allpa?" Qora offered. "Quya Urpi has never shown any loyalty to Sumaq. In fact, she seems to defy everyone and everything. I bet she'd be sympathetic to our cause, especially since a war might affect Allpa the most."

"My name is refuge," the quya had told her.

"Maybe," said Ninan, "but being the smallest nation after

Tisqu, her resources are going to be limited, regardless of her feelings about this."

"If we assemble the right team," Kuy argued, "I think we could at least take down this base. We just have to get creative. We could knock out the staff with hushdust, Req could cook up some explosives, we send some guys in to steal dominite and maybe a few reptile eggs, then we get out and blow the place. It wouldn't fix *everything*, but it would certainly hurt the qhapaq's source, maybe delay his plans. And we can transport this dominite supply back to Qhusi where we can use it for defense, and have plenty more to test until we can figure out how to replicate it."

Qora hated the idea of decimating so many reptiles, whom the qhapaq had forced into existence against nature, but she supposed it was a necessary evil. It was better than allowing the qhapaq to unleash them on innocent people.

Sakay scoffed. "'Assemble the right team?' Do you remember what happened last time?"

"What happened last time?" Qora still hadn't heard the full story, or any details about any particular missions in which Sakay had participated.

"Like I told you at the masquerade, we don't have time for that," Sakay replied. "The point is, accomplishing a mission doesn't always bode well for the entire cause."

"You think the Razorclaws are to blame for *this*?" Wayra gestured at the base again. "There was no way we could have known the qhapaq would figure out a way to make soldier-slaves out of reptiles. That doesn't mean we should stop trying. That doesn't mean everything we do is going to result in something worse."

Req put a hand on Sakay's shoulder. "Blaming us—blaming

yourself—it won't bring Ramaya back."

Sakay shoved him off. "I'm not suggesting we stand by and do *nothing*. But we should at least not set ourselves up to make mistakes again. At least don't be too proud to consider involving someone with more resources. Qhapaq Izhi will be putting his own people first—as he should—but he knows hurting this army will be beneficial to all of Runaqa. The Razorclaws should work *with* him, not as a separate force. Everyone against this war should be on the same page, as far as strategy, if we want the best outcome."

Qora sighed. "Qhapaq Apo is right about one thing: Unity is power. If we don't work with Izhi, our efforts could inadvertently hurt his, and his could hurt ours, and we could all end up worse off for it."

Kuy, Wayra, Req, and Gorgo all exchanged glances.

Wayra raised her eyebrows. "Qora has a point."

Kuy rolled his eyes. "I guess."

A few more looks between everyone and Ninan finally said, "So we're all agreed? We take this to Izhi?"

With hesitant pauses in between, everyone nodded their assent.

Ninan crossed his arms. "Great. We'll see him at the gala in Port Waqta next time the *Velosaura* makes port. At the very least, it's convenient timing."

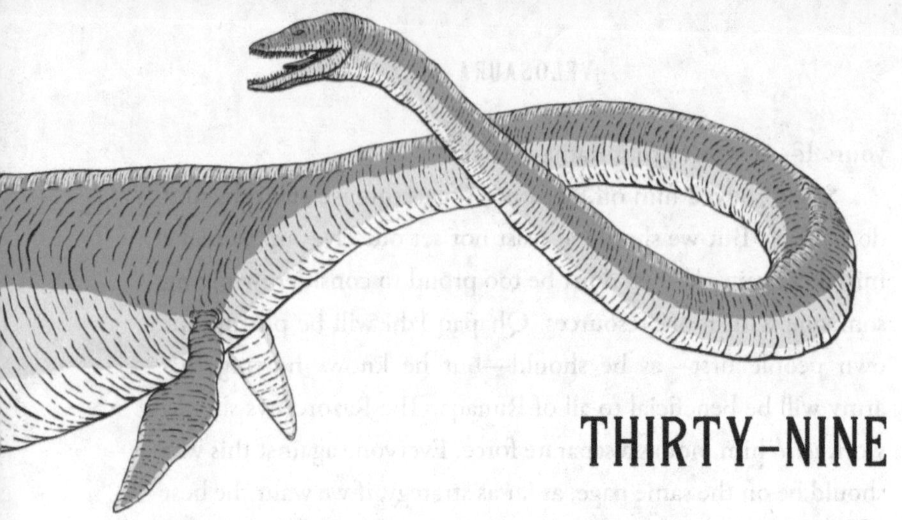

THIRTY-NINE

NINAN ADJUSTED THE CUFFS OF HIS SLEEVES. His stomach roiled. There were only three days left until his wedding, and meanwhile he was dealing with an increasingly burdensome amount of information that could cost him his life. Suddenly his collar seemed too tight; he pulled at it to loosen the buttons, although this did little to calm him. As with so many situations lately, he'd simply have to endure.

The gala was to take place in the glass pavilion of the governor's cliffside villa—a rare and exotic venue since, even among highborns, few could afford glass windows, let alone glass walls—which featured a dramatic ocean view.

This time, Ninan left Tuko in his cabin, with a pile of inqa-nuts swiped from the galley. Although Ninan had come to depend on the pteromorph at these events, tonight he had too many other things to worry about, and didn't need to be wondering whether he was crushing the little reptile in one of his pockets.

Ninan met Paqari and offered her his arm. Without looking at him, she took it, and together they entered at the announcement of "The Third Prince of Sumaq and the Second Princess of Tisqu."

Entering the glass pavilion was especially dramatic, with the whole of the external wall made up of hundreds of windowpanes. The pavilion also appeared to be a sort of greenhouse—with enough plants to rival the jungle, Ninan thought. And while the glass maintained a conventional warp, it was the smoothest he'd ever seen.

Ninan swept Paqari into one of their rehearsed dances and, as had been the trend since Qora had left the *Velosaura*, they didn't speak. If Ninan wasn't so familiar with the steps, it would have been difficult to follow them considering all that was on his mind. Casually, he glanced at the other guests looking for Izhi; if the qhapaq wasn't *already* here, the announcers would make his entrance known later, but it was possible he had arrived before the *Velosaura* passengers. Ninan also kept an eye out for other familiar faces.

Already being on the island with the Razorclaws, Qora had gone with them to the Den to discuss further plans, and the whole group had promised to meet Ninan at the gala tonight so that they could all speak to Izhi together. He wasn't sure whether it would be ideal for Qora and Sakay to make an appearance, but Paqari had not officially disinvited them, and at this point it might be Ninan's last chance to see her.

When the current musical piece came to an end, Ninan and Paqari politely parted ways to mingle with the other guests. A few minutes later, the announcer's voice echoed through the pavilion, saying, "Their Majesties Qhapaq Izhi and Quya K'acha of Unu," and all heads turned to the large double doors, and then the guests bowed and applauded.

Ninan waited a moment for the attention to die down and for the guests to return to their conversations before easing his way over to where Izhi greeted a few of the other guests of honor.

Izhi looked up and subtly noted with his expression that

he'd seen Ninan. Beyond that, Ninan could only continue to wait.

It was at least fifteen minutes later when one of the staff approached and handed him a slip of papyr, with a message for him to meet Izhi at the observatory on the hour.

From what Ninan had seen pulling into the harbor, the observatory was the uppermost level of the villa, with a dome made of windowpanes like the glass pavilion, but extending overhead for a view of the sky as well. It wasn't nearly as large as the pavilion, and with everyone dancing and socializing here below, the observatory should be relatively private.

"Qora Kanchaya, champion of the fifteenth quinquennial Runaqan Venture, also known as the Raptoriva, attended by her guardian, Sakay Ch'ak of Qhusi, Sumaq."

Stuffing the message into his pants pocket, Ninan looked to the doors again, taking in the sight of Qora standing there on Sakay's arm.

I won't be the one to try and take her from you.

Regardless of Sakay's promise, Ninan tightened a fist at his side to quell the jealousy flaring in his chest.

Qora wore a sea-blue dress with pearl accessories and her hair tied to the side in a knot behind one ear. Her gaze landed on him almost immediately, and they held a mutual look for what surely must have been longer than was appropriate, before Sakay led her deeper into the expanse.

Hesitant, but all too aware of the time, Ninan went over before the guests could swarm them and said, "Izhi wants to meet at the observatory on the hour. Where are the others?"

"Nearby." Sakay cast a darting glance over his shoulder. "On the premises, but lying low. Should we rally them?"

Ninan nodded. "I only wanted to inform you. But we

should split up for now. It's probably not the best idea for me to be talking to—"

"Look who decided to join us again," said Paqari from behind him.

He clenched his jaw.

Qora gave a forced smile and a little bow once Ninan stepped aside to allow Paqari to participate in the conversation.

"I hope you don't mind," Qora said. "I know I left without saying goodbye. Under the circumstances, I wasn't sure how to—"

"It's fine," Paqari told her firmly. "You are clearly in demand"—she pointed her head at the group of guests that had accumulated around them, presumably all eager to see Qora—"and I am not one to deny my people. Please, enjoy yourself."

Ninan extracted himself from the group while Qora began to address her admirers, and caught up to Paqari, who had already distanced herself by several paces. "I wasn't expecting her," he said. It wasn't entirely a lie. He *hadn't* expected Qora at this event, until the previous day when he'd run into her as part of the Razorclaws in the desert and they'd hastily decided to meet here.

Paqari stopped to take a tiny glass of coconut wine from a tray. "I believe you," she said right before she took a swig.

"You do?"

She downed the wine. "You haven't been remotely subtle about how her departure has affected you, so I can only imagine that the champion has continued to behave unpredictably. How could you possibly have known if or when she'd return? Anyway, I don't care. I'm eager to finish this tour and make our meaningless vows and be done with it."

"Except we won't be *done* with it ..."

"You know what I mean. We'll have plenty of time to sort out the heir-production problem later. Not that your family will *need* any heirs, between your two brothers and their multiple wives."

If only that were enough, Ninan thought. However much his father might despise him, Ninan's virility and fertility were a reflection on the entire Kallpa household, so it didn't matter that Kallpa House didn't need his help in producing a future qhapaq; it was still expected of him to procreate in the traditional sequence and therefore to *marry* in the traditional sequence.

"Right." Ninan didn't want to argue. Besides, he needed to get lost in the crowd and slip out again without anyone noticing.

He and Paqari danced once more for the guests and once more went their separate ways, while Sakay seemed to have managed to sneak away. Ninan caught Qora's attention long enough for her to give an apologetic shrug as guests continued to vie for her attention. Worst case scenario, he could brief her later. Five minutes before the hour, he excused himself from a group of highbornmen discussing the ethics of patronizing controversial artists and fell in line with a few servants making their way back to the kitchens before he broke off toward the staircase that led to the observatory.

He arrived before Izhi did, and so did the Razorclaws, all dressed up to blend in with the guests should anyone see them. Kuy, Wayra, Req, Gorgo, Sakay … and Qora's brother, Ollan. Ninan wasn't sure whether Ollan had officially joined their ranks, but he sensed that, having lost four years thanks to the qhapaq's experiments, it was an easy decision to participate in the cause.

Gorgo looked entirely out of place in a dress jacket, with his hair combed in an almost degrading style when compared to his typical—and apparently preferred—state of disarray.

"Nice to see you all again," Ninan told them.

He stared at Ollan, looking for Kanchaya familial similarities. Ollan and Qora had the same chin and cheekbones, Ninan noted.

Wayra folded her arms. "A glass room doesn't seem like the most discreet location for a meeting like this."

"Maybe that's the idea," said Req. "It's away from most of the witnesses, but if Qhapaq Izhi is caught here, he can always say he just wanted to look at the stars."

"I do so enjoy looking at the stars," said Izhi as he reached the top of the stairs and sauntered in, using his scepter like a walking stick.

They all bowed.

He stopped in their midst and curled his jewel-ringed fingers around the scepter. "What I don't enjoy looking at are five strangers who shouldn't be here. The champion's bodyguard is already a stretch, particularly without the champion herself."

"Your Majesty," said Ninan. "I apologize for the surprise, but I promise you they're all trustworthy. More importantly, we have information for you."

"Information you could not have conveyed to me on your own?"

"The Razorclaws want the same thing you and I do: to stop my father. Independently, they've been working on gathering intel and developing resources for the cause. But after what we've recently discovered—they and I together, along with the champion, who is currently being detained by her fans—we think it would be best if we all combined our efforts."

"I'll consider it," said Izhi, "depending on what you have for me."

"We found the base," said Ninan.

Izhi raised an eyebrow. "Without the tracker?"

"The tracker didn't lead us astray," Ninan told him. "We misunderstood his clues. Qora determined that he meant to lead us into the Aquchay Desert, and she mapped a route using that information and two points of reference based on the Sumaqi pteranodon headed for Sut'u. I separately took Tuko to Aqu Aqu, in hopes that he could guide me from there—and he did."

"The Aquchay …" Izhi rubbed his chin.

"In a hidden area surrounded by plateaus, Your Majesty," said Req.

"Using the heat as an egg incubator, and Sut'u's aquaferns for hydration," Wayra added. "Training hatchlings and juveniles—and accelerating their growth somehow—before sending them to other locations."

"To camps," Ollan said. "More than likely at the border close to your capital, and possibly elsewhere."

Izhi took a moment to consider all this, inhaling deeply, slowly, and analyzing each of them in turn.

"Your Majesty?" Ninan urged.

Finally, Izhi said, "Your small band of rebels has managed to glean more valuable information in the past few weeks than my spies have in months."

"I'm closer to the source," Ninan reasoned. "As are many of the Razorclaw insiders. And, aside from wanting to protect everyone from a senseless war, I think we all have personal reasons to fight this."

He glanced at Qora's brother, the one with the most recent cause for seeking vengeance. As much as Qora must have been grateful for Ollan's return, Ninan ached over the time she'd lost with him, over the hurt he'd seen in her eyes after years of blaming herself for his death. Those were scars that would never fade.

"How do you propose we combine efforts?" Izhi asked.

Kuy came forward. "I imagine you'll want to destroy that base, Your Majesty?"

"That would be the obvious solution," Izhi replied. "I must destroy Qhapaq Apo's military outposts as well, but since we have yet to discover their exact locations, the best course of action is to cut off the breeding and training grounds so that he can't expand that army any more than he already has. We must stab the heart of the operation; of course there will still be blood in the veins, so to speak, but it will be a limited amount compared to what Apo could continue to pump out with a functioning base."

"In that case, we believe we have some things that might be of use to you," said Kuy. "Creative weapons you might not have developed yet."

"And why, with all my financial power and resources would I not be able to match anything you have?"

Req puffed out his chest a little. "Can you knock out a grown man instantly with a puff of dust?"

Izhi raised an eyebrow.

"What about deploying a flash of light that will temporarily blind anyone within a mile? Or a smoke bomb that can dampen sound?"

"We've also discovered a method that might allow our own reptiles to withstand the influence of dominite," said Sakay.

The Razorclaws had briefed Ninan on their tactics, as well as the fool's silver—which Wayra had insisted on observing carefully to ensure it had no negative side effects for the reptiles, while Req had examined the elements further on a chemical level. They had also brought an ample supply of hushdust from Sumaq, and were currently storing most of it with their friends at the Den in Aleta. Ninan hoped that with all his father's focus on breeding the dinosaur army, there had been little manpower left to focus on matching these kinds of tactics.

The continued silence on Izhi's part was answer enough.

"With all due respect, Your Majesty," said Kuy, "That's what I thought. With all your 'financial power and resources,' it's easy to just throw your massive troops and your myriad weapons at your problems. When you have armies and armories, you don't need to resort to underhanded tactics. But people like us? That's all we've got."

"If you send in a flyer unit," Wayra added, "the guards will be prepared to shoot it down. They've all got military bows on their backs, and no doubt a practically limitless supply of ammo."

"But if we *combine* our tactics and your resources," Ninan said, refocusing the conversation, "we'll have plenty of money, manpower, *and* a few things to make the whole process go a lot more smoothly."

"It's hard to hit a target when it's lost in a light flash," said Req.

"And hard for guards to defend their post when they're knocked out," said Wayra.

"Instead of dropping firebombs and hoping they hit the right places," said Kuy, "we can help get your unit safely down onto the base within the compound walls, where you can strategically plant mechanical time-elapse gearbombs—and plant *enough* of them—to get the whole place up in flames quickly. You'll lose fewer operatives, expend less effort, and do much more damage."

"And what's in it for the Razorclaws?" said Izhi. "I don't believe destroying the base is all you seek."

"We also want a significant part of the dominite from the base," Req said, "so that we can continue to test it, as well as keep it on hand to defend Sumaqi civilians, in case destroying the base doesn't keep our warmonger qhapaq at bay."

"I can't grant you that," Izhi told him. "I have a Terrain to protect as well—one that will be at the *mercy* of your warmonger qhapaq, as he attempts to gather other Terrains under his empire."

"Then give us a place under your protection," said Wayra. "Employ us and fund our expertise. Give Req a proper set of equipment to work with, and finances so that he can do what your elementalists haven't."

"I think it's clear that our skills are not being fully utilized," said Kuy.

Qhapaq Izhi gripped his scepter more tightly. "Very well. I will agree to your terms—on the condition that this mission goes as planned. If we do not succeed, you have no deal."

Kuy nodded. "Great."

Ninan took a deep breath. He wasn't sure this would work, but he told himself there was a much higher chance at success if the Razorclaws had Izhi's power to bolster them.

"When do we make our move?" Req asked.

"I should think that would be obvious too," said Izhi. "There is a particular event coming up that will provide the perfect diversion for most anyone who would try to deter us."

The Razorclaws all looked at one another, then slowly turned toward Ninan.

Ninan shook his head. "No." He turned on Izhi. "No—you led me to believe we could stop this *long* before I had to marry Paqari. Now we're three days away and you're not even going to *try* to keep from sealing my fate?"

"I made no promises," said Izhi. "I merely told you what was at stake, and that if there was any *opportunity* to break your arrangement, I would require your intelligence efforts."

"I've given you everything I could," Ninan told him.

"And it wasn't enough. It came too late. That's the reality of it. But that doesn't mean you can't be useful. With you at your wedding, captivating your father and more highborns than we can count, your friends and my military will have the opportunity to strike undeterred. Everyone's eyes will be on you and the princess, and the majority of your father's and Qhapaq Achik's staff will be dedicated to the event, which will significantly dilute their attention on the base and on other reptestrian military pursuits."

"You won't even let me ride with you …"

It was a ridiculous notion, Ninan realized as he said it aloud, his participation in the attack. What had he expected? Helping gather intel didn't make him a Razorclaw. If anything, he was an employee of Qhapaq Izhi, a reluctant double agent. Like always, he couldn't belong where he wished he did.

"You will do much more good by fulfilling your duty," said Izhi. "Consider the wedding a sacrifice for your people—to make way for this team to accomplish what is necessary to keep these lands from war."

⟫⟫⟫

When the others had gone, Ninan remained in the observatory for a few minutes, watching the waves churn in time to that familiar churning inside of him.

It was really going to happen. He was going to have to marry Paqari. Another string to tie him to his father—first through blood and heritage, now through the fortification of an alliance on Qhapaq Apo's behalf.

What would become of him then? If his father did wage war, Ninan would be forced to feign loyalty even more fiercely than he had since the Venture. He would have to stand before his own people and pretend to agree that reunification was the right course of action, while every cell in his body disagreed. He would have to give speeches supporting the Restored Empire. And of course that wasn't all he'd have to pretend …

It was fitting that the view of the sea extended high through the windows, because he might as well have been sinking into its depths from within a glass box, while water slowly trickled in as he waited for the pressure to build and the panels to shatter and the waves to sweep in and bury him.

Ninan pressed his hands to the glass, his breath fogging the transparent surface, and shuddered. He closed his eyes and tried to calm his increasingly rapid breaths, when footsteps drew his attention to the stairwell.

Qora emerged, likewise breathing heavily, only for the exertion of her climb.

She paused and glanced around the room. "I missed it …"

He went to her but stopped just short of where she stood, knowing if he were to touch her he might not be able to let go. "Qhapaq Izhi has agreed to combine efforts—to destroy the base."

"When?"

Ninan lowered his head slightly. "On … my wedding day."

Qora's lips parted for a moment before she replied. "You won't be attacking with us."

He didn't have to answer, because it wasn't a question. Qora was too intelligent not to realize how things would have to be.

"Izhi thinks that's where I'll be most helpful. Even if we attacked tomorrow, it wouldn't do any good to have me far from where I'm supposed to be, so close to when I'm about to—" He curled his fists. "I … already risked too much looking for the base yesterday. Luckily no one questioned me when I returned, since I had plenty to say about the geoglyphs and I came back all burnt and sweating like I'd toured the desert, since I *had*, only not the way they thought. It makes sense to attack when everyone's focused on an interterrenally important event."

"Yes. It does." Qora bit her bottom lip.

"It's ironic," Ninan added. "Ruining my father's plan was supposed to set me free from this, and yet, now that we finally have the information, the means, a method … the only way to serve the greater good is for me to go through with it."

A long moment of silence passed between them.

Qora's chin trembled. "I shouldn't be here alone with you. Especially not if the success of the attack hinges on your loyalty to the princess."

Ninan grabbed her wrist before she could leave. "Please don't go. I just … want to talk to you. I mean, if I'm honest, I want to do *more* than talk, but … it seems like there's so much still to say, and no time for it—like the way the sands in a sand timer seem to flow faster when there are fewer of them."

"Nothing either of us can say will change what's about to happen."

"I know. But I don't like how we left things that night in Qaqakuna. I wanted to say I'm sorry—not for touching you or kissing you, but for the hurt I caused with my weakness when it comes to you.

"And on a different subject, I wanted to say that I know what it must mean to you to have your brother back, but I also know how angry you must be. If I know you at all, I know that while you're grateful, you're beyond furious at what happened to him, at what was taken from you both, and that you're likely angry with yourself for *being angry*, because you think you should *only* be grateful. I wish to all gods I could be with you while you feel those things and sort them out."

"Thank you ..."

The look in her eyes was glossy, watery, and Ninan knew his own timing was as terrible as the timing to which the gods seemed to have subjected him. But the emotions stirring in his chest could not be silenced, were in fact fighting to break out.

"And, since I'm sure this is the last time we can speak privately," he said, "I need you to know how I feel."

"I do know ..."

"No. I haven't been brave enough to admit it to myself sooner, but right now I realize I've fallen so much further than I realized. More than what I've already told you. So before you fly away from here and I never see you again, there's something I have to say. Qora Kanchaya, I—"

Her fingers on his lips silenced him. "Don't say it. Please. Whatever you think you feel in this moment, you can't possibly know for sure."

"But I *do*."

"You can't swear to me that you would mean it, that you would even *think* to say such a thing, under other circumstances. Can you? It's the result of desperation. It's the gravity of everything, weighing on you, making you want what you can't have."

"Qora ..."

She shook her head. "It doesn't matter. Even if you mean it, what difference does it make now? It does nothing but hurt us both. In three days, you're going to be married, Ninan. And that's the *best* case scenario—because we don't know what else your father has planned. We don't know that destroying his base in the Aquchay will be enough to keep him from attacking every major city he hopes to control."

"Yes, the world is ending!" Ninan threw up his hands. "That's exactly my point! So if this is the last time I ever lay eyes on you, the last time I stand on my own two feet as a relatively free man, then by all gods I'm going to *tell you*—"

Qora wreathed her arms around him and pressed her face to his chest. She was silent, but within seconds her tears soaked into his dress shirt, dampening his skin through the material.

His chest rose and fell while he calmed himself, while he did his best to hold back the sting behind his own eyes. How had he ended up this way? Why had he ever dared to try and win back his place in Kallpa House when it only came with such a torturous price?

If he hadn't, though, he never would have known Qora, he reminded himself. Unless he'd continued prizefighting and somehow, through glimpses at the Underground, he might have realized what he did now—that he didn't think he could live without her. But would she ever have felt the same? Did she even feel the same now? Had she been correct when she'd questioned whether their bond had merely been the result of the fear and the fighting they'd endured in the jungle?

If there were nothing keeping them apart, and no impending continental conflict, would he feel the urge to tell her what he wanted to?

Ninan was still certain he would. But he knew Qora well enough to know she wouldn't believe him.

And so he wrapped his arms around her too, and held her for a long while, and when she released him, he thumbed away the more prominent tears from her cheeks, and she whispered goodbye.

"The embroidered cloth does not reveal the tangle of threads that holds the image together from the underside."

Suyana Kanchaya

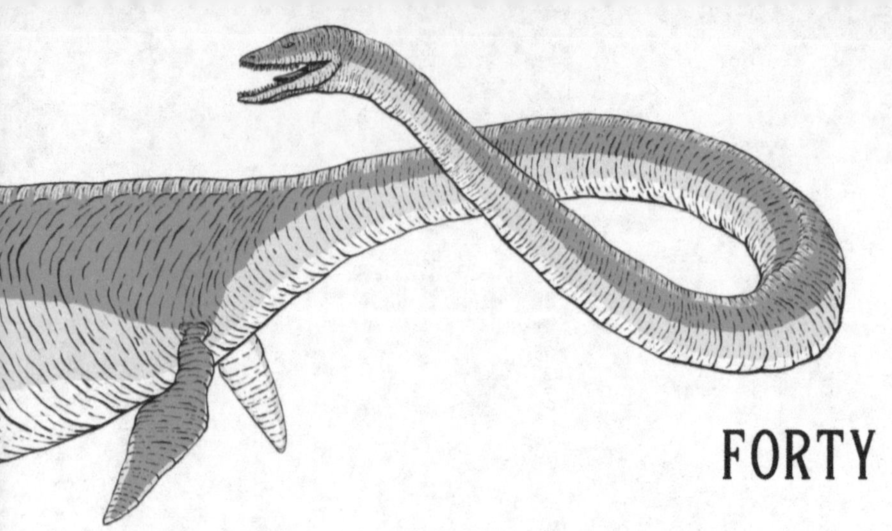

FORTY

AFTER HAVING CRIED HERSELF TO SLEEP at the Den, Qora set out early with her brother and the Razorclaws.

With several hours in the air, Qora's thoughts drifted over memories of the past few weeks, and wove in between the possible outcomes that lay ahead. She thought about everything that had led her to this point, wondering how her life had changed so drastically in such a short time.

A few months earlier, she was no one, a girl killing rhamphos in the woods for food and trading mystical dinosaur bones and rare, scaly leathers for extra silvers. Winning the Venture should have given her more freedom, but the qhapaq's attention made her and her entire family a potential target, should she ever openly rebel against him. She thought about how Ninan knew that fear too, beholden to his marital arrangement because of the threat against the people he cared about in Thak.

As Qora flew across the ocean and came upon the coastline of the mainland, she began to imagine how everything would play out with the upcoming attack, how the qhapaq would react when he eventually learned of the destruction. Even with the team's discretion, Qhapaq Apo's intelligence forces might be able to determine that the Unuvians were responsible, and maybe even that Qora was involved. It was impossible to know the extent of their power. With that in mind, she couldn't be sure what level of risk she was about to take—but she also knew she didn't want to back out.

If she participated as expected, she would be setting her family up for great danger. Which meant that she would have to plan ahead to keep them safe.

The group made it back to Qhusi by late morning. The qhapaq was expecting her to appear at the Revelry the day after Ninan's wedding, but she wasn't going to be there. In fact, she planned to never attend another event as the Raptoriva again.

She would, however, have to accept her summons to Kallpa House this afternoon to *prepare* for the Revelry. Fine-tuning her costume, rehearsing a few words that the qhapaq would expect her to say to everyone, maybe even briefing her to announce some of the matches—as marital matches were certain to be made between highborns inspired by the newly wed royal partners. The gondola would be here to retrieve her at the afternoon Fourth Bell. Which meant she didn't have much time.

The second she'd hitched her pteranodon to one of the reptile posts on the property, Qora tromped into the house and took out several traveling packs and began to fill them with clothing.

Ollan came in after her and stood in the doorway of her room. "What are you doing?"

"Start packing your things too," she told him. "I know you didn't bring much, but you're going to need all of it. Get Hakan's and Rimaq's things when you're finished, and I'll get Mamáy's."

"You just got this land and this house back—and almost died trying. *I* just got back. Now you want us to leave?"

Stuffing another shirt into the pack, she said, "I'm not stupid enough to think we're going to be safe here. Not after we help destroy that base. If the qhapaq finds out—which he probably will—he'll punish us. And if he can't punish you and me directly, he'll hurt Mamáy and the boys. He's basically doing the same thing to Ninan as we speak."

She thought, at the very least, that those people would be free from the looming presence of the qhapaq's guards once Ninan was married. She had spared few details when informing Ollan of all the history he'd missed in his absence.

"I remember," said Ollan. "But where can we possibly go?"

"Allpa."

⟩⟩⟩

When Qora's mamáy and younger brothers returned from the market, they arrived to see two pteranodons on the front lawn, saddled up with everything essential they owned.

The alpacas were gone, and so were most of the compies except for two—Rimaq's favorites—that remained in a crate.

"What's going on?" her mamáy demanded as she dismounted her rhabdodon.

"I know you're going to hate me for this," Qora said, "but we can't stay here. Ollan and I have packed anything we knew you couldn't part with, and I've donated the animals—including the rhabdodons, which we'll deliver later—to neighbors who could use them most."

Hakan, who was still sitting on one of the rhabdodons with Rimaq riding behind, gripped the reins. "What? Why?"

"Come inside," said Ollan. "We'll explain everything."

⟩⟩⟩

"I don't like leaving you behind," Ollan told Qora.

After having briefed their family on recent events and what would be occurring with the base they'd discovered, everyone had reluctantly agreed that Allpa was the best option. It was too risky to stay here. Maybe one day they might return, if everything was still standing, but for now, they required the shelter of a foreign power.

My name is refuge.

Qora had insisted that her mamáy wear the rose-gold smilodon medallion—the one Quya Urpi had lain around Qora's neck at the Venture homecoming ceremony—in hopes that the quya would see it as a message, a plea.

Her mamáy was in the saddle of one of the pteranodons with Hakan, while Rimaq sat on the other, waiting for Ollan to join him. They all fidgeted, already holding on tight even though the flyers were still grounded.

Qora bit her lip. She remembered her first pteranodon flight, the clench in her belly at takeoff. It hadn't been unbearable, though. Well-trained pteranodons like these were gentle; Wayra had made sure of that. Besides, it was the tricks and all the showy swooping that were the difficult part, and they wouldn't need to do any of that; the rest was just knowing the commands, and how to properly nudge these beasts in a way they understood. That much she'd already conveyed to her mamáy and brothers in the quickest lesson she could manage.

"Two to a pteranodon is already pushing the limits," Qora told Ollan, grateful at least that Hakan and Rimaq were lighter in weight than fully grown adults, "and if I'm not here when the qhapaq's gondola arrives, he'll get suspicious. I have to make him believe I'm still loyal for the moment, and in the meantime, you will see that Mamáy, Hakan, and Rimaq get safely under the quya's protection."

Ollan sighed and scrubbed his hands over his face. "I know you're not a kid anymore, and I respect that you've won the Venture; you are more than capable. But you're still my little sister."

"I wish that's *all* I had to be. For a few more days, though, I have to be the Raptoriva too." She hugged him tightly. "I'm sure Quya Urpi will be generous, especially when you deliver my message. I'll stay with the Razorclaws until you join us, and then after the attack you and I will go back to Allpa together."

Ollan glanced warily at the others. "Promise?"

"I promise."

〰〰〰

Before delivering the last rhabdodon, Qora rode to the Underground to meet Sakay and borrow his pteranodon. She explained her plan, and then flew over the great chasm that separated Qhusi from Kallpa House on its adjacent mountain, soaring through the mists until she touched down on one of the landing pads.

An attendant greeted her. "Miss Kanchaya. It's been a while since we've seen you." She offered a thinly veiled grimace as she sized up the black pteranodon. "You've ... procured your own flight transportation?"

"Yes. Please keep it waiting for me—no need for the shelter. I don't expect to be long."

She went to the guest hall. Jaylli and Michiq, her female attendants since the Venture, received her first and took her to the dressing room.

Once in a while the qhapaq would commission a more special version of Qora's green jacket, made from silk, or embroidered with shimmering threads, or he might order another pair of boots with a daintier shape. In preparation for an event like the Revelry, he would have already had these items tailored to her now-well-known measurements but still expected her to come in for a fitting just to be sure.

"It's good to see you again, Qora," said Jaylli. "I can't believe you've been traveling with the prince and princess. Are the islands just wonderful? I heard there were several eventful days on board the *Velosaura*. Did you really have to fight a terminonatator?"

Meanwhile, Michiq brought several items of green clothing and began to lay them out.

"The islands are incredible," Qora told them. "And yes, unfortunately, we were attacked by *three* terminonatators, but—" Her eyes went wide at the sight of five gowns, in differing lengths and cuts. "What are *those* for?"

Michiq frowned. "For you. For the Revelry."

"But ... I thought I was supposed to wear my Raptoriva clothes." No matter the updates to the style, it was always a jacket and boots and a blouse and fitted pants. Here there were only draping satins and velvets and lace.

"Yes, well, the qhapaq requested only gowns this time," said Jaylli. "I know it's unusual. But I think he has something else in mind for you. He hasn't prepared you a speech, or even any notes."

Qora's pulse quickened. What could he possibly have in mind for her?

Numbly, she let the women dress her, laying the gowns against her to see which looked best with her features, and selecting a particular look and styling her hair and lining her eyes. Not so different from what Paqari's beautician had done, only this time she would be under more scrutiny.

And then they presented her to the qhapaq in the summit hall.

Qora and her ladies bowed.

The qhapaq sized her up and gave a brief nod to Jaylli and Michiq. "Perfect. You're both dismissed."

The ladies each subtly released breaths of relief before removing themselves from the qhapaq's presence and leaving Qora to speak with him alone.

"I appreciate the attention to detail," Qora told the qhapaq, "although I have to say I'm … a bit confused about the gown."

"Yes. It is a drastic change from your usual attire. However, you will not be attending the Revelry as a public figure, as you have other events."

"Then .. what am I to be?"

His lips curled into a condescending smile. "Many of the girls and young women of Sumaq have become enamored with your … persona. And while I aim for all to admire you as my champion, it has also come to my attention that the inspiring nature of your tale is causing a bit of a … disruption."

"Disruption?" Qora couldn't imagine that a surge in the production of green jackets or raptoriva figurines could be a problem.

"Young women are getting … *ideas*. Losing sight of their roles in our society. In the beginning, I didn't mind; these trends tend to fade eventually, and then it's back to business as usual. But with some great changes on the horizon—the details of which I won't bore you with—I need everyone to know their place. Many women are allowed the privilege to serve in our military, or to compete in our more grueling events, but they must be the exception. You understand."

Of course. Girls couldn't be thinking it was best to abandon their domestic duties and learn to shoot. They couldn't be trying to emulate any behaviors that would jeopardize the natural order. Not when the qhapaq needed a body of people suited to a full empire that would serve him efficiently.

"I believe I do," she told him.

"With that in mind, I expect that you'll also understand why I've decided to make a very special match that I will announce publicly during the Revelry."

Qora clenched her teeth behind closed lips, keeping herself steady. *A special match.*

She wasn't a highborn, and certainly not a member of the Kallpa Household; it wasn't a common practice for the qhapaq to make marital arrangements for anyone else. But it wasn't unheard of. And when the qhapaq ordered a union, those involved could not deny him.

"Everyone will agree it's a match to rival even that of my son and the island princess," said the qhapaq. "Two Venture favorites united."

"Venture favorites?" Qora's throat went thick.

"From this moment forward, consider yourself betrothed to the beloved competitor of the third quinquennial Venture from Qolqe: Thalu Machaqway."

〉〉〉

Now back in her regular clothes, Qora hurried through the corridors, heart pumping. Keeping her wits about her in front of the qhapaq had left her trembling the second he'd dismissed her. But she reminded herself she would not be back. She would not attend the Revelry. She would not marry Thalu Machaqway. She was leaving Qhusi before the wedding, and flying to Allpa the second the dinosaur army base went up in flames.

There was just one last thing she had to do before she left Kallpa House.

Entering the menagerie, she went straight to the raptoriva.

The little flyer cocked her head at Qora and made a warbling noise.

The raptoriva's tether hung on a hook beside her cage, a cord of twisted fibers attached to two leather straps that would encircle the raptoriva's tiny ankles. Metal jump rings were attached to each strap, tied to the forking cord that ended in a larger clip that would attach to a perch mounted in the field. Qora used all her strength and pressed her thumbs against one of the jump rings—it was flexible, but only under extreme pressure from a specific angle—where the two ends met, twisting the metal away from itself to form a small opening, not very noticeable but enough that the tether cord could slip out under the right amount of resistance. She repeated this for the second jump ring, then lifted it up to the raptoriva so that she could see it.

Miña squawked once.

"Do you understand?" Qora whispered.

Slipping her snout through the bars, the raptoriva gently bit the metal, as if testing its strength.

Qora nodded and replaced the tether on its hook, then stroked the raptoriva's tiny head. "Goodbye, my friend."

In two days, the handler would take Miña out for exercise. Qora hoped it would be the last time Miña ever had to see him.

FORTY-ONE

THE RAZORCLAWS MET IZHI'S UNIT in a forest clearing in Aqu Aqu one day before the wedding. They would finish preparations here, and hide close to the base so that they could attack early and fast.

Sometime during the waiting period, Sakay went off under the pretense of relieving himself, but instead paced a quiet section of the trees. It was all he could do to keep his limbs from going numb at the very thought of what he and these other fighters were about to do. Up until now, he'd held himself together, but with so few hours left before the group would have to fly off for the desert, he felt an increasing pressure building within him.

Flashes of his earlier days with the Razorclaws gnawed at his mind—gathering around maps and blueprints, marking entry points, watching Req prepare chemical weapons.

And among those flashes, Sakay kept seeing her face.

Ramaya.

Eyes like polished obsidian and lips drawn tight in concentration.

Sakay wrapped his fingers around the dinosaur tooth that dangled from his neck.

"Use your teeth."

Ramaya had once threatened to stab him with this tooth.

After her death, he'd ached to know what it would have felt like plunging into his heart—and had had half a mind to do it himself, just so he could be wherever she was. If she was nowhere, he wanted to be nowhere. If she ceased to exist, he likewise would prefer to cease existing.

Somehow, he'd become numb to the memory over time. The Underground had always been busy with traders eager to challenge his intelligence and his skill, which had been a welcome diversion. Meanwhile, there had been Qora, challenging his patience, keeping him on his toes.

If Qora—or any of the Razorclaws—were to be lost during the attack on Qhapaq Apo's base, Sakay didn't think he could bear it.

Kuy was right; Ramaya wouldn't have wanted him to stay in the shadows, to just keep pushing liquors and leathers at the Underground, when there was still so much to be done about the state of affairs in Runaqa. She would have said to fight, no matter the cost. Although he wondered how she would have felt if she could know that her own sacrifice had not been enough— that it hadn't been worth it. What if *this* wasn't either?

The ache in his chest began to spread.

"Gods, I miss you," he whispered, hoping that Ramaya's spirit could hear him from the High World, if the High World was as real a place as he'd always been taught.

The more he thought of her, the more he ached *everywhere*. Deep in his bones, he ached. How could he feel such physical pain when he sustained no wounds, no injuries? It was too familiar. Too like the moment he'd watched the color drain from Ramaya's cheeks. Such an ache that he'd wanted to pierce his own heart just to make it stop.

I should have cut ties with the Razorclaws a long time ago, he thought. Because, while he wanted to fight for what was right, he also couldn't help feeling as though his participation in this was unearthing things he swore he'd buried.

In the distance, the fighters and the other Razorclaws chattered amongst themselves, arguing about the campsite and how to arrange things.

Sakay tuned them out and gazed up at the bits of blue between the treetops. He wasn't sure how long he stood there, staring upward, but at some point someone came shuffling through to where he was.

"There you are," said Ollan. "Qora's looking for you. Everything … alright?"

Sakay stood and brushed off his pants, offering Ollan a solid handshake. "Never better."

Ollan glanced at their clasped hands, then at Sakay's face. "Listen. Since I don't know if I'll get the chance to say it later, I want you to know how grateful I am to you."

"For what?"

"You know for what. My sister might not be alive if it weren't for you."

"Well, I don't know if I deserve any credit for *that* …"

Ollan smiled wanly. "You do. She's told me about everything you've done for her. I hate that I wasn't there, but …" He shook his head. "You have no idea how glad I am that you were."

"It was my pleasure," Sakay said quietly. "She's done a lot for me too. More than she realizes."

"I'm glad to know she didn't just give you a hard time these past four and a half years."

Sakay chuckled faintly. "Can't say she didn't. But I'd be lying if I said I didn't enjoy it."

"I know what you mean. I've missed her. Now that I've seen

to the rest of my family's safety in Allpa, I don't plan on letting her out of my sight."

"Sounds like she's back in good hands."

>>>

Sakay pulled himself together while Izhi's commander gathered the fighters and went over the plan.

"We'll fly out to the base half an hour before dawn and station ourselves on the viewpoint plateau—what we believe to be the closest we can get without being spotted. In darkness, we will arrange luminate canisters along the near-side pinnacles, with fuses primed for ignition. Meanwhile, during this preparation, we will have ensured that all of our reptiles have received doses of alluvial fool's silver to fortify them against the effects of the dominite and keep them under our own control.

"As the hour of the wedding in Aleta arrives, we will protect our eyes and deploy the luminate, which will flash like the sun's anger and give us approximately fifteen seconds to close in while the guards and handlers wait for their vision to clear. When we reach the perimeter of the base, the Razorclaws will deploy muters to dampen the sound of our arrival for guards who might be trained well enough to shoot blindly using our noise as a guide. This will also disorient any dinosaurs within the enclosures.

"With these protections in place, we will fly directly over the base and dispense our individual allotments of hushdust from the air, ensuring no further human activity that would deter our efforts. We expect that the dinosaurs will remain somewhat disoriented, even though the hushdust won't affect them.

"Once we're on the ground, the First Team will loot dominite crystals from unconscious handlers to keep dinosaurs at bay as needed while the Second Team spreads out and—on my count—winds the gearbombs and distributes them in designated areas based on our rough schematics. Simultaneously, the Third Team will collect and load as much dominite as possible onto their flyers, and the Razorclaws will fly laps around the base to keep watch for external threats until we finish the job.

"Gearbombs will explode within three minutes, so *do not waste a single second.* Keep your activities tight, like we practiced in drills. Then we fly out as fast as we can before the base blows, leaving nothing behind but rubble."

Sakay had to admit, while he didn't love this mission, the very idea of watching Qhapaq Apo's base go up in flames set alight a blazing fire in his own heart. With Ramaya so prominently on his mind today, he leaned into the fury, more than ready to see the tyrant leader pay for the losses he'd caused.

The fighters applauded and cheered.

Sakay squeezed Qora's hand. "Let's end that bastard once and for all."

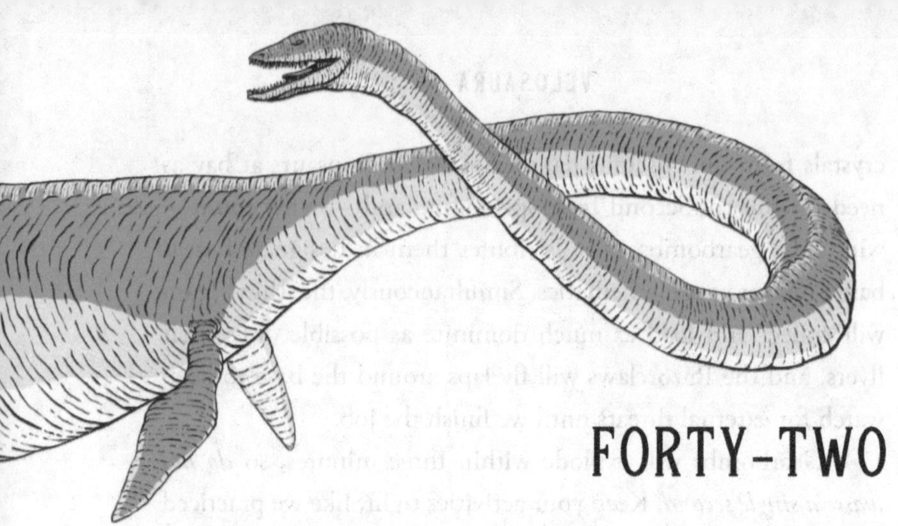

FORTY-TWO

SPARSE CLOUDS ABOVE THE SEA caught the light of the descending sun in pink and purple hues as Ninan looked out from the main deck. This would be the last time he saw one of these views, since the *Velosaura* would be back in Aleta in a couple of hours to conclude the tour.

He sat upon a barrel, plucking the strings of his charango—the one Qora had left for him—and inhaled the sea air, thinking of how clear and abundant it was, thinking how little "breathing room" he would have when this was all over, and tried his best to savor it.

Soon, Paqari joined him—silently at first, letting the wind blow loose strands of her hair over her forehead. Then she said, "At least try not to look *so* disappointed when we exchange vows tomorrow."

He plucked a few more strings, emitting the vague melody of an old song his fingers still seemed to remember. "I really am sorry about the other night."

For a moment, she almost seemed to appreciate his music, inclining her ear toward him. When he slowed the tempo, she said, "You weren't my first choice either, you know."

"I know. I mean … I wouldn't think I was. And I don't blame you."

She folded her arms. "Your little speech, though, last week below decks … about manipulation, and determining the essence of who you are and all that nonsense …"

He placed his palm across the strings to silence their vibrations, and raised an eyebrow. "Yes?"

"You and I aren't so different. When your father discovered your behavior wasn't in line with what's expected of a qhapaq's son, he sentenced you to death by wilderness abandonment. When my father discovered my failures, he forcibly removed the man I *really* wanted to marry … and then engaged me to you."

"By all means, compare an engagement to death by abandonment."

She rolled her eyes. "I'm not saying it's the same. I'm only saying that what you and I do wrong never goes unpunished. And whatever went on between you and the champion, your father saw fit to stamp it out by delivering you to my ship."

"And, what did your father do to … the other guy?"

"The other 'guy' … was a watchguard. I never could have married him, obviously. I wasn't even in my right mind to *get* married, but, if I'd had the ability to choose …" She pursed her lips. "Well, I still can't say. I was sheltered, and naive, and he … opened my eyes, I'll say that much. Anyway, my father sent him away. I didn't know where at first. It took me weeks to find out, bribing attendants and digging through posting orders. When I finally learned where he'd gone, I stole away into the night all cloaked like some criminal, and on a megaraptor no less … only to find him at a towndwelling, married to a seamstress. A woman already with child by him."

Ninan thought how he would feel if he were to discover Qora married to someone else. His stomach formed a hard knot.

"Later," she added, "I learned that my father had *wanted*

me to find him then—allowed me to—to punish me, so that I'd stop pining."

"That's despicable."

She took a deep breath and erected her shoulders. "This is just what we have to endure. This is the life of a royalborn. It might seem heroic to fight against the forces that control us and squash our whims, or to try and get what we want against all odds and live life as we please, but … there's strength in doing our duty, too. Especially when it's not what we want. There's honor in sacrifice."

That sounded an awful lot like Qora, Ninan thought.

"Maybe that's just the sacrifice we have to make. To tamp down the raging fires we hold inside."

"If I had fought harder for the watchman," Paqari said, "he might have ended up dead, rather than relocated. Likewise, the champion is safer by not being with you. Not everyone will understand what we endure for them, but many will be better off for it. Remember that."

It hadn't occurred to Ninan that Qora would be better off without him, although it should have. But regardless of how significant she was to *him* personally, in reality she was only a small thread in a much larger tapestry—a tapestry that was comprised of his friends in Thak, and every other citizen of Sumaq, and all those who dwelled upon the farthest reaches of Runaqa. With every agonizing step toward the altar tomorrow, he would have to think of all of them.

Izhi had said that too: *"Consider the wedding a sacrifice for your people."*

Hesitantly, Ninan nodded. "You're right."

"It comforts me to know that I am not alone in this burden," Paqari told him. "Perhaps through our years together, we can build upon that."

At this moment, Ninan caught a glimpse of something past Paqari's smooth, bronzed skin and silky hair and red lips—all of which he could objectively appreciate—to the depth of her strength, to what she had become after all she'd endured. It wasn't the same as what he loved about Qora, but he could appreciate this too.

If marrying this young woman, whose hardened mask gave her the confidence to wake up every day and live through her obligations, could make way for Izhi and the Razorclaws and Qora to safely move forward with their plan to prevent continental conflict, then he would do it.

He would be like the creature whose namesake had transported him all over these islands, and alter his very skin so that he could blend in to the environment he'd been born for, accepting it and becoming it and concealing his true colors so that "Ninan" disappeared and Apo-Kimsa Kallpa stood proud before the people who would never truly understand what he'd given them.

"Yes," he said. "Perhaps."

The small and swift oryctodromeus burrows into the ground and creates a network of tunnels for shelter, food storage, and safety. The true key to its survival, however, is the construction of multiple burrows—in other words, multiple escape routes from predators.

Excerpt from *Survival of Prey*

FORTY-THREE

A GOLDEN BAND OF LIGHT STRIPED THE HORIZON.
Qora watched as Sakay placed a canister on the surface of the plateau and gave its fuse a gentle tug to test it.

"That's the last one," Sakay said.

Along the plateau's upper surface, which stretched about a quarter mile across the desert and shielded the base, members of Izhi's unit and the other Razorclaws manned nine more luminate canisters distributed evenly for maximum coverage.

Prior to the attack, Wayra would imitate the cry of a wild flyer—high-pitched and sharp and loud enough that all could hear, but authentic enough that anyone on the base would think little of it—three times, and on the third cry, assigned operatives would light their fuses with a friction match and shield their own eyes.

As the canisters shot the luminate into the air, a soft *pop* would sound, but by the time anyone on the base could react, it would be too late.

Those on the base, and anyone within at least a mile radius, who viewed the flashes without protection would be fully blinded for up to thirty seconds and would likely experience afterimages for up to a minute.

Meanwhile, on pteranodonback, the Razorclaws and Izhi's

military teams would close in.

"I can't believe we're really doing this." Qora took a shuddering breath as she observed the setup—what little of it she could see in the dim dawnlight. Her heartbeat seemed a constant murmur, one that had kept her on the brink of waking throughout the night preceding this event.

Sakay rubbed the back of his neck. "It's not often we have this kind of information *and* advantage at the same time."

He had been quiet since Qora had arrived at the camp, Qora realized. Not quite himself. Although he hadn't really been himself consistently since the start of all this—since Kuy had shown up at the Underground. If that girl, Ramaya, had died as the result of Sakay's last mission with the Razorclaws, this must be torture for him.

"At least Ninan is alive."

Remembering that sentiment, Qora tried to be grateful, to acknowledge what Sakay must be suffering. Still, in the back of her mind—where she'd intentionally banished it—was the thought that, by the end of all this, Ninan would be married to Paqari. Considering everything else, it was only a cut among gaping wounds, but it hurt nonetheless.

As always, her doubts about her feelings for him persisted, fueled by the continual suspicion that she'd only grown so attached to him because of all they'd endured together in the Venture, and now by the suspicion that it was perhaps only the forces keeping them apart that made them long for one another, a natural opposition to what they both faced today.

Qora must have been lost in an obvious daze, because Sakay then said, "You're allowed to mourn him, you know."

"Am I?" she asked. "When there are so many lives on the line? So many loved ones lost already?"

He seemed to understand how his experience factored in.

"My bleeding doesn't negate your bruises."

Over his shoulder, Qora spotted Ollan approaching them. Her eyes welled—in part for Sakay's compassion, in part for Ollan's survival.

When Ollan reached them, he said, "Everything alright?"

Qora shook her head, but stood between them and took one of each of their hands. "No," she said. "But I'm glad you're both here with me."

My brothers.

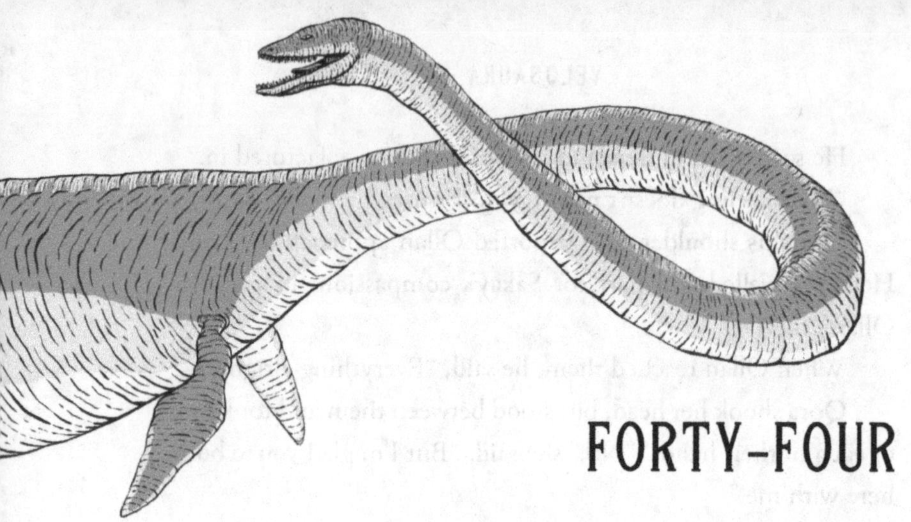

FORTY-FOUR

EXTENDING FROM ALETA'S COAST was an enormous jetty made of piled rock, wide at its connection point and tapering on a curve. An aerial view would have revealed the shape of a reptilian claw. Additional rocks were piled around its start, forming the claw's tubercle. All along its top surface, paved with flat stones, Huapaya House attendants scurried back and forth in preparation for the wedding, which would take place at the apex of the jetty.

Arrangements of orange inqa-lilly, pink kantuta, and yellow amancay flowers lined the outer edges of the walkway. Small ships gathered around the apex, full of spectators, who were bustling and chatting with excitement.

Guards patrolled the jetty as well, and the surrounding coast, with vigilance, should enemies think to disturb the bliss of such an occasion.

Ninan watched from the third floor of Huapaya House. The surrounding bluffs were already cluttered with thousands of middleborns and lowborns who had come to witness the union.

In a few minutes, the qhapaq's chief attendant Mullu would arrive to escort Ninan to his doom.

With trembling fingers, Ninan adjusted the cuffs of his dress shirt, and flinched when a knock rattled the door of his dressing chamber. He scooped Tuko—who had been perched on the edge of the desk—into an open drawer and slid the drawer shut.

The tailor, who had altered so much of Ninan's clothing aboard the *Velosaura*, poked his head in. "Apologies, Your Highness, but there was a last-minute adjustment I wanted to make to your vest."

"Oh?" Ninan said.

"Yes. I find that simple, uh … *comforts*, can be helpful," the tailor explained, gesturing to the red velvet vest draped over his own arm.

"Comforts? Helpful for what?" Ninan's tone was verging on indignant and he had to clear his throat to cut the tension.

With a flat, knowing smile, the tailor went before the gilded mirror and held the vest open.

Ninan waited for further explanation, but at the tailor's continued silence, he joined him, turning his back and slipping into the armholes.

From behind him, the tailor brushed the sleeves so that the nap of the velvet was all aligned to pick up the light the same way. Ninan watched himself in the mirror as the tailor reached around and lifted the left panel of the vest to reveal a pocket on the inside.

Ninan flicked his gaze at the tailor in reflection, meeting his eyes. "Why … ?"

"I don't presume to know why that little flyer is so fond of you, or why you're so fond of him, but I imagined you might want to keep him close today."

For a moment, Ninan pressed his lips together, trying to keep emerging tears at bay. It was such a small gesture, and yet …

"I … That's …"

"Don't worry. It's just between us." The tailor patted his back and left him to finish getting ready.

As soon as the door closed within its frame, Ninan carefully removed Tuko from the drawer and slipped him into the inner vest pocket. He took another look at his reflection, partly to ensure that Tuko's shape was fully hidden behind the velvet, and partly to get a final glimpse of himself before he stepped outside and fused his soul—at least, that was how the High Shaman would describe it—to Paqari's for the rest of his pitiful life.

A sense of fearful energy flooded his veins, dizzying his mind. Every breath released with a slight shudder. His mouth went dry. For a moment, he had to brace himself on the desk and close his eyes.

I can do this.

He thought of the base, dotted with obedient dinosaurs, a mere fragment of what his father had in store.

He thought of Qora, riding on pteranodonback with the Razorclaws and Qhapaq Izhi's unit.

He thought of the people in Thak—of Pidru and Tamya and their mamáy who had taken him in—working under the watchful eyes of his father's guards.

He thought of other citizens, from every Terrain and every walk of life, and imagined a war-torn land around them ravaging their trades and industries and crops, decimating their homes and families.

After all he'd been given, this task was the least he could do.

"We've both already won more than we deserve."

When Qora had left him in the observatory in Port Waqta, she'd whispered goodbye, but Ninan had said nothing in response. He hadn't been able to bring himself to repeat the word, to say it out loud. That would have made it final.

Now, it was the only thing left to do.

Although she wasn't with him this time, he went to the open window and, trusting the air spirits—if they were even real—to carry the sentiment all the way to the Aquchay and touch her heart, he said, "Goodbye, Qora."

The next person to come to the door was Mullu.

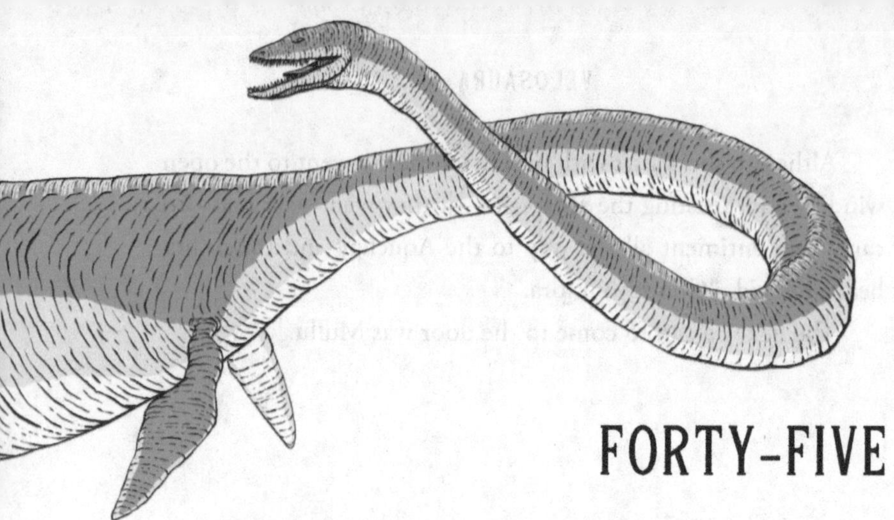

FORTY-FIVE

AS MORNING CAME IN FULL FORCE, drawing out the majority of the dinosaurs and their handlers, Qora waited with the Razorclaws and the Unuvian operatives, sitting atop their pteranodons behind the spires of the plateau. A few of the Unuvian officers manned the luminate canisters, and would follow soon after the first wave.

All fighters were armed with military blades and crossbows.

The pteranodons had had an hour to get their fill of fool's-silver-laced water so that they might be resistant to the dominite on the base.

Qora kept her eyes fixed on Wayra, who stood at the center of the line and raised both hands to her mouth, intertwining her fingers and cupping her palms and forming a shape that would channel the sound appropriately. Then Wayra took an enormous breath, puckered her lips, and blew into the opening, creating the first shrill cry.

FORTY-SIX

IN BETWEEN EACH OF THE THREE CRIES, Sakay's heart thumped in a syncopated rhythm.

The sound Wayra made was identical to that of a wild pterodactyl, sharp and reverberating.

As the last cry rang out, all ten fighters lit their respective fuses and everyone covered their eyes. Within seconds, the lit fuses ignited the contents of the canisters, which each shot up simultaneously. The soft explosion let the fighters know the flash had deployed, but the light was so bright, it still penetrated Sakay's fingers, even with his eyelids closed. How blinding it must have been to witness with no protection, Sakay thought.

And now it was time to ride.

Sakay opened his eyes and kicked off with his flyer. All other airborne fighters were up and away with him, a burst of dark figures from the earth.

Dinosaurs in the distance screeched and shrieked in response to the aftereffects of the flash.

The Razorclaws headed the group and soared across the distance between the plateau and the base, closing in fast and readying the muters. Kuy went first, then Sakay and the others, tossing the copper incendiaries that were indistinguishable from firebombs but for their hidden contents. On impact, the casings bloomed clouds of thick smoke, and silence flooded Sakay's ears. The sounds of screeching dinosaurs died instantaneously. Sakay's pteranodon opened its mouth and cried out, but it fell upon deafened ears.

One by one, the airborne fighters crossed the outer wall, pteranodons flapping just a few feet above the base enclosures. Everyone gripped their saddles with their thighs and used both hands to aim and deploy each powder cannon of hushdust over the disoriented guards, handlers, and trainers as they clamored silently in the dissipating smoke.

As if affected by some god of sleep, the people on the base began to drop where they'd stood. Sakay followed Kuy, with Wayra, Req, Gorgo, Qora, and Ollan close behind, circling the base to observe.

The adult dinosaurs within their own enclosure ran wild, rearing and bucking at the commotion. The juveniles and hatchlings, unaffected by the dust, gathered around their trainers, still entranced by the dominite crystals they kept.

As soon as the dust settled, Kuy shouted, "All clear!"

The Unuvian military touched down, dismounted, and dispersed.

In the heat of the fire, one may be forged
or one may be consumed.

Unuvian Proverb

FORTY-SEVEN

NINAN FOLLOWED MULLU to a designated starting point until the man stopped to face Paqari's attendant. Then Mullu and his counterpart both stepped aside to allow Ninan and Paqari to see one another for the first time on this blessed day.

The princess was a vision in royal purple silks with flowing sleeves, and a gold collar necklace and a diadem on her head made of small, gilded liopleurodon teeth that pointed like rays of sun beaming out of her hair. Her skin was aglow with a shimmering powder—the luster of a goddess—while rubies dangled from hoops in her earlobes.

She raised her chin with a defiant gaze, reminding Ninan silently that they were both to accept this fate with dignity. He nodded at her once, slowly, solemnly.

A look of understanding passed between them.

And then he took her hand.

FORTY-EIGHT

THE FIRST TEAM RAN to the fallen trainers for dominite crystals while the Second Team took their places and prepared to wind the gearbombs. The Third Team rushed to the storehouses, opening large burlap sacks to fill with more dominite.

Sakay's thundering pulse slowed as he looked over the fallen workers and guards, seeing them still and useless. He searched the skies around the base and found them clear.

While time was of the essence, there was no one here to hinder the fighters' progress; all initial deployments had gone as planned, and it was now a matter of seizing dominite and leaving this place in ashes.

As the muter smoke thinned, the silence lifted in a crescendo.

The Razorclaws formed a circle in the air, visually checking in with one another to ensure the status thus far.

Storehouse doors were open.

Gearbombs were in place, ready to be wound.

The First Team fended off small theropods to get to the fallen trainers for dominite.

Sakay hovered his pteranodon and focused on the First Team. Every trainer among them was limp and flat on the sand face down, as expected, and coated in a sprinkle of white dust.

Wait—Face down? Sakay thought. *Every single one of them?*

The more he stared at them, the more their forms looked … strange. Not like what he'd seen in Ika, when the Razorclaws had put the dockworkers and guards there to sleep, with their awkwardly splayed limbs and gaping mouths and random undignified positions.

These people lay with their limbs closer to the body, hands positioned near the chest in a way that Sakay imagined someone would if they were to trip and catch themselves before taking the full impact of the ground as they fell. Or, worse yet, if they were to—

"Storehouse is empty!" Qora pointed to the Third Team as they emerged with drooping burlap sacks.

Upon closer inspection, hundreds of clear, white, depleted crystals littered the ground surrounding the storehouse buildings.

The First team had begun to push through the juvenile dinosaurs to get at the trainers when Wayra said, "These are different dinosaurs …"

Sakay tightened his grip on the pommel, struggling to catch his breath, and squinted.

Stripe patterns differed in vibrance, each dinosaur's overall color differed slightly from the next, and the size variance among them was much greater than groups that would have hatched at the same time.

Ruck—she's right.

Before the First Team could search the trainers, every man or woman that had been lying face down now "awoke" and sprung up. The trainers stripped skin-toned masks from their mouths and noses, and then one of them shouted, "Advance!"

Portions of every inner wall below the thatched awnings separated from the main blocks. The dusty, coarse texture morphed to forest-green scales. Riders wearing camouflaged uniforms emerged from behind the newly revealed dinosaurs and mounted them, raising loaded bows.

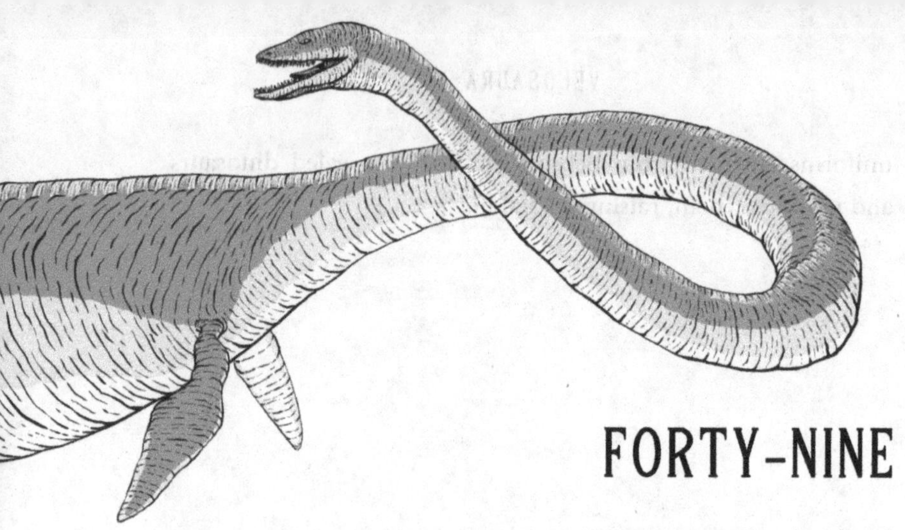

FORTY-NINE

HIGHBORNS AND PRIVILEGED ATTENDANTS bordered the walkway that led to the apex of the claw-form jetty, all of whom bowed as Ninan and Paqari began their procession, while Mullu and Paqari's attendant trailed them.

With every step, Ninan took a steadying breath, trying to focus on the ground beneath his feet instead of his runaway thoughts about the attack on the base and how he would much rather be flying into battle with the Razorclaws. The fact that others were risking their physical safety and even their lives right now while he made a spectacle of himself among flowers and fawning had a special kind of sting to it.

Nearing the end of the line, Ninan and Paqari passed the royalborn guests of Qolqe and Unu. Ninan shifted his gaze quickly so as not to linger on Qhapaq Izhi—so as not to betray their silent alliance.

The Allpan quya was absent, however, and Ninan wondered if perhaps she hadn't been invited. While most royalborn events were open by default to other royalborns for diplomacy's sake, he could also believe that his father might not appreciate the "spiritual discord" someone like Quya Urpi might cause with her attendance. Someone whose leadership defied convention surely was not welcome on a day like this.

All other guests watched from the decks of anchored ships positioned to provide a good vantage point, while the highborns on the jetty came forward from behind the couple and gathered near.

As Ninan and Paqari reached the apex, both their fathers were already standing on either side of the altar, with the High Shaman of Huapaya House between them in his purple robes. The altar, plated in gold, supported a sculpture of Tisqu's emblematic liopleurodon, forged with an open mouth and a hollow belly so that bundles of holy wood might burn from within while the head spewed smoke in a silent roar.

Members of both families formed a semicircle on the outer edge of the apex, facing the approaching couple, with the Kallpas to one side and the Huapayas to the other. Ninan paid no attention to his brothers and their wives, or the other quyas, but exchanged a glance with his mother, who wrung her hands. She had to know what this day meant for him—from the memory of her own wedding, from the maternal instinct she possessed.

Ninan felt Tuko's tiny claws at his chest, right where his heart pounded, as if the pteromorph were trying to calm him. That pounding must have been a strange sensation, causing Tuko to react, but Ninan liked to think it was an intentional consolatory gesture.

"Welcome, esteemed guests," the High Shaman said in a booming voice that even the persistent crash of the ocean didn't overpower. "Let us begin."

In the beginning, there was the Energy. The Energy shaped the Worlds, and all those therein that flourished. The Energy remains among us, between us, within us. We may direct and redirect it, absorb it, become transformed by it, or it may break us to pieces.

The Sacred Forces, Record I, Script I

FIFTY

FIGHTERS FROM QHAPAQ IZHI'S UNIT sprang back with arrows in their chests.

Sakay juked with his pteranodon as an arrow soared past his ear.

More arrows zipped up toward the Razorclaws, who quickly abandoned their circular formation to dodge them.

One minute the fighters had had everything under control. The next, megaraptors had emerged from the walls as though born from the bricks themselves. How had they shifted their very skin to blend in like velosaurs? What sort of biological sorcery was at play here?

Meanwhile, the juveniles within the enclosures had all the signs of wild gangs—not uniformly hatched trainees.

"How can this be happening?" Req swerved beyond the bounds of the base for a moment.

The thatched awnings had covered the megaraptors from an aerial view, Sakay realized. From the ground, the camouflage effect—paired with the unit's singular focus—had been sufficient to allow the threat to go unnoticed.

"Qhapaq Apo must have evacuated the dinosaurs we saw before, or replaced them," Qora panted. "Except for these megaraptor hybrids …"

The teams below drew their own weapons and shot back, spewing arrows in all directions.

"How could the qhapaq have known?" Kuy said.

Sakay had a sinking feeling as he watched the trainers' discarded masks trampled in the chaos—the masks that had kept the hushdust out of their lungs.

"I don't think he did," Sakay told them.

The Razorclaws had revealed their hand—or at least one of their most valuable cards—almost a month ago. The qhapaq hadn't known who had attacked in Ika, or even that his dominite had been the target, but he would have eventually learned someone had put the workers to sleep with powder cannons.

Our fault—again.

"But he was ready for it," Wayra said.

"Except he didn't have protection against the flash," Sakay replied. "Or the muters."

A look of understanding passed over Qora's face. "He was being cautious. Because of what we did at the docks."

"He knew today would present an opportunity," Ollan concluded.

Sakay nodded. The qhapaq might not have suspected *exactly* what the fighters had been planning, but it didn't matter; it had taken less than a minute to recover from the flash, another half minute for the muters' effects to fade, and the trainers had played unconscious for longer than that, easily—recovering just in time to ambush anyone who might descend on them.

FIFTY-ONE

AFTER SEVERAL INTRODUCTORY PHRASES, the High Shaman said, "The couple will separate, and each will take his or her place with the qhapaq to whom he or she belongs."

Paqari went to her father while Ninan went to his.

The High Shaman nodded. "The qhapaqs will now begin the rites."

"My brother under the Sky," said Qhapaq Apo.

"My brother under the Sky," Qhapaq Achik repeated.

"With this union we maintain the Mother's balance," said Qhapaq Apo.

"As the water spirits float from the great bodies and upon the Sun's heat rise to the clouds …" said Qhapaq Achik.

"… so do the water spirits fall again to the place from whence they came," said Qhapaq Apo.

In unison: "And so in equal parts disperse their blessings upon our land."

Each of the qhapaqs produced a large, gold coin, which they exchanged. They pocketed their identical, equal measures of gold, and then presented and exchanged their respective children, so that Paqari took her place beside Ninan's father and Ninan took his place beside Paqari's, with his back to the bluffs. He was grateful, at least, to not have to face the enormous crowds that had gathered there.

In front of the sculpted liopleurodon, as smoke billowed gently from its mouth, the High Shaman placed a golden bowl. He then withdrew two gilded daggers and handed them to the qhapaqs. "With these, you will draw the blood of your lines."

Ninan had seen this during his brothers' weddings, and once when he'd attended the wedding of a Qolqese cousin. Paqari's father would cut his hand—a clean line across his palm—and then guide him to the bowl, while his own father would do the same to Paqari, and together the bride and groom would each squeeze three drops of blood into the golden bowl. From that moment on, they would be joined before the gods and all these people in an unbreakable blood bond.

As the qhapaqs took their respective daggers, the High Shaman lit a piece of holy wood and circled the four of them, wafting the smoke as he spoke a cleansing chant in one of the old languages.

Ninan presented his upturned palm, sucking in a breath as Qhapaq Achik gripped his wrist. Across from him, Paqari stood firm and unflinching. No matter the pain or the fear or the dread or the injustice, she did not cower.

In that moment, Ninan followed her example and held his head high as his future father-in-law dragged the blade in a diagonal, and a red line materialized on his skin.

I can do this.

He looked at the foreign qhapaq with a numb, resigned sort of peace. The qhapaq guided Ninan's fingers into a curled position, a loose fist that he would then bring to the bowl. Then Ninan looked at Paqari and bowed his head in respect. When he raised it, she glanced upward at something behind him—and a tiny smirk played over her lips.

Everyone gasped.

Every guard drew a weapon.

"Get down!" the High Shaman shouted.

Ninan spun around to see two dozen airborne pirates soaring down from the bluffs.

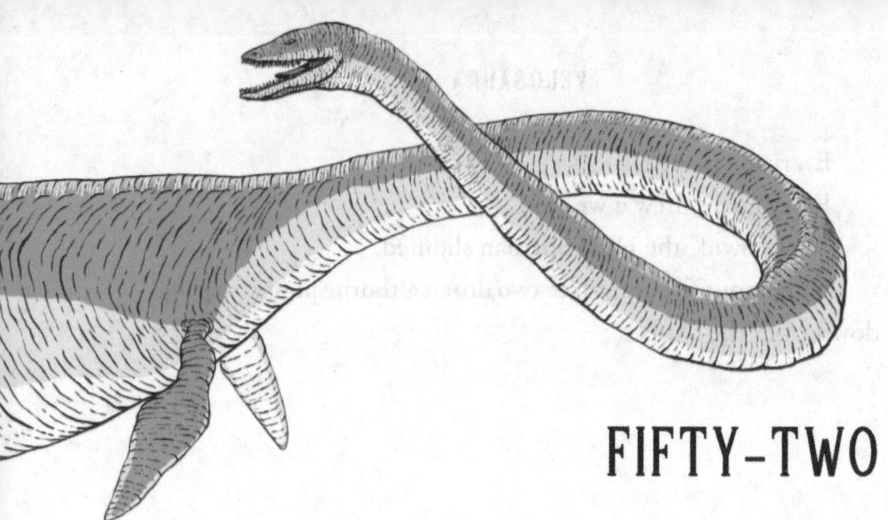

FIFTY-TWO

SAKAY TRIED TO KEEP HIS WITS ABOUT HIM as everything continued to unfold.

Qora and Ollan drew their crossbows from their high positions and shot downward, both taking out riders and trainers with lightning speed in between dodging shots against them.

Kuy swooped low and flung knives until he'd exhausted his supply.

Req wove in between the other Razorclaws, taking cover behind them as they defended themselves, then re-emerging to spew remnants of hushdust at unmasked enemies. As ammunition dwindled for everyone, however, forcing those on the ground into hand-to-hand combat, their proximity to one another made it difficult for Req to knock out trainers and ground riders without dosing his own people.

Dinosaurs ran amok to stay close to the handlers with the glowing purple crystals. Only the megaraptors remained in any kind of formation under the command of their riders, while the wild juveniles followed crystals blindly and without logic.

As the rebel fighters overpowered more of the enemy, the riders shouted new commands at their raptors.

"Target!" A rider pointed his crystal at one of Izhi's fighters and the raptor charged forward, pinning the woman to the ground and clamping its jaws over her neck.

Another rider sicced her raptor on a separate fighter just as he was a breath away from plunging his blade into a murderous trainer.

It only now occurred to Sakay that the trainers weren't trainers at all, but military in disguise.

His breath stalled.

How had he been foolish enough to think this would work? Qhapaq Apo was too powerful, too knowledgeable. There was nothing the Razorclaws or any army on Runaqa could do to overpower him. If all other Terrains were to combine against Sumaq, *maybe*, but the qhapaq had spent the last two decades slowly chipping away at their unity—taking a Qolqese woman to wife, marrying off his second son to the Qolqese ambassador's daughter, and now forming an alliance with Tisqu through Ninan's marriage to the island princess and building rapport through the engagement tour. The man was unstoppable. Anyone who tried to fight would not only *not* win the battle, but they were fated to lose something or someone dear to them.

The scene below became a dizzying blur. Sakay's vision tunneled as his sweaty palms slipped on the pommel. Pressure mounted in his chest, and despite his best efforts, his lungs refused to fully inflate. He squeezed his eyes shut for a moment, deferring control to his flyer.

"Sakay?" Qora said, sweeping past him. "Sakay …"

She steered her pteranodon to fly parallel, keeping a steady gaze on him.

He tried to focus on her, tried to focus on the rhythm of his flyer's wings.

What was wrong with him? He'd faced criminals at the Underground—many of whom would have taken his life if he hadn't been so savvy—and he'd infiltrated the walls of the qhapaq's facilities before with the Razorclaws. Since then he'd also faced pirates and terminonatators. How could he lose composure at a time like *this*?

Qora's closeness should have comforted him, but instead he only imagined her young face drained of color, her flesh marred by an enemy blade. She shouldn't be here. Neither should any of the Razorclaws. Just like before, they had worsened the situation. He knew it. Every bone in his body knew it.

"Stay with me, Sakay. Please." Qora had to pause to take another shot. "Sakay?!"

Her voice came at him like a soft and distant cry, muffled by his own pulse pounding thickly in his ears. He wavered on his pteranodon, his vision darkening at the edges.

FIFTY-THREE

THE GUARDS THAT LINED THE JETTY aimed their crossbows high, but the pirates had already begun to fire their own bows.

Ninan shoved between guards to get to his mother. "Come on," he told her as he led her away.

The Head of the Guard shouted, "Shields! Now!"

The guards surrounded the royalborns and raised their shields collectively to create a roof as they ushered everyone toward the beach.

The pirates lowered their pteranodons and dismounted. "Laps!" the pirate captain called. The two dozen pteranodons returned to the skies and flew circles around the site, while the pirates below swarmed the crowd and mingled among them, snatching the highborns' jewelry and silk scarves.

Launching from the bluffs was a strategic choice, Ninan thought, as flying over the water would have made them visible from miles away. Regardless, the guards seemed to have been more preoccupied with the guests on the ships, as though they'd expected a threat from among them instead.

Mullu stood before Qhapaq Apo and made a weapon of the skyrock-tipped staff he always carried. He swung the staff, its shaft striking one of the pirates with a sickening thud. He spun on his heel, driving the staff against another pirate's ribs, and another's spine, sending their blades clattering on the stones beneath their feet.

Once Ninan had ensured that his mother was safe beneath the shields, he withdrew himself from their protection.

With the guards divided between fighting off the pirates and protecting esteemed guests, the pirates managed to wreak havoc despite their small numbers.

Although the pirate attack on the *Velosaura* had been weeks ago and had happened quickly, Ninan had been in close enough contact with many of them to be able to say with certainty that these pirates were not the same as those. Maybe these simply hated all royalborns and highborns. Maybe they saw this gathering as an opportunity to get their hands on prized jewels and gold. Maybe—

Ninan wrestled a pirate to the ground and maneuvered her blade away, but as he kept her pinned, she only grinned at him, struck him with a knee to the groin, and willingly dove off the edge of the jetty into the water. As Ninan grunted and clambered to his feet, he paused to catch his breath and quell the wave of nausea that crested in his belly, observing the whole scene as if in slow motion.

The pirates ransacked the crowd, tearing valuables from necks and wrists and ears. They dodged weapon attacks, slipped out of headlocks and ducked under swinging fists, stole weapons and flung them into the sea—or fired them only in the vague direction of one or more guests or guards without hitting anyone. Every action that wasn't theft appeared to be self-defense or merely for show.

What in the Five Terrains...

He remembered Paqari's face as the pirates had descended.

Had she known? Had she expected this?

Had she somehow … *planned* this?

These pirates were a menace, to be certain, but on some level they were almost … harmless. They didn't seem to have any specific target, or any specific purpose, other than to stir the people to panic.

Other than to disrupt this ceremony.

"Your Highness," a guard said to Ninan. "We have to get you to safety."

Ninan shook his head. "I can help. Let me fight." He twisted away from the guard's attempt to grasp him. A surge of fire spread through his limbs. Whatever god—or perhaps *girl*—had intervened to make this happen, it was an opportunity.

All this time, he'd only been reacting to the events in his life. His own people had dropped him in the wilderness and he'd wandered until someone had taken him in. The quinoa farmers had told him to cut stalks, so he'd cut stalks. Then his father had dragged him back to Kallpa House and thrown him into the Venture, so into the Venture he'd gone. Finally, his father had threatened his friends and forced him into an engagement, and he'd boarded the *Velosaura* with hardly a second thought, except for Izhi's instructions, which he'd followed with little deviation. The small choices he'd made for himself—helping Qora win, spying for Unu, assisting the Razorclaws—were always overshadowed by his more significant choice to do what he was told.

"You don't wait for permission to strike."

But how could he strike with so much on the line? He simply hadn't known how. With his fists, there was never a question. With his fate, however, he continually found himself at a loss.

"In the grander scheme of things … you just need to figure out new ways to punch."

It struck him now, almost as hard as a true blow to the head. Maybe in this case, the way to punch was to *not* punch.

He'd been keeping his fists up, trying to keep his fears and his enemies at bay, certain that his "opponent" was too big, too strong, unbeatable. He may have been skilled in a ring, but when it came to his father, the man's very shadow was enough to knock him flat. He'd bloodied his knuckles and bruised his ribs trying to attack in whatever underhanded ways he could think of and still came up wavering each time, with no hope of a win. His eyes had been too swollen to see the obvious truth, but he could see it now: There was a way to lose *in* the ring and still win *out* of the ring—but only if he was intentional about it.

He had to lose on purpose.

He had to throw the fight.

"The wind is a force beyond our control and thus, in the face of its wrath, we must adjust our sails to harness it—so that it may carry us ever more swiftly to our destination."

Captain Inkill Puyu of the Allpan vessel *Feathertip*

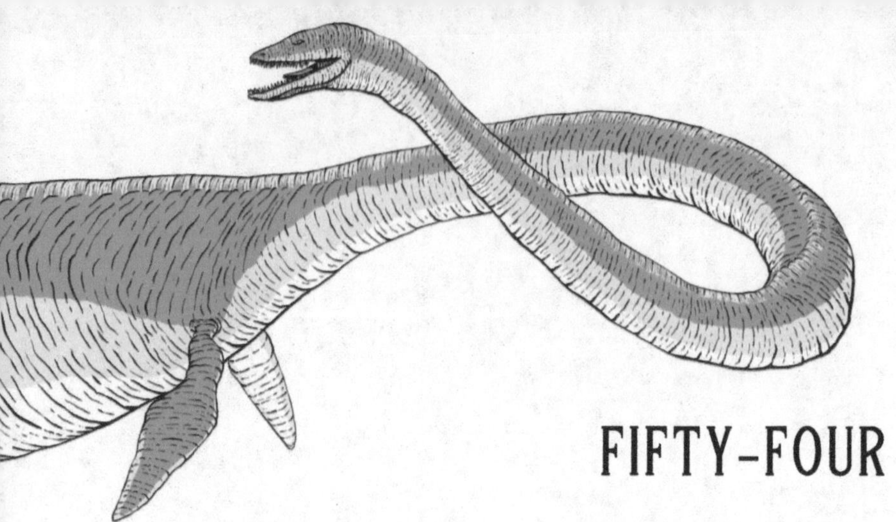

FIFTY-FOUR

AS SAKAY CONTINUED TO WAVER, he tightened his grip on the pommel, inadvertently urging the flyer into a sharp downward turn.

"Sakay!" Qora called from somewhere in his vicinity.

Sakay and his pteranodon dropped low over the base, where dozens of arrows zipped back and forth and a few shot high where the Razorclaws flew. Sakay was just present enough to release pressure so that his pteranodon leveled out—and it was then that the sight of a blackened hand caught his attention.

The beastlord.

While the faces of the base workers meant nothing to him, the evidence of such poison told him everything. There was still a chance something good could come of this. The memories of his last mission with the Razorclaws—when Ramaya had still been a part of their team—streamed through his mind, deepening his desire to redeem what he could from this one, strengthening the parts of him that were failing.

A flood of new energy seeped into him. Little by little, his muscles regained control. Air flowed freely and abundantly into his lungs. The darkness at the edges of his vision began to recede, giving him a clear view of everything before him. He took deep, steadying breaths. He swept over the base and guided his pteranodon to double back.

Qora seemed to be keeping him within her view, while also flying in a serpentine path to keep clear of any arrows. Now that Sakay had regained some sense of himself, however, Qora had stopped calling after him.

For an instant, Sakay locked eyes with her, then pointed his head at the beastlord with the blackened hand. Qora's gaze flicked to a scuffle below, where the beastlord grappled with one of Izhi's fighters.

Sakay didn't know if Qora fully understood what he was getting at, but she would recognize that hand too, and recall to whom it had belonged. For certain, it was a gamble—but Sakay was good at gambling. He'd watched people at the Underground, learned to understand human behavior, habits, instincts. And if this had been a betting opportunity, Sakay would have bet that the beastlord had recently received orders via microraptor, to send the trained dinosaurs to a specific location for safekeeping. If those orders were in the handler's uniform, the same as whatever orders he'd received the day the Razorclaws had discovered the base, then this was now an intelligence mission.

Qora mouthed the word "no" but Sakay had already positioned himself.

Sakay flew straight for the beastlord and drew up his feet so that he was crouching on the saddle. As the flyer came to a skidding stop on the ground less than a yard from the man in question, Sakay sprang up off the saddle and leapt forward, tackling the man and pinning him.

Before he could reach into the beastlord's uniform—where the corner of an orders papyr peeked out—the beastlord flipped them both and thrust Sakay onto his back. Sakay twisted his upper body to avoid the beastlord's fist coming at his face. As soon as Sakay situated himself to throw a punch of his own, the beastlord withdrew a dominite crystal and held it out long enough for its energy to capture the attention of several wild reptiles, then shoved it down the front of Sakay's shirt collar, and slipped away just as the reptiles converged. Sakay swatted and shoved and tried to shake the crystal free from the fabric against his skin.

A bolt from above pierced one of the reptiles, then another, giving Sakay the chance to retrieve the crystal and chuck it across the enclosure so he could get to his feet, where he waved a quick gesture of thanks to Qora as she reloaded, and caught sight of the beastlord snatching up a fallen bow and taking possession of an abandoned Unuvian pteranodon.

Sakay mounted his own flyer again and took off.

The beastlord soared over the base, taking shots at any fighter who had the upper hand on one of the guards. As Sakay gained on him, the beastlord looked over his shoulder and sped up. But it was too late; Sakay had taken a higher position and once again leapt off his own pteranodon and flung himself at the beastlord.

"Sakay!" Qora cried again.

Sakay was well aware that when Qora had done these kinds of acrobatics, she'd been flying over the water; for him, there was nothing but solid ground to break his fall—and break him it would, if he faltered. Regardless, the energy pumping through him seemed to dispel any rational sense of fear he might have otherwise had.

When he landed behind the beastlord, his own pteranodon continued to fly close, while the other pteranodon screeched under his sudden weight, dipping in flight. Sakay grasped at the beastlord's uniform from behind.

Qora followed their flight path from a few yards below,

struggling to maneuver while aiming her weapon. As Sakay and the beastlord grappled over the papyr that had come fully loose now, Sakay doubted Qora would have an easy time taking a good shot at the beastlord without interference. When she did shoot, the beastlord swerved at the same time, and the bolt only cut the dead air above his head.

"Ruck," Qora muttered, spanning the crossbow again and fumbling for another bolt.

The beastlord took back the papyr and threw an elbow at Sakay's face, sending a ripple of pain between Sakay's eyes as the nasal bone cracked. Blood oozed from his nostrils and past his lips, forcing him to taste it before it cascaded down his chin. He wiped it on his sleeve, taking quick breaths through his mouth, then wrapped an arm around the man's neck and tightened his hold while the beastlord clawed to break free. Twisting and flailing and threatening to unseat Sakay, the beastlord gagged as the pteranodon tilted with the abrupt and unsteady motion of its riders.

Finally, the beastlord's strength withered, and at that moment, Sakay reached again for the papyr. But then the back of the beastlord's head thrust against Sakay's broken nose and his vision blurred. Sakay loosened his grip on the man's neck, muscles slack in the wake of cresting agony.

With a wicked grin, the beastlord twisted his body so that he could grab Sakay by the front of his shirt, then heaved him off the saddle. In what felt like mid-air, Sakay managed to clasp his fingers over the corner of the papyr one last time and tug it free—just as all security fell out from under him.

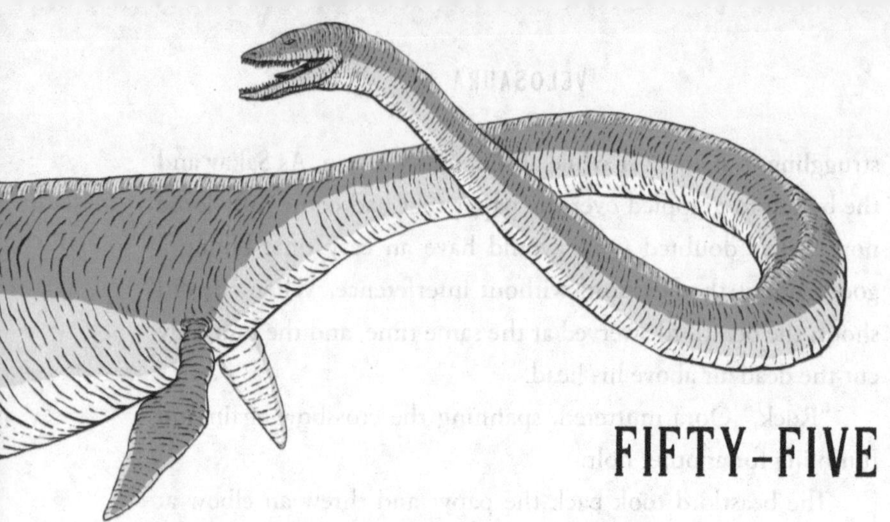

FIFTY-FIVE

THROW THE FIGHT. FAKE A LOSS. *Let them think I'm completely out of the game.*

If Ninan played this right, he could win this round against his father. He could get to Kallpa House while his father was here in Tisqu. He could get supplies and transportation and—his chest fluttered with something he didn't dare allow to take full hold of him, but continued to entertain the strategy now flourishing in his mind—he could keep the people in Thak safe from his father. But only if he could get off this damned jetty.

Ninan had to push through screaming guests to get to another pirate wrestling over a crossbow with a guard. Now that the pirate was within reach, Ninan wreathed his arms around the pirate's torso, dragging him downward. He grappled with the man, a lighter-skinned thirty-something with hair in a tail at the nape of his neck and sun-damaged cheeks and a worn floppy hat. The pirate struggled underneath him, but Ninan kept him in place with a hand on his neck and a knee on his belly. Ninan glanced over his shoulder, where everyone was either scrambling away or fighting uselessly, then leaned close to the pirate's ear.

"Kidnap me," he told the man.

The pirate furrowed his brows. "I beg your pardon?"

"Call your flyer back and kidnap me." Ninan released

pressure and allowed the pirate to sit up—part way—before shoving him back down with artificial force.

"I know who you are." The pirate panted. "Why in the Grave World would you want me to do that?"

Ninan let up again, then grasped the front of the man's shirt and pulled him into a roll on top of him. The pirate, now with what looked like the upper hand, tried to climb off, but Ninan yanked him back down.

Tuko squawked from within Ninan's vest, reminding Ninan he was still there.

Ninan winced at having put pressure on him, but looked up at the pirate. "I'll get you your weight in gold, but you need to get me *out of here*."

"You and the island princess must really hate each other …" The pirate only hesitated for an instant before he shrugged and punched Ninan in the face. "Land!" he shouted at the flyers in the sky.

One by one, the circling pteranodons descended back on the jetty.

The pirate dragged Ninan up into a standing position, wrenched both of Ninan's arms behind his back, and held him by the wrists, then drew a long dagger and pressed it against Ninan's throat as a pteranodon tucked its wings and landed beside him, scattering everyone that had been in its place.

Guards fired bolts, but the pirate tugged Ninan with him behind the pternodon's hulking form, using it as a shield while he and Ninan scooted precariously along the jetty's edgestones. Bolts stuck out of the pteranodon's scales like spikes, but it only grunted and hissed at the guards, snapping its toothless beak at them as the pirate shoved Ninan into the water, flung himself up onto his saddle, and kicked up into the air while more bolts fell short behind him.

The icy water bit Ninan's skin as he broke through the surface and plunged into its blue embrace. Light beamed through the clarity, but he could only squint at it as the sting of the saline forced a pained gurgle from his mouth. The second his body settled and the downward force of his fall no longer worked against him, he kicked and paddled his arms to help buoy himself back up, breaking out and gasping for breath just in time to see the pirate pteranodonback speeding toward him.

From the air, the pirate winked at Ninan, then shouted, "Retrieve!"

FIFTY-SIX

"RETRIEVE!" QORA SCREAMED at Sakay's pteranodon. A wave of dread washed over her.

As a battle raged on below, Qora kept her eyes fixed on Sakay's plummeting form in the air. She leaned into her own flyer's forward motion, urging it to get to him.

Sakay's pteranodon dipped sharply, intercepting his fall and snatching him up with its long beak. Somewhat limp, but alive, Sakay grunted as the flyer tore him from his fall, face up in its toothless grasp.

Thank you, Sky Mother.

Izhi's commander shouted at the fighters on the ground to fall back, and retrieved his flyer as he signaled everyone still standing to do the same. They were losing too many too quickly. The Razorclaws had done what they could from the sky, with Ollan firing bolts like storm-hurled rain and depleting his backup ammunition at a terrifying rate, but despite the aerial assistance and the numbers they'd started with, the fighters on the ground were fading.

Qora caught up to Sakay, moving ahead of his pteranodon so she could command it to follow her to safety, but before she could anchor herself, a sharp rush of air crossed her cheek.

Sakay cried out as an arrow jutted from where his abdomen

was exposed between the pteranodon's mandibles.

Qora sucked in a breath. "Sakay!"

The beastlord loaded another arrow.

With a blazing fire in her veins, Qora spanned and loaded a bolt, bracing herself with her elbows on her pteranodon's neck while she worked. She curled her fingers on the trigger. As the beastlord pulled back to shoot, he jolted sideways with Qora's bolt in his head, slumped from the saddle, and plummeted to the ground where he landed with a crack.

Sakay grimaced and panted, pressing the place where the arrow protruded from his flesh as blood seeped from the wound. The lower half of his face was almost equally bloody, his nose swollen and bluish.

"Align!" Qora told his pteranodon.

Still carrying Sakay, the pteranodon trailed Qora as she went after the other fighters that had retreated to the skies. She spared a glance at the base, where the majority of Izhi's fighters lay dead among some of the base workers, and wild reptiles fed on their corpses.

Less than a dozen fighters escaped the chaos, with arrows still flying at their backs as they ascended toward the plateau. Qora counted the Razorclaws—Ollan first, then Wayra and Kuy and Req and Gorgo. For the moment, Sakay's status was indeterminate. *No*, she corrected herself. *He'll be fine. He has to be.*

FIFTY-SEVEN

NINAN PADDLED TO KEEP HIS HEAD ABOVE WATER.
Tuko made a gurgly cry and stuck his head out of Ninan's vest pocket, sputtering until his tiny throat seemed to clear.

The pirate had to steer his pteranodon at Ninan so that it understood it was to retrieve someone other than its own rider, who of course already sat upon its back. Dipping low, the pteranodon twisted its head sideways and opened its beak. In one fluid movement, the upper and lower beak clamped around Ninan from his chest to his knees, and rotated him laterally. The water that had soaked into Ninan's clothes now gushed from the pteranodon's beak, peppering the sea as he rose into the air.

The other pirates seized whatever last-minute goods they could and got back on their own flyers, kicking off toward the sky.

It certainly wasn't the most dignified position, Ninan thought, being carried in a large reptile's mouth like a fish snatched from the rapids, but it was efficient. He wondered if his father would even send anyone after him; it must have been a lot of effort to arrange the wedding and the tour—surely more effort than the most powerful qhapaq in Runaqa would like to have spent—and Qhapaq Apo could still say he'd held up his end of the bargain with Qhapaq Achik while forces beyond his control had forcibly removed the groom from the altar. Better yet, he could blame Tisqu's flimsy military for the security breach, and at the same time be rid of Ninan for good. And still better, Ninan couldn't be blamed—as far as his father knew—for the abduction. Ninan had let the Tisquvian qhapaq cut his hand, fully ready to mingle his blood with a girl he didn't love, just as he'd said he would. Still, he didn't trust his father to leave the quinoa farmers alone, and that's why he'd had to get off the jetty—and fast.

When they'd soared a mile or so from the jetty, leaving nothing but angry human specks behind, the pirates landed on a jagged cliff and set Ninan down, all twenty-four members of the group dismounting and gathering around him.

"Would you care to explain this, Yaku?" the pirate lord demanded.

The one apparently called Yaku said, "Relax, Kunaq. The little prince promised me my weight in gold—and I'm a solid hundred and eighty pounds, so ..."

"I asked him to stage an abduction," Ninan explained, while several of the pirates stared perplexedly at the pteromorph head that stuck out from within his vest. "It took me all of two minutes to realize your little band of pirates had likely been *hired* to sabotage my wedding. So since you can be bought, I'd like to pay for a few additional services."

Kunaq raised a brow. "First of all, we're not pirates."

"We're bandits," a woman cut in. "We were only acting as pirates for this job. I'm Tika, by the way, and I would just like to say that I was a big fan of your Venture performance—"

Shooting her a silencing look, Kunaq continued: "Second of all, I only agreed to a deal with the princess, to come down on the ceremony, pick off some valuables, ruffle some feathers, and get out. And only because she assured us that she had planted suspicion among the guards, toward some disgruntled former suitor aboard the viewing ships who might be carrying concealed weapons. I didn't agree to involve my entire gang in treason."

Ninan scoffed. "Attacking dozens of royalborns at the wedding of the year isn't considered treason?"

"Not the same as abducting a prince," said Kunaq. "Especially a prince of Sumaq. I have no desire to stir your father's particular brand of wrath."

"So you're aware what he's capable of," said Ninan.

Tika raised her chin. "We've seen some pretty ruckish things over in your land, to say the least."

"What if I told you his anger at my kidnapping will be nothing compared to what he's already started here on these isles?" Ninan asked. "What if I told you the whole continent will be at war soon, and that I might be able to help stop it now that I'm free?"

"We'd say that's none of our business," Kunaq replied. "People like us are disposable in big conflicts. As much as we hate the sovereigns, it's best we don't get involved."

"You'll end up involved whether you like it or not, if this thing gets out of hand. Everyone will. As we speak, my friends are attacking a military base where my father has been breeding thousands of vicious hybrid dinosaurs and controlling them with a skyrock product that turns them into slaves incapable of defying him. When he attacks, it won't be with human soldiers but monstrous creatures that will bow to his every whim."

The leader narrowed his eyes. "Why should we believe something so ludicrous?"

"I saw it for myself. And it was only the beginning of what he probably has growing somewhere else. I've been working with the Unuvians to get more information, and I'd like to continue fighting except there's something I have to do first, but I'll need transportation back to Sumaq and there's not much time. This is my only opportunity to get to Kallpa House alone; everyone who could reasonably stop me is still on the jetty."

"Your castle doesn't have guards?" asked Tika.

"I have ways of dealing with them. Especially if your team can assist me." He looked from one to another, and another, and another. "I promise you'll be compensated beyond your wildest dreams. In fact, you can take whatever you'd like from Kallpa House while we're there."

"How do you plan to deal with the guards protecting the castle?" said Yaku. "Whatever your fighting skills, you surely can't keep them *all* off our backs."

"I know of weapons even my father's military doesn't have. Something that can knock out a hundred men in a matter of seconds."

"You're bluffing," Kunaq said.

"I'm not."

"*That* I would like to see …" Yaku scratched his chin. He and Kunaq exchanged a glance.

Yaku raised his eyebrows.

Kunaq rolled his eyes and sighed, turning back on Ninan. "Alright. If you're serious about this *weapon*, and if you're serious about the gold—I expect you to provide *my* weight as well— then we'll help you."

"Good. Then we'd better hurry," said Ninan. "We'll need to make a quick stop on the way out of Aleta."

"Fine." The leader grabbed his pteranodon's pommel and pulled himself up.

The other bandits went to do the same.

"Hop on with me," Yaku told Ninan. "Unless you want to

ride in the beak again." Once Ninan was on the saddle behind him, he said, "Where to?"

Ninan braced himself behind the man. "Ever heard of the Den?"

The soul is stitched to the body by a few fine threads. When those threads begin to fray, we must prepare to return to Sky Mother's embrace.

From "Woven Breaths" by Hatun Walla

FIFTY-EIGHT

A MILE WEST FROM THE BASE, the Razorclaws and fighters landed at the foot of another plateau in a rare shadow zone.

Qora and Ollan landed before Sakay's pteranodon and waited below to receive him. Normally the pteranodon would fly low enough and tilt its head to allow a rider to simply land on their feet, but Sakay was in no condition to hold himself upright.

Together, Qora and Ollan lowered Sakay from the ramp formed by the pteranodon's open beak into a reclined position on the sand, while the other Razorclaws gathered around him. Qora knelt at his side and put her hand over his, where he clutched the arrow that pierced him.

Ollan removed his shirt and handed it to Qora. She bunched up the material and pressed it to the wound, sobbing as it reddened like wool submerged in a dye bath.

Sakay parted his dry lips.

"Water," Qora told Ollan, who fumbled among saddlebag supplies until he produced a canteen. She put it to Sakay's lips and let him drink from the careful trickle. As he drank, she cupped his clammy, ashen face. "It's okay. We'll fix this. You're going to be *fine* …"

Ollan knelt beside Qora and placed a gentle hand on her

shoulder. "Qora …"

"We just have to stop the bleeding. We've got flyers—we can stabilize him and get him to the city in a matter of minutes. He—"

"It's …" Sakay rasped. "It's alright." His gaze was unfocused, almost distant. He swallowed with difficulty.

"Don't try to talk right now," she told him. "You'll have plenty of time to lecture me later." Teardrops streamed down her cheeks.

"I'm … I'm ready."

"Ready for what?" Qora said.

Despite his bleary stare, he seemed to lock onto her visually now. "You know … for what."

She shook her head. "Stop. Don't say that. You're just—"

He put his bloody hand on top of hers. "Ninan … did the right … thing, but … you …" He swallowed again. "*Kantuta* … you don't wait … for *anyone*."

Qora's heart pounded and her tears fell on him like the start of rain, dappling his shirt. "Please, Sakay …"

"Don't let fear … or the …qhapaq … or even … *hope* … keep you in a cage." His eyes welled, and he arched his back against whatever internal sensations plagued him. He tightened his grip on Qora's hand. "You're too … majestic … not to … fly free." Then he guided her hand to a spot on his chest, pressing her fingers against the shape of a long tooth.

Panting, Qora felt around his collar for the leather cord and tugged it free, lifting his head slightly to pull the necklace off of him. She handed him the tooth, and he clutched it, shivering.

"I love you," she whispered.

"I love you too, *kantuta*." Blearily, he looked around at the Razorclaws, whom Qora had not realized had gathered even more closely, each touching a part of him—a limb or a shoulder. With the faintest voice, and with a breath he seemed to have held so that he could say these last words without pause, he told them, "Use your teeth, friends."

As Sakay's eyelids fluttered and his breaths began to still, Qora kissed his cheek, his face a blur through her watery sight. She put her ear to his chest, listening to his fading heartbeat, one soft throb and then another, further and further apart until the next one didn't come.

And that's when she knew a small part of her would never wake again, either.

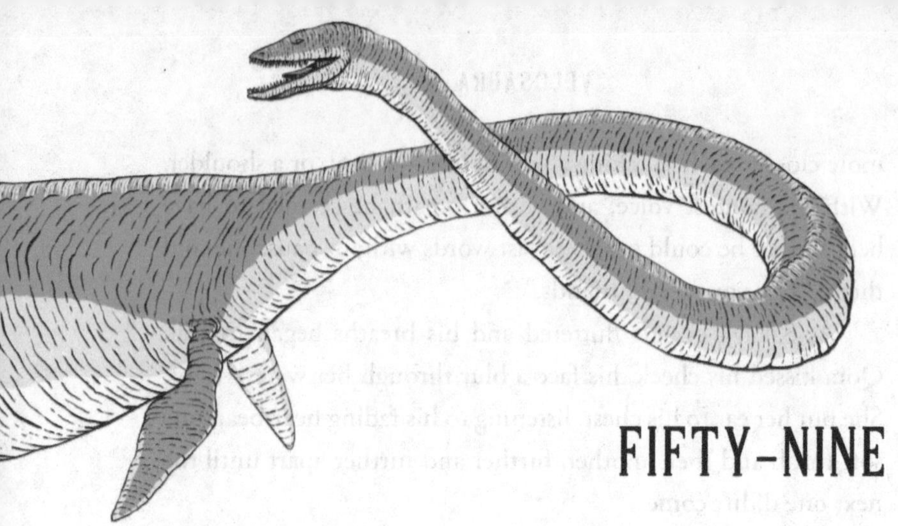

FIFTY-NINE

THE DEN HAD A SIMILAR LOOK AND FEEL to the Underground, although it was smaller, and there were no prizefighters on the premises. Although the area technically pertained to the vast city of Aleta, it was located at the western reaches, along one of the more obscure, unofficial trade routes.

It hadn't occurred to Ninan that the arrival of twenty-four bandits and a now-well-known prince might set the Den into a bit of a frenzy. Buyers and traders were divided between gawking at the prince and scattering in the wake of so many dark-clad flyer-riders. The noise drew the owner to the forefront, who paused before Ninan with a piercing gaze.

"Everybody out," she said.

All traders, gamblers, and other patrons—along with all bandits except Kunaq, Yaku, and Tika, filtered out of the space.

Atuq stepped forward, glancing warily at the bandits. "Your Highness. To what do I owe this great pleasure?"

"I'm a friend of the Razorclaws," Ninan told her. "I know this may come as a surprise, but I've also been working with Qhapaq Izhi to gather intel on my father—and with the help of these bandits, I've managed to escape my own wedding. Now I've got a matter of hours to return to Sumaq to try and save my friends before my father kills them for my betrayal, but to do that, I'm going to need something from you."

She sized him up first, then his companions, and folded her arms. "Like what?"

"The Razorclaws mentioned you were helping them store a fairly large supply of one of their more useful weapons." He only hoped there was enough left over after what they'd taken to the base.

"They told you …"

Ninan nodded. "You know they wouldn't have, unless I'm on their side. On *your* side. I know you want to stop my father— and so do I."

She twisted her pursed lips as she considered, and then after a moment said, "Come with me."

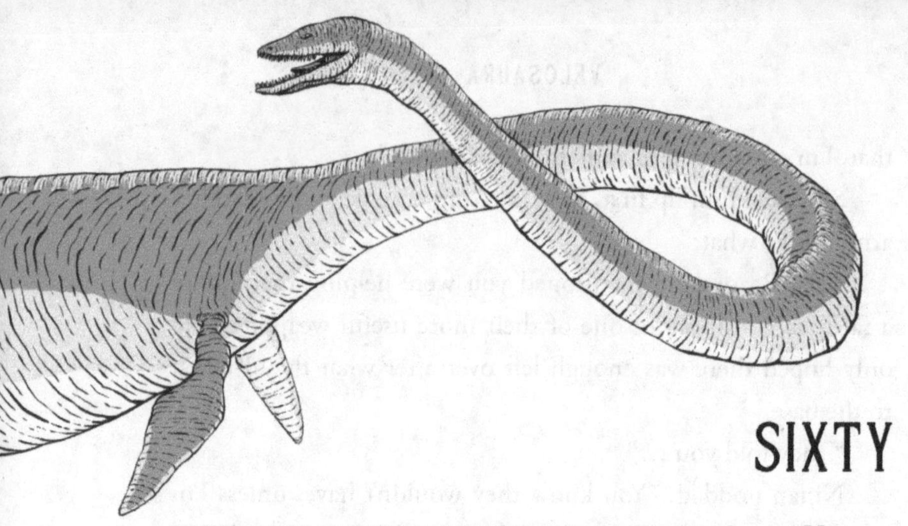

SIXTY

IZHI'S REMAINING FIGHTERS RETURNED to Unu as soon as they'd caught their breath. The Razorclaws, however, remained at their makeshift site for nearly a half hour, to process Sakay's death.

When Qora finally peeled herself away from Ollan's embrace, made all the more sweaty by his lack of shirt, it struck her that the group had a difficult task ahead of them.

She wiped her eyes. "We have to get Sakay's body back to Qhusi."

Wayra nodded numbly. "The pteranodon can carry him in retrieval pose, as before. But we should try to wrap him—at least keep his arms and legs tight against him."

Qora shuddered as she imagined the indignity of transporting him in this state, and how much uglier it would be if he were to dangle with his limbs loose. But he obviously couldn't ride in the saddle.

"Req and I can go back to the campsite in Aqu Aqu," said Kuy. "There might be blankets or other materials we can use."

That would only take maybe another half an hour round trip, Qora thought. "The rest of us can try to clean him up in the meantime."

Their water was precious here, but she couldn't stand to

406

leave Sakay so bloody, even if it was just until they could get him home. She didn't want his uncle to see the severity of his appearance, either, when they arrived. The news itself would be bad enough.

While Kuy and Req flew off into the distance, Wayra tore a strip of fabric from the bottom of her own shirt, leaving her midriff bare. Ollan handed her the same canteen he'd given Sakay to drink a while earlier.

Qora swore she saw Wayra blush—at Ollan's state of undress, perhaps—but it was difficult to be sure when all their faces were flushed with the heat of this climate.

Wayra poured a bit of water onto the fabric and knelt next to Sakay's head, gently cleaning the crusted blood from his nose and mouth.

Qora looked at him and choked on a dry sob. Some part of her mind had closed off for the last few minutes, allowing her to feel as though he were only sleeping, but the reality of his death struck her anew.

She removed Ollan's bloodied shirt—already almost completely parched by the desert air—from Sakay's abdomen, and snapped the arrow shaft so that it no longer stuck out of him. She didn't think she could bear to try and remove what was inside, but at least now it wouldn't be in the way when they wrapped and transported him.

Ollan went to the other end and drew Sakay's feet together, lining them up evenly.

Then, as Qora positioned both of Sakay's arms on his chest and prepared to cross them, her fingers brushed the fine edge of a papyr, crumpled within his left fist. She sucked in a breath.

Carefully, she uncurled the fist and withdrew the message, pulling it apart and flattening it against her thigh.

To: Beastlord Wasqar, Aquchay Base, Tisqu Isle, Tisqu
Subject: Immediate Evacuation

This order mandates the precautionary evacuation of Sumaq's Aquchay Military Base due to potential enemy attacks during interterrenally significant events.

Execution: Cease breeding and training activities. Transport all dominite stores and reptilian trainees via routine methods, dispensed in equal measure to the following locations.
* Camp Ñansa
* Camp Wood Ridge
* Camp Wayaqa
* Camp Kawsay

Timeline: Between the Dark Hours 0 and 5, prior to Fifthday at dawn

Additional Instructions:
* Receive decoy reptile shipment and release to enclosures once trainees have been dispersed.
* Receive Sumaq's deployment of special operatives and allow them to operate as instructed.
* Conduct a sweep of the base to ensure no personnel or critical assets are left behind.

Final Comments:
Engage with enemy forces as potential situations require.

Operational Commander Sallqa

"What's that?" Ollan said.

Qora handed it over. "It's what Sakay died for."

He scanned the information. "Gods in the High World. They were evacuating dinosaurs that very night … while we were camped in Aqu Aqu. They would have just finished when we arrived at the plateau to set up the luminate."

Wayra stood and looked over his shoulder at the papyr. "It lists the camps." She looked at Ollan meaningfully. With his Sumaqi military experience …

Ollan nodded as if to answer the question she hadn't asked aloud. "And I know where they are."

When the velosaur could hide no more—for the mosasaur had a sense of smell too keen—the velosaur had no choice but to come forth into the open water. Remaining within the darkness of the massive shadow, he darted under the belly of the mosasaur where the flesh was more delicate. From here, he delivered an electric shock—brief but sharp—and in the flurry that ensued, the velosaur slipped away.

**Excerpt from "The Velosaur and the Mosasaur"
from *Asiri's Apologues***

SIXTY-ONE

ARMED WITH POWDER CANNONS full of hushdust, Ninan and the bandits flew over Kallpa House from the north side, where the mountain would shield their arrival until the last possible second.

They allowed the watchtower guards to see them—the horrific sight of twenty-four dark pteranodons descending on the castle—for long enough that the guards would call out for reinforcements.

And that's when they struck.

"Now!" Ninan commanded from his place behind Yaku.

He and the bandits dusted the watchtowers, all visible staff, and the swarm of military protectors that filled the courtyards and baileys and balconies shortly after, and watched everyone collapse like puppets with their strings abruptly cut. Bolts and arrows faltered mid-air as shooters fell to the ground. Shouts and screams tapered to silence. Bodies thumped against the ground-bricks in small heaps.

Kunaq, Tika, and Yaku touched down on a stone landing pad among unaffected Kallpa House pterobeasts. Ninan jumped off, let Tuko out onto his shoulder, and said, "While the others make sure everyone's down, I'll show you where to get your gold."

"Spread out!" Kunaq told the bandits above as he and Tika

411

dismounted, powder cannons raised for any other staff that might emerge.

The airborne bandits dispersed over the vast property, over every wing of the castle and its additional sections and the adjacent tiers of land, and dusted anyone within range.

Ninan raised his own cannon and strode through the body-strewn courtyards, past the great hall and the main keep and the grand staircase that led to the summit hall.

A few of the staff members who had remained inside for cover murmured from their cowering spots as he passed, but he ignored them; none was trained to best him in a fistfight, and he was certain most would be more worried about staying alive than protecting this place from him.

It pained him to be the source of their fear, but there was no time for guilt; there wasn't even time for him to think about what had become of Qora and her brother and the Razorclaws, although they'd crossed his mind many times on the flight from Tisqu, and he refused to accept that they hadn't been successful.

If he was going to do this, however, he had to maintain a singular focus.

Ninan led Kunaq, Yaku, Tika, and seven additional bandits to the treasury, where a long hall lined with iron-gated vaults remained in near-darkness until Ninan lit a lantern at the entrance. The flame of the first lantern, connected by rope-wicks to other lanterns that dangled in front of each vault, grew and caught on the rope, spreading along to the others and filling the enclosure with light—and the warm, musky scent of sauropod oil. Tuko ruffled his sceathers as if in delight of the effect.

A minute later, Ninan found the treasurer in the courtyard, demanded his keys, and returned to the vault. He tossed Kunaq a thick, iron ring with several oversized keys attached to it. "Load up as much as you can carry. I'll meet you out front in a few minutes."

⊃⊃⊃

First, Ninan went to his father's scriptorium. Inside, the air was thick with the scents of aged books and ink and papyr, and beeswax candles and more sauropod oil. In the recesses of the ceiling, squares of stained glass cast an ethereal multicolored light upon the stone walls, causing the entire space to exude a sense of reverence in which Qhapaq Apo did not deserve to dwell.

It took Ninan only a moment to locate his father's spinosaur-and-shield signet stamp, which rested among several documents and an inkwell, with its signet face down and its black-marble handle plumb. He would need it later, as part of his grand plan. When he picked it up, he glanced at a sheet of embossed edict papyr with only three short paragraphs of text inked onto it. His father often took weeks to draft letters or announcements regarding trade or diplomacy, and left them half finished here while he tended to other matters. But several of the words on this particular letter stood out to Ninan's vigilant eyes.

I, Qhapaq Apo Kallpa, sovereign of Sumaq, the First Terrain, do hereby address the peoples of Runaqa concerning a matter of magnitude.

In the aftermath of the hostile acts of our own Second Terrain of Unu, which has threatened the peace and prosperity that we have strived to uphold, I must meet force with force.

In defense of my Terrain, and all other Terrains under my protection, I declare my intent to unleash the might of our newly bred protectors, the Sauroguard, to restore our honor and ensure the safety of

The text ended there, and so did Ninan's train of thought as he stared at the papyr.

Sauroguard. Meet force with force. Intent to unleash …

It was as though he were being swept away by a dark undertow, the opposite current dragging him away from the surface of his consciousness.

His father had to have begun drafting this edict *before* departing for Tisqu—hours before Izhi's unit attacked with the Razorclaws—and yet, it seemed he already had plans to deploy trained dinosaurs in retaliation.

The unit may have destroyed the source that was feeding this "Sauroguard"—gods, he hoped they had—but there was still much to fear. And he had to warn Izhi, as soon as possible.

🌙🌙🌙

With his pulse thrumming like a parade drum, Ninan sprinted to the pteriary tower on the eastern grounds. A robust stone archway opened into the space, with cylindrical walls three hundred feet tall. Thick timber beams crossed its diameter at various heights, where pterobeasts and pteranodons could perch and roost. Natural light streamed in through open windows. Large troughs displayed slabs of meat, on which a trio of pteranodons fed as Ninan entered.

Directly through to the other side, another archway led to an open field and a waterfall that spilled into a pterosaur drinking pool before spilling into a second waterfall that spilled into the misty gorge below Kallpa House.

Ninan gazed up at a few of the pterobeasts perched above him, avoiding the splatters of guano on the floor, which staff members might be cleaning right now had he not forced them into an untimely slumber. Mentally, he did the math for how many pterobeasts he would need, as Tuko burrowed into his collarbone at the sight of so many flyers so much larger than him.

A pterobeast could lift around fifteen hundred pounds comfortably, which equated to ten to fifteen people (averaging weights). There were around two hundred people in Thak; some of them were hefty men, but some were small children. If Ninan were to use multiple gondolas, he would need twelve to transport all of them at once—but that would be too difficult to coordinate, as would multiple trips with fewer gondolas. The trip he had in mind would take nearly seven hours. Regardless, he would need multiple flyers, but it was possible for them to share a larger load because, thankfully, these flyers were trained to synchronize their wingflaps.

Moving on to the tack warehouse, Ninan located multiple long, lightweight vessels, used for delivering large numbers of additional guards over to the city center for important events—such as the Heritage Festival, or Venture sendoffs.

Ninan calculated that with three of these arks, each carried by six coordinated flyers, he could divide the people between them fairly evenly, and even have additional support for the weight of some of their belongings. The plan would work. This way, he would only need three pilots—and he knew just the ones.

〉〉〉

"You want us to do what?" Yaku asked.

"They follow the same commands as pteranodons," Ninan said. "'Rise,' 'retrieve,' 'align'—all of them. Anyone with pteroflight training can handle it. I'd conduct one myself, but

I've just learned that I need to get to Unu as soon as possible. Qhapaq Izhi will be back at his capital by the time we pass it, and I have to let him know his people are in danger. As soon as I've ensured that the people from Thak are safely on their way out of Sumaq, I'll stop in Yupa to deliver the information, then join you and my friends immediately afterward."

"We do sort of owe him," Tika pointed out. "We're set for life after this."

As they spoke, every member of their team of bandits was securing saddlebags full of gold on the backs of their pteranodons.

Ninan nodded once. "Great. Because I'll need all of you to help me get eighteen pterobeasts harnessed to their arks. And we only have about half an hour left before the hushdust wears off."

ↃↃↃ

Guards began to stir, sleepily scrambling to their feet and aiming their weapons at the bandits, who were already mounting their gold-laden pteranodons for the last time, while Kunaq, Yaku, and Tika each conducted an empty gondola lifting off behind Ninan, who rode Yaku's pteranodon solo, flanked by Kunaq's and Tika's pteranodons.

"Tell your qhapaq we appreciate his generous donation!" Yaku called back.

As Kallpa House shrank behind them, Ninan took a final look at the adjacent tiers of land, where handlers were waking from the hushdust in the midst of reptiles that had gone rogue under their lack of authority. That's when he caught sight of a little green flyer who, having apparently broken loose from her tether, flitted toward the edge of the mountain overlooking the gorge. When she leapt off, Ninan's heart leapt too, and he

416

watched her glide across the expanse to freedom.

⊃⊃⊃

With impressive speed, Ninan and his three pilots soared on the chilly winds to Thak, splitting off from the other twenty-one bandits who would return to their hideout on Tisqu to store the gold.

As the quinoa fields came into view, Ninan sped ahead on his own, catching the startled attention of the workers with the mere sight of a single flyer-rider—unusual for these parts.

The sauropod ribcage tunnel marked where the community and its twenty-five adobe homes were settled along the edge of the crops, which would have been sown only a few weeks ago, with each plant just beginning to produce its fourth leaf. The young plants were small, tender, and green, forming rows that striped the countryside, while the soil was dark and moist from the irrigation channels.

Ninan inhaled the earthy aroma, and felt a pang at the familiarity of it. For a place he'd lived less than a year, its essence struck him in an unexpectedly visceral way.

His father's guards fired up at him without hesitation, but he swooped out of their bolts' trajectories and doused every uniformed man or woman in hushdust as the arks appeared behind him like otherworldly invaders.

Below, the farmers froze from between the rows of quinoa. The women and children, who had been spinning wool or hefting water buckets or preparing food, had initially begun to scatter or retreat into the houses, but paused as the stationed guards collapsed before their eyes. Although the approaching flyers and arks told of Kallpa House terror, surely it was clear to all, Ninan thought, that this was no invasion.

The wingflaps of a dozen and a half pterobeasts was enough to force wind through the commune, jostling the leafy fields and wafting the smoke of small fires.

With an ache in his chest, Ninan brought the pteranodon to a halt at the central gathering area and dismounted, staring at dozens of confused, sun-bronzed faces.

He hadn't known every single one of them well, but everyone in this community—at least by now—knew who *he* was. What they didn't know was why he'd returned.

The bandits landed the arks in the minimal open space beyond the gathering area and the pterobeasts dropped in regimented lines parallel to the arks' lengths, tucking away their wings with harness lines sagging on the ground.

A young man came forward with a seething glare, approaching Ninan with a stride that made each step feel like a punctuation of his mood. Despite his familiar, slight frame and weary eyes, he was menacing.

Ninan parted his lips to speak, but paused when the young man stopped and took a knee before him.

"Your Highness …" the young man bit out.

The title was like a dagger to the chest. Ninan's breath caught in his throat. "Pidru."

SIXTY-TWO

ONE YEAR AND FOUR MONTHS AGO

PIDRU STEPPED OUT of his small, adobe house into the darkness. His mamáy and younger sister Tamya were fast asleep on their bedmats inside, oblivious to his activity. He'd have to explain himself eventually, he thought— they'd figure it out at the end of the month when the taxes came due—but for now, he had no choice but to swallow his dread, and face his demons.

Sighing and rubbing his eyes, he picked up a lantern, lit it, and dragged himself to the large wooden dinoshelter to the east of the community buildings, where he took one last breath of fresh air before the pungent scent of ruck assaulted him.

Rhabdodons stirred at Pidru's entry, grunting with each strike of his foot against the floor.

"Yeah, yeah ..." he muttered as he hung the lantern on a hook that dangled from a chain attached to the ceiling. The flickering glow revealed nothing but an empty floor.

They're late, he thought. For a moment, he wondered if—or hoped, really—they weren't coming. But he knew it wasn't likely.

Listening to a few of the rhabdodons continue to stir, and with what were likely to be at least a few minutes of time on his hands, he slipped on a pair of gloves and snatched a pitchfork from the tool rack and went to one of the stalls.

He'd have to be up at dawn to clean the ruck anyway. Might as well get something done while he waited.

Within the first stall lay the smallest of the rhabdos, a little female positioned on her side with her limbs stretched out, so relaxed that she appeared to be dead. All the rhabdodons had this way about them when they slumbered, and Pidru chuffed at her as he stabbed the pitchfork into the straw.

Once he'd cleaned that stall, he skipped the next one, which was empty for the moment, after its inhabitant had died after getting loose and eating from a patch of surmanta yew leaves.

When the straw shifted, Pidru froze.

He peered through the half-open gate. The stall was empty—no rhabdodon, of course, but likewise no stray compies or any other creatures that he could see. He crept into the stall and raised his pitchfork high, heart racing.

The straw shifted again.

"Who's there?" Pidru demanded.

Slowly, a head emerged from the mess, with pieces of straw falling from all sides of it. A dark, smudged face took shape, along with dark, mussed hair.

It was a boy who appeared to be Pidru's own age, a youth on the cusp of manhood. Pidru didn't know him, however—and because the community was small, he knew *everyone*. This boy had to have come from somewhere else.

His complexion was sallow and drained, his eyes accentuated by dark circles.

"Who are you?" Pidru demanded. "What are you doing in here?"

The boy parted dry, cracked lips with difficulty. "Um …"

Outside the stall, heavy boot-thuds played the planks of the floor like a marimba.

Pidru froze. He glanced at the boy in the straw, who furrowed his brows at the sound. Pidru put a finger to his lips, then whispered, "Stay here. Don't make any noise." He slipped out of the stall and closed the gate, turning to face the source of the footfalls.

A tall, twenty-something man in dark clothing stood before him, with three others behind him of similar age and size, and similarly dressed. "Sorry we're late. Got held up at our previous stop. But we're here now." He held out his hand.

Hesitating, Pidru's own hand twitched at his hip, inches from where the coppers sat in his pocket.

"Come on," said the man. "You can give it to me, or I can take it. Up to you."

"Haven't you taken enough?" Pidru asked. "Is this really how you want to get what you need? By harassing workers who barely make a living?" He wanted to mention that he had a mamáy and younger sister to worry about, but he didn't know what kinds of sinister ideas guys like this might get if they knew he was the only one protecting the women of his household. He wasn't doing the best job protecting them financially at the moment; physically, he'd be even worse.

The man stepped closer to Pidru, a full head taller than him. "This is your last warning."

Pidru didn't want to take this kind of treatment, but the pain that still ached in his ribs—pain which had made his last two weeks cutting quinoa quite difficult—reminded him what would happen if he didn't. Still, it wasn't like this could go on; if he didn't pay the taxes, he'd end up indentured, and then what would his mamáy and sister do?

"Look," said Pidru, "Maybe we can just—"

The man thrust a fist at his gut, doubling him over. In

Pidru's hunched position, the man shoved him into the middle of his group of companions and within seconds they had him on the floor.

The fine fractures in Pidru's ribs radiated a new pain as one of the other men fished around in his pockets and removed all the coppers, jostling them in a cupped palm.

"I think next time you're going to have to owe us a little extra," said the man. "For our trouble." He grabbed Pidru by his hair and held his head up, pulling back a fist.

Pidru cringed, bracing himself for impact.

Another hand clamped around the man's wrist.

The boy from the stall stood over him, his cotton shirt smeared with dirt, with bits of straw clinging to it.

The man growled and released Pidru's hair and tried to wrench out of the boy's grip, but the boy held firm and threw a punch that split the man's lip.

With a raging glare, the man swung his fist at the boy, but the boy dipped under it and threw an uppercut. The man's companions converged on the boy, but he slithered between them like smoke, like he could predict their moves, and then it was a blur of fists and elbows, twisted arms and knuckles smashing into faces. Heads snapped back and men doubled over, and soon they were little more than a groaning heap, and Pidru's coppers were scattered across the floor with one final coin wobbling in a precession before completely losing momentum and falling flat.

Panting, the scraggly boy retrieved the coppers, then extended his hand to Pidru and pulled him to standing. He turned to the men on the floor. "You have thirty seconds to get up and walk away from this place, or I'll make sure you never walk again."

The men stumbled out, glowering at Pidru and the boy on their way, but soon were gone.

Pidru looked at the boy, who offered back his coppers. "Thank you."

"No problem."

Sizing up the boy in his stained cotton shirt and splotched face, Pidru said, "Why don't you come inside and get something to eat?"

》》》

By the time Pidru returned to the house with the boy, his mamáy was awake, with a lantern flickering on the kitchen table.

"Where have you been? It's well after dark and—" she paused at the sight of the strange boy. "Who's this?"

"Found him in the dinoshelter," Pidru said casually.

Pidru's mamáy analyzed them both, and it was only under this scrutiny that Pidru suddenly felt hyper-aware of the bruises burgeoning on his skin.

"Gods and spirits," his mamáy remarked. "What's happened to you?"

"A few men attacked me. This boy stepped in. I'm alright."

"Alright?" she repeated. "Come, sit down, both of you. And *you* ..." she said to the other boy as she urged him into a chair, "You look like you've barely slept or eaten in days. What were you doing in the dinoshelter?"

The boy didn't answer.

Pidru's mamáy waited, but when it was clear he had nothing to say, she turned back on Pidru. "Better yet, what were *you* doing in the dinoshelter? At this hour?"

Pidru didn't answer either.

The woman sighed and went to the pantry, where she unwrapped a bundle of corn bread—still fresh, as she'd made it for the evening meal—divided it, and slid a plate toward the other boy, then poured the contents of a dented, metal pitcher into a cup. Goat's milk, which Tamya had brought in that morning.

The boy held back for only a moment before he began shoving the bread into his mouth, chugging milk between bites.

Pidru's mamáy took a jar of clay—used for sealing small cracks that would sometimes appear in the adobe walls—from the cabinet and began to cake it onto her son's bruises.

Reveling in the chill of the clay on his skin, Pidru gave the boy a moment to get his fill of food before he said, "Where do you come from?"

After a heavy swallow, the boy—to Pidru's surprise—replied. "The city."

"And where's your family?" Pidru's mamáy asked.

"I don't have one." The boy took another swig of milk, draining the cup.

Pidru looked to his mamáy for direction, not sure whether he should prompt the boy further. The boy could have been on his own from the beginning, a runaway from some establishment for orphans, or perhaps his family had been recently killed.

His mamáy put away the jar of clay and produced a cloth, which she dipped in a bucket of water. She went to the boy and put a hand under his chin, tilting his head this way and that as if to get a better look at him. Finally, she took the cloth and began to wipe the dirt from his face.

"They cast me out," the boy added. "I'm dead to them."

Pidru's mamáy finished removing a particularly stubborn spot of dirt from along the boy's jaw. "I'm sorry to hear that."

It was ironic, Pidru thought, that his mamáy's methods for treating bruises had been to *add* a substance of the earth, while for this boy her method was to take such things away.

"Not as sorry as they'd be if they found out I'm not actually dead," the boy muttered.

"They ..." Pidru cleared his throat. "They tried to kill you?"

The boy looked down at the crumbs that remained on the plate in front of him. "In a manner of speaking."

"And who, exactly," said Pidru's mamáy, "was trying to kill *you*, Pidru?"

With a new crackle of pain in his ribs, Pidru shivered. He moved to the fireplace and piled a few more pieces of wood on the dwindling flames.

"Seemed like a band of common thugs," said the boy.

"Of course," said the woman. "That's why no one in the community is supposed to go out after dark. Thieves and bandits like to harass vulnerable countrypeople—and it's been getting worse, with the higher tax rates. Everyone's desperate. Some take it out on others." She crossed her arms, waiting for Pidru's explanation.

Pidru tossed one more piece of wood on the pile, then looked over at her. "Alright. Fine." He sighed. "A couple of weeks ago, just after getting my coppers, I came home and sat down on the old rocking chair and fell asleep. Do you remember that night, Mamáy?"

She nodded.

He turned to the boy to give some context: "We've increased the yield from the previous year, trying to meet the qhapaq's quinoa demand, but our workforce has basically remained the same, so ... you can imagine how that's been wearing on us." Then, to both of them: "Anyway, when I woke to the sound of rain pattering on the shutters, and suddenly remembered I'd left my tools outside, I rushed into the darkness, despite the warnings against it—because rusty tools are a poor worker's demise. But before I'd finished gathering everything and storing it in the tool shelter, those four men cornered me and emptied my pockets. I tried to resist, but then I found myself flat on my back with a bloody nose and cracked ribs. They said I'd better meet them in the dinoshelter, at the same hour every week, and pay up, or they'd find me and give me the same treatment—and that if I told any of the community's elders, they'd trash the fields and make sure *I* was blamed for it."

"Spirits …" His mamáy put a hand on her chest.

"I didn't have the courage to say what had happened. I was … ashamed, I guess. Those guys had already taken most of my pay twice, so … it was only a matter of time before you figured it out. And if I'd been alone out there tonight, I …"

"It was fortunate," his mamáy said to the boy, laying a hand on his shoulder, "that you sought shelter among our dinosaurs. I can't thank you enough."

"I'm glad I could help."

"Will you tell us your name?" Pidru asked.

"My name …" The boy stared into his milk cup like he might find the name there. He looked up at Pidru, but never finished the thought.

"If you need work, we're short a cutter," Pidru added, as though it might better entice him. "Well, we're short a *lot* of cutters, but one of our guys just left a few days ago to join the Guard—since it pays better—and it's harvest season, so, that's going to hurt us. Unless …"

"I've never cut before. I'm not a farmer. Can't say how much help I'd be."

"You can learn. I'll show you," Pidru told him. Then he raised his brows at his mamáy. "Maybe ... he can ... stay? I know I'd feel *safer* if ..."

She chewed her lip for a moment, watching the boy.

At seventeen or eighteen—as the boy appeared to be—he wasn't exactly a child, Pidru thought, but he wasn't fully grown either. Being around the same age, Pidru couldn't imagine what it would be like to have to wander the countryside without a steady meal or a mamáy to come home to, even as a young man capable of getting by one way or another. Tough as it had been cutting quinoa, at the very least Pidru had always had a place to lay his head.

Whatever the boy's family had cast him off for, he didn't seem to be a criminal; he could have easily taken Pidru's money, and any other money those thugs had collected, but he hadn't.

Pidru wondered if his mamáy was having a similar train of thought, and she must have been, because she then said, "If you'd like, we can make you a bedmat. I can't guarantee you'll be a good fit with the cutters, but it's worth a try. Would you like to stay a while ... and see how it goes?"

The boy nodded slowly. "I think ... maybe ... I would."

"Alright," said the woman. "Let me see what comforts I can gather for you for tonight, and tomorrow we'll stuff a proper bedmat for you."

"Thank you," said the boy.

Pidru and the boy sat in silence for a few minutes, and Pidru poured more milk and cut more corn bread—some for himself as well. When they'd both consumed their portions the boy stared into the fire, almost entranced.

"Listen," Pidru said, "If you're going to stay, you'll have to at least tell me what to call you."

After another long moment, gaze fixed on the flames, the boy finally turned to Pidru and met his eyes. "Call me Ninan."

SIXTY-THREE

"GET UP," NINAN TOLD PIDRU, who still knelt on one knee. "Please."

The other members of the community exchanged wary glances and bowed regardless.

Tamya appeared within the group, her face ashen and her eyes wide as she clung to her mamáy—and the two of them bowed as well.

Ninan took a step backward. "Stop. All of you. This is ridiculous."

"I agree," Pidru said. "It *is* ridiculous." He stood now. "Ridiculous that you would dare show your face here after everything."

"There will be time to discuss that later, but right now I need you all to gather your things—only what you can't live without, nothing more—and board these arks."

"Where are we going?" someone said.

"You expect us to *leave?*" said someone else.

Pidru crossed his arms. "We're not going anywhere. Especially not with you."

Ninan scrubbed a hand over his face. "I know you're angry. You should be. I lied to everyone, and then I disappeared, and then my father's guards took *you*, specifically, in the dead of night, without explanation, and brought you to me in chains as a piece of leverage. And up to this point, you've all been living under threat of this patrol." He gestured at the sleeping guards. "Because of *me*. I know that. But eventually they're going to wake up, and when they do, you all have to be gone."

"This is your idea of making things right?" Pidru spat. "To tear us from the only home we've ever known?"

"A home where you're treated little better than slaves!" Ninan protested. "Where you're forced to grow crops for my father's government and severely underpaid for the grueling work you put in. And then so much of that pay is taxed away from you."

"You know nothing about us. The year you spent here didn't give you the slightest glimpse of what this place means to us."

"Maybe not, but I can say from experience that it's easy to believe your home is a refuge even when it's wrought with misery and abuse. I believed that enough to accept my father's offer to compete in the Venture—thinking I actually had some choice in the matter—so that I could return to my *own* home, and only too late did I come to the conclusion that I never should have longed for it in the first place. I know you love your land, but your home is within you, among you, and in the way you live *together*. That's something you can take anywhere you go."

Pidru scoffed. "What a lovely platitude."

"You will never know how sorry I am. But I can take you somewhere far away, where you can start over, and provide crops for *yourselves*. You can live free of the constraints of Sumaqi agricultural laws, without the threatening, watchful eye of the qhapaq."

"Where exactly do you expect to take us?" said a woman. "You want us to leave the Terrain entirely?"

"I'm considering an incentive program for agriculturists ...

Allpans don't have the same knack for quinoa as your people do."

"I am certain that we can take refuge in Allpa," Ninan explained. "It's the only safe place at a time like this. And from what I know of the quya, she will be sympathetic. She has ambitions to cultivate her land for quinoa, and is eager for Sumaqi expertise. But she isn't like my father; she will be fair, and generous in exchange for what you can do."

"But there's no guarantee …" said one of the farmers.

"No," Ninan admitted. "Only my faith in the quya, whom I believe is a woman of integrity."

Another farmer came forward. "You said, 'it's the only safe place at a time like this.' What do you mean by that?"

"At a time when we lowborns become collateral damage," Pidru supplied, "in the vicious political games of the highborns."

"You're not entirely wrong," Ninan told Pidru. "But this is no game. My father has bred and trained a dinosaur army, using a refined skyrock product called dominite that can captivate any reptile and convert them to an unflinchingly loyal soldier. He means to start a war, to support his ongoing efforts to reunify the Terrains under one empire that he alone will rule. With an army like that, he'll finally be able to do it."

The people exchanged worried glances and began to murmur amongst themselves.

"So what?" Pidru asked. "We can't stop it. And we're already under his rule anyway. What difference does that make to us?"

Ninan shook his head woefully. "If you think he's a tyrant now, just wait."

"We've managed this long," said Pidru.

"Stop being a stubborn pachyceph," Ninan said. "You're furious—I understand. But you can't stay here. Soon my father is going to realize what else I've done that should upset him, and he'll come after *all* of us."

"And what have you done this time, *Your Highness*?"

Ninan ignored the sting of the title again. "For starters, I joined forces with these bandits"—he pointed his head at Kunaq and Yaku and Tika—"and bribed them to abduct me from my wedding. And that was *after* months of complying with my father's terms to keep his blades off your throats, all the while risking my life daily to act as a spy for the qhapaq of Unu in hopes of getting enough information about my father's dinosaur army to try and put a stop to what will surely be one of the bloodiest conflicts this land has ever seen.

"All the while, not a day has gone by that I haven't thought of you, and ached for your suffering at my hands, and longed for an opportunity to make up for what I've done." He sighed. "Even though I can't change the past, I *can* ensure a future for this community. At the very least, I need you to let me try."

When everyone stared at him silently, he added to Pidru, "Never in my life had I experienced the care and acceptance I did from your family, the only exception being my mother who was so often kept from me at Kallpa House. You gave me what she could not, and what the rest of my family *would* not."

He addressed all of them once more. "So, please … get in the arks, and fly away from this godsforsaken place, before my father catches up to all my sins against him and sees fit to destroy everything and everyone I love." His mother was only safe because of the marital blood oath, which Ninan knew his father would honor. "You deserve the chance to pour your rage upon me—but you have to stay *alive* to do that."

Now Pidru seemed to have lost the ability to speak. Tamya clung to her mamáy's arm with tears in her eyes. Their mamáy pressed her lips together.

Two of the elders who made most of the decisions for the community whispered rapidly to one another, before they turned back to everyone. "The Third Prince is right," one of them said. "We must go. There is nothing for us here. This quinoa does not belong to us, and hasn't for decades, although we practically give our lives for it. These homes are falling apart, and we do not have the time nor the energy nor the means to maintain them. Our children grow hungrier each day, and the taxes on our lots grow increasingly high every year. The qhapaq's guards occupying this land were only salt in the wounds he had already inflicted upon us. If there is an opportunity to improve our situation, we must take it."

𝄞𝄞𝄞

Despite Ninan's initial concern about adding too much weight to the arks, he was quickly humbled by the community members' lack of personal possessions, and even more so by the very few which were actually of value to them. It made him sick to think how he had cared so much for recreational megaraptors and dino steaks and ornithomimid-feather mattresses. These people brought dried fruits and jerky for the trip, a few clay pots, and the farmers brought their sickles and a few other small tools, but otherwise it was little more than the shirts on their backs and the worry they carried perpetually on their shoulders.

Pidru and his family did not speak to Ninan as they loaded their change of threadbare clothes and a stack of collected papyrs and a bundle of corn bread. Tamya kept casting wistful looks at him, with an expression torn between hurt and affection. Ninan had missed her, a feeling made so much worse by the thought that she might not forgive him for this.

There would be time to explain himself, to apologize profusely, he told himself. But the safety of these people was his first priority. He continued to help carry bundles of goods and tools, as well as heirloom quinoa seeds that could hopefully soon be sown on Allpan soil. He and the bandits double-checked the flyers' harnesses and the gondola attachments to ensure everything was still in working order before takeoff.

Everyone boarded before the hushdust wore off. Some of the guards moaned, although they were all still too drowsy to get on their feet or make any moves to stop the people from leaving.

Kunaq, Yaku, and Tika each headed their own ark now filled with people. One by one, they commanded their flyer teams to rise, aligning in an airborne caravan with Kunaq's and Tika's pteranodons in tow. Because of the full loads and the need to allow the pteranodons—with their smaller wingspans—to keep up, they flew at a slower speed. Again, Ninan rode Yaku's flyer, following close behind for nearly four hours, until the caravan passed through Yupa, the capital of Unu, where Ninan turned into a downward sweep, waving his temporary goodbye.

As soon as he was finished in Unu, he would meet the bandits and the ark passengers in Allpa, where he would return Yaku's flyer so that the bandits could fly back to their hideout on Tisqu Isle. For now, the bandits carried a message from Ninan to Quya Urpi—begging her to find a place for his friends, with the promise that he would be there in person within a few hours to discuss it further—along with the Kallpa House signet seal so she would know the group was arriving on his authority. He hoped she would remember her words to him at the embarkation of the tour.

With a pained flutter in his chest, he also hoped he might find Qora and the Razorclaws in Unu, safe and sound under

Qhapaq Izhi's protection. The Razorclaws had made a deal with Izhi, after all. Qora likely had her own plans, but she was close to them, and might have accompanied them. While matters of his own heart were of so little consequence when compared to all the lives at risk, and while he had no idea what would come next, he wanted Qora to know how he felt about her.

It is only in darkness that the stars are visible to the human eye. Without it, humankind would know nothing of them.

From *The Book of Dawn and Dusk*

SIXTY-FOUR

QORA DIDN'T BREATHE EASILY until Sakay's pteranodon lowered his body to a steady resting place. She and Ollan and the Razorclaws delivered him to Wayra's house on Mount Qaqra, where they placed him on an open rhabdo-cart so they could more comfortably transport him to one of the funerary slabs throughout the countryside that surrounded Qhusi. The raised, rectangular surfaces were made of concrete, available for public use as needed.

The Razorclaws flew off to call for a shaman, as well as to deliver the harrowing news and bid friends and family to attend the ceremony that would soon take place, while Qora and Ollan stayed behind to hitch the cart to two of the rhabdodons in Wayra's dinoshelter.

As Qora helped Ollan position the rhabdos and line up the cart behind them, she choked on another sob. She couldn't believe Sakay was just lying here, lifeless, nothing but pounds of flesh with no spirit to move them. It was only a few hours ago that she'd stood on the plateau, holding his hand, and Ollan's hand too, so grateful to have them both—but no, she couldn't have them *both*, could she? The gods had forced her to trade one for the other, like there was no room for so much goodness in her life and some of it had to spill out.

Of course she didn't love Sakay as much as she loved Ollan, but Sakay had occupied a much larger space in her heart than she'd realized.

Ollan flinched like he wanted to comfort her, but Qora was sure he knew her well enough to give her some space for now, and he held back. Instead he got to work on one of the rhabdodon's harnesses while Qora started on the other.

They worked in silence for a few minutes, and as Ollan slid a bit into his rhabdodon's mouth, he quietly said, "I was just thinking about when you were eight …"

Qora paused and looked up at him, waiting for him to elaborate.

"Back when you used to collect tree frogs and moths and ladybugs … pretty much any little living thing you could get your hands on."

She sighed, not in the mood to reminisce. Ollan was trying to distract her with good memories, with the simplicity of childhood, but it only made her feel like a fool— a fool for ever living in such ignorance to the ways of the world. She'd been digging up earthworms while the qhapaq had probably been drawing up the early plans for his special dinosaur breeds. Like an idiot, she'd been imagining shapes in the clouds, not realizing she'd one day be soaring among them while enemies pelted her with deadly bolts and arrows. That version of her had no idea what would be coming, no idea that a storm had been brewing on the very horizon that had shown her so much beauty.

"That spring, we had that ephemeral pond in the meadow," Ollan continued. "Do you remember? It rained more than it ever had in my life, more than it ever has since."

She didn't answer, but of course she remembered. That was when she'd learned about ephemeral ponds—temporary wetlands that could form in low-lying areas after heavy rainfall.

"Anyway, you came back to the house every day like you'd struck gold, with a bucketful of tadpoles or fairy shrimp. The dragonflies were harder to catch, but you loved to watch them hover over the water."

"What's your point, Ollan?" Qora attached the lines to her rhabdodon's bit.

"At the end of the season," Ollan said, "it all dried up."

Qora nodded slowly, remembering how the water had begun to evaporate, making the pond smaller and smaller each day. Until there was nothing but grass and mud.

"And it never filled up again," she murmured.

"No, it didn't." He secured the breastcollars on both reptiles. "But there was so much life there that spring. Life and beauty and happiness that wouldn't have ever existed, had it not been there … even if only for a season. Even though it only happened once."

A heavy look passed between them.

Qora dammed up her tears as she thought on Ollan's meaning, on the weight of what he had said. He was just like their mamáy sometimes, putting together allegorical phrases and stories. And just like their mamáy, he said them at the time Qora least wanted to hear them. "You think you can just tell me that my friend's life is like some stupid pond from when we were kids? You think that you can tell me life is fleeting but somehow we can manage to find joy in the brief moments we're allowed, and we should just be grateful it ever happened instead of sad that it's gone? That's not *enough*, Ollan." She stopped what she was doing and clenched her fists.

"It has to be. I'm sorry, Qora. I'd do anything to take away your pain right now, but I can't. All I know is that *nothing* is promised; *nothing* lasts forever. And we can either hold onto what we have for as long as we have it, and remember it with gratitude when it's gone, or we can spend our lives in agony over every loss."

"We've both already won more than we deserve." She'd said that to Ninan. It had seemed wise at the time. But she didn't feel wise now. She felt … lost.

"I'm not asking you to not be sad," Ollan said. "I'm not asking you to pretend you don't feel what you feel. I'm only telling you that your friend gave you something no one else could—hell, he gave *me* something no one else could, when he helped keep you alive—for a season. And that season is over now, but because of it, you're still here. It wasn't in vain. Maybe someday, a long time from today, once you've had a chance to heal—even though I know you probably feel like you'll *never* heal—you can come to believe that, and find some semblance of peace in it."

Despite her standoffish posture and the rage that must have been written all over her splotched face, Ollan went to her and swathed her in his arms, and she sank into him, soaking him with her tears.

SIXTY-FIVE

THE CITY OF YUPA, UNLIKE QHUSI, was located in a vast, emerald-green valley nourished by the waters of Lake Umiña. The lake was the largest on the entire continent, and if it hadn't been for Ninan's past several weeks at sea marking the grandiosity of water bodies in his mind, it would have seemed like a sea in its own right, albeit a still and silvery one in the midst of endless meadows and deciduous trees.

Tuko peeked out of Ninan's vest enough to let the wind caress the sceathers on his head, but kept the rest of his body flattened and tucked away.

Villca House was a circular citadel at the center of the city, with its main keep surrounded by concentric walls forming a small circular courtyard and two ringed baileys. Four watchtowers rose up from the outer bailey, distributed evenly around the ring. The outermost wall formed the ramparts.

From the ground, the walls would have appeared much too high to see anything within, but from the air, Ninan had a view not unlike a diagram, detailing each layer.

Another tower hosted the citadel's front gate—a huge, wooden thing built into it with an arching shape, drawn up to close off the city beyond. The upper half of the tower, however, was a pteriary, with large openings to permit the flyers in and out, and a platform on top for arrivals and departures. Izhi didn't have as many transportive devices as Apo, but his gondolas and flyers were regal nonetheless in their decorative, blue-velvet drapings and bardings.

As Ninan swooped toward the platform, a dozen guards raised their crossbows.

"I am Apo-Kimsa Kallpa," Ninan declared. "I seek refuge from Sumaq, and an audience with Qhapaq Izhi."

The blue-clad guards hesitated a moment, but as Ninan flew closer, somewhat bedraggled in his royal wedding clothes—the materials of which a lesserborn man could not afford—they slowly lowered their weapons and cleared the way for him to land. When he dropped out of the saddle, he showed the emblem inked on the back of his neck, and received a nod of approval from the Head of Watch.

"Welcome, Your Highness. Apologies for the confusion. Please allow us to escort you to the qhapaq."

Tuko clawed his way to Ninan's shoulder as Ninan followed a pair of lower-ranking guards inside.

)))

Ninan had to wait in the parlor, sitting upon one of the cushioned chairs tapping his foot while Tuko tried to chew on a pillow tassel.

After what felt like an eternity, Qhapaq Izhi entered.

Ninan stood and went toward him so abruptly, he almost didn't catch the shift in the qhapaq's usual demeanor. The second he did, his heart sank. "What is it? Is everything alright? The attack ... Was it ..." He couldn't even finish the sentence.

The qhapaq stared at him, surely confused that Ninan was

here right now after having witnessed a band of pirates carry him off. Nevertheless, he answered the question. "I'm afraid our mission was ... unsuccessful."

At those words, Ninan felt like the blood was slowly draining from his body. "Unsuccessful ..."

So they hadn't destroyed the base, but ... Qora? Ollan? Sakay? The Razorclaws? Izhi's unit? What did that mean for them?

"It appears your father anticipated that someone might try to take advantage of your wedding as a distraction. He prepared his beastlord and handlers and guards against airborne tranquilizers, and fortified the base with additional, camouflaged military personnel. Some of our methods were effective, but not beyond the initial landing."

Ninan trembled. "And my friends? Are they not under your protection?"

"The Raptoriva made it out alive, I know that much. Those from my unit who survived brought word when they returned. It seems one of the Razorclaws was lost to battle—I can't be sure which, as I did not witness the event."

"You couldn't be sure even if you'd been there," Ninan seethed. "You don't know a single one of their names, do you? Even though the Razorclaws agreed to help you, to work with you. You only care about your own people. The rest of us are just a means to your end. Even though I came all the way here to *warn* you ..."

Izhi's attendants came forward as if to restrain Ninan, but Izhi raised a hand without looking at them and they stepped back to their places, exchanging a glance between them.

"Warn me of what?"

"My father is planning to come to Yupa with his Sauroguard.

That's what it's called: the Sauroguard. He's in the process of drafting a declaration of war—I saw it in his scriptorium—and you're the first target. Because of the attack on the base this morning."

"What do you mean 'in the process of drafting'? How could he have begun to draft such a document before he left for the wedding, when I had not yet even deployed my unit?"

"I think he's been waiting for you to attack, to commit an act of war. He wanted an excuse, and now he has one."

"I see," said Izhi. He seemed to reflect for a moment on the gravity of this. "It is a great advantage to have this information, and for that I truly thank you. I will have my military fortify the Unuvian borders. We should have a few more days at least, before your father makes his official declaration. At that point, perhaps we can negotiate a less hostile method of resolving our conflict."

"And if he demands that you cede to his authority?"

"It all depends on what we're up against. At this point in time, we simply don't know the full extent of it. Ultimately, I will do what is best for my people—and yours."

Ninan didn't reply to that. The implications were too great. If Sumaq came to occupy Unu and eventually conquer it entirely . . .

No. He couldn't think about it right now. He took a deep breath before he said, "What information do you have about the whereabouts of my friends?"

"None, I'm afraid. I imagine they would have wanted to perform final rites on the one they lost. The Razorclaws are to come to me eventually, to continue developing relevant military tactics, but for the moment, they could have gone anywhere. I do know, from one of my posted sources, that the girl evacuated her family a few days ago, although no destination could be determined. Perhaps she, at least, has gone wherever she sent them."

Of course, Ninan thought. He shouldn't have been surprised at that. Like him, Qora was well aware that his father could go after loved ones as punishment, especially after what he'd told her about his friends in Thak. If her part in the attack was revealed, all the Kanchayas would be targets.

"I have to go find her." Ninan strode past Izhi.

Izhi scoffed and turned his gaze to follow him. "You'll scour the whole of the continent without a lead? After the day you've had?"

Ninan paused at the entryway.

"Don't be ridiculous," Izhi continued. "Allow my culinarium to provide you some nourishment. Lay your head down for a few hours at least. In all likelihood, the Raptoriva will see to her friend, return to her family wherever they are, and then surely she will send word to me. Or you might at least wait for the Razorclaws to arrive; perhaps she'll be among them, or they will know her whereabouts. Then you can go to her with a fresh, rested mind, knowing exactly where she is."

At the mention of food, Ninan's stomach clenched, and only then did he realize he had eaten nothing today. He hadn't been able to bear the idea of breakfast before the wedding, and since his escape he'd hardly had a moment to think, let alone eat. But how could he eat when Qora was out there suffering?

Which Razorclaw had been lost in the attack? Gods, he hoped it hadn't been Ollan. Not that he wished it on *any* of them …

Regardless, his strength waned. Simply standing here required more willpower than he would have liked to admit. His consciousness was fuzzy at best.

"I'll eat," he finally said, "but I doubt I'll be able to sleep."

SIXTY-SIX

IN A MANNER FAR TOO SIMILAR to their preparations for the attack in the Aquchay, Qora and Ollan and the Razorclaws waited in darkness just before dawn.

Funerals, when possible, were to begin a few minutes before the rising of the sun, and end as dawn lit the sky, to symbolize the passage from one world to the next.

The shaman's assistants removed the wrappings that kept Sakay's limbs bound, as well as his shirt and shoes so that his chest and feet were bare. One of them went to remove his tooth necklace but Qora said, "No. Leave it. Please." And so they did, positioning it centrally to keep with a dignified pose.

As the shaman arrived, guests gathered around holding small sauropod-oil lamps. Shaman Achirana—the same who had treated Rimaq in his illness—laid pieces of holy wood around Sakay's body. She took another piece of holy wood and held it upright, lit it, and chanted the funerary prayer:

Oh, Grave World, where the ashes lie,
Oh, High World, where the spirits dwell,
Nourished by that which falls and shines from our skies
And by that which grows from where our bodies bid farewell.

With water do we rise like wilted flesh against the pull,
In fire do we shrivel and succumb to nature's cleanse.
This spirit we do send beyond our world, in full,
That he may find his way to where eternity amends.

As the shaman spoke these words, she wafted the smoke of the holy wood over Sakay to cleanse the pyre for his soul, and then laid the wood at Sakay's feet to continue smoking gently— for an uninhibited journey into the next life. She then withdrew a small pot of sky-blue paint, dipped her thumb into it, and drew a thick line across Sakay's forehead.

"That his memories may remain with him as he departs."

Then a spot on Sakay's heart.

"That his deeds will earn him an eternity of peace."

Then on the soles of his feet.

"That he will swiftly find his way to his ancestors and to those he loved who have since departed."

Ramaya, Qora thought. That's what Sakay had wanted. That woman had seemed to be all he'd cared about, in secret, for the past two years. Qora wished she could have known her too.

She imagined, now, Sakay's soul waiting at the gates of the High World, where other souls stood for his arrival, with Ramaya among them. Suddenly everything she'd been taught her whole life about spirits and souls and the afterlife sounded too good to be true, and she wondered if they were. Or if death was only darkness, and forgetting. It was hard to imagine not existing, not thinking or feeling or … fearing. Maybe, if nothing else, it was a relief, a mercy to cut short the suffering of humankind. Dread pooled in her belly.

She'd been young enough when Ollan had disappeared that it hadn't occurred to her to question such things. And regardless, she hadn't actually *seen* him die—which she now knew had been indicative of the great secret of his absence all these years. But this was different. Sakay had been alive one minute, and the next, his body had turned still. Permanently. As she stared at him lying on the pyre, it was becoming more real to her. More severe.

"For those of you who have brought an offering," the shaman said, "you may place it now."

Sakay's uncle went first and stood beside Sakay for several minutes, stroking Sakay's head like a father might a little boy's. For however emotionally detached Sakay's uncle might have been, he'd raised him, taught him everything, relied on him as a partner in their trades. Finally, the man pressed a gold coin into Sakay's curled hand, then planted a rough, shaky kiss on his painted forehead.

The Underground workers took turns next, each saying a few parting words, a memory they'd shared with him, and leaving some of his favorite things on the pyre—spicy ornithomimid jerky, pteroleaf cigars, a bottle of Huandoyan pisco, a swatch of woven cloth with his preferred color and pattern.

Then the Razorclaws went, contributing items of a similar nature. A book of riddles, a bracelet of aquilops vertebrae.

When it was Qora's turn, she had to will her feet to move. She went forward in a daze, the figures around her blurring. Her eyes welled as she laid her offering on his chest: A single, red, kantuta flower.

"Kantuta, you don't wait for anyone."

Everyone drew back to give the shaman space now, as he drizzled the finest sauropod oil—Qora had insisted—from a narrow bottle, followed by a drizzle of the high-proof botanical spirits always used for this very purpose. The alcohol in the spirits would ignite at once, while the oil would sustain it, and the wood would provide the final, lasting fuel, enough to fully cleanse the body by fire.

With a friction match, the shaman lit the pyre from the head, and within seconds the flames engulfed Sakay's body, releasing his soul to the world beyond.

"For an entire generation, we, the quyas of the late Qhapaq Pawllu of Allpa, have borne only daughters, unable to provide sons to inherit the terrenal seat of power and continue our succession of heirs. At this time, we implore the tribunal to consider a new path to government: That I, primary quya to our beloved qhapaq, and mother to the first child that carries his blood, may act as regent until the child, Urpi Qhispina, comes of age and takes her rightful place at the head of the Terrain.

"Furthermore, I propose that my daughter maintain the right to rule without deference to her husband, should she marry; and should she fail to provide a male heir, that the line may continue as her own, through the firstborn, regardless of sex.

"For guidance in your decision, I point to the symbol of our great Terrain. Within a smilodon pride, it is the females who lead, who band together to pursue sustenance, while the males remain at the den to protect and defend the young.

If nature proves the capacity of the feminine, how can we deny opportunity to one of rightful blood among our kind? How can we justify a ruler who does not share Qhispina blood, when my daughters, and the daughters of my quya companions, are ready and waiting to fulfill their father's legacy?"

Quya Mayua's address to the Allpan Tribunal of Succession

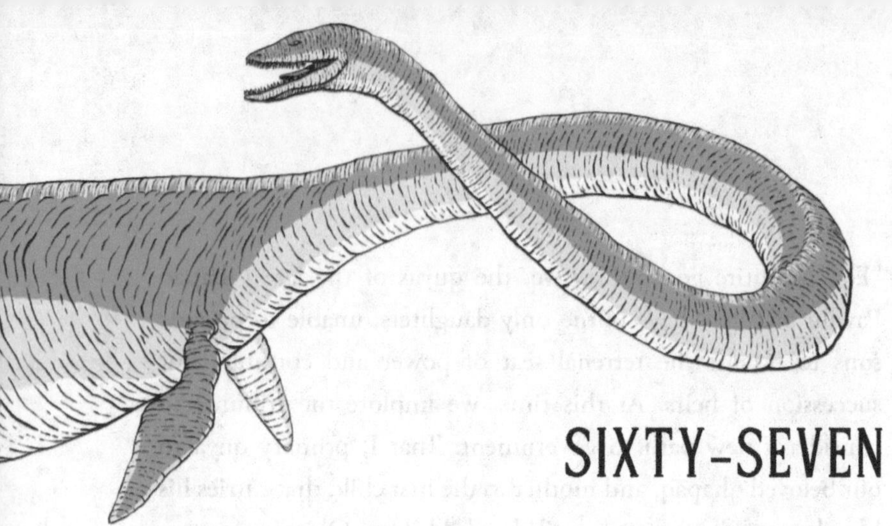

SIXTY-SEVEN

NINAN HAD GORGED HIMSELF on spiced eudimorphodon wings, arapaima ceviche, corn cakes, fried yucca strips, and caramelized plantains with sweet cinnamon cream on top, all the while feeding bits of everything to Tuko as Izhi looked on with frightened fascination. When attendants had shown Ninan to a guest room, he'd flopped onto the bed with the intention of only allowing himself to digest such a large amount of food for a few minutes, but despite his best efforts, he'd drifted off to sleep.

In the dim light of dawn, he woke on his belly, face smashed against the blue bedspread, with a trickle of drool at the corner of his lips. Tuko hopped around on the bedspread before stopping to nip at the hair that had fallen into Ninan's eyes. With a groan, Ninan pushed himself up and stumbled to the vanity, where a porcelain bowl of water was placed before the mirror, and splashed his face and dragged his fingers through his mussed hair. In reflection, his skin was sallow, with dark spots under his lower eyelids.

How the mighty have fallen, he thought.

Not that he'd ever felt mighty. But this certainly wasn't one of his better moments—an escapee from his own wedding, still wearing the same clothes only now they were tattered and spattered with dirt, a traitor in his father's rival's house.

He raised an arm and sniffed, wrinkling his nose. It wasn't the worst he'd ever smelled; the Venture had drawn out some of his most pungent odors. And of course those first several days in the wilderness after his disinheritance had left him reeking and disheveled. But something about today, far beyond his scent, felt worse than both.

Maybe it was that some part of him had believed those days were in the past—the days of fleeing for his life, hiding, pretending to be someone else. He'd still been fleeing, only in a different way, more mentally than physically. As far as pretending, well, maybe he'd *always* been doing that, even before his father had disowned him. Pretending to belong among Kallpas.

A knock at his door startled him from his thoughts.

"Come in," he said.

An attendant entered. "I heard you stirring, Your Highness." Ninan raised a brow. "And?"

"And His Majesty Qhapaq Izhi asked that I tell you to join him on the vantage hall balcony as soon as you awoke."

ꝹꝹꝹ

Attendants escorted Ninan up a spiraling stairwell along the inner walls of the main keep—whose height rose above the rest of the citadel—to its highest level, likely the only part of Villca House visible from below besides the pterosaur landing platforms, through what Izhi's staff called the vantage hall. Ninan gazed around the large space, which had more windows than walls, and dozens of chairs and sofas for taking in the view. Then he stepped onto the immense, tiled balcony.

Despite the early hour and the minimal haze of light on the horizon, Izhi was fully dressed, with sharp posture and an alert gaze. He sipped a dark, steaming liquid from a goblet made of blue glass.

"Good morning." Izhi snapped his fingers at an attendant, who produced a second goblet and delivered it to Ninan. "This kaphiy is an ancient blend. Unlike anything you've tasted before."

Ninan took a sip and nodded. While most kaphiys were bitter, this had a certain fruity sweetness to it, with notes of cacao. The warmth slid into his belly, an unexpected comfort. "Do you always drink your kaphiy overlooking the qhapaqdom like some god surveying its creations?"

Tuko perched himself on Ninan's wrist and tried to dip his head into the goblet, but Ninan clicked his tongue to deter him. The pteromorph made a displeased trilling sound.

"Every single day," Izhi replied. "I find this particular hour to be ... empowering."

Ninan rolled his eyes.

"I'm preparing troops as we speak," Izhi told him, despite the attitude, "with the intention of sending them out this very morning to fortify my border at every vulnerable point. For now, that's the best we can do, until we receive more information."

"And the dominite?" Ninan asked. "Any progress on that?"

"My elementalists are testing it day and night. They've learned that it's made up of the very same elements found in skyrock, with no additional materials. It's simply a ... reconstruction." He took another sip of his kaphiy. "As far as which other element, elements, or conditions cause it to restructure, they can only guess. Thus, they are guessing—and putting each guess to the test one at a time, isolating variables and so forth. But of course there are more than a hundred elements, and many sets of conditions with temperature, humidity, and pressure in isolation *and* in combination. Worse, we lost a portion of our samples to sun exposure before determining that the crystal energy wanes under light."

"We're certainly not likely to get close to another shipment again any time soon," Ninan lamented. "My father was already viciously protective of his activities. Now that you've attacked his base, I can't imagine how much more security we'd have to deal with."

Izhi offered a sardonic grin. "Well, we might not have destroyed your father yet, but you *were* able to avoid your wedding, at least."

Ninan nearly spit the liquid from his mouth but caught himself, wiping his lips. "Yes, no thanks to you." Oddly enough, he had Paqari to thank. He hadn't had the chance to consider those details further, but he wanted to. She must have gotten the idea from the first round of pirates, the real ones. After all that destruction, it had been a logical solution, and he wished he'd thought of it himself.

"Forgive me if the matters of the royalborn youth are not my *utmost* priority," Izhi said.

Ninan rubbed the back of his neck, thinking of the emblem there. No matter where he went, no matter who he pretended to be, it would always mark him. Right now, in a foreign Terrain, having betrayed his land and his family, it was all the more a stain against him. He wondered if his father would think to look for him here, if he would make the connection between the attack on the base and Ninan's disappearance from the wedding, or assume Ninan had merely taken advantage of the chaos already in place. Either way, his father would know Ninan had raided Kallpa House and evacuated Thak; from there, it wasn't a far jump to connect him to everything else.

"We're not finished yet, Apo-Kimsa," said Izhi. "Your father is formidable, but he's not infallible. We *will* determine his weaknesses—and exploit them."

"I hope you're right."

Izhi glanced over the balcony. "Of course. It's only a matter of—"

Blue glass shattered on the tile floor, spewing kaphiy in a starburst.

Flinching, Ninan's gaze then fell to Izhi's trembling fingers, which curled over the gilded railing as the man stared wide-eyed into the distance.

"What's—"

Ninan's breath caught in his throat when he looked out.

Along with the light that spread across the skyline, so too did several thousand dinosaurs.

SIXTY-EIGHT

QORA SWIPED AT HER EYES in between tightening the saddlebag on her pteranodon outside the Underground. This pteranodon would be hers now, Wayra had said. No point in trying to figure out the logistics of returning it, since Qora would need it to get to Allpa, and there was no telling when she and Wayra would see each other again.

Ollan's pteranodon—also officially his now—was hitched next to Qora's, awaiting takeoff. "Thank you," he told Wayra. "We couldn't have done any of this without you."

"My pleasure," Wayra said. "I'll miss them, for sure, but I've got a dozen more to keep me busy."

Their eyes seemed to meet for longer than necessary, Qora thought, but she had too much else on her mind to pick apart the nuances in their body language. She stroked her pteranodon's neck and took a deep breath to compose herself. Her eyes were burning as it was, and she willed herself to stop tearing up, at least for a little while.

"You have to deal with your demons one way or another, kantuta."

Never had she thought it would be Sakay's absence that haunted her.

A few seconds later, Req, Kuy, and Gorgo (who had

accompanied Sakay's uncle home after the funeral) suddenly came rushing from down the street outside the Underground.

Req held a chronicle sheet—a long papyr covered in text providing the daily news. "You two need to see this."

Qora accepted the sheet and unfolded it while Wayra peered over her shoulder to read along.

UNU ATTACKS SUMAQI ARMY BASE ABROAD, UNPROVOKED

In recent years, Qhapaq Apo of the Sumaqi House of Kallpa has commanded a private military training program with the intention of guarding against extracontinental threats, the evidence of which has become clear through various foreign dinosaurs appearing on the isles of Tisqu and terrorizing local villages. Qhapaq Achiq of the Tisquvian House of Huapaya was an early supporter of the plan, and provided a secluded place within the Aquchay Desert for special forces, covertly known as the Sauroguard, to be trained.

However, yesterday morning, with highborns and the Tisquvian Guard focused on the wedding between Apo-Kimsa Kallpa (Third Prince of Sumaq) and Paqari Huapaya (Second Princess of Tisqu), a unit of Unuvian operatives, along with a band of Sumaqi rebels, attacked the secret military base without cause, destroying much of the grounds and killing hundreds.

In anticipation of such an attack on this interterrenally important day, Qhapaq Apo had fortified the base with additional personnel, which proved insightful, as it is believed that these reinforcements prevented complete destruction and allowed base operatives to drive out the attacking troops.

It has come to attention that a network of Unuvian spies, under the direct instruction of Qhapaq Izhi of the Unuvian House of Villca, have infiltrated several Sumaqi industries and gained access to classified information, which they then used to determine the location of the special military base.

The Unuvian attack comes without cause or provocation, and is considered not only a direct attack on Sumaq and its ally Tisqu, but an affront to all the other Terrains of Runaqa who would have received protection under these special forces.

Qora curled her fingers into fists, crumpling the sheet. Before her haste, she'd glimpsed a second header, ROYAL WEDDING SPECTACLE BEYOND WORDS, but she didn't need to know what a grand show the wedding had been, how opulent and gorgeous with its seaside locale and highborn guests trimmed in gold. Although she wished it was *only* the wedding that was souring her stomach now.

"He's going to use this as an excuse," Qora said of the qhapaq. "I wouldn't be surprised if he actually *wanted* Unu to attack, if he's been silently provoking Qhapaq Izhi all this time."

"Even *allowing* bits of information to surface …" Wayra suggested.

"Do you think we're in any immediate danger?" Req asked Kuy.

Kuy sighed. "Hard to say. Qhapaq Apo might want to give it some time, to let this … *story* … sink in, circulate, get people riled up in his favor."

"Or he could retaliate immediately," said Qora.

"We should head to Yupa right away," Wayra said to the men. "To start working on a new plan."

"Because the plan went so well the last time?" Gorgo asked.

Wayra folded her arms. "We'll just have to do better. With Qhapaq Izhi's money and manpower, we can scale up. Better equipment, more precise experiments—bigger bombs, bolder innovations. And we have Sakay's contact for the fool's silver; Izhi can buy it in bulk."

"We can't rely on Izhi alone, though," Qora argued. "Whatever resources he has, they haven't been enough. We're going to need more than one royalborn on our side. I'm going to make sure Quya Urpi knows what we're up against. From what I've heard, she doesn't take well to deals with the qhapaqs—and I think the feeling is mutual—but maybe in this case, she'll make an exception for an alliance with Unu."

"Let's hope so," said Kuy.

Qora looked at each of the Razorclaws in turn. Fuming with rage and ravaged with grief, she was grateful for them. She understood why Sakay hadn't been able to distance himself from them completely, even after what had happened to Ramaya. She knew she could count on them for anything—and she was certain she'd have to eventually.

Wayra pulled her into an embrace. "Fly safe."

"Thank you," Qora said. "For everything."

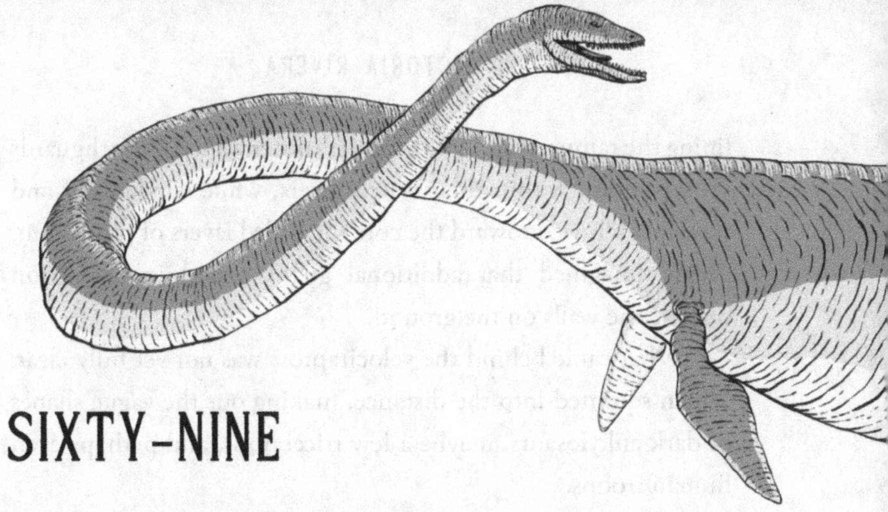

SIXTY-NINE

NINAN'S KNUCKLES WENT WHITE on the railing as thousands of velociraptors advanced through the city streets, evoking shrieks and screams from any citizens who had braved the early morning.

These velociraptors were twice the size of any Ninan had seen before—at least four feet high instead of two. And instead of fiery orange scales and feathers, these were bare and brown but for their feet, which were red as blood.

Beastlords punctuated the horde, one for every few hundred velociraptors, shouting commands. They wore collared necklaces of dominite crystals strung together like glowing, purple sun rays bursting from their throats, as they sat atop night-black megaraptors covered in scutes.

Scutes? Ninan thought. Somehow, his father had managed to breed *armored* megaraptors? He surveyed the sections of the citadel, heart pounding heavily. Here, at the innermost layer, he was the safest he could get, and yet … he didn't feel safe in the slightest. There was no way out other than to fly, but the pteriary was all the way over at the gate. Although velociraptors posed little threat to walls so high, Ninan knew this was only the beginning of whatever his father had in mind.

The onsite Unuvian Guard assembled with impressive speed,

lining the ramparts along the citadel's outer wall. All watchguards took position within their watchtowers, while citadel staff and residents scurried toward the core for added layers of protection. Ninan imagined that additional guards stood in protection outside the walls on the ground.

What came behind the velociraptors was not yet fully clear. Ninan squinted into the distance, making out the vague shapes of dark ankylosaurs, maybe a few triceratops, and perhaps even human troops.

As soon as the velociraptors advanced within shooting range, the Unuvian commander shouted for the guards on the outer grounds to fire.

The beastlords shouted, "Assail!" at the reptiles.

Hundreds of mechanical clicks echoed off the stones as the guards fired—but whatever bolts had struck hadn't been enough. Guards cried out as the velociraptors overwhelmed them, painting a picture in Ninan's mind that made the blood drain from his face.

"There are too many," Ninan choked out.

Izhi's upper lip twitched. "Perhaps. But the reptiles will not be able to cross the walls."

The qhapaq kept a firm stance, but Ninan could see the cracks in his facade. This army should never have gotten past the freestanding Unuvian watchtowers near the borders—at least not without them relaying a warning beacon first. How had they done it?

"Maybe not the velociraptors," Ninan said. "But they're wearing down your outer defenses. What about the dinosaurs that come *after* these?"

"Incoming!" shouted the commander. "Overhead!"

Something like two dozen pteranodons—an unusual mottle

of gray and off-white skin nearly lost against morning clouds—
came swooping in without riders. An airborne beastlord
followed, wearing the same dominite collar as the beastlords on
the ground.

Tuko squawked and clawed his way back into Ninan's vest
pocket.

"Get my quyas and my children into the south passage!"
Izhi told his guards.

Several of them nodded and disappeared back into the
vantage hall.

The few guards who had remained to protect Izhi began to
usher him and Ninan back into the keep, holding shields over
their heads like the Tisquvian Guard had done at the wedding.
Ninan could scarcely see the few feet in front of him, and he and
Izhi hadn't even made it to the doors when a screeching sound
rattled their ears and all four guards collapsed around them.

Ninan, too, collapsed under the weight of the now-
unsupported shield. He got to his feet, still holding the shield by
its grip, and gaped at the heap of guards writhing and screaming
on the balcony floor tiles while their uniforms were slowly
disintegrating in patches as something bubbled and ate away
at them, reddening the flesh beneath and releasing gases that
slithered up like steam. Ninan gagged at the smoky, acrid-meat
odor.

Qhapaq Izhi had made it to the shelter of the keep and
beckoned Ninan from the doorway. But another screech
prompted Ninan to look up as one of the pteranodons swooped
low, opened its beak, and spewed yellow liquid.

Raising the shield, Ninan blocked the flow before it could
touch him, and watched it drip from the metallic edges. It gave
a soft hiss as it hit the tiles, quickly corroding their surfaces as a

feeling of dread corroded Ninan's insides.

"Apo-Kimsa!" Izhi shouted. "We must get to safety. There is a tunnel system to escape the citadel, but you have to come with me now!"

Had the guards known what was coming, Ninan thought, they could have handled this with their shields, but as none had been expecting acid-spewing pteranodons—and why should they have?—many were collapsed throughout the citadel, cluttering the courtyard and the ramparts while their comrades aimed crossbows high.

The grayish pteranodons swooped and soared, taking hits that didn't penetrate their flesh, and raining more acid. As usual with creatures this formidable, there seemed to be only one way to take them down.

Ninan picked up one of the fallen guards' crossbows, spanning and loading it with trembling hands. He had to pause and raise the shield again to avoid another splash of acid from the sky. When he was ready, he put himself directly in the path of another pteranodon and, just as it opened its mouth to screech, he cringed and fired straight down its throat. Its cry cut off into a gurgle and it threw back its head, careening from its flight path, crashing into the courtyards and skidding across the pavingstones.

Somehow in this dreadful chaos, Ninan had an instant to wish Qora had just seen him. *Probably couldn't hit the broad side of a triceratops.* Gods, he ached to be wherever she was now, listening to her mock and berate him. He would have taken her meanest, vilest words if it meant she was near.

Guards that were still standing began to follow his example, aiming into the pteranodons' mouths, shouting at others to do the same. A few weren't quick enough, getting doused in acid as their bolts flew out, but several managed to take out a pteranodon in one or two shots, leaving half as many in the air now.

At this point, Qhapaq Izhi had disappeared into the main keep, leaving Ninan to himself.

Ninan went to the railing again to see the rest of the Sauroguard coming well into view. He'd been right—ankylosaurs, black ones, with extraordinary club-tails, commanded by beastlords riding gray triceratops.

His father must have bred them in muted tones, Ninan thought, so that their species' otherwise-vibrant colors would not be a marker for their arrival.

They thundered through the streets, which citizens had cleared many minutes ago. It would only be another minute or so before the reptiles reached the citadel, and Ninan had a fairly good guess as to what they would do when they arrived.

"They're climbing the walls!" someone screamed.

Or maybe not.

Climbing?

Turning his attention to the sound, Ninan spotted the first of those blood-red velociraptor feet coming up between the battlements. Within seconds, hundreds of velociraptors swarmed the ramparts, terrorizing the officers. Some continued up the watchtowers, retracting their claws and pressing their red feet against the exterior stones and scuttling upward like insects.

Bile rose in Ninan's throat.

How had his father accomplished such a thing? Whatever was on their feet allowed them to keep their grip, to practically defy gravity.

Worse, Ninan and the Razorclaws hadn't seen any of these dinosaurs—or pterosaurs, for that matter—when they had surveyed the base. Like the qhapaq was sending different species through the base in batches. And as far as those they *had* seen, what fantastical features would they possess once they were fully mature? If these could spit acid and climb walls, what had the qhapaq bred the others to do?

Ninan shuddered.

The beastlord on pteranodonback seemed to be in charge of the velociraptors now, as the beastlords on megaraptor had to remain outside the walls. Thank the gods the megaraptors couldn't climb, Ninan thought, although after everything else it hardly seemed to matter.

As his pulse thrummed in his ears, Ninan raised his crossbow and scoured the skies for his next victim when the airborne beastlord hovering over the main keep made him pause. The beastlord was only maybe thirty feet above where Ninan stood, and if there was a stairwell that led to the keep's roof—

Ninan rushed into the keep and scanned the space until he located an opening at the opposite side, beyond the polished floors and velvet sofas and mounted triceratops heads. A dark stairwell spiraled around the inner perimeter of the keep, leading Ninan upward until the top of his head came upon a hatch. Carefully, he pushed it open, splitting the darkness with a crack of light from the sky. While the beastlord shouted at his reptilian squadron, Ninan emerged from underneath.

Trembling, Ninan fired at the beastlord, striking him with a bolt to the shoulder and sending him tumbling down to the roof. Not a perfect shot, but it had been good enough.

Before the beastlord, clutching his bloody wound, could get to his feet, Ninan threw three punches to his face and tore the collar of dominite crystals from his neck. Tuko peeked out, eyes wide and unblinking in the purple glow.

"Land!" Ninan commanded the pteranodon.

Without hesitation, the pteranodon touched down and allowed Ninan to mount it.

"Rise!"

Ninan steered the pteranodon toward the ramparts. Fighting guards cowered under him.

"Here!" Ninan broke off one of the crystals and dropped it in their midst. "Command them to 'cease'!" He flew over the rampart and distributed more of the crystals, repeating his instructions.

Entranced, as expected, the velociraptors obeyed, but only those within a certain range. Many more had already moved beyond the ramparts and were well into the bailey, and onto the bridges, and down in the courtyard, clawing in through the low windows of the keep.

Then, the walls began to shake. Thunderous rumblings and lightning-sharp cracks sounded from the base of the outer wall.

Ankylosaurs.

The velociraptors and the pteranodons had bought them all the time that their big, slower bodies needed to reach the walls— and now they would knock them down in a matter of minutes.

With only two crystals left, Ninan struggled to get the pteranodon to take him beyond the citadel wall to get a better view.

Ruck, I shouldn't have given so many away.

A beast this size needed more dominite to remain loyal to someone who wasn't its known trainer.

Beyond the wall, hundreds of ankylosaurs swung their oversized club-tails at the stones simultaneously, busting pockmarks into the surface that grew deeper and deeper with each connection. Some had already turned to holes, revealing the bailey within.

"Strike!" the beastlords shouted. "Strike!"

As soon as holes formed large enough to allow passage, human troops poured in to comb through the lower levels. Ninan didn't know how, but he was sure his father knew about Izhi's tunnels; he just hoped Izhi had gotten far enough into them to have a good head start before the troops located the entrances and infiltrated those too.

The pteranodon twisted against Ninan's rein-hold.

"Come on," Ninan muttered. "Don't be like that." He dangled the remaining crystals on their thin chain in the flyer's periphery, but it jerked its neck, trying to tug out of Ninan's grip. It seemed determined to fly west.

When it defied him so aggressively that the reins bit into his palm, he grasped the pommel and held tight as the pteranodon swept toward another flyer just like it—with a rider wielding a dominite collar.

Another beastlord.

Ninan's pteranodon fixated on the beastlord's collar. Tuko, wriggling in Ninan's pocket, prompted Ninan to stuff the remaining two crystals in with him so he didn't fly out in search of more.

"Come!" the beastlord told Ninan's pteranodon.

Just a few more yards, Ninan thought, picking up the reins again, clenching his thighs around the saddle, and pulling the pteranodon off course just enough to angle toward the keep to the inner wall. *A little more. Right … there …*

He urged the pteranodon low enough that he was ready to take a risk. He flung a leg off the saddle and turned himself so he was dangling from one side. As the pteranodon dipped slightly, Ninan launched himself onto the bridge.

His feet touched the pavingstones for an instant before he

curled his body so that his shoulder and back took the fall at a roll and ended with him in a stumbling crouch. He had to withdraw the dominite again as he found himself in the midst of several snarling velociraptors, but as he looked past them, he quickly realized he had a bigger problem.

Sumaqi officers and reptiles surrounded him from both sides of the bridge.

A general—as evidenced by his uniform—stepped forward. "Apo-Kimsa Kallpa: You are under arrest."

SEVENTY

AFTER SEVEN HOURS IN THE AIR, Qora and Ollan soared across the border between Unu and Allpa in the afternoon. While a standard map caused the capitals of Sumaq, Unu, and Allpa to line up in an almost perfect diagonal across the continent, the most direct route between Qhusi and Amachakuna had Qora and Ollan passing through Unu approximately thirty miles east of Yupa. As they did, Qora glanced in a westerly direction, wondering if she and her brother ought to take a slight detour and stop in Unu's capital to discuss the aftermath of the attack with Qhapaq Izhi, but she was too eager to get to her mamáy and younger brothers, especially only having had a few days with them to appreciate Ollan's return.

It was another hour or so before the city of Amachakuna greeted them in the dipping sunlight, where Qhispina House stood like a flame on the only hill for miles. As if in direct contrast to the red-orange plastered castle walls, the Kuchuna River gushed through an arched tunnel where the castle extended over the base of the hill. It took a more focused look to see that the two columns flanking the tunnel each formed the shape of a downward-pointing sabertooth, that the rounded-square stones framing the arch formed a row of smaller teeth, and that the apex formed a nose, with eyes and ears carved into the surrounding stone—a smilodon face.

Qora wasn't sure whether the river's path occurred naturally this way through the hill and the Allpan royals had simply designed and built their fortress over it, or whether the hill itself was some elaborate construction to allow such a thing, but she gaped nonetheless.

For all her visits abroad, even to Allpa, she'd had yet to visit the capital, until now.

"Spirits …" Qora said.

Ollan, whom Qora had almost forgotten had already been here to deliver their family, managed a smile. "It's certainly a beautiful sight, after what we've just been through."

Quya Urpi's flyer port was located at the top of her pteriary. The tower, with its massive diameter, had large windows on the upper half for flyer entry and exit, and was topped with a flat, paved circle for takeoffs and landings. All perches must have been in the lower half, Qora thought, and it appeared that a team of saddlers remained below while pilots and riders summoned the flyers from above.

When Qora and Ollan flew close, every guard and staff member paused to look up. For a moment, Qora feared they would be on the defensive, as neither she nor her brother had anything on them that hinted at their importance—and other than her status as Venture champion, she couldn't say that she was anyone especially important anyway—but soon they began to applaud.

Receiving staff stepped aside to allow the pteranodons a place on the circle.

Qora and Ollan landed nearly side by side, as everyone gathered and helped them down.

"You already know who we are?" Qora might have expected

this of the quya, whom she had met in person, but not of her workers.

"Quya Urpi has made it a priority that we know you both by sight," said a female attendant. "She's been awaiting your arrival. Come."

The staff ushered Qora and Ollan across a bridge adjoining the pteriary to one of the main keeps and inside, leading them through passageways draped in green velvet and gilt-frame portraits of past royalborns and taxidermied theropods poised as if for attack.

They stopped in a long hall, further tiled in white squares, with onyxwood shelves extending the length of it from floor to ceiling, filled with tomes. Two smilodons lounged on velvet cushions at opposite ends.

Quya Urpi paused, her fingers lingering over text on a page, and turned toward her guests. She closed the book and came toward them.

Qora and Ollan bowed.

The quya was probably about twice Qora's age, but her eyes spoke of wisdom beyond even those additional years.

Today, Quya Urpi wore a simple, mauve gown that draped without voluminous undergarments. Her hair was fixed in a single, long plait down her back. Her rose-gold diadem was narrow, and without gems.

"The Raptoriva lives," the quya remarked, placing a hand on one of Qora's shoulders. She pressed her cheek to Qora's briefly.

"Thank the gods," Ollan replied.

"Welcome back," Quya Urpi said to him.

"Thank you for receiving my family," Qora interjected. "I apologize that I could not be here the first time, to ask for your assistance in person. I apologize with even greater intensity if

I misread your words that day at the Venture homecoming in Qhusi, and if we are intruding on your kindness."

Urpi smiled. "Not at all."

"Good," Qora said. "You told me that your name is 'refuge,' so now I'm here to tell you that mine ... is 'exile.'"

⟆⟆⟆

Qora and Ollan waited in Quya Urpi's grand library while attendants went to fetch the other family members. She motioned for them to sit on an arrangement of velvet-upholstered chairs with high backs, surrounding a polished onyxwood table. A smilodon curled up beside her feet, taking up more space than was polite.

"I hoped you would understand my meaning," Urpi told Qora, "and I'm glad you did. I seek to provide what others in my position cannot, or will not. In fact, I've already received a small influx of refugees that my people are currently placing on a swatch of countryside for cultivation, as their permanent residence. Sent here by Apo-Kimsa Kallpa, in fact."

Qora's heart practically seized in her chest. "Apo-Kimsa?" It was a strange sensation to use Ninan's true name—but stranger still to think he'd had the means to send refugees across two borders. "How ..."

"It seems he commandeered a trio of pterobeast arks to transport the entire community, along with three bandits to pilot them since he obviously couldn't bring them himself. Still ... gods only know how he managed it, with everything he's had going on, and with the Terrains' eyes on him leading up to his wedding. We're still awaiting news on *that*, of course, but I can't say I care much for all the fanfare of such things."

473

Ninan's friends in Thak ... Qora thought, her throat thickening. He'd been able to save them after all.

Try as she might to convince herself he was still a spoiled prince, she couldn't seem to support her own argument. Not when he'd suffered abuse and neglect at the hands of his own family; not when he'd given up trying to win the Venture to make way for *her* to win; not when he'd used his position to help Izhi. She couldn't help but ache at the knowledge of what he'd risked, stealing Kallpa House arks and sending them abroad. Even *without* considering that, Ninan had married Paqari because staying in his father's good graces would continue to allow him the rank and access he needed to fight with Izhi and the Razorclaws, and because it would keep the Terrains' attention and security focused and hopefully allow the attack on the base to go smoothly.

How could she have ever been so frustrated with him? How could she have ever thought so little of him? She clenched her jaw, trying to calm her breathing. The worst part was, it didn't matter. He was far away now, and married, and a prisoner to his station. He would spend the rest of his life fighting secretly from within. She might never get to see him again, might never be able to tell him everything she realized now.

Her only consolation in this moment was the fact that Ninan's friends—his family—were safe, and so was she, and so were her mamáy and brothers. Qhapaq Apo couldn't threaten them anymore.

Not yet, at least.

With trembling fingers, Qora produced the chronicle sheet she'd crumpled before departure, flattening it and then presenting it to the quya. "Have you had news of *this*?"

The quya examined the sheet, bringing it closer and squinting. "No ..." she breathed. "I'm afraid I have not ..."

After giving the quya a moment to read the first several paragraphs, Qora said, "It's false. I was there. I've been working with that 'band of rebels', as well as with the Third Prince and Qhapaq Izhi, to destroy the source of the Sauroguard—that much is true—but Qhapaq Apo didn't create that army to protect Runaqa; he created it to force reunification. He's been breeding special dinosaurs and controlling them with dominite—surely your own spies have learned about dominite?"

Quya Urpi nodded, folding the chronicle sheet and setting it on the table.

"But he's been staging attacks with his own dinosaur *creations* to instill fear in the Tisquvians so that they'll spread the word that everyone else should harbor the same fears too. And it's possible that he *wanted* Izhi to find out, so that Izhi might try to stop it with force, and justify the start of a war."

"Your part in the engagement tour …" Urpi said. "I caught word of that. You're telling me it was an act of espionage?"

"Not intentionally. I was helping the Razorclaws, before they joined forces with Qhapaq Izhi, but my friend Sakay and I discovered that Ninan—Apo-Kimsa—was following the same trail of clues. When the princess saw us together, she insisted I go aboard the *Velosaura*, to please her people."

"That must have been quite tense," Urpi said, "if those rumors about your 'alliance' during the Venture are true."

Ollan flashed Qora a sympathetic look.

"Well, that's over now—clearly." Qora fought back tears, the sting of which came with double the intensity after the day she'd had.

"In any case," Urpi said, "I can't fairly say that I am equipped to be the one to go up against your qhapaq and win. My military is strong, but it was already no match for Sumaq's even *before* he established several units of reptilian soldiers. The only thing that has kept him from forcing reunification thus far has been the defiance of the other Terrains *combined*. Qolqe's loyalty to him was expected, but the rest of us outnumbered them both together. Until now, when he's ensured Tisqu's loyalty too."

Qora produced the second important document she'd brought—the orders Sakay had stolen from the beastlord. "We know some of the locations where Qhapaq Apo is keeping his dinosaurs. This gives us a chance to prepare. If we share this with Qhapaq Izhi ..."

The quya looked over the papyr and sighed. "It's a start—and vital information to have, for certain. The only problem is that with *this* narrative"—she tapped the folded chronicle on the table—"Qhapaq Apo makes a villain of Unu, which will make our alliance much more complicated."

"But you can do whatever you want," Ollan said. "You always do."

For as long as Qora could remember, Quya Urpi's reputation preceded her. Ever since Urpi's mother had secured her ability to rule.

"I can," Urpi agreed, "but you'd be surprised how important it is to have the majority of the Terrain's people behind your decisions, even with power like mine. When a population is not, at least for the most part, unified in its ambitions, it affects everything. Division breeds rebellion, riots, treason—all of which are detrimental during wartime.

"Imagine a household, which has fortified itself against the wild monsters of nature—shut up the windows and triple-bolted the doors. Everyone who lives within agrees, 'We must protect ourselves.' But should a single one of them sympathize with the creatures outside, and perhaps reopen a window, or crack the door for a moment, those lying in wait will seize the opportunity to infiltrate the household … and all is lost."

"So, what do we do, then?" Qora said. "We can't just sit by and expect that Qhapaq Apo won't fight his way to us eventu—" Her mamáy and younger brothers entered the library and she forgot all about the discussion, standing to go to them immediately and embracing each in turn—first Rimaq, then Hakan, and then holding to her mamáy fiercely as tears overwhelmed them both.

"They killed Sakay," Qora sobbed against her mamáy's shoulder.

"Oh … Qora …" She held her even more tightly in response, cradling the back of her head.

It was everything Qora needed right now—her mamáy's healing energy, and then her three brothers coming to embrace them both. It dampened the sting, enough for her to endure another moment in this world and all of its monsters, then another moment, and another moment. Maybe one day, the pain would fade. Her rage, however, would not. She didn't see how it could.

"Your Majesty," said one of the attendants. "A document has just arrived for you. Would you like to review it privately?"

The quya stood and extended her hand to accept it. "No, thank you. I will review it now."

Qora looked up long enough to catch a glimpse of the quya removing the seal on the correspondence—and the horror that passed over her face as her eyes moved over whatever was on it.

"This … further complicates things," said Quya Urpi. She met Qora's eyes meaningfully.

"What is it?" Qora released her family.

"Qhapaq Apo has taken Unu."

Qora sucked in a breath and squeezed her mamáy's hand. "When?"

"This morning," said the quya. "He details much of what you've shown me in your chronicle. He considers the attack on his Sauroguard an act of war. Now he demands that I side with him or risk 'occupation.'"

"'Occupation,'" Ollan repeated bitterly. "A euphemism for 'terrorizing and seizing control.'"

Urpi nodded. "And If I make an ally of Unu, I will appear a traitor to the Five Terrains. On the other hand, if I make an ally of Sumaq, it is a subtle shift to putting myself under its rule. With all other Terrains either manipulated or battled into compliance, my Terrain's defiance may very well be the last stand against reunification."

Qora's breathing went ragged as heat flared within her, a thick pulse pounding in her ears. It was like she was staring down that spinosaur again, only this monster was human. Little by little, the qhapaq was ripping away everything that mattered to her.

Her papáy had died building one of Qhapaq Apo's city walls. Ollan had lost four years of his life—and nearly his life in general—because of the monsters that had resulted from Qhapaq Apo's breeding program, while Qora had spent all that time blaming herself. Sakay was dead, at the hands of the qhapaq's Sauroguard beastlord. Ninan would be forever out of her reach. Her entire family had had to leave their home to avoid his wrath. And she never would have risked her safety and sanity in the Venture if it hadn't been for the qhapaq's exploitative laws.

But it wasn't just everything she and her family and friends had suffered at the hands of that man—it was what everyone on the continent had suffered, and would soon suffer, at his hands if they didn't stop him.

"What can we do?" Qora said. "There has to be something. What about extracontinental allies?"

"Extracontinental nations have no motivation to get involved," the quya reasoned. "And that could be much more dangerous than helpful, if they discover the development of dominite. Many of the Terrains have already had to fight off foreigners who covet our skyrock. Can you imagine what would happen if they knew about the crystals?"

"Even if we could rally additional military forces," Ollan said, "they'd still be no match for the Sauroguard—not if what we saw in the Aquchay was any indication of what we're up against. Perfectly obedient dinosaurs that can camouflage themselves, bred with impenetrable scales …"

Qora thought of the spinosaur again, with its likewise impenetrable scales. She imagined that even the dinosaurs she saw at the base would scurry in the shadow of a creature like that. "Maybe we just need bigger dinosaurs."

Ollan scoffed. "Sure. But where would we get them? Even Qhapaq Apo doesn't seem to be employing them, despite his resources. They'd be too difficult to transport and keep fed, they'd take up too much space, they'd probably require more dominite to control them regardless of how powerful that stuff is, solely because of their size."

The bigger the breed, the more you need. That must have been true with dominite too, otherwise the qhapaq might have considered the big theropods in his army. But he, of all people, knew what a challenge they were, having procured one for the Venture.

"I've wondered since the Venture where he got the spinosaur

he planted at the ruins of Utula," Qora said. "I've had my suspicions, but …"

"There's only one place they still exist," the quya replied, "and I imagine he sent someone there to steal eggs many years ago, for his handlers to raise and use for hybrid breeding. I believe it came from the Tail."

The tiny peninsula at the southernmost point of the continent flashed in Qora's mind, the way she'd seen it on continental maps her entire life, thick on one end and tapering like a reptilian tail.

It was a no-man's land, an unwanted territory that the Five Terrains had agreed to leave independent. There were no resources to be claimed, no naturally magnificent landmarks, and the travel routes were rigorous through the Pirqa Mountains, requiring flight for any kind of transportation of goods—which was limiting when it came to heavier resources like timber or stone. It was simply too much trouble, an unnecessary appendage that the qhapaqs of old would have physically removed if they'd had the ability to do so.

"I assumed he'd stolen it from here in Allpa," Ollan said. "From somewhere within your Tukukuq region. I heard there was a decent population of them."

Right, Qora thought. There was a bit of land past the Pirqas that belonged to Allpa, before it narrowed to the isthmus connecting the Tail.

"Those theropods have been dying out, and they're not nearly as large," said Urpi of the southern region of her lands, which were practically a no-man's land themselves but for the sacred Mount Wiru where certain religious fanatics would trek— despite the alleged dangers of the apparently-not-that-large tyrannosaurs, spinosaurs, allosaurs, giganotosaurs, and so forth.

The Pirqas served as a protection for the nearby populated zones and everything that lay north of them, as the giant theropods seemed to have no more desire to cross those mountains than most humans did.

"A few Allpan explorers traveled to the Tail a few years ago," Urpi explained. "They returned with very strange and interesting tales of what they had seen there. Enormous theropods—and people living among them, but up in the trees, which grow much higher and hardier than anything within the Five Terrains. Strange, foot-propelled flying contraptions that mimic pterosaurs. Brutish, woolly mammals. I couldn't be sure how much of it was true."

"They live *among* the enormous theropods?" Qora asked.

"Yes, I found the account difficult to believe. But the explorers insisted it was true, that a peace existed between the humans and the reptiles, even a certain coordination of their separate lives."

"They know how to handle them," Ollan concluded. "And ... without skyrock?"

"Apparently," said the quya.

"We have to go to them," Qora said. "We have to seek their help. If they could teach us, if we could *utilize* dinosaurs of that size ..."

"Logistics, though ..." Ollan reminded her.

"That's exactly why Qhapaq Apo wouldn't expect us to do it. Besides, the people of the Tail obviously know things we don't."

The quya shook her head. "Why should they care to be involved? A war between the rest of us would not affect them."

"It could," Hakan said.

Everyone looked at him in surprise. He and Rimaq had been so quiet, it had been easy to forget they were listening.

"I'm just saying," Hakan continued, "if Qhapaq Apo sent someone to get an egg, he must have some idea what else is down there. It might not have been anyplace to brag about a few centuries ago, but clearly the people have made something of it. He's not just going to ignore that. If there's anything worth having, he'll want a piece of it—won't he? He'll conquer them, too."

Qora put a hand on his cheek. "So we have to get to it first. We have to warn them, and beg them to help."

"The young man is wise," said Quya Urpi.

The thirteen-year-old boy blushed.

"Ollan and I will go." Qora took note of the look on her mamáy's face—the sudden deepening of the creases on her forehead, the pursed lips. "I know our family has only just come together again, but … we have to 'use our teeth,' Mamáy."

The woman sighed. "I know." Even though she likely wasn't familiar with the phrase, she would be familiar enough with those *kinds* of phrases to understand.

"I'll assemble a team for you," said the quya.

"What will you do in the meantime?" Rimaq asked. "What if Qhapaq Apo invades Allpa before there's a chance to get help?"

Quya Urpi stroked her smilodon's head between the ears. "Surely you're aware of the sharpness of these saberteeth …"

The Kanchayas nodded.

"Although these cats are small compared to many dinosaurs, their teeth are one of the few things that can cut through thicker scales. A smilodon can often best a bigger dinosaur that way, provided the feline is not outnumbered."

"Is it true that the point of a sabertooth is sharper than what the human eye can detect?" said Hakan.

"It is," said the quya. "Not to mention that its length allows for the deepest dental puncture among known creatures—not including those with horns or tusks, of course."

Ollan raised a brow. "You're going to make an army of smilodons?"

Quya Urpi chuckled. "*Make*? No. I already have one. And it's no small achievement, I'll tell you. Have you ever tried to impose your will upon a *feline*? Even a common housecat?" The smilodon leaned into her strokes, its throat rumbling.

Housecats must have been more common in Allpa, Qora thought. She couldn't imagine how a pet like that would play out with all the compies back home.

"You might not say 'army,'" the quya clarified, "but I do keep a reserve of trained cats available in defense of my city. The guards patrol with them at night; you'll likely witness a few of them while you're here."

"And do you think you'll train more?" Rimaq asked.

"We must use every resource at our disposal," Quya Urpi replied. "It is not lost on me that dominite has no effect on mammals."

TREATY OF THE EXTENSIVE LANDS OF RUNAQA

Preamble

We, the representatives of the Five Terrains hereby establish this treaty concerning the governance of the land known as The Tail, situated at the southernmost point of the Runaqan continent.

Article I: Recognition

The parties to this treaty acknowledge that The Tail, a small peninsula extending from the southern point of the continent, is a unique and distinct region which currently possesses features insignificant to Runaqan trade, tourism, and culture. The parties agree to respect the geographical and cultural peculiarities of this land at this time.

Article II: Status

The Tail shall remain an autonomous territory, free from direct governance or intervention by any of the Five Terrains. The Tail is to be recognized as self-governing and shall retain full sovereignty over its internal affairs.

Article III: Non-Interference

The Five Terrains agree to refrain from territorial claims, administrative control, or military presence into The Tail. No Terrain shall engage in any action that might infringe upon the sovereignty or autonomy of The Tail.

SEVENTY-ONE

SEVERAL HOURS LATER, as Ninan's back began to throb from sitting on the floor against the stone wall of the iron-barred cell within the citadel's underkeep, keys jangled from the distant corridor. He swallowed, trying to wet his throat; the meager bit of bread and water he'd received a while ago had not satiated his hunger, nor quenched his thirst, especially since he'd bitten off small pieces of that bread and spat them down the front of his shirt for Tuko to slip out of his vest pocket and catch.

Ninan twisted his wrists within the iron cuffs that bound them, connected by a chain of five links.

One of the Sumaqi generals approached and shoved a key into the small gate directly facing Ninan, opening the cell with a creak. Four guards filed in—two of them flanking Ninan and dragging him up by the underarms, while the other two supervised.

"Your father is here to see you," said the general.

A chill shot up Ninan's aching spine.

The guards marched Ninan to one of the upper levels of the main keep, forcing him up the hundreds of stairs that spiraled the interior. Ninan's muscles tightened beneath their firm grip on his biceps. Of the two additional guards, one marched ahead while the other marched behind.

Four isn't so many, Ninan thought. He was surprised his father hadn't sent more, although he imagined there was quite a mess outside and it would be difficult to spare personnel when securing the occupation of the entire city and citadel, dealing with the blood and the guts. It was likely as well that his father had not expected him to be here; although Ninan had shown a clear betrayal to his own House and people, his whereabouts had remained unclear.

Qhapaq Izhi had been the prime target—of course—and his escape through his tunnel system had left Sumaqi retrieval forces in a frenzy, splitting up and spreading out in attempt to intercept Izhi at one of several potential escape junctions. As yet, they had not captured him.

Ninan's eyes flicked to each of his own surrounding guards in turn. All wore light armor, with a longblade strapped to the right hip—no crossbows. The guard ahead of him kept a steady but hesitant pace, as though he were wary of potential threats lurking in the shadows.

Ninan strained his ears for a moment, listening to the guards on either side of him. One had a sort of irregularity to his footfalls, a slight favoring of one leg over the other.

Injured.

Subtly, Ninan glanced at the other, whose left glove showed extra signs of wear on the leather at his palm.

Left handed.

Soon the light from the floor above spilled onto the stairwell, and the guards shoved him into a type of ballroom, with polished floors and an enormous chandelier of triceratops horns fused together. A few more Sumaqi officers restrained surviving Unuvian guards and what appeared to be citadel residents, all of them sweaty and bloodied and gashed.

In the center of the room, with the chandelier above him like some gaudy, oversized crown, stood Qhapaq Apo.

"If it isn't the fruit of my loins," said the qhapaq, holding fast to gilded scepter with a splay of sharp prongs at its head. "Rotten to the core, as I always suspected."

"Except …" Ninan replied, "it was the tree that cast me to the ground for the rotting in the first place, wasn't it?"

Mullu was not in the room to strike Ninan this time, and so it was his father's scepter that doubled him over as the shaft of it came against his navel.

"You are finished," said the qhapaq. "No longer will you walk upon the lands of my empire. No longer will you use your highborn knowledge to betray your own Terrain and its people. No longer will you make a mockery of your lineage. You will die today."

"If you kill me, you'll only make me a martyr," Ninan replied through a groan.

"That is a consequence I am willing to accept. While you deserve no such esteem, your death will finally allow you to serve a purpose."

Panting, Ninan managed to say, "And what purpose is that?"

"Uniting everyone against a common enemy. When the Sumaqi people learn that their beloved, newly redeemed prince—a hero of the Venture—died *at the hands of Qhapaq Izhi*, after brutal torture following abduction from the wedding, they will unite with a vengeance. They will curse the Unuvians, and stand with me in this war without question."

Ninan's legs began to tremble, but he tightened his muscles, keeping himself as rigid as possible. "Always more lies …" he bit out.

"People don't know what's good for them. They're like

children; some things are beyond their full comprehension. Despite evidence, they will not see reason. If I must depict it for them in a way that allows them to better understand, so be it. But if it's truth that concerns you, then you need not fret; I've already arranged for Qhapaq Izhi's executioner to perform the task." He snapped his fingers and a pair of Sumaqi officers shoved one of their prisoners to the forefront, a tall but weary man with part of his uniform—and his skin—eaten away by acid. "Let us begin."

Everything within Ninan's body wanted to resist. His instincts urged him to throw elbows, to drag his feet, to drop every pound of his weight to the ground, to twist and flail and scream. But instead, he clenched his teeth, took in meaningful breaths through flared nostrils, and curled his fists.

Not yet.

It would do no good to struggle against the officers when he was indoors, with more officers in the periphery, with exits that could be easily blocked, with Unuvian hostages who might be cut up right in front of him to prove a point.

No. For now, he let the officers manhandle him back to the stairwell and up another level and then out onto the very balcony from which he'd first seen the Sauroguard advancing on the citadel.

Blood streaked the railing. Slain Unuvian guards littered the black-and-white tiles, fallen weapons and shields beside them. One of the gray Sauroguard pteranodons lay in a lifeless heap, with a bolt protruding from its soft palate and a stream of fresh acid still trickling from its mouth into a puddle that continued to eat away at the surface on which it had begun to spread.

Qhapaq Apo pointed to a spot and one of the guards from the underkeep—the one favoring an injured leg, Ninan noted—

shoved Ninan into a kneeling position, holding him by the scruff of his vest. At the movement of the fabric, Tuko twitched inside the pocket.

Two more officers dropped an execution block in front of Ninan, forcing him to stare down the scarred wood with its rounded notches carved out on the near side for the chest and on the far side for the chin—a last, ironic "comfort" before the blade would kill him.

The Unuvian executioner came forward with a single-blade obsidian axe that glinted in the afternoon sun.

A royal execution.

Even with all the shame Ninan had brought upon his father's house, he would receive a death befitting a royalborn. After all, the emblem on his neck remained sacred, and must only be destroyed with the finest of blades—and the finest of blades this was. It was a blade so fine, it could only be used but once, because the volcanic glass, while forming the sharpest cutting edge known to humankind, would be too brittle to withstand the force of the block. Such blades had the power to sever one head before shattering on the wood.

The chains between Ninan's wrists clattered against the tile as the guard shoved his head down. Tuko stirred again, but thankfully didn't squawk.

Sumaqi officers stood with their hands bracing the hilts of their sheathed blades, should the executioner try to turn on them.

The executioner raised the axe.

"'Justice is swift upon the body,'" recited the executioner, "'but its penalty will last throughout the eternities.'"

Face-down, panting, Ninan tried to formulate a plan. If he utilized the element of surprise, he might be able to throw his head back forcefully enough to startle the guard that held him in place. He had enough flexibility in his cuffs to push off the ground, and from there he might duck to avoid the axe, deliver a justice-swift kick to the guard's injured leg, then use that same guard as a shield, or perhaps shove him into the other guards that would surely lunge at him in that moment and—

He flinched at the sensation of tiny claws digging into the shirt fabric at his chest.

Tuko, no … Please … Not right now …

But the pteromorph was already making his way out.

No one seemed to think much of Ninan's twitching reaction to this—and why should they? Anyone who was about to lose their head would be twitchy, trembling, short of breath.

Tuko dropped down with a soft tap of his claws on the tile surface directly below where Ninan's chest was positioned parallel to the floor.

Okay, Ninan thought. *New plan.*

The executioner took a hesitant breath. Although Ninan knew this man was no stranger to killing, it obviously wasn't every day he was forced to kill a royalborn—let alone by command of a qhapaq that was not his own.

But if Ninan had anything to say about it, he wasn't going to die today. At least not like this.

The man's gruff voice rang out clearly as he began to enunciate his final words. "'May your soul—'"

"Tuko," Ninan said quickly. "Sting!"

The pteromorph streaked out from under Ninan and sunk his tiny teeth into the executioner's hand.

The executioner cried out as officers drew their blades in a chorus of ringing metal.

Ninan thrust his shoulders forward against the execution

block, pushing off from his knees, and—with a grunt—tipped the whole bulky thing and flung himself over it, tearing his neckline from the grasp of the officer and rolling onto his feet. Officers converged on him, but he leapt at the executioner, who had loosened his grip as he tried to fling Tuko from his torn, bleeding flesh.

Even with hands chained close together, Ninan managed to snatch the axe and swing it in a wide horizontal arc, cutting into five advancing officers—clean through their thick uniforms—before the sharp points of the obsidian blade began to break off.

And now, it's a bludgeon.

Amid his kicks and feints, he struck officers across the back of the head, between the shoulder blades, direct to the groin, across the shins, behind the knees, and finally buried the blunt axe in someone's abdomen just in time to deter a longblade headed for his chest.

With the majority of the officers injured now, the executioner picked up a fallen longblade and fought with Ninan against those that remained. Ninan's fisticuffs suffered under his restraints, but with the executioner's help, they finished off the last of the Sumaqi officers in a matter of minutes. Tuko flitted around, having apparently flown up out of the chaos and landed back on Ninan's shoulder once he'd deemed it safe again.

Taking heavy breaths, Ninan glanced around to ensure that all officers were down, and then faced the executioner with an ironic sense of gratitude. "Thank y—"

A blade sprouted from the executioner's heart.

Blood bloomed at the base of the puncture.

The man's gaze went bleary and he wavered for a moment before collapsing in a mound of uniformed blue, with a longblade's hilt in his back.

And there, standing behind him, was Ninan's father.

Ninan stumbled back a step, shaking his head. But before he could say anything, his father's gilded scepter came swinging around from the side, connecting with Ninan's skull and knocking him flat.

He found himself with his face against the cold tile, while Tuko hovered over him, squawking. He pressed his cuffed hands down and got onto his knees, but the scepter came again, sending a surge of pain through his ribs.

"When are you going to learn?" said the qhapaq.

The qhapaq struck him again.

And again.

And again.

Ninan stifled a whimper, panting as he dragged himself gracelessly across the floor on his shaky elbows and forearms, knowing he couldn't be fast enough to escape the next strike—at least not until the pain of the last ones faded.

This was how it was always going to be, wasn't it? A poor, pathetic princeling hoping to crawl out of range of his father's wrath, but ever victim to it, ever crippled *under* it.

"How I ever sired such a worthless creature, I will never know," the qhapaq seethed.

It was coming again. Ninan knew this. That hard metal that already had bruises flourishing under his skin, the rod that threatened to crack his bones. It was inevitable. He'd already heard it whooshing through the air, pulling back in preparation to come down, building momentum for an even more menacing strike.

But maybe ...

The slain pteranodon's dead golden eyes seemed to lock on Ninan's. The acid that still dripped from its open mouth gleamed, adding to the puddle accumulating in a corroded hole.

It was only a few yards away.

With trembling legs, Ninan bent his ankles to form right angles, and pressed his toes to the floor, giving himself enough leverage to get his knees under him again, and pushing off so that he might take at least two off-balance strides toward the pteranodon before the scepter touched his ribs.

This time, the prongs cut into his clothes. Ninan hissed at the sharp, hot pain, but he landed back on the floor in a dive, his body sliding the rest of the way to his destination.

Ninan adjusted the cuffs carefully, so that the chain alone dangled into the acid puddle, completely submerging three of the five links, all blocked from view by his head and shoulders.

"Perhaps I should have made one of these flyers your executioner," said the qhapaq. "Such a beast would not have fallen for your antics."

"My antics that fended off *all* your officers …" Ninan panted heavily to disguise the sizzling of the chains in the acid, pushing out each breath with exaggerated sharpness to dissipate the gases and also to keep from inhaling them. The black iron lightened to a reddish brown, its surface turning rough and textured as bits of metal flaked off and floated within the puddle.

He hadn't expected it to work so quickly, but he supposed full immersion was more effective than a splash or a spew. The acid had, after all, put a fairly deep hole into these tiles.

"And what did that award you?" the qhapaq asked at Ninan's back. "Are you free? Do you have the upper hand?"

Ninan subtly raised his chain from the acid, allowing the excess to dribble. The chain links were porous now, and matte with brittleness.

"Do you?" his father repeated more forcefully.

At the whoosh of the scepter, Ninan rolled onto his back and raised his fists, taking the brunt of the strike against the taut, corroded chain between them.

The iron links fragmented and Ninan's wrists shot apart. He crossed his arms, trapping the scepter against his chest, its prongs mere inches from his cheek. He then gripped the scepter and spun it so its prongs pointed at his father like a multi-headed spear ready to strike.

"Go ahead," the qhapaq told him.

With aching bones and leaking cuts, Ninan forced himself into a standing position, keeping the scepter's prongs trained on his father.

Tuko landed on Ninan's shoulder once more, squawking at the qhapaq as if in rebellion.

The march of officers echoed from the stairwell, at least a hundred footfalls.

"Whatever your skills," the qhapaq said, "you are no match for my numbers. You may kill a few, but eventually your strength will falter, and my officers will overwhelm you, and you will *beg* for death. In this world, one is either predator or prey—and I'm afraid you are a natural victim."

Ninan thought of velosaurs, the small thalattosaurians with their sleek agile bodies and their ability to blend in.

"Prey are quick," Ninan argued. "Prey are clever."

He was feinting, of course, as he did in a fistfight. It was clear he hadn't been quick *enough*, or clever *enough*. He may have slithered into a crevice and found temporary refuge there, altered his skin to take on the color and the texture of the surrounding rocks, but now he was trapped.

He was trapped on this balcony, too high up to jump off, and there was no direct bridge to the pteriary where he might obtain flight transportation. The officers were coming; their footfalls told him they had already reached the top of the spiral stairwell and were crossing into the vantage hall.

"They *must* be quick and clever," Qhapaq Apo agreed, "to compensate for *weakness*."

His father was right, Ninan thought. He was weak. When faced with everything the man could put up against him, he was nothing. Less than nothing.

Still, like the prey his father looked down upon, Ninan couldn't help but want to survive—couldn't help but feel *determined* to survive. He had to; he was the only one that truly knew this predator's lair from the inside. He couldn't dwell on his inadequacies at a time like this—and he shouldn't.

"The wild ones don't wallow."

As he considered whether he ought to stab the prongs into his father's heart—whether it would make any difference to this war, or if his brothers would simply rise up to take Apo's place and move forward as planned—a distant cry rang in his ears.

"Apo-Kimsa!" called a female voice amid the screeching of a slate-purple pteranodon.

Ninan and his father both turned their gazes upward as the pteranodon flew over the outer wall in their direction. Its rider leaned forward, urging the flyer into a high-speed pose.

"Paqari ..." Ninan rasped.

The princess was in full riding gear—trousers, gloves, goggles.

The Sumaqi officers filed onto the balcony. Ninan backed away from them, stopping only when the railing pressed into the sore spots of his flesh where his father had struck him. He glanced outward, then up at Paqari with only seconds before the officers reached him.

She nodded at him like she knew what he was thinking.

No. It's insane.

But of course nothing about any of this was sane.

He climbed up onto the ledge and dropped the scepter.

"Seize him now!" Qhapaq Apo told the officers.

As Paqari approached, Ninan leapt.

"Retrieve!" Paqari commanded.

For an instant, time seemed to stop as he hung in the air.

His heart clenched.

His breath hitched.

His head swam.

He imagined the invisible tendrils of death twisting up out of the Grave World to receive him.

Tuko's claws dug into his shoulder.

And then, the thick, toothless beak of the pteranodon closed around him, dipping under his weight but rising again to compensate.

"Get me to the pteriary!" Ninan shouted.

Paqari nodded and guided the pteranodon to the tower over the gate, hovering at one of the large windows until Ninan climbed out of the beak and into the pteriary's upper level. Within, he located Yaku's pteranodon, mounted it, shoved Tuko back into his pocket, and burst up out of the window on the opposite side, as Paqari flew spirals waiting for him.

"Hurry!" she told him.

The flew fast, but back at the pteriary, beastlords were already racing to mount Sauroguard pteranodons.

In seconds, there were six beastlords in pursuit.

"Ruck ..." Ninan said. He'd been so close to a clean getaway.

Not considering, of course, all the blood and guts he'd just left behind, much of which he was responsible for.

He didn't have the energy for this. And fighting in the air was an entirely different situation, for which he was most definitely not prepared. He wasn't a Razorclaw, or a pirate, or even a bandit. He was just some stupid—

He gasped, suddenly glancing at his saddlebag.

He did have one advantage.

This flyer had gone to Kallpa House with him, ready to take out the guards there, and thus it carried the very weapon he needed right now.

Ninan strained his muscles to reach back into the saddlebag, where his fingers came upon one of the powder cannons. He grabbed it and waved it around to get Paqari's attention. "Catch!"

When he flung it to her, she fumbled, causing the pteranodon to waver under her hasty movements, but she managed to secure her grip on it. She looked at it and furrowed her brows.

"Watch me!" Ninan told her, reaching for another one.

By the time he had it ready, the beastlords were gaining on them.

He waited until they were closer, his back and shoulders tense at the thought of them closing in and their flyers ready to spew acid. But he had to make sure they were in range, that the beastlords would take the brunt of the dust and get enough of it into their lungs.

Three ... two ... one ...

He blasted the dust, watching it cloud up and fan out behind him.

Paqari followed his lead.

The beastlords flew directly into it, coughing and trying to waft it away, but it was too late. One by one, they drooped in their saddles, sliding limply off and plummeting into the trees below.

Branches split and snapped. Leaves rustled. Birds and small

pterosaurs shot out from the commotion.

The Sauroguard pteranodons dove after their riders, using the glowing dominite-crystal collars as guides, while Ninan and Paqari raced off toward the heart of Unu.

SEVENTY-TWO

AFTER A MEAL, during which Qora devoured three plates of food, her mamáy pulled her aside and led her to the fibery, where several stitching machines sat in little rows, and mannequins lined the far wall wearing dresses or uniforms at various states of completion. One station, with its onyxwood and cast-iron stitching machine, had an olive-green garment draped over it.

Qora's mamáy lifted the garment by its shoulders, allowing its long sleeves to hang straight. "The quya has allowed me to do whatever work I please here." She laid the garment against her own chest, facing outward, showing off the four pockets distributed over the front panels. The sleeves also had small, square pockets along their length. She opened one of the front panels to display additional pockets within, one of which was tall enough to fit a handful of crossbow bolts. "I know you said you didn't want another one, but ..." She held it open and came to Qora's side, motioning for her to try it.

Tentatively, Qora allowed her mamáy to slip it onto her, then pulled her hair out from under the collar so it could hang freely down her back. She turned to a freestanding mirror among the mannequins and stared at her reflection. The material on her was lightweight, but with a strong, tight weave. The sleeves were attached with laces, something she realized she could pull loose to convert the jacket to a vest. She brushed her fingers over the brass buttons.

The girl looking back at her was someone else, she thought. Yes, she was wearing a green jacket like the Raptoriva, but there was more to her now. The muted tone of this green aligned with the muted tones of her heart, those which had once been vibrant with hope. But all of its compartments aligned with the notion that she must go forward and gather weapons and resources, hoarding them and hiding them close to her until the time was at hand to fight.

After so many months trying to distance herself from the Raptoriva, she had never been able to escape her entirely. Maybe that was because it simply wasn't possible to separate herself from her own skin. She understood now. That's what the Raptoriva was; not a costume—a skin.

"It suits you," her mamáy said over her shoulder.

Qora raised her chin and fastened the button just below her breasts. "It does."

"Do you think you're ready to wear it?"

Nodding slowly, Qora pulled up the hood of her jacket and narrowed her eyes. "If Qhapaq Apo wants a raptoriva … that's what he's going to get."

SEVENTY-THREE

ONCE THE RUSH OF THEIR ESCAPE HAD WANED, Ninan and Paqari settled into a well paced flight.

Ninan glanced over at the princess, sighing, and felt his lips quirk up. "Gods ..."

Even *she* couldn't help smiling. "I know ..."

They let the freedom sink in for a moment, and then Ninan motioned for her to land in an upcoming field.

"Why did you come for me?" Ninan asked when they were both dismounted, leading the flyers on foot behind them. Tuko squawked at Paqari from Ninan's shoulder. "How did you know where I'd be?"

Paqari scowled at the pteromorph, perhaps realizing now that he'd had a bigger role in Ninan's exploits than she might have previously thought. "The bandits told me. I paid them half up front, and promised the other half after. Impressive that you figured out I hired them, by the way. Not so impressive that you thought anyone who knows you well would believe you could be abducted so easily, but ..." She shrugged. "Anyway, the bandits came to collect after the wedding, and told me what you did—raiding Kallpa House and sending your friends to Allpa while you went off to Unu to deliver some warning to Izhi. Not long after that, news spread about Unu's attack on the base in

501

the Aquchay, and word got out about the Sauroguard that is supposedly a protection against external threats."

"It's not."

"I know. I'm the daughter of a powerful man, too, remember? I'm familiar with propaganda, and underhanded military strategy. I'm not stupid enough to think there's no danger in having an army like that."

"My father won't share his power with yours. Not at the end of all this."

"I wouldn't have spent all day on the back of a pteranodon if I thought he would. When I heard early this morning that Sumaq was sending part of that Sauroguard to Yupa in retaliation, that's when I came to find you. I arrived at that godsforsaken citadel right as you finished off the Sumaqi officers. I didn't expect your father to start beating you; I wasn't sure if you were feigning defeat—given your track record—or if I should interfere, so I waited on the outer edge of one of the watchtowers until it was clear you were going to need me."

Ninan chewed the inside of his cheek. "I … don't know what to say."

"You don't have to say anything. You saved hundreds of people; I only saved one. To be fair, you did most of the work."

"I guess I don't understand, though, why you didn't just write me off as a traitor."

Paqari scoffed. "Please. I know better than almost anyone else how easy it is to act in opposition to a qhapaq—especially one who's your own father."

"Right. Of course. Hiring pirates to sabotage your royal wedding and all …"

"Bandits," she reminded him. "I learned my lesson the first time—on the way to Rikracha."

Ninan started to nod, then jerked his gaze toward her. "Wait—*what*? Rikracha? I thought those pirates were real …"

"They were. I paid someone to tip them off as to where our ship would be sailing that day. I thought the guards aboard the *Velosaura* could handle them easily, but clearly I was mistaken. For the wedding, however, I wanted to better control the chaos—hence, the bandits."

"So you tried to sabotage the tour as well?"

Paqari nodded. "That's why I wanted the champion to come aboard. I saw you sneak off after you left the governor's estate in Kicai that first night, and then I waited for you to come back. I watched you from outside the kantina and decided to burst in like it was spontaneous, but really I just wanted to see the look on your face when I caught you with her. I thought if I brought her with us, that eventually you'd slip up and ruin the whole engagement. Same thing with the masquerade, when I arranged for the two of you to find one another."

"You arranged that?"

"At the last minute I changed my gown, and of course I realized this color wasn't suited to the ankylo, so I switched it, and I completely forgot to inform you."

"I have to admit, it was … more painful than I expected, when my plan actually came to fruition. Finding you together below decks, knowing you'd been out for a while doing … similar things."

"But you didn't use it to your advantage." Ninan raised a brow. "You …"

"Like I said before the wedding, your words in Qaqakuna affected me. I caught a glimpse of this desperate, aching boy who truly cared for the champion. So, despite the hurt I felt that the champion would go behind my back like that—when

I'd thought we were becoming friends—I decided I still had other methods of sabotage I might pursue, rather than inflict punishment on the two of you."

"I … appreciate that."

"I also knew you were both up to something from the beginning—of course I didn't know *what*, specifically—but I went along with the little scavenger game because, well, I do like puzzles, and I figured if it helped you make a bigger mess of things, that would be a win for me." She laughed bitterly. "Trying to lure terminonatators to the *Velosaura*, however, was a bit more difficult, and not quite how I'd planned for it to go."

Ninan's eyes went wide. "How would you *even* …"

"Ferosquid ink. The squids release their ink to distract and confuse predators like terminonatators and other large elasmosaurians, but when the ink properties decay—long after release—it becomes a marker, revealing that ferosquid have been nearby. It draws elasmosaurians to the site as they hunt them, from nautical miles away and even in deeper waters. I made sure it was mixed in with the tar during routine waterproofing before we set off on the tour. There were traces of ink all over the upper hull. I knew it was a long shot that we'd attract anything, but when we hit that storm after Masi, everything coincided to make it effective."

Ninan paused again to piece this together. The reason the terminonatators hadn't been sufficiently deterred by the skyrock-tipped tridents, why they had been insistent on attacking the ship—because there had been something stronger drawing them to it. And then, why Paqari had been so insistent on helping the crew, why she'd refused to stay safe below decks—because she'd felt responsible for what had been happening.

"Are you out of your mind?" he asked. "We could've all died!"

"I do genuinely regret that. I'm not often genuine, I'll admit it, but I really only thought the terminonatators would cause minimal damage to the ship and delay the tour. I didn't anticipate the storm would drive away their food source and make them hungrier for *us*. I didn't intend for anyone to get hurt."

Ninan rubbed the back of his neck. "So you're some sort of evil mastermind …"

She raised one shoulder. "Well, I wasn't raised to be *good*, that's for sure. Mastermind? I do try. But mostly I wanted to wreak havoc in any way possible."

"You just want to watch the world burn."

"The world I was born into didn't do me any favors. In it, I'm only a bargaining chip. It doesn't matter what I want or whom I love or how I'd like to live. That world doesn't deserve my mercy."

"What about all that talk of 'honor in sacrifice' and 'strength in doing our duty'? You said it was more heroic to accept our fates."

"I meant every word of what I said."

"I doubt that."

"Alright, not *every* word. But, during those rare times when there's truly nothing that can be done, we must find solace in accepting our circumstances with dignity, and finding the benefit, even if that benefit is not to us. I couldn't be sure that my final effort would produce the desired effect—and if it didn't, I had to prepare myself. So did you."

"That's true, I suppose." He sighed. "What are you going to do now, though? Surely you're not flying all the way to Allpa with me."

"I am."

He furrowed his brows. "You? *Allpa*?"

"Why not?"

"I don't know. I guess I didn't peg you for a runaway. And to the smallest of all Five Terrains …"

"It's not like it's Qolqe."

Having seen the dry, barren lands between major cities there, Ninan couldn't argue with that. "You're really not going back to Tisqu?"

"Quya Urpi approached me once. Two years ago, at a Sky Temple groundbreaking. She complimented my gown, and then told me I ought to visit her sometime. It seemed an innocent enough comment, but … there was a special quality in her gaze that struck me. It lasted a beat too long, perhaps, or her tone was unusual. I'm not sure. But I'm certain she was trying to tell me something."

"She has that way about her," Ninan agreed. "Like she can see through to your soul."

"Or maybe she simply recognizes a prisoner when she sees one. I only know I've often imagined Allpa as a sort of haven; I simply didn't have the courage to find out for certain—until now."

"Well, I don't know how long I'll be staying. I have to see to my friends, and to thank the quya for her help. Then I have to find Qora."

Paqari frowned. "What do you mean?"

"I have no idea where she is. Izhi said she made it out alive after the attack on the base, but beyond that, he had no information. I don't want to go back to Sumaq, but if I have to—"

"Oh, you sweet, *adorable* little idiot …"

"Excuse me?"

"You need look no further, Apo-Kimsa. You're headed straight to see her now."

Ninan gaped. "I … don't understand. She's in Allpa? How do you know?"

"Because she confided in me once that Quya Urpi offered her refuge as well. I'm positive that's where she is."

With a flutter in his chest, Ninan gazed out at the way forward, at the miles of verdant foliage that led to Allpa's grasslands, and for the first time in a long time felt a surge of true hope.

The destruction behind him was only the beginning of what might occur, but at least for the moment, he was free, and he might soon have Qora.

)))

Darkness fell before Ninan and Paqari reached Amachakuna, but Qhispina House glowed from within, its lit windows dotting the towers. The swell of the river through its tunneled base came like a maternal shush.

Attendants received them at the paved circle atop the pteriary, greeting them by name. "The quya has been expecting you," one of them said.

The head attendant led them to a grand salon, where multicolored rugs in geometric patterns with golden tassels covered much of the floors. Multiple onyxwood-and-velvet sofas and chairs created seating areas throughout the space, while woven tapestries lined the walls, mostly featuring smilodons among leaves and flowers.

The quya entered before Ninan and Paqari had even taken a seat. Both bowed and said, "Your Majesty" in unison.

Quya Urpi stood before them and bowed her head briefly. "Your Highnesses. Welcome." She took one of each of their hands and squeezed. "You both look the worse for wear, I'm afraid. Please sit."

They seated themselves on a sofa adjacent to a chair that was large, with ostentatious floral carvings on its wooden frame—clearly meant for the quya.

One of her domesticated smilodons sauntered up to her, pausing to fixate on Tuko, who sat on Ninan's knee. Tuko squawked. The smilodon growled.

Ninan scooped up Tuko and put him back into his vest pocket, although the pteromorph peeked out with a glower.

"Thank you," Ninan told the quya, "for receiving my friends. I'm sorry for sending them on without me, and for not sending word beforehand. It's been—"

"No need for explanations," said the quya. "I'm aware of the circumstances. We are not in a situation that grants us much time, or room to plan ahead. Your friends are already making homes for themselves in my highlands; I had some very proficient builders construct a series of temporary, timber homes on the croplands in a matter of hours. Your ark pilots are with them as well, awaiting you."

The tension in Ninan's shoulders began to ease. He imagined everyone from Thak settling into new houses, preparing food amongst themselves, looking over vast new lands with no guards surrounding them. It wasn't Sumaq, of course, but they were free, and safe.

"I must say, though," the quya continued, "I didn't expect the two of you to arrive together. Not after what I've just read about your wedding."

"Well, we didn't leave it simultaneously," Paqari said. "My groom cleverly decided to stage his own abduction so he could return to Sumaq."

"Which explains how he had time to commandeer three arks to evacuate two hundred people," the quya mused. "Clever indeed, Apo-Kimsa."

That name was suddenly more grating on Ninan's ears than ever. When he thought of those velociraptors climbing the walls of Izhi's citadel and the pteranodons spewing acid and the ankylosaurs busting through brick—their defiance of nature in their enhanced features and the ruthlessness of their attacks—his insides felt rancid. How could he share the heritage of a man who would force such atrocities on innocent people?

"Forgive me, Your Majesty," said Ninan, "but … since I have now willingly abandoned my Terrain and political station … I prefer 'Ninan,' if you don't mind."

She looked him over. "'Ninan.' As you were called in the Venture."

"Yes."

"I assumed your father only gave you that name as part of your pretense."

He shook his head. "I chose it for myself, while I was hiding in Thak."

"Interesting. Why that name?" Quya Urpi asked.

"When my friends took me in, they asked me what they should call me, and I didn't know what to say. Being stripped of my former self, I was sort of … nameless. All I knew was that I wanted to burn everything I touched."

"Ninan means fire," the quya said knowingly.

Ninan nodded. "Turns out, though, I'm a lot of smoke and very little flame."

"I don't know about that," Paqari said. "You helped the champion finish the Venture. When your father forced you to perform an engagement tour, you turned it into a spy mission.

You got yourself out of a royal wedding—"

"With your help."

She smiled slyly. "Still. You saved everyone in that little farming community—while stealing three arks and nearly twenty pterobeasts from the most powerful monarch in Runaqa. The bandits told me you even let them raid the Kallpa House treasury."

"Shame they couldn't clean it out completely," Ninan said. "Anyway, I'm sorry to change the subject so abruptly, but"—he turned a pleading gaze on the quya—"I was hoping to speak to Qora Kanchaya. Please tell me she's here."

The quya's optimistic demeanor seemed to wither at that. Ninan's spirit withered too, at the thought that Paqari had been mistaken.

"Unfortunately, she is not," said Quya Urpi. "I'm afraid she just left—not three hours prior to your arrival."

Ninan shot up from his seat. "To where?"

Paqari grasped his wrist and tugged downward. "What—are you going to go after her *now*? In the dark? Don't be dramatic. Sit."

He did not sit, however.

"She and her brother have gone to the Tail," said the quya, "with a team of my guards, in hopes of warning them of your father's war, and imploring them to share resources."

"What resources?" Paqari said.

"We don't know for sure. Giant theropods, perhaps, as well as innovations we might not have developed," the quya explained. "I'd be happy to expand upon the details, but perhaps the two of you should get cleaned up first, eat something, rest a bit ..."

"Last time I did that, I woke to the Saurogaurd advancing on Qhapaq Izhi's citadel." Ninan clenched his teeth. How he had managed to sleep that night while the Sumaqi Guard had been preparing to send a full army of dinosaurs in his direction, he couldn't fathom. He should have known, should have sensed it somehow.

"Ninan …" Paqari's voice managed to reach him through the thickening fog of his thoughts.

The unusual tenderness of it, and the fact that she'd called him "Ninan" drew his focus. He glanced at her, took a slow breath, and sat down again, curling his hands into fists.

"If you don't think you're 'fire,'" the princess added, "you're even more of an idiot than I thought."

"Thanks," Ninan replied bitterly.

Paqari met his eyes. "You're *pure* fire, and your father was a fool to try and contain you. But fire dwindles without fuel. You've been burning through yours with impressive speed. If you don't slow down, you're going to burn out completely."

"The princess is right," said Quya Urpi. "Give yourself a while to recover. You have endured much these past few weeks— even just today. I promise we will employ every available resource to stop Qhapaq Apo. In time, you may travel to the Tail as well, if you so choose. When you do, I will provide a pterobeast and gondola."

"That would be lovely," Paqari said.

Ninan furrowed his brows at her. "'Lovely' why?"

"Because I've just spent most of the day on pteranodonback and my hindquarters are killing me. I have no desire to go to the Tail on a saddle."

"Wait a second—"

"I'm going with you, scute-brain. Obviously."

The quya smiled at them both. "Obviously."

"I didn't come all this way to sit around," Paqari clarified, "and it's become apparent that you're going to need someone to keep explaining things to you."

Ninan wasn't sure how to respond. After everything, he'd never expected to be here now, with Paqari, thinking of crossing the Pirqas into the mysterious territory to the south. Nothing made sense, and the world was falling apart, but for the moment, he was safe, with people who were ready to fight the monsters with him. His friends were safe, too, and Qora was almost within reach.

"Alright," Ninan finally agreed. "But as soon as I've seen my friends, we're going to the Tail to find the girl I love. And when we get back, I'm going to make sure my father regrets everything he's ever done." His heart pounded like a war drum as he spoke to the two royal women before him. "Because I'm going to do what *fires* do: I'm going to burn that man to the ground."

ACKNOWLEDGMENTS

Once again, I want to thank my dino babies, Rocco and Bellamy. Thank you for helping to inspire this story world, and also for continuing to be patient with me, and for getting excited about this series even though you aren't old enough to read it yet.

Nano, as always, you are amazing and I couldn't do this without your love and support. Thank you for listening to me ramble incoherently about writerly things, for dragging me to brunch when I need a break, and just generally being awesome. I love you so much. "You … disturb me." And I mean that in the context of this book, and also in the context of you constantly interrupting me ♡

Zach, Walker, and Jacob: Thank you for being so consistent with writing group and for giving awesome feedback. I'm so excited that you've all had the chance to move on to *Velosaura* with me.

Thanks again to TrifBookDesign and Daniel Brown for the cover and internal artwork. It makes me extra proud to show off my books!

Brooke: Thanks for being my best friend and sending me text messages to brighten my day and always checking on how I'm doing with this whole writing thing. This book was especially crazy to complete and I felt like you were with me through so much of it, cheering me on from the sidelines.

To all my TikTok friends, you are incredible! Thank you so much for liking, commenting on, sharing, buying, and reviewing *Raptoriva* and being excited about *Velosaura*. If you've made it this far, it means the world to me!

AVAILABLE NOW!

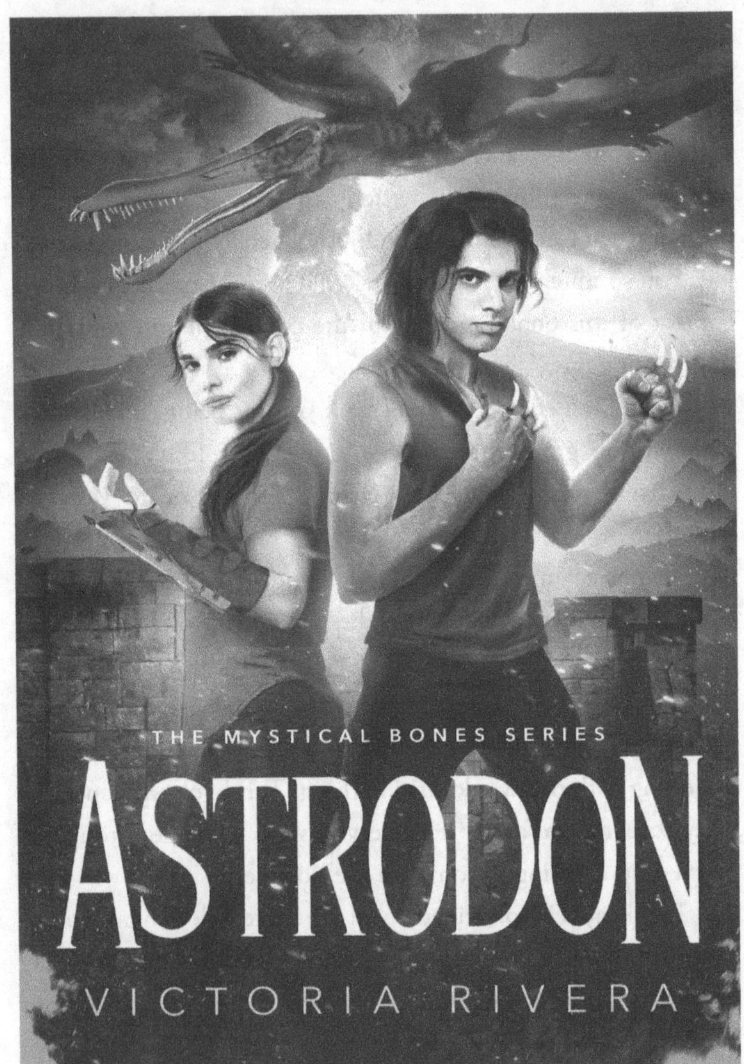

ABOUT THE AUTHOR

VICTORIA RIVERA is a graphic designer and mom of two kiddos. She has a bachelor's degree in English and has worked as a copy editor, proofreader, and designer at newspapers and magazines.

She was born and raised in Oregon but currently lives in northern Utah and misses the rain.

When she's not writing, she enjoys doing DIY projects, playing Beat Saber, rage-cleaning to good music, and reading (obviously).

For updates on books, **subscribe to her email list at www.toririv.com**. Follow her on **TikTok (@tori.riv)** for a glimpse into her day-to-day activities and other bookish things.

If you enjoyed this book, please leave a review on Amazon and/or Goodreads. Your feedback is greatly appreciated!